The Jam Factory Girls

Mary Wood was born in Maidstone, Kent, and brought up in Claybrooke, Leicestershire. Born one of fifteen children to a middle-class mother and an East End barrow boy, Mary's family were poor but rich in love. This encouraged her to develop a natural empathy with the less fortunate and a fascination with social history. In 1989 Mary was inspired to pen her first novel and she is now a full-time novelist.

Mary welcomes interaction with readers and invites you to subscribe to her website where you can contact her, receive regular newsletters and follow links to meet her on Facebook and Twitter: www.authormarywood.com

BY MARY WOOD

The Breckton series

To Catch a Dream
An Unbreakable Bond
Tomorrow Brings Sorrow
Time Passes Time

The Generation War saga

All I Have to Give
In Their Mother's Footsteps

The Girls Who Went to War series

The Forgotten Daughter
The Abandoned Daughter
The Wronged Daughter
The Brave Daughters

The Jam Factory series

The Jam Factory Girls

Stand-alone novels

Proud of You
Brighter Days Ahead
The Street Orphans

The Jam Factory Girls

Mary Wood

PAN BOOKS

First published 2020 by Pan Books
an imprint of Pan Macmillan
The Smithson, 6 Briset Street, London EC1M 5NR
Associated companies throughout the world
www.panmacmillan.com

ISBN 978-1-5290-3346-5

1 3 5 7 9 8 6 4 2

A CIP catalogue record for this book is available from the British Library.

Typeset by Palimpsest Book Production Ltd, Falkirk, Stirlingshire
Printed and bound by CPI Group (UK) Ltd, Croydon, CR0 4YY

To Juan Del Olmo, Aurora Del Olmo and Ascen Fernández, who helped me through the coronavirus lockdown in Spain when I was unable to get home. They didn't hesitate to allow me to stay on in their holiday villa in the beautiful, tranquil setting overlooking the coastline of Isla Plana. During my time there, relaxed and safe, I was inspired to write two novels. Thank you, muchas gracias *– forever grateful x*

Chapter One

Elsie

OCTOBER 1910

At the unearthly hour of 6 a.m., when Elsie had to rise, the stars were still twinkling and the night air still bit, making it difficult to shift herself. Turning over, she tried to ignore the scratching on the window. Shivering and with her belly rumbling, she tucked the old coat – the only covering she had – around her body, but it didn't help.

Her brother Cecil, one year younger than her at seventeen, lying next to her, grumbled incoherently about the disturbance as he threw off the threadbare counterpane he'd been snuggled under and climbed out. 'I'll let the knocker-up man know we're awake, Else.'

She muttered a sleepy, 'Ta, luv. I'll be up in a mo.'

When the window opened, the shout came in, 'Six o'clock and the wind's enough to cut you in two, Cecil.'

'Ta, Mr Munster.'

They couldn't afford to pay Mr Munster, but he made sure they were awake anyway, because he knew no one else would, and if Elsie was late at the jam factory, she'd lose her job to any one of the women who stood outside the factory gates, hoping to get set on.

With just two weeks to go before Swift's Jam Factory closed at the end of October until Christmas, when the oranges from Spain would arrive and the marmalade-making would begin, Elsie needed the six shillings she could earn in a week, and wanted to be sure of being set on when the factory opened again.

Cecil needed to be on the Surrey dockside early, too, to see if he could get taken on by one of the costermongers. Sometimes he got lucky and was given a day's work and could earn a few bob, depending on what the stall made that day; at other times he only got a couple of hours helping to set up one of the market stalls and brought home a farthing, a couple of pounds of potatoes or something of that nature.

'Come on, Else – it ain't so bad, once you brave the cold.'

She grinned as she looked up at Cecil. 'So it's all right that you're shivering then, is it?'

'I fibbed. Look, I'll nip through and see to setting the fire going. That wood me and Jimmy collected around the docks last night'll be dried out by now.'

Elsie nodded and looked over to her mum's bed in the corner of the room. 'I see Mum's in, then?'

'I'd have thought the stench would have told you that.'

Cecil wouldn't mean this in a nasty way, but his joke did cause Elsie to take in the smell of alcohol and fags – something she should be used to, but which always turned her stomach.

Flapping her hand in front of her nose, she gently prodded her other two brothers with her foot. Having just one bedroom in their ground-floor two-roomed home, plus a scullery and a lav – one of forty similar flats in the tenement block on Long Lane in Bermondsey – meant that Elsie and her three brothers had to top-and-tail in the sagging old bed. But they were luckier than most, as some similar flats had nine or ten living in them.

'Jimmy, Bert, come on. You've to get dressed now. And keep the noise down while you do so, as Mum's asleep.'

Bert, always as bright as a button the moment he awoke, shot up into a sitting position and grinned at her. He'd been a joy in Elsie's life since his birth four years ago. She'd taken care of him even then, seeing to his feeds during the night and making sure he was kept clean and warm. But Jimmy, poor Jimmy, he'd been the worry of her life – always ailing. At eight years old, he wasn't half the size he should be. His hacking cough as he woke up went right through her, and Elsie sent up the prayer she always did, asking God to make her brother well.

'You didn't get much rest then, Jimmy?'

He shook his head and rubbed his crusted eyes.

'I'm sorry for you, Jimmy. I don't want to send you out today, but you know as another lad'll soon take your round off you, if you have too many days off.'

Jimmy sat up. Bert jumped on him and cuddled him tightly around the neck.

'Gerroff, Bert.'

'Shush!' Pain creased Elsie's stomach as she swung her legs off the bed and stood up, but she tried to ignore it. Eager to help Jimmy, she took a piece of cotton cloth from the hoard she had under her pillow. Often, when on cleaning duty, she'd slip the bit of rag she'd used into her pocket, and then boil it when she got home. 'Use that for a hanky, Jimmy.'

'Ta, Sis.'

'I'll try to take you to see Dr Stanley when I'm laid off.

He's a good bloke and don't charge the likes of us. Ooh . . .' Elsie clutched her stomach.

'You need this rag more than me, Else. Keep it for . . . well, you know what.'

'I've got some rags in the pocket of me cardi. I'll be all right.'

Having your monthly was no secret when you lived this close to each other, but it was a comfort to Elsie that her brothers understood and did extra chores to lighten her load when they knew she was on.

Now fully awake, Elsie slipped her long brown frock over her liberty bodice, wishing she had a corset, like the one her mum had, to support her bust. Her breasts were bigger than those of most girls of her age, and their soreness at this time of the month only increased her discomfort.

Pulling on the only pair of bloomers she possessed, which she had to wash out every other night, she shivered as their dampness chilled her. Clamping her lips together, she knew she just had to get used to the feel of them until they dried out on her body. With this determination spurring her on, she stuck her feet into her oversized shoes – the only ones she was able to get from the second-hand stall down Petticoat Lane market – and tried not to think about how her toes chafed on the scrunched-up newspaper that she'd stuffed into them to make them fit better, although she still had to tie the laces under her foot to secure them.

'I'll light the candle, as the gas lamp'll go out in the street soon. But don't be long coming through, Jimmy. And blow the candle out when you do, then it'll last another night. Oh, and bring the piddle-pot with you – it's your turn to empty and swill it.'

They all used the piddle-pot if they needed to go in the

night, as the trip to the lav across the living room and into the porch near the entrance of their flat wasn't easy to manage in the pitch dark, and they hadn't got a penny for the gas meter, so they couldn't light the lamps inside the flat.

The light from the match illuminated the corner where her mum was. Elsie looked down on her – oblivious to everything, Mum had her face squashed on the pillow as she lay on her front, with one arm dangling to the floor, her fingers almost touching the empty gin bottle. Her red hair fell in long ringlets down her back.

Although she hated her mum working the streets, Elsie hoped the gin bottle indicated that she'd had at least a couple of punters, because that would mean they would eat tonight and maybe even buy a bit of coal from one of the neighbours.

Elsie's wage, and whatever Cecil brought in, just covered the rent and paid the tallyman. If they didn't pay him, they wouldn't be able to borrow any more money when they needed it, or get Mum a new blouse, or Cecil, Jimmy and Bert some shoes, which, as growing lads, they always seemed to need.

Mum only had a new blouse every six months or so, and Elsie accepted that this was essential for her. 'I'm sorry, darlin',' she'd say, 'but I ain't getting any decent punters. I need to look the part to attract them.'

What Jimmy could earn before he went to school, delivering groceries for Mr Gravers, on the corner-shop owner's bike, enabled them to put a copper in the meter to last them a few days and bought some candles. Sometimes Mr Gravers gave him some toffees, and they would all sit on the step, huddled together, and share them when Mum was out.

Mum could put more into the pot if it wasn't for her gin and fags, but with what she did to try and make ends meet and feed them all, Elsie thought she deserved her little luxuries.

Jimmy kicked his legs out from under the blanket and swung them over the side. Elsie was glad to see that he was making the effort. She gently took hold of Bert's arm. 'Come on, buggerlugs, let's get you by the fire.'

Bert jumped up and down, reciting, 'Me buggerlugs', then went into a fit of giggling in a way that was infectious and had Elsie laughing with him.

When he was awake, Bert wanted everyone else awake, too. Elsie shushed him, preferring her mum to sleep a little longer, at least until she'd got everyone sorted. Then she'd take her mum a cup of tea and make sure she was all right, before she left.

Lifting Bert up, Elsie hugged him. He grinned at her as he grabbed her cheeks in his chubby hands and kissed her nose. 'Cold nose, Else.'

'Mmm, but look at this!' Opening the door to the living room bathed them in the warmth that the fire gave off. Even the linoleum floor didn't feel as cold as it usually did. As soon as Elsie put him down, Bert scampered over to the rag rug in front of the hearth – a favourite squatting place of them all, and something Elsie was really proud of, as she'd made it herself, with a little help from her brothers. They would say they'd made it, too, but more often than not, as she sat toiling away on the step during the long summer evenings, the lads would go off to play football in the street with their mates.

Having been shown how to make the rug by Mrs Potter, who lived in the next-door flat, Elsie and the lads had found the hessian they needed around the back of the grain mills. The night-watchman had seen them and chased them off, but not before they had a couple of sacks each, which, when opened up, made a good-sized base for the rug. They'd cut up two of their gran's old coats – her red one and navy one – to make pieces to push through the hessian. This made the rug extra-special, because it was like a memorial to their lovely gran, who Elsie was proud to be named after.

There wasn't much else in the room besides the fireplace, which was also their cooker, with its side-oven, hot plate and grate that swung over the flames to boil the kettle on – just an old sofa and a table and four chairs.

They used to have Gran's piano next to the fireplace and, standing along the back wall, her lovely dresser. But Mum had sold them both. So now their bits of china were on a shelf in the scullery. Elsie felt sad about this, because she'd loved polishing the dresser and thinking of her gran as she did so. And she'd loved to play the piano, too, because Gran had taught her how.

It had been a sad day when Gran died. Elsie missed her so much; she was always cheerful and full of tales of her youth, when she'd been a music-hall entertainer, playing the piano and singing. Elsie had loved to listen to her. Some of her songs were a bit bawdy and would have everyone in fits, and Mum would tell Gran off, but she would be laughing as she did so . . . Happy times.

Then one day Gran didn't call in, and Mum went along to see if she was all right, but she'd gone. Sitting in her chair, Mum said, as if for all the world she was waiting for a cup of Rosy Lee, as Gran called her cup of tea. A real old-fashioned cockney, Gran was; she rhymed everything, like a lot of those around here did. She'd call Jimmy and

Bert the tin lids – the kids. She was funny. She'd come in and, if Mum was looking down, she'd say, 'What's up with your boat race? You look like you've lost a penny and found a farthing.'

As she went through to the scullery now, Elsie had a smile on her lips at these memories. When she passed Cecil she told him, 'I soaked some oats overnight, Cess, they're in the pantry. Get them on to boil up, will you?'

She didn't wait to see if Cecil did as she asked, but nipped out through the passage and fetched the enamel bowl from its hook outside the back door.

'I'll use some of the hot water you've got in that kettle for us all to have a wash while the porridge is cooking. Jimmy'll be through in a mo.'

'All right. But I ain't washing – I've got me clothes on now.'

'At least swill your face and clean your ear 'oles out, Cess. And get rid of that tide-mark around your neck as well, mate. If you don't look respectable, none of the costermongers'll take you on.'

By the time they had all washed, and Elsie had used the water to scrub the front doorstep – not wanting the gossips in the block to slag her mum off for not having it done – the water resembled sludge. She tipped it down the drain, shivering as she hung the bowl back in its place, and went to hurry back inside, but was stopped by Mr Wright, the neighbour on the other side to Mrs Potter.

'Is that you, Elsie, girl?'

Impatient to get inside and go to the lav, Else called out, 'Yes, Mr Wright. I'm in a hurry this morning.'

This didn't deter him and, as it turned out, Elsie was glad.

'Right-o, matey, but I just want to tell you that me missus 'as baked some bread, so if you send one of your brovvers round, she's got a loaf for you.'

'Ooh, ta, Mr Wright, I'll do that. And tell her I'll be round on Saturday to do her step and her windows, as usual.'

'Ta, you're a good girl, doing that for her. She likes to do something in return, and while she ain't good on her pins these days, she still likes to do her baking.'

'Give her me love . . . see you later.' With this, Elsie closed the door behind her.

Feeling relieved after her visit to the lav, Elsie found her brothers sitting cross-legged on the rag rug, eating their porridge. She didn't like to disturb them, but didn't want to go and fetch the bread herself, as Mrs Wright was like her husband – one for keeping you talking whenever she spotted you. Cecil went without grumbling, the thought of fresh bread being a good incentive.

Her own porridge went down well, even though it was lumpy, as Cecil hadn't stirred it, as she was always telling him to. But then although he was good in many ways, he thought himself too big to carry out women's work.

He'd refilled the kettle, though, and it was now filling the air with its shrill whistle. Elsie tipped the dried-out tea leaves from the cup she'd made last night into the teapot and poured boiling water onto them. She knew there wouldn't be much strength in the tea, but she had a drop of milk and some sugar, so that would improve the taste. Handing Bert half a mugful, she ruffled his blond hair. He looked up and his lovely blue eyes shone with love for her.

'When we go, you're not to leave this room, mate. Don't go outside, and don't move the guard from the fire. Just wait in here till Mum gets up, or go and lie with her. Now promise me.'

'I promise, Else.'

'Good boy.'

None of her siblings looked like her, but then they all had different fathers. And none of them knew who their fathers were. Jimmy stood in complete contrast to Bert's fair looks, as he had dark hair and almost-black eyes, and his skin was an olive shade. Cecil was different again, with his sandy-coloured hair, though he did have their mum's lovely hazel eyes. Cecil didn't look like Mum, though, but Elsie did. She had red hair and her mum's features, but her eyes were a dark brown, though a lighter shade than Jimmy's.

Even her gran hadn't been able to give Elsie a clue as to who had fathered any of them.

But in Elsie's and her brothers' eyes, this wasn't their mum's fault. Yes, she had many failings, but they all adored her. She was always funny and kind. She'd help anybody and often brought one of the women from the street in for a warm-up and a bite to eat, and she did her best to provide for her family. Sadly, though, Mum was often lonely. Her only friends were the other prostitutes, because the women living around here were wary of her and didn't approve of her way of life, probably thinking they'd be looked on as being the same as her if they mixed with her, or they were afraid of losing their husbands to her.

Often Elsie would see her mum just staring into space, holding a fag, but not smoking it. At those times a tear would trickle down her cheek, but she'd wipe it away before more could follow, and Elsie would give her a hug, without asking what was wrong. She'd long since learned that Mum wouldn't tell her, because she never spoke about her life.

Elsie knew, from her gran, that her mum had worked at the jam factory when she was a girl, but had lost her job when she became pregnant and morning sickness made her late for work. Her place was taken by one of the women who stood at the gate hoping to be set on. Mum had a hard time of it after that, as she married her boyfriend, who, although he wasn't the father of her child, said he'd take her on. But he'd become bitter and violent soon after they were wed. Then, not long after Elsie was born, he took his own life.

The action of pouring a mug of tea for her mum stopped Elsie brooding on who her father was – something she often did when she was thinking everything over, as she was doing this morning.

Bert joined her as she was going through the door to the bedroom. 'I wanna be with Mum on her bed, Else.'

'All right, buggerlugs, come on then.' Glad at this turn in events, Elsie felt safer leaving Bert in bed with Mum, even if she was fast asleep. And besides, the fire was dying down and he'd get cold after a while in the living room. This thought prompted her to call out, 'Cess, bank the fire up with some slack, there's a good 'un. It'll be burning through then by the time Mum gets up.'

With her free hand Elsie shook her mother.

'Mum. Mum, we're going now – here's your mug of tea.'

Groaning as she stirred, Mum didn't open her eyes. 'Ta, darlin', put it on the floor.'

'Bert's here to sit with you till you get up, Mum. He's had his breakfast, and there's half a loaf of bread left that Mrs Wright baked – it's in the pantry, so you can have some of that. We've all got some to take with us.' Still her mum didn't respond with more than a nod. 'Have you any money,

Mum, so that I can call at the butcher's tonight and get a bag of bones to boil up?'

Her mum turned over and pointed to her bag. 'In me purse. I had a good night. Leave me some to get me fags with, Else, there's a darlin'.'

Elsie sighed. What Mum called enough to get her fags would probably be most of what she had. But she was surprised to see a lot more than usual in her mum's purse.

When she went to kiss her goodbye, Mum was properly awake at last. She giggled and ruffled Elsie's hair. This brought joy to Elsie. 'You're happy, Mum?'

'I am, me darlin'. For more reasons than having enough money to have a night off. And I might have a few of them now. Things could look up a bit for us, me darlin'.'

Her arms opened and Elsie went into them. Her heart warmed. There was nothing like a hug from her mum to make her feel better about the world – that was, if she held her breath and didn't take in the stale alcohol and baccy fumes.

As she let go of Elsie, Mum pulled Bert to her and tickled him, then looked up with a smile on her face, which made her seem beautiful. Her hazel eyes were the largest Elsie had ever seen and, despite not always looking after herself, Mum had skin that was soft and a lovely creamy colour, which was enhanced by her freckles.

Elsie smiled back. 'Well then, I'll get pie and mash for supper, shall I? Ma Baker comes into the factory at dinner-time to get everyone's order now, as she says she can't be doing with the rush.'

'That old hag. She more than likely wants to make sure it's her as gets the business, and not Curly down the road from her. Go to him, Else – he makes lovely liquor. Ma Baker's pie ain't got no taste.'

Curly, a big black man, owned a pie-and-mash shop at the end of their road. Elsie didn't want to give a thought as to how her mum knew he made good liquor – the parsley-flavoured sauce they all liked with their mash – so she didn't ask.

A lot of whites wouldn't go to Curly's shop, though she knew he did well among his own people, as he also made hot and spicy dishes, which they loved. It wasn't that he wasn't liked, as he was a lovely man, always happy and grinning and making everyone laugh, so it was hard to fathom why people wouldn't eat his food.

'All right, Mum. Curly's it is. If I see him when I walk by on me way to work, I'll order them ready, then it won't be too late for little Bert to eat.'

'That's good, darlin'. We'll have a grand night: pie and mash and cocoa. I won't get any gin, I promise, and you can play the piano, cos I'm going to get that out of hock today. And I'll ask Ronnie to get one of his men to bring it home on his dray, and to drop some coal off, too; he owes me a bag or two. I don't know why I bother with him half the time. Something for nothing, that one.'

Ignoring this, Elsie released the deep breath of happiness she'd taken in, on hearing about the piano. 'Oh, Mum, you only pawned it? I thought you'd sold it.'

'No, I wouldn't sell me ol' mum's piano. She held on to that through thick and thin, and I'll do the same. Besides, it's your piano now.'

Wanting to clap her hands with the glee she felt, Elsie hugged her mum. 'You're the best mum in the world, and I love you.'

'Well, that's a thanks an' a half, Else.'

'I've missed playing so much. Ooh, I can't wait for home time, but I'd better get going now.'

'Yes, get off now, me darlin'. And ta, Else, for all you do. And no more worrying about the next few weeks – we're going to be all right, girl.'

Elsie skipped towards the door, her mind too full of what was happening that evening to wonder why her mum sounded so positive. But once outside, the October chill made her pull her shawl around her against the onslaught of the wind, and she soon caught up with Jimmy and Cecil. For no matter what tonight was going to bring, there was the toil of the day ahead to get through first.

Chapter Two

Elsie

They hadn't gone far along Long Lane when Dot appeared from the next tenement block.

'Morning, Dot . . . Oh, Dot, look at your face! Your dad been at you again, mate? What for this time, eh?'

A tear dripped off Dot's eyelashes.

'Come here, love. Let's give you a cuddle.'

Dot was like a sister to Elsie. When Dot hurt, she hurt. They'd been mates all of their lives, even though their mums didn't speak to each other – another thing Gran couldn't throw any light on, as she'd said that Mum and Beryl Grimes had been inseparable as young girls.

'What set him off this time then?'

'I don't know, Else. It don't take much. Something to do with me boots being left near the door. But I always leave them there, ready for when I come outside – as me mum does with hers. He said they were in his way, just as I am. And . . . and he called me a bastard again. Me mum didn't say anything, even when he hit me and sent me flying. I – I don't reckon as she loves me, Else. I've never felt that she does. I always feel in the way and can never please her.'

Elsie had heard this so many times along the years and knew it to be the truth. She could think of nothing to say as she let go of Dot and they walked along towards Staple Street. Dot's parentage was another subject that had always given the gossips fodder, because her mum had become pregnant not long after Elsie's mum; she'd married her boyfriend of the time, but it was said he'd got drunk one night – as he often still did – and had cried, saying that his girlfriend was up the duff and he hadn't touched her. This was believed more as each year passed and no other children were born to the couple.

'When I'm ready, I'll sort your dad out for you, Dot,' Cecil said. 'I'm training meself to be a boxer. Mr Wright helps me with me technique; he used to box in the army and he's got medals for it.'

'Ta, Cess.'

Elsie didn't tell Cecil off for boasting in this way, as she secretly hoped he would beat up Dot's dad. Instead she added her pennyworth to cheering up Dot. 'And you can come to ours for tea tonight. We're having pie and mash! How about that, mate, eh? Warm the cockles of your heart, that will. I've got the money and I'm going to order it from Curly as we go. It's all down to me mum having a good earner last night.'

'Sounds lovely, Else. But Curly's?'

'Yes, why not, eh? Me mum likes his pies best, and she did the hard work to earn the money for it.'

Dot shrugged. She was never one to argue the toss.

Feeling guilty at having snapped at her friend, Elsie linked arms with Dot and snuggled up close to her.

Cess lightened the moment. 'Anyway, to top that, Elsie's going to play the piano! Mum's rich enough to get it delivered back home today. And you can share me pie and mash with me if you want, Dot.'

Dot smiled at Cecil, and Elsie saw him blush. She knew he was sweet on Dot, and somehow him being a year younger than her didn't matter. Cecil was taller than Dot, and looked and acted older than his years.

But then Dot was tiny – dainty, and pretty, too, with her mound of dark curls and eyes the same colour as Elsie's. Dot didn't resemble either of her parents, which fuelled the probable truth of what her dad had told everyone in the pub that night. But to Elsie, having made his decision to take Beryl on, Mr Grimes should have got on with it, and not got all bitter about it and made Dot's life a misery. She'd felt glad many times that the man her mum married had gone forever – not only because she knew that he knocked Mum about, but because she was sure he'd have acted the same way to her as Dot's dad did.

As they came up to the shops that lined the road on the corner of Long Lane, they saw Curly outside his cafe, sweeping the path, although Elsie wondered why he was doing so, as the wind swirled the rubbish straight back where it had been.

'Good morning, me rays of sunshine.' His mouth stretched into a wide grin, showing his lovely white teeth as he called this out to them.

Dot dodged behind Cecil, and Elsie heard her say, 'Walk on, Cess.'

'What?'

'Come on.'

Cecil walked on with Dot. Embarrassed, Elsie hurriedly gave her order, and the money to pay for it, to Curly.

'Don't worry about that, Missy. That's not Dot's way;

that's her dad scaring her. Me and him don't see eye-to-eye. Now, Missy, your order will be ready and waiting. But mind you return me bowls to me, as some don't and I'm out of pocket then.'

'I will, Curly. See you later, eh?'

When they reached Staple Street, Jimmy, who hadn't said a word, turned to go into the shop that occupied the whole of the corner of Long Lane. He looked so miserable that he wrenched Elsie's heart.

'I'll see you later, Jimmy. You'll be all right, mate. Keep that scarf around your neck.'

Jimmy gave a half-hearted wave and Elsie wished she could send him back home, but that wasn't an option – Mum had found new fortunes before, but these had come to nothing before too long, so Jimmy would have to carry on until they were sure they could manage without his job.

As they turned the corner, the smell of different foods, and the stench from the leather factory, assaulted her nostrils. Bermondsey had a great intensity of food factories, producing jams, pickles, cakes and pies, and was known as 'London's Kitchen'. And this was besides housing umpteen other factories, distilleries and mills.

Elsie felt mixed emotions assail her, for although she was thankful to be part of the workforce, she hated the conditions that she worked under. And in particular the busiest weeks of the summer when you never knew, as you entered the factory, what time you would leave it. Sometimes she and Dot had still been working at nine o'clock at night.

But the surge of bodies jostling around her took these thoughts from her, as they were caught up in the throng of folk calling out to one another, their boots clattering on the pavement against the backdrop of the clip-clopping of horses' hooves, the grinding of carriage wheels and the smelly, noisy engines of motor vehicles as their drivers wove in and out of the crowd. All of them had one aim: to get to the factory where they worked on time – the workers on foot, the bosses in their carriages or cars.

Usually this was the point in her journey when Elsie's heart dropped, as she dreaded the day ahead, but not today; nothing could daunt her today – she had her pie, mash and liquor to look forward to and, best of all, she'd have her piano back. Life didn't get much better than that.

But even the excitement of the coming evening didn't help, as the daily grind got under way. Clocking-in and getting to your allocated station was the first scramble of the day. For Elsie and Dot, that was jam jar washing. A back-breaking task.

Steam filled the tiled sluice room, where large tubs of boiling water bubbled on one side. Elsie scooped a bowlful from the largest tub and carried it to the sink. Tipping it over the jam jars that stood in rows of four, six deep, she rolled up the sleeves of her overall, which were constantly unravelling, and, lifting the skirt of her pinny, wiped her sweating brow with it. Her back ached; and the wet, sticky rag in her knickers chafed her thighs, rubbing them red-raw. Trying to ignore the discomfort of that, and of wanting a pee, she plunged her hands into the thick rubber gloves and began the task of brushing the jars and standing them upside down on the draining board, building row after row of them until she had a pyramid.

Being so hot, the jars dried very quickly, and Elsie was able to tray them and stack them into boxes, then load them onto trolleys for the carrier to haul into the main part of the factory to be filled with jam.

The washing of the jars was one of Elsie's least-favourite jobs, second only to her most hated task of sorting out the boxes of fruit. After discarding the rotten fruit, the topping and tailing of the berries caused blisters on your fingers, and the juice that seeped into your broken skin stung until it brought tears to your eyes.

With a batch of jars stacked ready, Elsie straightened her back and tucked a stray curl into her mob cap. As she did so, she caught sight of Chambers, the foreman, leering at her. He immediately covered it up by bawling her out. 'What're you messing about at, you useless article? Get on with it or you'll find yourself out of the gate!'

As Elsie hurriedly turned away, she saw Dot struggling to lift a full crate of jars. She willed her to manage it, as she daren't go and help her. Chambers meant every word when he threatened them, especially if he thought them incapable of doing their job.

Somehow Dot found the strength and swung the crate onto the trolley. Elsie saw the tears running down her sweat-reddened face, but had to wait for Chambers to leave the room before she could go over to her friend. As soon as he did leave, Elsie stopped what she was doing and hurried to Dot's side. 'Are you all right, luv?'

'Me back's killing me, Else.'

'Look, once you've got a crate loaded, swap places. I'll lift them onto the trolley for you while you carry on washing my jars, eh?'

'Ta, Else, but don't get into trouble on my account.'

'I won't. We'll keep an eye out for Chambers. But as long as the work's being done, he's got nothing to complain about, has he?'

Elsie's own back ached and her stomach dragged, causing

her pain that she couldn't bear at times, but Dot needed her, and that was all she cared about.

Lifting the fourth crate of the last hour creased her in two. Losing her grip on it, Elsie stumbled and almost fell, as it slipped from her and crashed to the ground. The room fell silent as women stopped what they were doing to stare. Elsie looked down in horror as broken glass surrounded her feet, and the tingling stings of cuts to her legs made her wince. Lifting her skirt, she stepped over the shards, hearing those she couldn't avoid crunch under her shoes.

Dot was by her side in a flash. 'Get back to your own station, Else. I'll take the blame. It's my crate.'

'No. Chambers ain't heard it. Come on, let's clean it up as quick as we can – we might get away with it.'

'I'll help you, girls. You go and fetch the broom, Dot. Come on, Elsie, help me pick out the jars that aren't broken. And cheer up, girl. Worse things happen at sea.'

'Ta, Lucy.'

Elsie didn't know much about Lucy or where she lived. A lanky young woman who never put an ounce on, no matter how much she ate – and she was known for always putting something in her mouth – she was also generous, for if she thought someone was hungry, she'd share what she had. She was liked and, Elsie would say, respected by everyone, for the way she would fight the corner of anyone being put upon, and the way she tried to make a difference to the conditions they worked under. Chambers labelled her an agitator and did all he could to trip her up, so that he could sack her, but Lucy was too clever for him.

From what Elsie did know of her, Lucy lived alone. The talk was that her elderly parents had died in poverty, even though she'd done her best to keep a home going for them.

The general feeling was that Lucy was a born spinster, as she hadn't much in the looks department. Her face was sort of pointed, with her nose jutting out and looking too big for her other features. She didn't help matters by scraping her hair back off her face and coiling it into a tight bun at the nape of her neck. She was what you would term 'worldly-wise'. Folk turned to her for advice, and Lucy had a kind of magnetism when she spoke out, as she often did about the National Federation of Women Workers – a union formed to improve the lot of female workers. But although they listened intently and hung on Lucy's every word, not many of the women took up her plea to join the union. Elsie liked the idea, but, like the rest of them, felt the penny-a-month fee was too much for her.

'There, that's done, and it'll soon be dinner break, girls. Get back to your stations. I doubt Chambers'll even know anything happened.'

'Ta, Lucy. You're a good 'un.'

When the bell went for their dinner break, Elsie had never felt more relieved. 'Dot, go to the canteen – I'll be with you in a mo.' Pushing her way through the crowd of women heading for the lav wasn't easy, but the magic whisper of having the curse let Elsie get to the front.

Feeling less in pain now, and more comfortable, having relieved herself and managed to change her sodden rag, she made her way to Dot.

'I bought a mug of tea between us, Else – it's all I could afford. Have you got anything to eat?'

'Yes. I've a doorstep of bread, ta. So you can eat all your own sandwich, love.'

As they munched away, Elsie thought of the coming evening and her spirits lifted, so much so that she burst into song –

'Heaven Will Protect the Working Girl', a song about the kind of work her mum did, but still poignant to everyone here. Someone joined in, and before Elsie got to the end of the second verse and on to the chorus, all of the girls were belting out:

'From temptations, crimes and follies,
Villains, taxicabs and trolleys,
Oh, heaven will protect a working girl.'

'Ha! What d'you reckon, Ada? Is there a God?'

'I've not seen much of him lately, Gladys, unless it were that beggar who pinched me bum the other night in the pub. He offered me a bountiful grace by way of a feel around the back after closing, but I hit him where it hurt. And when he got up, he didn't have no halo, I can tell you, but he did have two red eyes.'

This sent the women into a fit of giggles, and then moans, as the bell rang and they all piled back into the factory.

For Elsie, the afternoon passed quickly, as her stomach ache eased and she got into the swing of the jar-washing. But she couldn't wait for home time.

'Listen up, everyone.' Dread entered Elsie, on hearing this. Chambers stood in the doorway, a list in his hand. 'No one is to leave until we have another six crates full. We've a rush job on, and you haven't kept the fillers going. So get on with it, and no slacking.'

Elsie's heart sank. She could almost taste her pie and mash, and her fingers were itching to play the piano.

'Come on, girls. Six crates won't take long if we put our backs into it.'

'Says you, Lucy. Me back's killing me, and I can't put it into anything.'

'You'll be all right, Dot. Let's work in the team way that I'm always on about. Elsie, you fetch the box of dirty jars – them returns near the back door – as I noticed a few had been rinsed. You get an empty crate, Dot, and I'll get the boiling water. Then as I wash them, you two pack them; they'll be dry by the time they get to the fillers.'

In no time the three of them had done three crates and were helping the other women with the crate that each had on the go. Ada protested at the method, but when she saw how quickly the job was done, she soon mucked in.

'There! Seven o'clock – not bad. Though I might stay longer and help the fillers, but you all go home. I've nothing to hurry home to.'

'Ta, Lucy. And you should talk to Chambers about your method, as that were far quicker and easier.'

'He won't listen. You know what he's like. But we can work in that way whenever we think we can get away with it, if you're all in agreement?'

As the women filed out, some said they would, but most said they'd only do it if it was overtime, as Chambers would have left by then. Elsie wondered at this. And at the way everything had to be done as it had been for years, when there were better ways. But to be relieved at last, after twelve hours of slog, was enough for now. She'd more to do than put the world to rights.

Grabbing her coat and helping Dot on with hers, Elsie took Dot's hand and made for the door. Taking a deep breath, she said, 'Fresh air at last, Dot.'

'Ha, you sure about that? Me throat's full of smog. But I don't care – we're done for the day, and me legs have a new lease of life. Let's run to Curly's and, while you pick the tea up, I'll nip home and let me mum know that I'm coming to yours.'

'She won't stop you, will she, Dot?'

'No. She'll be glad to have more of what she's cooked to give me dad, and to have me out of the way. I think he treats her better when they're on their own.'

When they turned the corner, they found Cecil waiting for them. 'You're late.'

'We've done overtime – not that we'll be paid for it, but we had no choice. You go on, Cess. You're quicker than me. Run to Curly's, and I'll meet you at home, eh? Me feet and back are killing me.'

'All right. See you in a mo. And you, Dot.'

As Cecil left her, so did Dot. Elsie noticed that Dot could move all right now, and smiled to herself as she saw her catch up with Cecil and watched them hurry along together. Digging her cold hands into her coat pockets and putting her head down, Elsie forgot her tiredness – her only thought was to reach home as fast as she could.

Mum had the little flat looking lovely when she arrived. And, joy of joys, the piano was back in its old place.

'Oh, Mum, I can't believe it. And a cabinet!'

Bert and Jimmy were so caught up in the excitement of it all that they ran at her and nearly knocked her over. Ruffling Jimmy's hair and kissing his cheek, Elsie bent down and picked up Bert. His little arms squeezed her and his lips planted a wet kiss on her face, but she didn't mind and held him tightly to her.

'I missed you, Else.'

She couldn't answer as her heart swelled. Her mum was now telling her, 'Sorry it's not Granny's old cabinet, luv, but this one was in the pawn shop and up for sale for a shilling, so I told him to put it on the dray for me. The china looks nice in it, doesn't it?'

'It looks lovely.' Elsie admired the glass-fronted dark-wood cabinet and suddenly she felt she had a home again. A real home, with a crackling fire and furniture. She twizzled round, making Bert squeal with laughter. It was then that she caught sight of another item. 'An armchair! Oh, Mum, a chair as well.'

'Ha, I thought you'd never notice. It don't match the sofa, but it were cheap. So yes, I bought that too, and still have some money left. Anyway, it means that none of us need sit on the rug, unless Phyllis and Rene come to see us. Now, the pie and mash, where are they? I thought you'd never come.'

The door opened and the delicious smell that wafted in answered Mum's question.

The next few minutes were taken up with everyone scurrying around, laying the table and dishing out the food. Giggles filled the room, and Elsie thought she'd never felt happier. But then, with her belly full, she felt an even greater happiness as she sat down to play the piano and they all sang along.

Her cares left her and her heart swelled. Especially as Bert decided that he wanted to play and climbed on the piano stool with her. What he did surprised them all, as his little fingers soon found a rhythm and Elsie knew that, like her and their gran, Bert had a natural talent. She would make it her mission to teach him. Who knew – one day it might lead to bettering his life. She hoped so. She hoped that Bert, Cess and Jimmy would all have a better life than this one to look forward to.

Chapter Three

Millie

'Millicent, you really are a headstrong girl – and often not to your own good! I forbid you to go anywhere alone again, and especially not near St George's churchyard gardens! Your father was mortified to be passing by on his way from the factory and see you stop to help that woman with her shopping. What on earth were you thinking of, mixing with such people? You are meant to be a lady.'

'I didn't do anything unladylike, Mama. The woman had a child in a pram and a toddler and she was trying to carry a bag, which didn't contain shopping by the way, but coal. Coal that she'd collected from the merchant, as she couldn't afford to have a delivery.'

'None of that was your concern. You shouldn't have been there in the first place; but as you were, you should have passed on by.'

'I'm sorry. I needed to escape for a while. And then when I saw her, I couldn't leave her to struggle – she was exhausted. So I helped her to her home, Mama, which was a flat in a block and she only had one bedroom for all five in her family. And do you know what? I found out that her man is out of work, and she had just finished her shift working in Papa's factory and had collected her children from her mother's. Is that why Papa didn't stop when he saw me? Was he ashamed that I would find all this out, if the woman acknowledged him as her boss? Well, I found out anyway, and I am appalled. If she works the hours she does, why can't she afford to have coal delivered?'

'You did what? Millicent, are you mad? You drove your horse and trap into the slums?!'

'They are not slums. Her flat was very clean, and all the others looked so, too. Well, most of them. I can't believe you are more appalled about me going there than you are about the terrible poverty our workers live in.'

'Don't be ridiculous. Of course I care, but we don't know their circumstances – maybe they spend their earnings on drink, or at least their husbands do. But there is nothing we can do about it. Berating your father and upsetting him, by acting the way you have, won't change things; it will only spoil your chances and goes against everything we are planning for you. We have spent hundreds of pounds preparing you for a gentle life.'

'Oh, Mama, why does all of that mean so much to you? Why can't you think of my happiness? Much as you both want me to progress in society, it isn't going to happen. Yes, you can afford to send me to schools that aristocratic girls attend, but that doesn't make me one of them. I am still the daughter of a self-made man from the North of England. And as such, I am often ridiculed. But for Bunty, I wouldn't have any friends at all. And even she stops short of inviting me to her home. So where do you think I am going to meet someone who will elevate my standing?'

'Lady Barbara – not Bunty! And she may do one day, my

dear. Most of the aristocracy are short of money and need to marry rich girls. With you being that, besides being beautiful and educated in their ways, it is very much a possibility that one of them will offer for you.'

'Oh, Mama, please try to understand. It won't happen. You just don't seem to care how unhappy I am, and how lonely. And that will only get worse in the future. I don't want to go to the finishing school you have put me down for. I know Bunty is going to be there, but she cannot save me from the snide remarks and humiliation that I suffer at the hands of the other girls; and from the teachers, which is sometimes worse. They have the attitude that I should be aiming at what they are doing, as upper-middle class or poor aristocratic women: teaching, not looking to progress to a higher class than my own.'

'Exactly! That proves my point. They cannot find husbands because they haven't the wealth to attract them – and that's what it takes to rise in the world. Anyway, that isn't what they think; that's your imagination. If they are offhand with you, it is more likely because they know you stand a chance, and they don't. You are much wealthier than any of those women.'

'Yes, I am. Papa's success has made us one of the richest families in the country, but do you know what Bunty said to me? She asked if I would one day consider being her live-in nanny-tutor, if I remain a spinster!'

Mama looked shocked, then lowered her head and her expression became a little sad. She often looked this way, leaving Millie to wonder at what problems she might have that she didn't know about.

The low autumn sun shone through the window, its rays highlighting her dark hair and her lovely pearl-like skin.

Millie knew that she took after her mother in these, but in every other way she looked like her father. She had his dark-brown eyes, though she'd often wished she had her mama's liquid-blue ones. And her features were more her father's, too.

After a moment Mama recovered. 'Things will change. I know they will, and you need to be ready for when they do. You must not behave in the way you have ever again, Millie.' On a deep sigh she continued, 'And now you've given me a headache. Go to your room. Your father will have to deal with you when he returns. I'm sure he will have plenty to say on the matter. You've disappointed me, Millicent.'

At nineteen years old, Millie considered herself a grown woman – far too grown-up to be sent to her room. She stormed out of her mother's sitting room, making sure that she slammed the door hard, to mark her contempt.

Barridge, their butler – a man in his fifties, who had been with them for as long as she could remember and was a good sort – jumped. He made a little noise that sounded like a muffled scream, then turned it into a cough. 'I beg your pardon, Miss Millicent.'

Millie couldn't stop to give him her pardon as she ran to her room, giggling. She had only just entered her bedroom when there was a knock on the door. 'Who is it?'

'Ruby, Miss.'

At Millie's bidding her to, Ruby, her maid, confidante and friend – the only one who kept her sane – came through the door, immediately dropping any formal address. 'Eeh, me lass, how did you get on?'

'Oh, you know Mama, Ruby. But it's not all over. She said she is going to tell Papa to deal with me.'

'Well, that's all right then. You've got him wound round your little finger.'

'I may not have in this. And in some ways I think Mama may be right about me taking a risk going to the tenement blocks alone. I was scared, Ruby. I got a lot of hateful looks, and one man spat on the pavement in front of me.'

'Eeh, I'd have pasted his lugholes for him, Miss. But aye, I reckon as you did do wrong. You should have told me you were going further than the green behind the house. Your father could sack me for not accompanying you.'

Millie sank down on the stool in front of her dressing table. *What have I done?* 'I'll talk to him, Ruby, I'll make sure everything is all right for you, I promise. I don't know what got into me. I was riding around and suddenly had this urge to go further. I knew I was doing wrong, but that made it all the more exciting.'

'I knaw, lass. You don't have a lot of fun – I'm not blaming you. But let's hope there's naw consequences that we can't handle, eh?'

'There already are. I can't get it out of my mind how those people, who work such long hours, have so little. And Papa is to blame! I want to help them, and I know I won't rest until I do. So, you see, I've unsettled myself, when I was making do with my lot and getting on with it all. Who am I to complain about my life, Ruby? I feel selfish and spoilt and . . . well, I want to change that, and I can't.'

'Eeh, don't blame yourself for them things, lass. You're none of them. I'd not even say spoilt, as you're forced to do stuff you don't want to. You're a kind-hearted, lovely young lady, and all of us downstairs love you.'

Millie felt her heart swell. To have the love of those who

called themselves 'the downstairs staff' meant a lot to her. 'Thanks, Ruby – at least someone does.'

Ruby grinned. A little older than Millie, she had a lovely round face. Her cheeks dimpled when she smiled and her eyes were a soft brown. Her uniform of a light-grey frock buttoned up at the front and a small white pinny suited her well, as she had what was termed an 'hourglass' figure.

With Ruby's reassurances making Millie feel happier, she rose and walked to the window. Her bedroom, in what Mama called their 'London town house', overlooked Burgess Park, which stretched around the back of their long garden and up to the Old Kent Road. A three-storey house, with the family rooms on the ground and upper floors, it had the kitchens and the housekeeper's office, which was shared by Barridge, on the lower-ground floor. These rooms could be accessed by way of steps outside leading down to them, so that the staff didn't have to traipse through the main house. Then there were the attic rooms, where the staff who lived in had their bedrooms. Ruby was one of those staff.

The stables at the very end of their garden opened onto the park, and Millie loved to slip through the gates on her horse and ride round the lovely lake. Today she'd wanted to practise driving the small trap that she'd been learning to handle for a few weeks now. She loved the feel of guiding the horse from her seat. It gave her more freedom than riding side-saddle. She'd never felt safe doing that.

'If you're all right, Miss, I'd better get on. There's still a lot to pack, and the staff are all at sixes and sevens. Some of them are going to Leeds next week, and everything that's going with them has to be ready.'

'Yes, I'll be fine, thank you, Ruby. At least we only have a few weeks left here, and then Christmas to look forward to, back home in Leeds, before we set sail for Belgium and that wretched finishing school.'

Millie loved Raven Hall, their sprawling country home on the edge of Ravensprings Park in Brighouse, a short drive from Leeds, although it felt like a different world from the busy northern city.

Leeds was where her father had begun his first venture, buying a confectionary shop with the money his grandmother had left him. He'd only been nineteen at the time, and although reasonably well educated, he hadn't had the benefit of coming from a business family because his father had been an engineer. But having a natural talent for reading the markets he dealt in, he realized that not many shops stocked jams and marmalades. And instead of buying in his stock, he employed an aunt who made lovely jams and preserves.

It wasn't long before he had to expand, as demand was high and he soon realized that his fortune lay in mass production. By this time he'd met Mama, a wealthy young woman born to elderly parents who had died and left her well off. With her money and what he'd made himself, Papa employed an agent who found a factory that was rundown and not producing to its full capacity. And so Swift's Jam Factory was born in Bermondsey.

Not that their name was Swift; they were Hawkesfields, from a long line of Hawkesfields hailing from the Leeds area. But Papa, when telling the tale of his rise, loved to relate why he picked the name Swift for his business. 'My rise was swift, Millicent. I was swift to see the potential of jam production, swift to act on my hunch, and I swiftly snapped up an ailing business and turned it around!' Then he would give his infectious laugh and she would end up in a fit of giggles.

She loved her papa; he always had time for her, and never, to her knowledge, lamented the fact that his only child was a girl. He had a charming way with him and made all the female staff giggle with his comments to them. And yet Ruby was wary of him and, yes, a little afraid – something Millie didn't understand. And he didn't make Mama happy, either. It was as if she tolerated Papa, but then was like a puppy being given a treat if he was particularly nice to her.

Doubts began to form in Millie's mind. *Is Papa all I think he is? What about that poor lady today? My own papa was the cause of her poverty.*

A strong urge overcame Millie to find out more about the workings of her father's factory and the conditions the workers had to endure. To this end, she decided to show an interest; to ask Papa questions and to be allowed to visit and be shown the process of making jam. That way, she would be able to see for herself and, hopefully, put her mind at rest.

It was at supper that evening that her father brought up the subject of Millie's foolhardy trip.

He'd greeted her in a cool manner, and they'd sat in silence while their first course of smoked-salmon pâté and buttered toast was served. He was sitting in his usual chair at the top of the table, his manner aloof, his slim, strong body held stiffly. Still dressed in his grey business suit, with a grey-and-silver striped waistcoat, he'd kissed Mama on the top of her head and apologized for not having had time to change. But to Millie, no matter what he wore, she saw him as a rakishly handsome man. Tall and elegant, he had dark-brown hair falling in soft curls to his ears and although he parted it in the middle, it always flopped over his forehead.

His upper lip sported a neat moustache, and his dark-brown eyes reflected his every mood – and this evening they were seething with anger.

As the staff left the room, Millie felt her papa's eyes on her. She looked up. 'Papa, I know you are angry with me, but I am equally angry with you.'

'What? Ha! Don't try to turn the tables, young lady. You have behaved very badly today and I will be having words with your maid. How dare she let you go out alone? But you, Millicent, put yourself in danger and have given your poor mama the fright of her life.'

'Ruby didn't know; she thought I was riding around Burgess Park, as I had told her I intended to. I am sorry. I know I behaved foolishly. I didn't mean to frighten you, Mama. I simply felt that I needed some freedom, and I took my chance, that's all. In that I was wrong. But, Papa, what I did in helping that poor lady, I will not apologize for. I am fit and strong, and she was weak and very tired. I did the decent human thing and helped her.'

The bang of her father's fist on the table made Millie jump. The anger in his face got her trembling. 'You stupid girl! Have you no idea what these people are like? They are dirty, thieving scavengers! They want something for nothing. And they wouldn't care what they did to get it – and that doesn't include working for it. They are lazy, disruptive and uncouth. They don't need your help, young lady; they need to be locked up in prison. Trying to keep up production, with them as my workforce, is a constant struggle. They want more, more, more – money, that is – but less work. How do they think I got where I am today – by being lazy? I worked fifteen or sixteen hours a day, and still do on many occasions. You don't simply take what you want in this life; you work for it. They don't know the meaning of the word.'

Although she was shaking, Millie had to make a stand. 'Papa, why don't I know all of this? Because you keep me away from the real world. And because you try to make me something I'm not.'

'What is it that you are not? A well-brought-up lady with manners? That's what I see. And I am not going to have this discussion with you about your life. I have heard it all from Mama, and I am appalled.'

Fired up now and unable to stop herself, Millie burst out, 'No, that isn't all I am. I am like a piglet. All you and Mama see is your advancement, through me. So you prepare me, you put me through agonies of unhappiness and loneliness for your own ends. Just as surely as the farmer fattens the piglet up for market, you are getting me ready for a non-existent marriage market.' Out of control now, she felt tears springing from her eyes. 'I hate you! I hate you both!'

Scraping her chair along the polished oak floor, Millie stood up. As she turned to run out of the room, she caught sight of her father's astonished face. His mouth was gaping, his eyes almost popping out of his head. She'd got to the door by the time he spoke. He didn't shout, but said on a sigh, 'Please come back to the table, Millicent. It seems we have a lot to discuss. Through what you said to your mama, you have made me see how your life is. I am ready to listen to you.'

Millie turned and ran into her father's arms. There she found the love she knew he felt for her, but rarely had time to show her.

He stroked her hair. 'Sit down, my dear. I listened to your mama, concerning which direction we should guide you in, and I shouldn't have done. I want to hear what *you* want to do with your life, my darling daughter.'

Mama hung her head. She looked broken. Millie went to her side and put her arms around her, but her mother stiffened, leaving Millie feeling rejected. 'Mama, I'm sorry that I can't be what you want me to be. I'm Millie. Yes, Millie – not Millicent. Bunty always calls me "Millie", and I like it. Millicent is the person you want me to be, Mama, but can't you simply accept me as I am?'

Mama's hand came on hers and patted it. 'Sit down as your papa has bidden you to, Millicent.'

Papa surprised them both then by saying, 'I like the name "Millie". Yes, I think it suits you. I will call you that from now on.'

'Richard!'

'Richie! I was always known as Richie, until you insisted on using my full name. Well, from now on, I will only answer to Richie! Millie isn't the only one rebelling today. I am, too. And while I am, I have made my mind up that Millie isn't going to that silly school to learn to balance books on her head, but is going to do as I have always wanted her to – come and work with me and learn the jam-making business, so that one day she can take it over.'

'No! Richard, are you completely out of your mind? I will not allow it.'

'Richard may have been out of his mind, but Richie is not. Now may we please eat our supper? You and I will retire to your sitting room afterwards, Abigail, and have the talk that we should have had years ago. But prepare yourself, because things are going to change in our lives.'

Millie had never seen her papa like this before; he'd become someone very different from the father she'd always known. *Poor Mama looks lost. Papa has always given her free rein when it comes to what happens to me and what direction my life should take.* But somehow Millie couldn't feel sorry for Mama, as she was too full of happiness for herself. *At last I am going to be allowed to be me!*

That happiness dissolved later as Millie lay on her bed, playing over in her mind all she'd heard her parents say to each other as she'd listened outside Mama's sitting-room door. Most of it shocked her to the core. Nothing was ever going to be the same again.

Papa's opening words had cemented the knowledge that she'd come to recognize earlier – Papa wasn't all he seemed, and said things he didn't mean, to suit his purpose. He'd begun his 'talk' with Mama by mocking her.

'Well, Abigail, are you going to loosen your corsets and become Abby?'

Millie had smiled at this, feeling in the first instance that Mama deserved to be brought down a peg or two; even the crudeness of it hadn't offended her. But then her mama's answer had shaken her. 'There are enough women loosening their corsets for you, Richard.'

From then on, what she overheard got worse, as Papa had retorted, 'I wouldn't have had to ask them to, if you had been freer with yours, instead of banning me from your bed.'

'That only happened after I found out about your infidelity. You humiliated me.' Mama's voice had trembled with emotion.

'I have told you a hundred times, that girl threw herself at me. What you saw was me coaxing her to behave herself.'

'Oh? Really? You were coming out of a kiss. And with

my maid! Your hand was on her breast. Is that how you coax somebody to stop? I think quite the opposite.'

'Look, Abigail, we have been over and over this, and it gets us nowhere. That shouldn't have happened, but it did. Your unforgiving nature and lack of understanding about how a man can be led astray have driven us apart ever since, when we were so much in love when we first married.'

'No, your action drove us apart. Yes, I know how men are. But there is such a thing as self-control, and not wanting to hurt the woman you say you love and have promised your life to. Didn't that count for anything with you? I will never forgive you, never!'

'And that is why I have to carry on my "infidelity", as you call it. I had learned my lesson, Abigail. I had been flattered and had been very foolish and wrong, but that moment of weakness cost me a great deal more than it should have done – not only losing your love, which meant the world to me, but also my chances of having a son. It was your duty to try and give me a son to carry on my name, and to take my business into the next generation.'

'Well, who knows how many sons you have out there! But I am not concerned with them; they are an insult to me, although it seems you have the idea that you can now use your only legitimate child, your daughter, for your own ends, and I implore you not to.'

How the conversation ended, Millie didn't know. With her heart breaking, she had run up to her room. Papa, wanting a son! *Am I not good enough?* And going with other women and having children by them. *Is it true? Do I have brothers and sisters?* The thought grew in her mind. *Where are they? Does Papa take care of them?* She'd always known there was a deep sadness in her mama, and now she knew why.

Well, she couldn't change what made Mama unhappy, but she would always try to make her happy from now on – though it wouldn't be by pandering to her wishes and making an effort to marry into a titled family. No, she had another mission to accomplish, which she desired far more – to prove to her father that she was as good as any son he ever dreamed of having.

Chapter Four

Kitty

Smoke from the cigarettes of the three sailors, who stood around a large cargo ship anchored in the Port of London dock, curled up to the lamplight. One threw his butt end on the ground and walked over to where Kitty stood with Rene and Phyllis.

The women were in their usual spot, leaning against a pile of sacks marked 'Brown's Flour Mill'. Whenever they tried their luck at the dockside they would make for this spot, as the sacks offered warmth and shielded them against the elements.

It seemed such a short time ago that Kitty had thought she'd never have to do this again. She had promised Elsie and her boys that she wouldn't, but she'd been let down again by a man who had declared he loved her – something that had happened to her more times than she cared to think about. So here she was again, just three weeks later, and loathing every minute.

'We're in luck, darlin's,' Phyllis giggled. 'One each – just right to set the night off.'

'I'll take this one. I like 'em big.' Rene laughed at her own joke. 'Which one are you having, Kitty?'

'I don't care as long as he pays well, Rene.'

The man Rene had chosen came over to Kitty. His skin was a swarthy, weather-beaten brown; his voice was thick with a foreign accent. 'Want to earn good money, lady?'

She nodded.

He indicated with his head for her to follow him.

Loathing herself, Kitty followed, looking back as she reached the ship to see Phyllis and Rene go in different directions, each with one of the other men who had approached them.

When the sailor reached the ship he stepped back and directed her with his hand to board the boat. This had never happened before. Nerves tingled in her stomach, making her hesitate for a moment.

'You go.'

'Look, mate, I don't feel safe. What if your captain comes and I'm taken for a stowaway? He's likely to fetch the Old Bill, and I'll end up locked up for the night.'

'Me am captain.'

Kitty's fear deepened. Something wasn't right. He didn't look like a captain. She wanted to turn and run, but the man positioned himself across the end of the gangplank and held the rope on one side. He could easily grab her with his free hand. Desperate to seek a way out she told him, 'Look, before I go on the boat with you, mate, you need to know that I only do normal sex. If you're looking for more, then I'll take you to Ma Sawyers's place. She's got girls who'll do anything you want.'

'No. You'll do. We want you.'

'We? Wait a minute, mate, I don't do no "we".'

Before she had time to react, he grabbed her and twisted her round, so that her back was against him. His arm came round her neck, his large hand clamped over her mouth and his finger and thumb pinched her nostrils closed. She couldn't breathe. In an instant he had bent and picked her up. Flailing her free arm and kicking her legs didn't help. Her head was held as if in a vice. Desperate to get some air, Kitty tried to bite him, but he was like a monster and nothing she did made the slightest impact on his hold on her.

As they reached the top of the gangplank, she could fight no more. Her head spun. Deprived of oxygen, her mind went blank.

A sudden drenching of cold water made Kitty gasp as she was shocked back into consciousness. With the intake of breath, she took in the stench of stale body odour. Looking around her, she realized she was in a cabin, lying on a bed. The man who'd carried her here and two others stood over her.

Frantically she rolled over and tried to lift her body off the filthy sheet. But hands grabbed her and pulled at her clothes. Her screams didn't deter them. She was powerless against their strength. The big man watched, slowly stripping himself, his menacing look silencing Kitty as fear and despair sank in. By the time she was naked, he was, too. When he moved, she shrank back, but he didn't get on the bed as she expected; instead he pulled his discarded trousers towards him and slowly slid the thick leather belt from the loops through which it was threaded. Kitty drew in a horror-filled breath as he coiled the belt around his right hand.

The first lash stung her thighs. 'No, no. Please, I – I . . . Arggh . . .' The searing pain made her gasp as the belt whipped her other thigh.

She was turned as if she was a piece of meat, and the sting of the belt on her buttocks had her begging for mercy.

Her tears mingled with her snot and her spittle as she gasped against the extreme pain.

'Please, please don't. Don't.'

Suddenly the onslaught stopped and she heard a moan of pleasure – a sound she'd heard many times – and knew, with relief, that the man beating her had reached his climax. Sobbing into the stinking sheet beneath her, Kitty thought it was all over. But she was still being held.

'Let me go now, please. I'll not be any trouble. I just want to go.'

'No. My turn.'

How much later it was when she found herself rolling downwards and thudding against the gangplank, clutching her clothes, Kitty didn't know. Nor did she mind the biting wind, as it soothed and cooled her burning, smarting body. All she cared about was that it was over: the rape, the unspeakably depraved acts the men had gratified themselves with, using her as if she was nothing – not even human. And that's how she felt: like an animal.

'Kitty, Kitty. Aw, mate. Come on, me darlin', let's help you up.'

'Rene. Oh, Rene, I can't move.'

'You've got to, love. You'll freeze. Here, give me your hand.'

Rene helped her to stand. Every movement caused Kitty pain, but slowly they made it to the flour store. There, as she shivered uncontrollably, Rene dressed her as if she were a child.

'Can you walk, Kitty, love?'

Though she didn't think she could, Kitty did manage a few steps, but then had to rest.

'Look, you stay here a mo. I'll nip to the inn and get the two blokes that me and Phyllis had. They were decent enough and'll help us.'

'Where's Phyllis, Rene? Is she at the inn?'

'No. She got another punter. I didn't want her to go with him, as he looked a dodgy geezer, but Phyllis needs the money. She's in hock to the moneylender again, and he's threatening her. You know what he's like. One of these days her way of going on'll be the death of her.'

It wasn't until Kitty found herself in front of a roaring fire in the Ship Inn, sipping a gin, that she gave more thought to Phyllis and where she was. The men Rene had fetched had carried her here and had apologized to her for the behaviour of their fellow countrymen.

Kitty hadn't said anything; she hadn't been able to, for all that they seemed decent enough. She knew they must have known what the other men were like, and what she'd been in for, but they'd done nothing; they'd simply pursued their own pleasure and left her to her fate.

'Well, well, Kitty, girl, you copped it this time,' Ma Sawyers said, a fag hanging from her mouth and the smoke making her screw up her eyes as she sauntered over. She looked a comic figure, as her attempt at making herself look glamorous only resulted in making her appear ridiculous, with her bleached-blonde hair caught back in a wide red band, and her face thick with pancake make-up. Her lips were bright red, the lipstick fashioned into a heart shape that left much of her lips bare. Around her mid-fifties, she was a small woman, with her bust drooping onto a protruding stomach, revealing a long, sagging cleavage. She somehow managed to make her purple frock look indecent.

'You should come in with me, Kitty. I've offered you

many a time. Now look at you, mate. You wouldn't end up like this if you were with me. I look after me girls, and this stuff only happens to them if they want it to. Then they get good money for it, and some care afterwards.'

'You know I've got kids, Ma Sawyers. I can't leave 'em. But ta for the offer.'

'Come back to mine now, eh, darlin'? I'll see as you get cleaned up. Hettie, one of me older ones, she takes care of me girls. She'll soon sort you out and make sure you don't get an infection in them wounds.'

When she woke up the next day Kitty couldn't move, as her limbs had stiffened. With extreme effort, she managed to ease her legs off the bed. She peered over at the bed next to her and saw that it was empty and tidy. This meant that Elsie and the lads had gone to work. She felt behind her, but couldn't sense little Bert. He must be in the living room.

Her movement had caused her foot to kick the empty gin bottle lying at her feet. As it spun round, Kitty let her head fall forward as shame washed over her at the memory of how, after she'd been cleaned up, she'd been given a good swig of neat gin to help her with the pain. That had set her craving more, and she'd borrowed money from Ma Sawyers to buy a bottle.

Her head shook from side to side as the implications of her actions last night hit her. Ma Sawyers was ruthless – you didn't cross her. She had henchmen who could do worse to you than the sailors had done to her last night.

Ma Sawyers's words came to her now. 'Here you are, ducky. Ten bob. Will that do you? I'll give you a couple of weeks to get it back to me.'

How am I going to do that! Disgust at herself hit Kitty as she remembered buying the gin. She'd gone round the back of the inn, as she knew the landlord ran a card school after pub hours and would still be serving late drinks. He'd charged her double the normal price, knowing her need of it. She'd bought two bottles – one for Rene for helping her – and they'd swigged it there and then, consuming almost half in a couple of gulps.

The next thing Kitty could remember was being in a cab and taking Rene to her own home, and crying at the thought of Rene living in such squalor. But then the rhythmic clip-clopping of the horse's hooves and the gentle sway of the cab had sent her into a booze-induced slumber.

She'd registered someone helping her to the door. But then . . .

Tears tumbled down Kitty's face as she tried to fight through the haze of her brain to sort out the events that followed. The salty wetness stung the open wounds on her cheeks and found a path down her neck, leaving a trail of soreness as they travelled over her cuts and bruises.

Sounds drifted to her from the living room, making her realize that no matter what it cost her to stand and move, she must go to Bert and make sure he was safe. He might take it into his head to play with the fire, or climb onto a chair and make his way outside.

As she stood, Kitty's legs crumbled and she sat back down again.

A feeling of trepidation hit her as the memory of arriving home returned – whoever opened her door had helped her to the sofa. She'd sunk into oblivion, but then a noise had woken her and she'd known there was someone in the room with her. She'd heard muffled sounds.

Oh God! My handbag! Looking frantically around her,

Kitty's fear deepened. Her handbag wasn't on the floor, propped against the wall where she would normally put it. Nor could she find it on the bed. Given strength by the fear that was running through her, she made it to the door, to be met by Elsie.

'Oh, Mum, look at you. What happened to you? You've slept all day.'

Through the mist of her tears, Kitty tried to sort out this information in her mind. 'Else? What time is it, then?'

'Gone four, Mum. Oh, Mum, you look awful – your face!'

'Don't cry, darlin', I'm all right. Have you been to work? What happened to Bert? Where is he, and where's the lads?'

'No, Mum, I'm laid off now, remember? Cecil went to the docks and isn't back yet. Jimmy's at school and Bert's playing out for a bit, as it's not so cold today. Come and sit down. Who did this to you? Oh, Mum. Mum . . .'

'Don't worry, me darlin', dry your tears. I just need me bag, then I'll rest.'

'It's not here. I've cleaned all up and didn't see it. I'll have a look in the bedroom; you might have kicked it under the bed.'

Though she didn't object to this, Kitty felt sure it wasn't there. *Oh God, it was going to be hard enough to pay back what I spent, but what if it's all gone?*

'It's not there, Mum. Did you leave it somewhere?'

'No, I must have had it, darlin', or I wouldn't have been able to get in.' She didn't tell Elsie her fear that someone had followed her in. Her shame was too deep. She'd put her kids' lives at risk – it could have been anyone.

'Aw, Mum, don't.'

But Kitty couldn't help herself. The floodgates were open and a deluge of sadness, fear and worry hit her.

Elsie cried with her, and together they rocked backwards and forwards.

'Mum . . . you'll be all right. I'll look after you.'

Elsie's cry got through Kitty's wrenching sobs. She tried to swallow, to calm herself.

'I'll get a cup of tea on the go, eh? Then I'll get the bath and fill it for you. You can have a soak in front of the fire.'

'No . . . No, darling. I – I, well, I've been beaten . . . It's all right, as I've had me injuries seen to, but I couldn't bear the water touching them. But yes, get the kettle on. That'd be good.'

'All right. And I'll use fresh tea leaves, so it'll be nice and strong for you. I ain't got any sugar, but I'll nip round to Mrs Wright's – she'll give me a cupful, as I've done a lot for her this week. Poor soul's getting worse with her arthritis.'

Once they sat drinking the hot, sweet tea, Elsie asked the question that Kitty had been dreading.

'What happened to change things, Mum? A few weeks ago you were so happy, and you brought in some good money. I thought you'd met a nice regular, who'd look after you and keep you for himself.'

'I can't talk about it, love.'

'But why, Mum? What makes you keep secrets?'

'Don't ask me, darlin'. Just accept that I can't tell you certain things.'

'Mum . . . Look, I've been meaning to talk to you. There are things you should tell me. Not about me, but about Dot. And what happened between you and her mum. Dot knows Mr Grimes isn't her real father, and he treats her like a dog. Do you know who fathered her? Dot's asked me to ask you, as she'd like to get away and go to her real father.'

'Oh, Elsie. Me and Beryl Grimes did a bad thing. But if

you knew, it would cause you more pain. And if it got out, then a lot more would suffer.'

'Was me dad married to someone else . . . Has he got other kids?'

The pain this was causing Kitty was worse than the pain of her injuries. She'd known that one day her daughter would want to know, just as her sons might. But she couldn't tell her sons about their fathers – not for sure. But who fathered Elsie, that she did know, although it was better that she never revealed the secret.

'Mum?'

'Let's leave it, darlin', please.'

'All right, but you're not being fair. There's someone out there who might think something of me; and someone for Dot, too. Maybe Dot's dad would take care of her and get her away from that brute. And mine might even help us out, now and again.'

'Elsie, love, get that out of your head, girl. He won't want to know you. I'm sorry. I don't want to hurt you, me darlin', but don't go imagining that he's a knight in shining armour. He ain't, and you're better off not knowing him.'

Elsie went quiet. Kitty could see this had upset her, but it was better that she knew the truth about the situation – well, the bit that knowing her father would only cause her more pain, so that she didn't get any fanciful ideas in her head.

But what Elsie said next shocked Kitty, and hit a raw nerve of truth.

'All right, but there's something more that I want to say, Mum. I want you to stop prostituting yourself. Now! We've had enough. *You've* had enough. All it's doing is causing pain and worry. We'll manage somehow.' From this cross, determined voice, Elsie softened. 'I – I can't bear to see you hurt like this. And what if it was worse, and you were murdered? Well, I can't cope with the worry . . . and the lads, but they deserve better. They need a mum.'

'I'm sorry, me darlin', I know as you're afraid, and I know as I neglect you, but I just don't know what else to do to earn some money. This is all I've done for years.'

'There must be something. What about cleaning?'

'Who's going to have me? No one. Everyone for miles around knows me reputation and they wouldn't have me in their homes.'

'You could go further afield to where the big houses are – you might get set on. And they won't know you. Or . . . well, you could wait at the gate of the jam factory. There's always somebody doesn't turn up because they're sick, or their time's come to have their baby. Most work until they drop their kid, but not all get back in, as their place has been taken and whoever took it is proving to be a better worker.'

'Not surprising. It's hard to work when your belly and your legs have swelled and the weight's dragging you down. No, I could never work there again.'

'Why? Why do you always say that? Things are not good there, but they have changed since your day, Mum. We have washrooms now, since that girl died. We no longer have to eat our sandwiches in the mucky fruit-sorting room without being able to wash our hands, and we have basins in the lav, too. Things ain't how you remember them.'

'I'll find something. I promise. But I'll carry on as I am until I've got meself straight. Look, Else, I don't want to add to your worries, but – well, I owe a bit of money.'

'Mum! No. How much?'

Shame overwhelmed Kitty as she admitted to Elsie how much she owed.

'To Ma Sawyers! God, Mum, what were you thinking?'

This started the tears rolling again. Exhausted, Kitty laid her head back. 'I'm sorry, I'm sorry. I—'

'Come on. We'll sort it. Look, we've nearly paid the tallyman, so when he comes tomorrow, we'll ask him for a bit more. I can pay it off when I'm back in work. And I've got some left from what you gave me, when you were doing well. We'll give that to Ma Sawyers and ask her to let us pay the rest off weekly, eh?'

Hope settled in Kitty. Maybe if she could clear the debt with Ma Sawyers, then somehow she could try and make changes to the way she ran her life. *I have to try. I have to.*

'Right, let's get you dressed now. The lads'll be in for their tea soon. I've got some potatoes. I'll put them on to boil and make a plate of mash for each of us. Then I'll play the piano and we'll have a sing-song, eh? We haven't had one since that night you first got the piano back.'

Though tired and in pain, Kitty sang her heart out and laughed as the lads did jigs and fooled around. Even Cecil, who had been distant with her lately, joined in and was caring towards her.

'You've got a lovely voice, Mum. You could do what Gran did, and work the music halls. You'd go down well. I'd come with you to look after you.'

'And I could play the piano for you. Cecil's right, Mum, your voice is beautiful. I was so used to it that I took it for granted. Sing that new one, "I'm Shy, Mary Ellen". It's lovely.'

Kitty's mind went to where she'd first heard the song a few short weeks ago. She'd never mentioned to the kids how she'd had a magical music-hall evening. How could she, when she couldn't tell them who had taken her?

But now the evening came back to her. And she thought of how she'd gone to Rene's and had dressed in one of her frocks – a wonderful seamstress, Rene had a few special frocks that she'd made over the years. This one had been long and sleek and had fitted Kitty's figure like a glove, showing off her curves. Phyllis had dressed her hair, coiling it up on the top of her head and letting it fall in one long ringlet at the back, and they'd been to the market and found a fur wrap. It had looked a bit manky, until they'd got it home and brushed it over and over again. Kitty had felt like a queen by the time the car picked her up. *But then he said his goodbyes to me at the end of the evening, and I haven't seen him since.*

Brushing this thought away, she let the magical sights she'd seen onstage enter her mind. She posed her body and fluttered her eyes demurely, just as the actress had done. The music started, and at that moment Kitty's imagination showed her the curtain rising and herself standing centre-stage in a beautiful pink gown that floated around her. Taking a breath, she let her voice soar, as she did the comic actions to the lyrics. Her pain vanished as she let the music seize her. When it ended there was silence, then Elsie jumped up from her piano seat.

'Mum – oh, Mum, that was wonderful. You could be a star, Mum; you could.'

Caught up in the excitement around her, for one moment Kitty thought it could happen, but then a banging on the door brought her down to earth and fear shot through her, as the sound made her realize that something dreadful had happened.

The door opened and Rene stood there, her face deathly white, tears streaming down her cheeks. Her mouth opened and closed, but nothing came out.

'Rene. Rene, love, what is it?'

She sank down onto the sofa, and a horrible groan came from her.

'Rene. Tell us, Rene, what is it?'

'Phyllis . . . Oh, Kitty. Phyllis's body was washed up on the bank of the Thames. She – she's dead, Kitty. Our lovely Phyllis is dead. The Old Bill said she . . . she was . . . murdered!'

Every limb in Kitty's body shook with the shock. For a moment she thought she wouldn't cope with it, and the need for a gin came to her mind, but she looked round at the faces of her kids, all white with terror, and somehow gleaned some strength from deep within herself and opened her arms to them. All four came to her.

'Don't be afraid, me darlin's. Nothing will happen to you, nor to me. The Old Bill will find who did this and put them away for a long stretch. Let's look after poor Rene. Get the kettle on, Else darlin'.'

'I don't want tea, Kitty. I need a gin. Ain't you got any of that bottle left?'

'No, Rene, love. I ain't never touching it again. Never. Oh, Rene . . .' She sank down onto the sofa next to her friend.

Rene took hold of her and hugged her close. Kitty could feel the love she had for her, but could feel her loss, too. 'It's like someone has severed us, Rene.'

The tears flowed then and loosened the tight knot that had gripped Kitty's throat.

'Mum, don't be sad. Mr Jollop died, and Mr Wright said he'd gone to a better place. A happy place.' Bert's bottom lip was quivering as he said this.

Kitty put her hand out and stroked his hair. 'He did, and so will Phyllis – I know that. But Mr Jollop were your friend, and you were sad that you wouldn't see him again. And Phyllis was my friend.'

Mr Jollop had been a lovely old man who lived a little way down the road from them. He and Bert had formed a deep bond, as Mr Jollop used to wave whenever he passed. Little Bert had been heartbroken when he died.

The kettle whistled for attention and Elsie, who hadn't spoken, busied herself. Cecil had stood as if turned to stone, as soon as Kitty had gone into Rene's arms; and poor, nervous Jimmy sat down, wringing his hands. Taking a deep breath, Kitty made a promise that she prayed to God she could keep. It was partly something she'd already come to a conclusion about, after her experience the night before, but now she had to comfort her children. As she spoke, the strength that she'd felt earlier became a great force and she believed her statement to be a truth.

'Me darlin's, listen to your mum. Nothing like what happened to Phyllis will happen to me. From now on, even if we're starving, your mum'll never work the streets again. And I'll never touch a drop of gin again, either. I promise you that, on me life.'

The children were all in her arms again, clinging to her, and for the first time ever Kitty felt the pain she'd put them through.

The tears that fell from her eyes were not all tears of

despair. Some were for the loss of lovely Phyllis, and some for the shame she felt, but at the same time they held hope for the way she saw her future shaping up in such a different way from her past. But while this gave her a sense of relief, the feelings assailing her were too much for her to cope with.

Chapter Five

Elsie

Elsie almost skipped along the road and up the stone steps to knock on Dot's door. Her stomach clenched as she anticipated Dot's mum or dad opening it, but she couldn't wait any longer to tell Dot the decision her mum had come to the day before. And how this morning Mum had got up early and done all the chores, and had a pan of porridge on, by the time Elsie woke – something she couldn't ever remember happening before.

There were only two weeks to go till Christmas and then the factory would reopen. How they'd get through till then, with Mum not bringing anything in, Elsie didn't know. But she didn't care. Just to have her mum back – for it did feel as though she'd been missing for a long time – was enough to make up for having days when it was likely they would have nothing but porridge to eat.

Thankfully, it was Dot who opened the door. Already wearing her shawl, she stepped outside. 'You're up for going for a walk then, Dot?'

Elsie had sent Jimmy up to tell Dot she'd be up later and hoped they could spend a little time together.

'Yes, but I can't be out long. Me dad's out at the mo. He got set on down the docks two days a week and might be back at any time. Where're we going, Else?'

'Let's go to St George's gardens. It feels like you're in the country when you're there.'

'Except for that big wall where the gravestones are. That makes me shudder.'

'Well, we won't sit for long in this cold weather, but near that is the best place – it's a bit of a sun-trap and shields you from any wind. I'll hold your hand, then no ghosts will get you.'

They giggled at this and linked arms. When they reached the park, they sat on a bench watching a robin hopping about, almost as if it was begging them to give it something.

'We've no food, if that's what you're after, mate,' Elsie told it.

'Are you hungry, Else?'

'Starving. There weren't a lot of porridge left, and we've no money to come in.' Elsie told Dot about her mum's decision. 'I've been sitting here trying to think how I can solve it all, but I don't know of a way, and I'm afraid that me mum'll not stick to her plan if our situation worsens.'

'Me mum's cooking a stew tonight. And she bakes bread in chunks, to have with it. I'll hide mine and sneak it out to you, if you like.'

'Ta, Dot. I'd want it for the lads, not me. I can manage. I can beg something from Mrs Wright, she's a good soul.'

'Here comes someone who don't have to beg.'

The clip-clop of a horse's hooves had prompted this from Dot. The rider steered her horse towards them and stopped by them. 'Hello.'

Shocked, Elsie looked up into a face of a girl she'd seen

before. Of a similar age to herself and Dot, she looked different, close up. Elsie had the strange feeling that she knew this girl well, but she couldn't think why such a notion should enter her head.

The horse shifted about and shook his head, snorting loudly. Elsie recoiled. The animal looked like a monster. It was huge. 'It won't hurt us, will it?'

The girl dismounted, laughing as she did so. 'No, he's the gentlest horse I know. Papa wouldn't let me ride him if he wasn't. Not that he likes me to ride as far as this, but I love to see something of life – real life, I mean, real people.'

'We're not a side-show. We're—'

'Oh no, I didn't mean that. I'm sorry if I have offended you. I just mean . . . well, Papa has a jam factory near here and I work in his office with him sometimes, but I don't get the true picture of things from up there. I like to see how those who work for him live – oh, that sounds even worse. Look, I'll go. I didn't mean to intrude.'

'No, you're all right. We can be a bit outspoken around here. We know your dad. I mean, we don't know him – nor him us – but he owns Swift's, don't he?'

'Yes. I'd only been there once when it was working, but I've been there a couple of days a week while it's closed. It's a good opportunity for me to learn how it all ticks over.'

There was something about the girl that fascinated Elsie. She liked her, but felt wary of her at the same time.

'We work at Swift's,' Dot said. 'It's not what you'd call a bed of roses, and the pay ain't good, but we can't wait for it to reopen, as we've got nothing without.'

Elsie held her breath, wishing Dot hadn't said this, as the girl might take offence and report them to her father. But she didn't seem put out by it. She looked ashamed, which made Elsie warm to her. But when the girl asked their names, she became wary again. 'If we tell you, you won't snitch on me mate for saying what she did, will you?'

'No, I promise – I'll do a pinky-promise, if you want me to.'

Elsie didn't know what this was. Curious to find out, she said, 'Go on then.'

The girl took off her glove and stuck out her little finger towards Elsie, who stared at it.

'Ha, it's nothing bad. Just link your little finger with mine and then I promise – and that's it. I never break it, but you have to promise me at the same time that you'll never mention to my papa that you met me here. He would be furious if he knew I rode around this park on my own.'

Elsie could understand this, as the girl wasn't safe around here. Linking little fingers amused her, though, as she never thought anyone of this girl's standing would ever touch the likes of her.

Elsie giggled, but Dot still sat as if she was a statue. Elsie could feel her fear of the situation. She nudged her and smiled, but Dot still didn't move.

'Me name's Elsie. What's yours?'

'Millie; well, Millicent, but I like to be called Millie. I'd sit with you, but I have to hold on to Fennie. Why don't you stroke her mane? She loves anyone fussing over her.'

Elsie stood gingerly, the horse moved and she jumped back. Millie laughed out loud. For a moment Elsie felt affronted, but Millie had such an infectious laugh and there was no hint that she was making fun of her.

'She will be wary of you at first. Just talk to her as you approach. Say something like "Hello, girl".'

Elsie tried it, and the horse eyed her. Determinedly she

persisted and was rewarded with a feeling of being at one with the huge animal.

'She's lovely.' As she said this, Elsie's stomach rumbled as if she had a motorbike inside it. Embarrassed, she coughed to cover it up and hoped Millie hadn't realized what the noise was.

'Are you hungry, Elsie? I've got some bread and cake in my satchel – you can have them, if you like. They're not stale, but I have them to feed the birds and the swans in the park behind where I live.'

Unable to resist, Elsie nodded. And she couldn't believe her eyes when Millie brought a tin out of the saddle bag slung over the horse and handed it to her. The tin was round and had a picture of a cottage on the top. Elsie didn't think she'd ever seen anything so pretty.

'Take it – you can keep it if you want.'

'Ta, Millie. I'll save some for me brovvers. Ta ever so much.' Simply owning such a tin was a joy to her, let alone the promise of bread and cake! Sitting back down, Elsie had a strong urge to open the tin, but knew that if she did, she would want to scoff the lot.

'How many brothers have you got?'

'Three – Cecil, Jimmy and little Bert.'

The more she chatted to Millie, the more Elsie liked her. Everything about her: her easy manner, with no side to her, and her sense of humour. It didn't seem like she came from a different class to Elsie, but as if they were mates. She was sorry when Millie said that she had to go. But then felt a relief that she couldn't explain when Millie said, 'Let's meet again. I really need some friends – life gets very lonely, being an only child. If I come here tomorrow, will you come and meet me? Only . . . well, our friendship will have to be a secret. I mean, I – I don't need it to be so for my own sake, but my parents don't think like I do and would not allow me to see you both, if they found out.'

'I'd like that, mate. And don't worry. I understand how it is and wouldn't let anyone know. What about you, Dot?'

'Oh, you're called Dot? Is that short for Dorothy?'

Dot smiled and nodded her head.

'Don't be afraid, Dot. I promise I won't reveal anything of what you said. As long as you two promise never to tell anyone about me.'

'Not even our mums, Millie? Only I'll have to explain where I got this tin of cake.'

'Better not. Say you found it. And I'll bring you some more tomorrow, if you like. Cook's a good sort; she'll get some ham and pie ready for me if I ask her, and she won't ask any questions or tell my parents.'

This was too much for Elsie to refuse. She'd think of something to tell her mum. Although, with how hungry they all were, she didn't see her mum asking questions.

'I tell you what: we can call ourselves "the black-eyed gang" as we've all got the same dark eyes.'

Elsie laughed at Millie. 'Ha, I feel like a kid again, talking of having gangs.'

'I know what you mean, and us being young ladies, too. I was only funning. Though why I say I understand is a mystery to me, as I have never had any friends to be in a gang with. Others formed them, but I was never allowed to join in.'

'Oh, why's that then?' Listening to how Millie had to attend a school with those of much higher class than her shocked Elsie. 'I never thought there could be anyone of a higher class than you, let alone them as would look down on you. I know how you feel, though, as it happens to us all the time. It makes you feel less than human at times.'

'I understand that exactly. Yes, that is how it makes you feel, and that is why I made my mind up never to behave like that. Anyway, I have to go. I've been away for too long. Someone might look for me, and then it will be discovered that I'm not where I'm supposed to be. I'll try to be here tomorrow. I hope you can make it. Bye.'

With this, Millie rode off, leaving Elsie and Dot staring after her.

'Did that really happen, Dot?'

'I know, I can't believe it. I was struck dumb, but you talked to her as if you'd known her all your life.' Dot pushed her playfully. 'Think yourself someone, Elsie Makin, don't you?'

Elsie retaliated by shoving Dot back, then put on a swagger. 'I do, as it happens, Dot Grimes. I'm Lady Duck Muck from Long Lane, don't you know?'

They collapsed in giggles and linked arms again. 'Come on, let's get back. I'll call for you tomorrow at the same time, eh?'

'What if someone sees us, Else?'

'We'll take our chances, but if this is going to be regular, then we might have to think about that. My mum won't mind, but I'm not so sure about your dad. I'd tell me mum about Millie, but for me promise.'

'That pinky-thing were a bit weird, weren't it? Did you feel daft?'

'No. I felt . . . Oh, it doesn't matter. Anyway, a promise is a promise.'

Elsie decided she would feel daft if she told Dot that she had a feeling of being the same as Millie, and that there was no divide between them. And something else: a sort of kinship with her that she couldn't explain, because for all her fancy notions, she and Millie weren't the same; they were miles apart. How she could tell Dot all this, she didn't know, and she was glad Dot didn't have time to press her, as her mum appeared, looking over the railings of the walkway that ran along the front of all the second-floor flats.

'Where've you been, Dot? You said you'd be five minutes! I was just coming to look for you. I need you to run an errand.'

Without looking at or acknowledging Elsie, Mrs Grimes turned and went back inside.

Dot sighed, gave Else a quick hug and ran towards the stone stairs at the side of the building. 'See you tomorrow, Else.'

When she reached home, Elsie called out, 'Come on, all of you – look at what I found!'

Opening the tin released a smell that Elsie had only previously caught when she'd passed by the bakery on her way to work. The slices of cake – five in all, so one each – were of a plain mixture, golden in colour, and underneath them were two doorsteps of bread. The cake had a lemon flavour and was the most delicious thing Elsie had ever tasted.

'I can't believe it, Else, girl – manna from heaven, and I love the tin.'

With her mouth bulging with cake, Elsie told her mum that she could have it, if she wanted it. But was glad when her mum said, 'No, you found it, darlin', you keep it, eh? You'll find a use for it.'

Elsie was bursting to tell them all about her new friend,

so she was glad when her mum changed the subject. 'I'm going with Rene to the Old Bill in a minute. They want to talk to us, as the last ones who saw Phyllis alive. Not that we can help. The boat them sailors came off'll be gone by now.'

Though this sounded feasible, Elsie worried that her mum might be heading out to earn some money or, worse, borrow money to buy gin.

'I'll come with you if you like, Mum.' Cecil beat Elsie in suggesting this, and she knew that he was worried about the same things she was. It was early days for Mum, and she could easily slip backwards.

'No, don't be so daft. I'll be all right, I promise. Don't eat that bread, though, as I might be back with some sausage or something, and it'll go nicely with that.'

This increased Elsie's suspicions. 'We can manage with the bread, Mum – don't worry. Besides, you're not well enough to go. Can't Rene tell the Old Bill that, and have them come here to talk to you?'

'Look, girl – and you, Cecil – I ain't going to do nothing wrong. Rene called earlier and said the Old Bill had been to see her and wanted to talk to us both. So I thought that if we went along to the police station, on the way back Rene could help me call in a few favours. There's a few tradesmen that I could worry, by threatening to tell their wives stuff.'

As Mum got her coat on, Elsie decided she would follow her, just to make sure.

When the door closed, the four of them were quiet and didn't move for a moment. Bert's hand came into Elsie's and his head leaned on her thigh. Rubbing her hand through his hair, she looked over at Cecil. 'Cess, did Rene call?'

'Yes, she did, but she whispered to Mum and I couldn't

hear what was said. Mum gave a lovely smile and clasped Rene's hand, as if something had excited her. She wouldn't say nothing when Rene left, but she seemed agitated about what time you'd be back.'

'Oh, bugger!'

'You shouldn't swear, Else. You'll have a sin on your soul now.'

'I'll have more than one sin on my soul, Jimmy. Anyway, who's been feeding you that stuff?'

'School. We have lessons from one of the brovvers who live in the big house next to the church. You know, them as wear them long brown frocks.'

Elsie smiled at this. 'Well, don't take everything they say as gospel – except when they're reading from the Gospel, of course.' Turning to Cecil, she asked him, 'Are you going anywhere, Cess? Only I think I'll follow Mum and make sure she doesn't get into trouble.'

'I'll do that, Else. I can look after myself, if anyone cuts up rough.'

'No, you stay here with these two. I want to do this. I can stop Mum, without getting myself into a fight. If they see a strapping lad like you, they might go for you – that is, if she is lying to us and she's going on the game.'

Cecil agreed.

Grabbing her shawl, Elsie ran out of the house and turned in the direction she'd seen her mum go past the window. She wasn't in sight, but Elsie planned to make her way to Rene's in Salisbury Street, in case that was where they were meeting.

Turning into the street, Elsie was amazed how people lived in these rows of small cottages, with no sanitation. Their lavs were back-to-back sheds with a board across a huge bucket that had to be emptied at night, and their water was drawn from a well. Sickness was rife amongst those who lived here, and newborn babies and infants died in their droves. Elsie wanted to make everything better for them, and thought the flat where she lived was a palace compared to these dwellings.

When she passed Phyllis's house she felt a deep sadness. Phyllis had never done anyone any harm, and would give you her last penny if she thought you needed it more than she did.

Once outside Rene's, Elsie hesitated. The house looked closed up and uninviting. The door of the house next to it opened. 'You looking for Rene, ducky? She went out earlier this morning and ain't come back yet.'

Elsie's heart sank. Had her mum lied? Or had Rene told her she would meet her somewhere? A deep fear entered her. What if Mum wasn't meeting Rene, but going on the street alone? A feeling of hopelessness washed over her. *Where do I start to look for her? No, Mum. Please, no!*

'Are you all right, ducks?' The woman came closer. Elsie had to swallow hard to stop herself retching at the odour from her body and clothes. She looked into her face and the woman grinned. The two solitary teeth that she had were black with decay.

'Yes, but I hoped to find my mum here.'

'I know who your mum is, just by looking at you – you've got her hair and her looks. Well, I ain't seen her around here today, ducks.'

'Ta. Not to worry, I'll find her.' Walking away, Elsie felt she'd been rude, as the woman had been kindly. She couldn't help how she smelt, or her teeth – no one who lived around here could help it. Turning, she smiled and waved to the woman and was given a lovely grin in return.

Hurrying along the street, Elsie didn't know what to do or where else to look, or whether to give up and go home.

It was as she turned back onto Long Lane that she spotted her mum. How she'd missed her, she didn't know, as she wasn't five minutes from home. Mum was looking up and down the street as if she was on the lookout for a likely punter. Elsie opened her mouth to shout out, when a car that she recognized pulled up beside her mum.

Held in a moment of disbelief, Elsie watched her mum move in a joyful way, giving a little wave to the driver and almost skipping towards the car, her former stiffness and pain now forgotten. *Mum knows me boss? Millie's dad, Mr Hawkesfield? But how?*

Before she had time to pull herself together sufficiently to do anything, the car had turned round and they were gone. For a moment Elsie didn't move as she tried to absorb what she'd seen. Was Mr Hawkesfield a regular customer? If he was, and Mum had someone of his wealth as her only punter, what would that mean for them? *Oh, why am I thinking like this? I don't want Mum selling herself to anyone, no matter how rich.*

The frustration with her mum, for going back to her old ways so soon, made her angry. Mum had to stop this, before it was found out. *Oh, Mum, you promised us!*

But then what Elsie had seen made her realize that her mum hadn't broken her promise. She wasn't prostituting herself, but looked more as if she had gone on a date. Was she Mr Hawkesfield's mistress? Was it him who had given her more money that time, when she'd seemed so happy and thought they were going to be in clover from then on?

Fear clutched at Elsie. If she was right, then it could only end in hurt for her mum. Men of Mr Hawkesfield's standing used people for their own ends. If it had been him before, then hadn't he already done that: given Mum hope, and then dumped her?

And what of Millie? What if she found out? She would be so hurt and wouldn't want to be friends any more. Strangely, this hurt a lot more than it should have done, having only met Millie once, but Elsie wanted nothing to spoil the excitement of having a friend like her. Sadness clothed her then, because she knew that their friendship was already spoilt. Knowing what she knew now, she couldn't go and meet Millie the next day, or ever again.

Chapter Six

Millie

Millie felt desperate. She'd been coming to the park as often as she could over the last four days and still hadn't seen Dot and Elsie again. She couldn't understand it, and felt as though she'd lost something that was special – something that was hers alone, and that she hadn't even shared with Ruby. Poor Ruby, she was at her wits' end at the way Millie kept duping her and going out on her own. But Millie trusted Ruby. No matter how worried Ruby was about her absences, she knew Ruby would never betray her.

As she was about to leave the park, a funeral party passed by. She halted Fennie and lowered her head a little, though she kept her eyes on the scene, unable to look away. Never before had she seen a funeral like this one.

The coffin was on the back of a rickety old dray. The horse pulling it looked like an old carthorse, and was dirty and exhausted. The coffin was no more than a crate, and bare of flowers. Behind this cortège the mourners were few. Two men were walking immediately behind, followed by two women and then . . . Elsie!

Millie wanted to call out her name, but knew that would

be disrespectful. Poor Elsie; so this was why she hadn't turned up – she'd suffered a bereavement. Her heart went out to her and she wanted to go and hug her. What should a friend do in such circumstances?

Dismounting, she tied Fennie to the gate and waited until Elsie came alongside her. 'Elsie, Elsie.' Her whisper sounded loud, in the hush of the moment. Elsie looked up and, impulsively, Millie went forward with her arms open. 'I'm so sorry. I didn't know you had suffered a loss.'

Elsie drew back.

'Elsie?'

'Go away, Millie.'

Shocked, Millie stood for a moment. Then one of the women turned – a beautiful woman, so like Elsie. On catching sight of Millie, the woman gasped. The look of horror on her face frightened Millie and she stepped back. The woman dropped back to Elsie's side.

'Elsie? What's going on, luv? Do you know this young lady?' Her voice sounded incredulous.

'I'm so sorry to have intruded. I didn't mean to. I – I, well, I haven't seen a funeral like this before and I wanted to give comfort.' Millie turned to Elsie. 'Forgive me. You must think me mad – a complete stranger offering you a hug. I just felt so sad for you. I'm sorry.'

Turning with as much dignity as she could muster, Millie returned to Fennie and, without looking back, mounted her and steered her homewards. The heaviness in her heart spilled out as tears. *Elsie, why? I thought we could be friends – close friends.*

The loneliness that Millie had thought was at an end crowded in on her again, as all her fears of the last few days were realized. Elsie and Dot didn't want to know her. They had probably laughed their heads off at her, thinking her a stupid, rich idiot. Or maybe they'd found her patronizing. Had she been that? Had she come across as this big benefactor who was going to make their lives better? Or maybe they were fearful, because of who her father was. *Dot in particular was afraid, once she knew who I was. Maybe I can still make this right. I could keep going to the park and hope to see them again.*

But then the thought occurred that, the day after tomorrow, she and her family were travelling to Leeds for Christmas. Impulsive as ever, she turned round. *I have so little time. I have to do something now!*

The funeral party was no longer in sight, but she knew they would have turned into St George's Church – she would attend and talk to Elsie; ask her why she had changed her mind about being friends.

It wasn't until Millie walked into the church that it occurred to her there was a possible simple explanation for Elsie's reaction to her. *I embarrassed her. I did the very thing I had asked them not to. I exposed our friendship in front of her friends and family.*

With this thought, Millie turned round to leave the church. But at that moment Elsie looked back at her with a desperate look on her face. Her head was shaking from side to side.

Feeling angry with herself, Millie gave a little wave and then, as quietly as she could, made for the door.

Outside she stood for a moment, wondering what had possessed her to attend the funeral, but she knew it had been desperation. She was lonely and hadn't wanted to lose the small thread of friendship that she had formed with Elsie and Dot, although now it looked as though she had.

'Millie. Millie.'

The whispered calling of her name made her heart soar. 'Elsie!'

They ran to each other. The hug completed Millie's happiness. 'Oh, Elsie, I thought I had lost you. I'm so sorry you have lost a loved one. If only I'd known, I could have helped you. Who is it – a relative? Your grandmother?'

'No. A friend of my mum's. A lovely woman. I loved her very much. Sh – she was murdered.'

Millie gasped, 'Murdered!' Something her father had said, as he read the paper at breakfast time one day last week, came back to her. He'd lowered the paper with a sudden movement that had startled her, and her mother. His face had gone deathly pale. Her mother had asked what was wrong. He'd shaken his head. 'Oh, I'm just shocked. There's been a murder not far from here. A prostitute, but still, it makes you feel unsafe.'

'Don't be silly, Richard. Those women put themselves in danger – they don't know who they are going with. They could easily be targeted by a maniac. It's sad, but that's how it is. You have no need to worry.'

Her father had looked very upset and had excused himself. Then she'd heard him call for his coat, and for his car to be brought round to the front of the house for him. Mother had risen and run out to the hall, demanding to know where he was going, but he hadn't answered her and had just left the house, as if in a great hurry.

As these thoughts raced through her head, Millie stood and stared at Elsie.

'I can see that you've heard about it, and that you know about her, but don't judge her, Millie – or any of us. We do what we can to survive – exist, even – though I often ask myself, why? Why don't we give up and be done with it?'

'Elsie, don't talk like that – don't. I know I can't possibly understand fully, but I want to, and I want to help you. Please let me.'

'I can't. I came out of church to tell you not to try and contact me again. Our lives are so different, Millie. I'd drag you down, and I can't do that to you. I know this might sound silly, as we only just met, but I think such a lot of you. And I'm afraid that our friendship would only cause you pain in the future.'

'No! It doesn't sound silly, as I feel the same. Don't send me away.'

'Look, our lives are miles apart, and it's impossible for us to be friends. Others won't let us. So we have to forget it. Forget we ever met, and leave it at that. You'll make other friends.'

'I won't, Elsie. And even if I did, I would never forget you. You have a hard life, I can see that, but my life is almost as difficult, in another way. My parents, with their stupid ambitions for me, have isolated me. The only friend I have is my maid. She is from the North, and she is lovely to me, but I live in fear that Father will get rid of her one day.'

'I'm sorry for you – I am. But please, Millie, we have to say goodbye.'

Millie felt her loneliness nudging her again. She couldn't let this connection with Elsie and Dot be severed. 'Don't – don't. I . . . Oh, Elsie.' The tears she'd tried in the last few minutes to swallow down burst from her in a sob. Why was she acting like this? Had her lonely life brought her to a place where she needed to beg someone who was almost a stranger – a girl from a world she knew nothing about – to be her friend? Turning, Millie ran towards her horse, mounted it and galloped out of the churchyard. She had to get away from the rejection. *Oh, stop this! What's wrong with me? I'm behaving like a child who can't have a new toy. Well, there are no new toys for me. I have to toughen up and deal with the life that I have.*

Without warning, Fennie reared. Millie couldn't hold on. Her body flew through the air and crashed to the ground. A haze overcame her and left her floundering, as she felt her body being dragged along the ground, and she felt a deep fear as she realized that Fennie was bolting and her foot was caught in the stirrup. A bang on the back of her head zinged through her, and then there was nothing but blackness – a swirling, painful blackness.

'You're all right, Miss, I've got you. Me mate's run for Dr Stanley – he only lives a few doors from here. Don't try to move.'

Two strong arms held her – saved her from drifting into the deeper dark place that she was afraid to let herself go to.

'Me name's Cecil, Miss. What's yours?'

'Mil – Millie.'

'Keep talking to me, Millie. And don't worry about your horse. Me mate works for the milkman and knows about horses. He's calmed her, and he held her while I got you loose. He's tied her up now. But as he left for the doctor, he said the horse isn't hurt, only shaken.'

'Th – Thank you.'

Something about his name made Millie think of Elsie, and this increased her pain as she tried to think why. Then she remembered: Elsie had told her she had a brother named Cecil. 'El – Elsie?'

'Elsie? Are you asking for an Elsie? That's a coincidence. I have a sister called Elsie.'

'Yes . . . Yes, your Elsie. Sh – she is my fr—' She stopped herself going any further. *It's a secret – I mustn't tell.* Thankfully, Millie heard Dr Stanley's voice then, and this stopped her from telling Cecil any more.

'Now then, what do we have here? Miss Hawkesfield! What in the name of the Lord are you doing here? Oh, dear me. Let me take a look at you.'

After a moment of being prodded and pulled, Dr Stanley, who tended all of Millie's family, spoke to Cecil. 'Can you carry her to my house, Cecil? She hasn't broken anything, but I need to get her warm and see to her cuts, and she is in danger of going into shock. Then can you go for her father? I will give you a penny for your trouble.'

'Yes, I'll do that, but me mate's the best one to go. He can ride, so he can take her horse back at the same time.'

'All right, but in that case a halfpenny each.'

Millie was aware of the doctor writing something.

'Here, this is the address where Miss Hawkesfield lives.' The doctor wrote something on another piece of paper. 'And give this to your mate to hand to the housekeeper. Oh, and tell him to make sure to go to the back door. Then you can bring Miss Hawkesfield along to my house.'

Millie felt a comforting hand on her shoulder.

'Don't worry, Millie. Cecil is very strong, and a good lad – you'll be in safe hands. I trust him.'

'Ta, Dr Stanley, that's a compliment. And you're not so bad yourself.'

'Ha! Don't be cheeky, lad.'

Millie felt herself relax. Elsie's brother was just as she had described him: lovely, cheeky, and willing to help anyone.

Opening her eyes, she could see the likeness to Elsie in him. At that moment he amazed her, because despite the cold, he took off his ragged jacket and put it over her. It was none too clean, but she didn't mind; it felt like a cloak of love, and its warm lining gave her a trickle of warmth, too.

When he lifted her, she felt safe in his arms. She thought of Elsie, and felt such a sadness in her at the loss of her friendship. Through Elsie, she could have helped her family – made sure they had food, and even given them money from time to time from her own allowance.

Cecil looked down on her and, with a lovely reassuring smile, asked, 'Are you all right? I know as this ain't got much dignity for you, but I'll be as quick as I can. You're no weight. I've carried sacks at the dock that were five times heavier and didn't drop them, so you're safe with me.'

'Thank you.' It was all she could manage.

'D'you know me sister then? Only back there, you seemed to.'

'I – I, she works at my fa – father's jam factory.'

'That place! Your dad should be ashamed of himself for the conditions he makes the women work under. Oh, I beg your pardon, Miss. Me tongue sometimes says what it wants to, before me brain catches up with it – or that's what Else says, anyway.'

This made Millie smile. She wanted to say something, but felt too weak to converse, so she just closed her eyes.

'You've a sense of humour, so that's good. Don't take any notice of what I said. Your dad's your dad – and we can't help who they are. At least you know who your father is. Me, Else and me two brothers don't . . . There I go again, telling you me business now. Good job we've arrived – you'll be wondering who the hell you ran into.'

Millie wanted to laugh out loud. Cecil was so funny.

Nothing he'd said had offended her and, if she was stronger, she'd tell him that she intended to improve things at her papa's factory one day. But she wanted to save herself to tell him one thing, because she trusted Cecil, and this was the time to break any promise made previously.

'Tell Elsie – tell her . . . I am still – and always will be – her friend, and Dot's. But please don't tell anyone else. No one.'

'Crikey! You a friend of me sister and Dot! Real, like, mates?'

'Please . . . don't tell anyone.'

'I won't. And I'll give your message to her, but she's got some explaining to do. Blimey, that's a turn-up! You wouldn't like to be my friend as well, would you?'

Again, Millie could only manage a smile. She turned her head and felt a relief to see the door to the doctor's house was open and Dr Stanley beckoning them inside.

'Thank you, Cecil. Please lay Miss Hawkesfield down on the couch. Good man; now, here's your penny—'

'Doc – Doctor, make it more, please. I – I will repay you. Please . . . give Cecil a crown.'

'What? Your father will go mad!'

'Please. I – I can pay you. Papa needn't know.'

The doctor shook his head. 'You've a heart kinder than anyone I know, Millicent, and a lovely nature. Don't ever change. But you mustn't be too generous. In this case, knowing Cecil, he would share with his mate; and the rest he'd give to his mother, as he has a kind heart, too, and will only think of the good he can do for his family. Not his mate, though – well, his half will go on cigarettes and be squandered to suit himself.'

As if he was desperate to get the money and not let the

doctor change Millie's mind, Cecil blurted out, 'I won't give it to my mate – not all of it. I'll give him a penny and then take the rest to his mum; she could really do with it, Doc – as we could. Elsie is still laid off and bringing nothing in; Mum's not working . . . I mean, well, you know, not in general. She only has the one punter now. And I'm having a short time of it at the dock.'

Millie hated to hear Cecil beg like this. She hadn't wanted that, but at least he managed to persuade the doctor. She had no idea what a 'punter' was, as his mother was supposed to have, and assumed it was someone she could earn money working for.

'Very well, I agree. Give me a moment. Sit outside in the waiting area while I make sure Miss Hawkesfield is all right. Then I will sort out the money in equal shares for you.'

When Millie's father arrived, he was furious with her, but was concerned in equal measure.

'Please, Papa, I have a headache. I know you are cross, but going on and on about it isn't going to change what has happened.'

His sigh was audible above the engine of the car. 'Why are you so fascinated with going to such places? I don't understand. You have been told it isn't safe, and given strict orders not to venture into that area, and yet you defy us – your parents – and continue to go there. I am afraid for you, Millie.'

'I know, Papa.' She slid across the bench seat and snuggled into him. 'I just need something in my life, as it is so humdrum.' Something stopped her from telling him that she'd met some friends.

'Look, you will be in Leeds soon. You love it there.'

'Aren't you coming, Papa? You said that as if only me and Mama will be there.'

'I have some business to attend to. I'll come on Christmas Eve. But you are to rest until you leave. You're very badly bruised and shaken, and Dr Stanley is worried about the bang you received on the back of your head. Thank goodness those boys were there to help you.'

'Papa, one of them is good with horses, and the other is a big, strong boy. They looked so poor, and yet they were polite and really kind. Couldn't you find work for them? One said he goes to the dock to look for work each day; and the one with the horse helps the milkman now and again.'

'Millie, here you go again! How on earth did you find out all that about these urchins? You should have been disgusted at being at their mercy, not asking about their lives.' Papa sighed heavily and shook his head. 'You have to toughen up. You have to see these people for what they are, and be aloof when you are around them. I worry about you carrying on with your training in the factory. Oh, it looks well enough when it's empty of workers, as you have mostly seen it. But when they are there, they have to work very hard, and their bodies sweat; they smell like rotting cabbage at times, and that is why I brought in the rule about sacking anyone who I could tell hadn't washed themselves.'

'That's harsh, Papa.'

'It isn't. They are working with food; and my factory has to be hygienic. If they introduce germs to a batch, it will turn to mould and, before you know it, I will have lost a great deal of money. They have to learn cleanliness.'

'But, Papa, from what I know of them, they can't afford food, let alone soap. Not even those who work for you. And yet sometimes they work up to twelve hours a day.'

'Next you will be telling me that you are joining Mary Macarthur's National Federation of Women Workers! I despair. I should have had a son who took after me. God knows who *you* take after. Not your mama, as there isn't a harder nut than she is. Get rid of all this soft-heartedness or you will be absolutely no use to me.'

This stung. Especially the reference to a son.

'Look, I'm sorry. I shouldn't have spoken like that, when you're not well. But please think carefully about your future in the business. Your behaviour makes me think it is true what most people say: that women have no place in the boardroom.'

To Millie, the opposite should be true, as she thought business would succeed far better if the workforce was happy, fairly treated and given incentives to work. Not just like slaves, grateful for every crumb. She made her mind up to find out more about this Mary Macarthur.

Chapter Seven

Kitty

To see her children so excited lifted Kitty. With what Richie Hawkesfield had given her, she'd been able to get some treats for Christmas Day in two days' time. She had plenty in for a nice dinner, and a little gift for each to wake up to, which she'd wrapped and which now sat in a row on the mantel-shelf. She had fuel enough for the fire, and the pantry was well stocked. Not only that, but Elsie and Cecil were getting dressed, ready for a treat.

Rene had made Elsie a long woollen frock in navy blue, with a navy-and-red checked cloak and a bonnet to match; and for Cecil they'd been to the penny market and managed to buy him some trousers and a jacket, which Rene had worked her magic on and now fitted him as if they were made for him. Both looked lovely, and Kitty realized they had grown up without her noticing it. Cecil looked every inch the young man and had even had his first shave tonight, and Elsie was a beautiful young woman.

Kitty had tickets for the Adelphi Theatre to see *The Quaker Girl*, starring Gertie Millar and C. Hayden Coffin. She couldn't be more pleased with herself, or feel happier than she did at this moment. It was as if all she had longed for had finally come true.

Richie had told her that, from now on, she was to be his one and only. He had taken a suite in the Barstow Hotel in south London, and that was to be their haven.

He'd made up his mind to do this a few weeks ago, when he'd set up a meeting with her, through Rene, and had seen how badly she was injured. 'I don't want you ever to go with another man, Kitty. My wife and I are now finished as a married couple. You are to be available to me whenever I need you.' He'd given her an allowance to get new clothes with. She'd bought a couple of things, but had then purchased material and had given some business to Rene, making it possible for her not to work the streets so often.

Rene was helping her in so many ways. Tonight she was going to look out for Jimmy and Bert, and Kitty had promised them that she would take them to a pantomime when the season started after Christmas. To make sure of this, she had already put the money aside.

They were in clover, and her next plan was to offer Rene a home with them. She had an eye on a fold-away bed that would fit neatly behind their sofa. Since Phyllis's death, Rene had been very lonely. She and Rene needed to be together now. To cry over Phyllis and to help each other out.

Kitty could feel a real change about to happen in all their lives as she thought of this and the other plans she'd been dreaming of.

A knock on the door interrupted her thoughts. She rushed to open it, to see Rene standing there with a big smile on her face. At that moment Elsie came out of the bedroom and, as Rene stepped inside and caught sight of her, she gasped, 'Aw, darlin', you look bloomin' smashing.'

'Ta, Rene, I feel . . . well, I don't know how to describe the feeling inside me. But you wait till you see Cecil – he looks like a real toff.'

Kitty had tears in her eyes when her son came through the bedroom door. She never thought to see the day her children would look as they did.

'You do me proud, me darlin's. Just look at you. Come on, let's go – we've to catch the bus on Staple Street. Be good, Jimmy and Bert, and Rene'll give you a toffee each. She knows where me secret stash is.' Winking at Rene, Kitty thanked her.

Rene put her arms out towards her. 'Give us a hug, love. I'm happy for you. And long may this continue. Maybe you'll end up getting out of this place and living somewhere nice.'

As they neared Curly's shop, he was standing in his open door. His low whistle of appreciation made Kitty smile. 'Don't you all look the business? And what business is that you're on, honey-child?'

His look made Kitty blush. Curly had propositioned her a couple of times, but she'd refused him. She had no qualms about lying with him, but she knew that while she was tolerated by those who thought themselves above her line of work, they would make her life hell if it got out that she lay with Curly. They might even hound her out of the area.

He stepped in front of her. 'Ain't my money white enough for you, Kitty, eh?'

'You know it's not that. Besides, I'm no longer for sale. Now get out of my way, Curly, we're in a hurry.'

Elsie saved the day. 'I never had you down as one that would use my mum, Curly. I'm ashamed of you. I thought you a decent fella.' Her courage shone from her.

Cecil wasn't avoiding getting involved, but thankfully he was heeding the warning that Kitty had seen Elsie give him.

'I'm only funning. What's a man to do, when a beautiful lady like your mum comes down the road, eh? Go on your way and enjoy yourselves. Old Curly don't mean any harm.'

As they reached the corner of Staple Street, Elsie linked arms with Kitty. 'You'll get that for a while, Mum, but just ignore it.'

'You can always call on me, Mum,' Cecil said. 'As big as Curly is, Mr Wright has shown me moves that would floor him in minutes. It's all in the footwork – dancing, Mr Wright calls it, but that sounds cissy to me.'

The incident had shaken Kitty. She smiled at her youngsters, but inside she felt afraid. Not of Curly, but of him ever thinking he could force things. She knew, from her last experience with the sailors, that if a man was determined, there wasn't much a woman could do about it. Putting it out of her mind, by telling herself that Curly wasn't like that, she was smiling by the time they boarded the bus.

The vehicle chugged along, blowing out black smoke and frightening the life out of them by backfiring when they least expected it. They were in a fit of giggles by the time they got off.

It seemed to Kitty that here, standing outside the theatre, they were in another world. She looked at Elsie and Cecil, and they seemed to be struck dumb as they gazed up at the magnificent building with its veranda shielding the front entrance, supported by columns that made it look regal.

When they entered the building, all three gasped at the beautiful interior and the wonderful canopied ceiling. The seating area looked vast, and Kitty was taken with a fit of nerves for a moment, because it seemed as though it would swallow her up.

'Move along, please, madam. Have you got your row number?'

'Yes, ta.'

The usher stared at her with an astonished look – her accent had given her away. He was obviously not used to her type coming here. But she wasn't going to let him intimidate her. Her money was as good as the next person's, so she lifted her head and guided Elsie and Cecil with confidence, hoping that she would find their seats quickly.

She hadn't got far to go, as she'd only afforded tickets in the outer lower circle, but even so, when she sat down in the armchair of red velvet, she felt that she was somebody. Elsie and Cecil looked out of their depth, but Kitty was determined they should feel at ease. 'There, are you both settled?'

They nodded, their looks those of a scared kitten.

'Just relax and enjoy it, me darlin's.'

The show was wonderful. Witty and, in parts, so funny that Kitty had tears rolling down her cheeks. When the curtain came down for the interval, she told Elsie and Cecil that she wouldn't be long. 'I've to find the lav. All that laughing has made me want to pee. Eat your toffees while I'm gone.'

When she rose, she felt as though the actress within her had entered her skin and taken her over. Her mind was buzzing with the music and the words, and in her heart she became one of the main characters, the French princess Mathilde, with all her elegance and poses and silly notions. A yearning overcame her to be on the stage herself. *How did I reach thirty-five years of age without having this dream before?*

Even though her mum had been embroiled in the theatre – this very one, when she was a young girl – Kitty had never been drawn to it. Maybe she would have been if she'd been taken along, but her mum always left her with a neighbour, saying that this world wasn't for her. *But it is. I can feel it in my bones. I even love the smell of the place!*

'Tell me, love, that you're the bricks and mortar of old Elsie Packer! You've got to be. Blimey, you gave me a right turn, there. I'm Gerry Flounder. I own an agency for singers and the like.'

Taken aback, Kitty turned and looked into the face of a man with a small, sharp-featured face. He lifted his bowler hat and revealed a bald head. His smile changed him from frightening and intimidating to friendly.

Kitty smiled back. 'Yes, I am – my name was Katherine Packer, known as Kitty. But I'm Kitty Makin now. So you knew my mum?'

'Had her on me books for years. A good little earner, Elsie was. I didn't want her to give up – she was wasted playing the piano in pubs. But she used to say there was no place for a forty-odd-year-old, so she just earned her bread and butter. A big loss to the theatre, she was.'

'She was a big loss. It was her heart that gave out. And before she was fifty. We miss her.'

'We all do, darlin'. And what about you – did you inherit her talent?'

'Not for playing the piano. My daughter takes after her granny in that and is named after her. But I can sing and I feel that, given the chance, I could act as well.'

'And would you like the chance? I could get you work.

You have a look of Lillie Langtry – in fact, she'd better watch out, as she's old in the tooth now.'

'Lillie will never be old. But to answer your question, mate: yes, I would.'

'Hold on then, girl. I've a card here with my address on. Come and see me as soon as you can. I can give you an audition. I have some understudy work going – always have in the winter. Actresses aren't robust; they catch a cold as soon as a member of the audience sneezes.'

Kitty had no idea what an understudy was, but she didn't care. This was a start for her. And who knew? One day she might rise and be paid enough to get Elsie out of the jam factory.

Excitement gripped her as she made her way back to her seat. The lights hadn't yet dimmed, and it did her heart good to see Elsie and Cecil giggling together like kids. She looked around at all those taking their seats again, and the feeling that clenched her stomach increased. She so wanted them all to be settling down to watch *her*. One day they might be. She had a feeling that everything was about to change for the better. For her, and for all her family.

When the curtain rose, Kitty lost herself in the musical once more. And when they stepped outside, she couldn't help bursting into song: 'When a boy came up to me and said – He loves me, and I love thee.' She was only brought down to earth when someone started clapping and a couple came up to her. The gentleman pressed three pennies into her hand, doffed his cap and walked on.

'Mum! What you up to?' Cecil looked mortified, but Elsie was laughing her head off.

'From rags to riches, and begging in no time, Mum!'

The funny side of how she'd embarrassed herself took

over and Kitty laughed along with Elsie, ruffling Cecil's hair, which she had to reach up to do, further annoying him.

'Gerroff, Mum.'

'I've had the best time, me darlin's. Did you enjoy it?'

'I did, Mum. It was wonderful – magical. Funny, but at the same time it took you to another place, as if you lived in Paris yourself.'

'That's what the theatre is all about, darlin'. And I'm going to be part of it.'

'What? Don't be daft, Mum – the likes of us don't get to be onstage.'

Elsie jumped in to answer this, from Cecil. 'Gran did, Cess. So why not Mum? You said yourself that she has a beautiful voice.'

'Could you, Mum? Is it possible?'

'It is, Cess. I'm going to make it so, and I'll soon get you out of that jam factory, Else, you'll see. And you'll be having proper boxing lessons, Cess. And, most important, Jimmy will get some proper medical care, and him and Bert a good education. It's going to be wonderful.'

She told them about Mr Flounder and his offer. This seemed to set them both on fire with excitement and, regardless of the crowds milling around them, they hugged her and the three of them did a little jig.

Kitty didn't think she'd ever felt so happy in all her life as she did at that moment.

Their happiness continued over the next couple of days, and now it was Christmas Day. Dinner was over, and what a feast it had been.

Looking around her, Kitty experienced a good feeling settling in her. Her home didn't look anything like it had done a few weeks ago. Now it was a cosy place, and the paper chains and sprigs of holly gave it a festive feel.

Rene had joined them and, as they sat together on the sofa having a fag, watching the boys huddled on the rug over a game of cards, with Elsie sitting in the armchair leaning over, helping Bert with his hand, Kitty had to laugh out loud when, out of the blue, Rene said, 'I tell you, girl, this is me first Christmas off. Me and you are usually that busy, we hardly have no time to stand up before we're lying back down again.'

This seemed a good moment to tell Rene of her plans, so when she had stopped laughing, Kitty said, 'Rene, forget work today. I have – and that kind of work, for good. And you will be able to, too, if I get my idea up and running.'

'Ain't it time you told me about that idea, girl? I'm that curious, as you seem to think you can change our worlds.'

'I can. Look, I'm thinking that with your talent as a seamstress, you could start your own business, and if I get some good work in the theatre and get known, maybe I could get you some commissions to make stage costumes. You could do it, Rene, I know you could.'

'It's all airy-fairy, girl. I know you think you can make it work, and I like the sound of it, but all that ain't for folk like us. No one wants us to rise. They have a boot firmly placed on our head and, the minute we pop it up, they'll push it down again.'

Kitty sighed. Rene had been through too much to let herself feel any hope. But Kitty knew that she would never give up, and she'd drag Rene along with her, if she had to.

'No, it's not like that, Rene. I've got a chance now, and I'm going to take it. I've done my best for me kids – sold myself to some of the most rotten blokes imaginable, and I didn't achieve anything other than dragging them, and mostly myself, into the gutter. There has to be another way. My own mum didn't sell herself. She used her talent to earn money to bring me up. Now I'm going to do the same.'

'Didn't you ever have a dad, Kitty?'

'Not that I knew, no. My old mum said that he died when I was a baby, and I left it at that.'

'Mine died in the workhouse – and my mum. I was raped repeatedly by the governor, and he used to sell us girls to the likes of the mayor, and them as run the council.'

'Rene! Oh my God, Rene. You've never told me that.'

'When have we ever been sober enough to chat, eh? I didn't know about you not knowing your dad. But of course I knew your mum and what she did, as we used to go into the pub for a warm-up, and she'd be playing the piano and she'd give us a fag each.'

'Yes, she hated what I did. But, Rene, we didn't have a choice. Where would we have got any other kind of work, eh? Neither of us had our own man – talking of that, I never asked you: did you ever fall for anyone?'

'No. I never considered myself worthy of being loved by a man, only used by them. I can give any pleasure they want, and have done a million times, but as for cooking, cleaning and washing for a man, I've never done that in my life.'

'Give us a hug, Rene. We're getting down in our spirits, and a hug always cures us. Come on, it's Christmas.'

When they came out of the hug, Kitty caught sight of Jimmy. He wasn't playing, but lying with his head in Elsie's lap and she was rubbing his chest. Bert was asleep next to them. The warmth from the fire was lulling them all into a dreamy state. 'Are you all right, Jimmy, darlin'?'

'He's not feeling well, Mum. He'll be all right, won't

you, Jimmy? He just needs to rest.' Elsie's concern set fire to a pain in Kitty's heart. Jimmy hadn't turned to her, but to Elsie. She'd never been there for him, her little son, who struggled so much with his health.

'Come and sit on Mum's knee, Jimmy, eh?'

'Put your fag out then, Mum. It makes him worse whenever he's near smoke.'

Feeling ashamed, Kitty stubbed out her cigarette in the ashtray. She should give that habit up as well, and made her mind up that she would try.

With Jimmy on her knee, she could feel how hot his body was. 'Have you a pain, Jimmy?'

He tapped his chest. His eyes had a far-away look.

'Steam's the best thing for that, Kitty. They used to do that to anyone with a bad chest in the workhouse, and I've done it ever since, whenever I get a cough. You fill a bowl with boiling water, then he holds his head over it and you place a cloth over his head, and over the bowl. This traps the steam in, and Jimmy breathes it in. It'll clear his chest in no time. I'll fill the kettle.'

'Ta, Rene.'

Jimmy's pallor worried Kitty, as did his breathing: short bursts of air that seemed sucked in, rather than breathed in.

'Mum'll take you to Dr Stanley, love, I promise. But we'll try Rene's cure first, eh?'

Jimmy nodded. Kitty felt at a loss. She hadn't seen him as bad as this before, but Elsie didn't seem worried.

As the room fell quiet, but for the hissing of the kettle, Kitty gazed down at her son. It pained her not to be able to say who his dad was, but she had an idea that it was Gravers – the bloke from the corner shop, where the lad now worked. Gravers used to have her regularly at the time, and he was none too careful. He'd never claimed Jimmy, but he was good to him, and Jimmy did look like him. Gravers stopped having her when she got pregnant, and had warned Kitty not to lay it at his door. It would ruin him, and he wouldn't take kindly to that. Like all men with a bit of money, he could call on folk to rough her up, so she'd never said that he was the father. But then could she be sure? There were others at the time. Not that she could remember many of them now.

She looked over at Bert. He was a mystery to her. She had no idea she was having him till he started to come out. So she had no chance of pinning him on someone. Cecil was different; Kitty felt certain that he belonged to the bloke who came round from time to time to sharpen the knives. He had this contraption with a grinder fitted to it, and he'd turn his bike upside down to fix the grinder to the wheel. When he turned the wheel, the grinder rotated and sharpened the scissors and knives.

A sandy-haired bloke, he used to call and pay her for a quick fumble – and he was no trouble, as he never took long, but just this once he wanted to go all the way. He had the money, so Kitty didn't object. He wouldn't stop when he neared the end; he was rough with it as well, hitting her across the head when she begged him to get off. She never saw him again after that and was glad, but before long she was visiting the bucket every morning.

Elsie – well, she was a love-child. A smile formed on Kitty's lips. She knew what true love felt like, and not just during lovemaking, which was something special with *him*, but all of her days, for she always loved Elsie's dad.

The kettle whistling made them all jump, except Bert, who could sleep through a thunderstorm. Elsie and Cecil started to giggle. They were proper gigglers, them two. She hoped they never grew out of that.

'Right, Kitty. I'll put the bowl on the floor at the edge of the rug, then Jimmy can lay face-down and hold his head over it. I've got this bit of towelling, which you had hung on the nail next to the grate. I'll drape that over his head.'

Kitty had to support Jimmy, but soon he was coughing and clearing his chest. She was amazed with what came out of him.

'I'll take over, Mum; your arm must be aching. This is a good thing, ain't it? I wished I'd have known about it before. Ta, Rene. I think this could be the saving of Jimmy.'

'Well, it's only one of the things you can do. But I would do as you say, Kitty, and get Jimmy to see the doctor.'

'I will. What's the other things, Rene?'

'Honey in hot water – that were another thing they did at the workhouse. Oh, and they mixed herbs, but I don't know which ones or what with.'

'We've got honey, Mum.' Cess surprised her with this statement. 'I got some given to me on the last day I worked. It's in the pantry. I forgot about it.'

'That's the measure of how much better-off we are – that wouldn't have lasted five minutes before.'

They all laughed at this, from Elsie. And Kitty was glad that although their new-found wealth was down to her punter, none of them asked her questions about who he was, and none of them objected to her going with him.

'Right, I'll mix that for you, Jimmy. Let's have a look at you.'

Jimmy lifted his head to Rene and gave her a lovely smile. Kitty saw Elsie hug him and he turned to look at her, his face beaming with love. Kitty sighed. She needed to earn that kind of love from her children. Oh, she knew they did love her, but they weren't used to being able to show her, because she'd always been absent.

She clapped her hands to dispel the moment. 'Well, now that Jimmy's better, let's have a sing-song, eh?'

As if on cue, a chorus of 'Hark the Herald Angels Sing' came soaring through from outside, and they all burst out laughing.

'Well, me darlin's, we ain't the Herald Angels, but we will sing.' And with this, Kitty opened the door and, ignoring the cold air rushing in, joined in with the carol singers. She didn't notice when they stopped to listen to her, until the end when they all clapped her; and then she knew without a doubt that, yes, she did want to go on the stage, as this applause was the best Christmas present she could ever have. And she couldn't wait for the day she went to see Gerry Flounder at the singers' agency.

Chapter Eight

Elsie

JANUARY 1911

Elsie couldn't believe it was 1911, despite all the happy partying they'd done to welcome in the new year. Things looked better all round than they had at the beginning of last year. Not that she felt any hope of much changing in her life. *Except, well, one thing I do hope changes – I so want my friendship with Millie to get back onto a good footing.*

Elsie hadn't stopped thinking about Millie. It had terrified her when Cecil turned up with a guinea that day and told her what had happened. The message had warmed her heart, as the day of the funeral of poor Phyllis had been sad in so many ways. But, somehow, having to break off any chance of friendship with Millie had been the saddest part.

The message Cecil had brought Elsie had made that better. Millie hadn't given up on her; but Elsie hated to think of Millie being hurt, and maybe still feeling the effects of the fall and the bump to her head. Her only consolation was that she hadn't heard anything about it from any other source, so she could assume that although Millie might not be completely better, nothing really bad had happened, otherwise she would know. Nothing occurred within a ten-mile radius that didn't make its way to everyone's ears. There was a chain of gossip through market traders and shopkeepers, and even stuff that happened further afield, and as far as abroad, filtered through from the docks.

Dot and Cecil were walking a little way ahead of her as they made their way to work. Elsie had lagged behind to be with her own thoughts and, as always, the dread of the day ahead caused her feet to drag.

'Come on, Else, or we'll be late.'

'I'm coming, Cess. I didn't want to play gooseberry with you two, that's all, mate.'

Cecil laughed.

When they reached the corner shop, she had to nip in to tell Mr Gravers that Jimmy wasn't coming to work at the shop any more. She hoped he wouldn't keep her talking.

Mr Gravers looked shocked. 'He ain't that ill, is he?'

'No, if anything Jimmy's a little better, but Mum feels he's not strong enough to come to work before school any more, or to be out in this freezing weather any longer than he needs to be.'

'You tell your mum to come and see me. The boy needs to see the doctor. I've heard that your mum's a bit better off and has given up her games. She should have spent some of whatever she's got – and from wherever she's got it – taking care of her son!'

Elsie sighed. No doubt it wouldn't be long before everyone knew who her mum's benefactor was, and why. 'She's doing that today, Mr Gravers; she's taking Jimmy to the doctor. Look, I have to go or I'll be late, but don't hold Jimmy's job for him – he won't be back. Ta-ra.'

As she walked out of the shop, it struck her how concerned Mr Gravers had been. She'd never seen him care about anything, other than making money. As a thought struck her, she dismissed it. What did it matter who was whose father? They were happy and they had each other – that's what mattered. Family.

Having said goodbye to Cecil, Elsie and Dot walked arm-in-arm the rest of the way to the factory and, as they clocked-in, Dot said, 'Another day in the rat-race. I sometimes think there's no truer saying, where we're concerned, Else. We're treated no better than rats.'

Elsie ran her nails in a scurrying action along Dot's neck. Dot screamed, startling into silence the chattering women who were filing into the factory. Elsie laughed out loud. 'I was just being a rat, that's all, Dot.'

Ruth, the troublemaker at the factory, was in front of them and turned to see what was happening. 'Are you all right, mate?'

Dot giggled. 'Yes, Ruth. It was this daft idiot scaring the life out of me.'

'You're lucky to have a mate to laugh with. Or to have anything to laugh at.'

Elsie grimaced at Dot, then felt sorry for Ruth. Her dour nature didn't help her to make friends, but then neither did her way of carrying tales to the supervisor. She was one to avoid at all costs.

Holding back their remarks, the two girls pushed their way into the factory. A contrast of smells assailed them, as the sorting-room doors were still open: rotting fruit, and the sweet smell of fresh oranges that were ready to go into the huge vat to boil with the sugar – sacks of which were piled up on their right. Over the boiling vat there was a narrow bridge to cross before they got to their stations:

the gigantic sinks. Next to these were boxes and boxes of jam jars ready for washing, which they had been told was their job today.

From their first days at the factory, they had progressed around it, from cleaning around the machines all day, picking up any spillages, to sorting the fruit – rotten from good – and washing the jars. Next they would be filling the jars, and then on to the jam-making itself, the most skilled of the jobs, for which the women earned a few extra shillings.

Having donned their long pinnies and mob caps, Elsie and Dot walked onto the bridge. The crush seemed worse today, as the women were all eager to be at their stations before the supervisor did his rounds. Not being so could result in instant dismissal, and in someone else from the gate being brought in to take your place.

Someone shouted, 'Who's holding up the queue? Bloody hurry up, will you, mate?'

'It's that bloody Ruth. She's arsey this morning – got out of the wrong side of bed again. Someone give her a kick up the rump, will you?'

Dot prodded Ruth. 'Get a move on, Ruth. What you doing, eh, mate?'

Ruth had stopped and was bending down. There was a gap in front of her. 'Me stocking's all twisted.'

Before Dot could answer, one of the women who'd shouted out before now said, 'Bloody sort it when you're over the bridge, will you? We've got to get to our stations. Push by her, Dot.'

'No, don't, Dot – you might cause an accident. Ruth, please move along, the mood's getting angry. No wonder you haven't any mates; you've got no care for anyone.'

Ruth stuck her tongue out at Elsie.

'Let me by. I'll smack her a bugger.'

'Ruth, just go! Peggy's getting her hair off, and you know what she's like . . .'

Elsie had hardly finished saying this when Peggy, a big fleshy woman, pushed her to one side. Nearly losing her balance, Elsie clung onto the rail, shivering with fear as she looked down into the boiling vat below her.

'Move, Dot.'

Peggy's shove caused Dot to fall onto Elsie, taking her breath from her. Her legs went weak and her head spun.

Dot grabbed her. 'Hold on, Else. For God's sake, hold on.'

Elsie did so, for all she was worth. Her knuckles went white with the pressure of clinging to the rail, which, being waist-height, meant the top half of her body was bent over almost at a right-angle and she nearly over-balanced. Terror gripped her. The bubbling mass of boiling water seemed to come up and greet her. 'Hold me, Dot, hold me!'

Mayhem broke out as the women screamed at Ruth, and then at Peggy, to stop. But it was too late. As Elsie stared down, Ruth's piercing scream filled the space around her. Her body hurtled past Elsie and crashed into the vat. Scalding water splashed her arms.

The silence that followed made Elsie feel isolated amid the shock of what she'd witnessed.

Though she kept her eyes on the bubbling, steaming vat, there was no sign of Ruth surfacing. The horror of her having been swallowed up left Elsie trembling.

A rush of women pushed and shoved, all panicking to get off the bridge, just as a screeching alarm blared out. Elsie and Dot clung to each other as bodies squeezed by them. Elsie felt they were both perilously near to toppling.

But suddenly, with enormous strength, Dot bellowed like a bull and stopped the rush single-handedly. 'You stupid buggers! Stop. Stop, right now!' They did so. 'Come on, Else. Lean on me.'

Everyone filed off the bridge, in a hushed orderly manner, led by Dot. Once they reached the other side, Elsie and Dot hugged each other. Their sobs mingled, their shaking bodies sweating from the fear they'd felt.

Mayhem of a different kind broke out then, as orders were shouted that everyone should get out of the factory. Once outside, they learned that it was Ruth who'd gone over the railings. Everyone was saying it was an accident.

One of the women came over to them. Elsie wasn't sure of her name, but thought she worked in the jam-making kitchen. 'Look 'ere, girls, if any blame is laid at Peggy's door – or anyone else's, for that matter – there'll be consequences. All right?'

Betty Grimble, from the fruit-sorting warehouse, was right behind her. 'That's right. No one saw nuffink.'

Elsie saw Dot nod, and she did the same. Then a raised voice caught their attention. Elsie looked behind her and saw Lucy giving a speech, the women gathered around her hanging on her every word. 'This can't be shouldered by any one of us. It happened because of the limited time between being allowed to clock-in and getting to your stations. This is a vast building and we should be given more time. We must all stick together on this.'

Elsie couldn't believe the callousness of the women. It was born, she knew, of desperation, but there was not a word of sympathy for poor Ruth.

'Anyway, when all is said and done, that Ruth deserved what she got,' another woman piped up.

'She did,' a chorus of other voices affirmed.

'Why did she bloody hold us up?' someone asked, and the answer came, 'Because she was out to get us into trouble. She was a troublemaker, that one.'

Though she felt desperately sorry that Ruth had lost her life in the way she had, Elsie couldn't defend her against what the women were saying. She'd seen the smirk on Ruth's face. And now she thought about it, Ruth was doing just what they said she was. Ruth knew what would happen if those at the back were late. She could easily have made it in time to her station, by running when she was ready, but if she caused a long enough delay, then a lot of them – especially those at the end of the queue – wouldn't have been able to.

'What do you reckon, Else? Should we tell what Peggy did?' Dot whispered.

'No, it wouldn't serve any purpose, except to cause more trouble. The women are like a mob – they'd kill us. But, oh, Dot, I can't believe what happened. Ruth, gone!'

'Hug me again, Else. I feel safe when you do. You're always so strong. But, you know, Peggy caused this. She did.'

They held each other more gently this time. 'Dot, we have to remember that Peggy's got six children, and her man is only in work when he gets set on at the dock. She works her fingers to the bone, taking any jobs she can get, when she's not at the factory. She keeps a spotless home, and her kids all fed. She's someone to look up to and protect. I know that's not the right thing to do, but Ruth's gone, and nothing will bring her back. I don't know what family she had; she was a quiet one, always looking for the main chance to get someone in trouble and to advance herself. I think this is when we tenement-dwellers should keep shtum and look after our own.'

'Yes, you're right. Peggy can be loud and say her piece, but she's a good sort.'

Above the babble of shocked women, loud sobs could be heard. Elsie looked in their direction and saw Peggy on her knees, her head in her hands. She ran over. 'Peggy, don't. Calm yourself. You didn't do it. It was everyone being anxious to get to their work, and Ruth causing an obstruction.'

Peggy looked up. 'You won't tell?'

'I have nothing to tell.'

Peggy wiped her eyes, stood up, looked round and muttered, 'I wouldn't have caused any harm to her. She was an annoying woman, but I'd never have hurt her.'

'We know that, Peggy,' Lucy spoke up. Everyone hushed, to listen to her once more. 'Like Elsie says, you didn't do anything; you just wanted to get to work. Ruth was causing trouble and got more than she deserved in return, but we can't undo that. What does everyone say?'

All the women answered Lucy by nodding or mumbling phrases such as, 'That's right.' And they all looked around as they muttered their assent. Elsie suspected that, like her, the other girls were wondering if the supervisor had come outside yet.

Lucy addressed everyone again. 'Look, how many times have I told you that we needn't stand for this, eh? Come on, mates, you've got to admit it. I'll repeat meself as often as I have to. What's happened today is as a result of rules that are killing us. We need to take this opportunity and use it as a way to make some changes round 'ere.'

'Not that Women Workers' Federation thing again, Lucy?'

'Why not, Janet, eh? Come on, mate, you tell them all: why not?'

'Because it costs a bleedin' penny every month, and we ain't got it to spare.'

'A penny! Who can't spare a penny? You all can – walk to work one day, instead of taking the bus or Underground; buy one less packet of fags; have one less pint of ale, or one less tipple of gin. Course you can afford it. And then we can take our issues to the Federation as fully paid-up members and they will fight our corner. It's bloody daft not to join.'

A voice at the back of the circle called out, 'When's that Mary Macarthur coming to the factory again, Lucy?'

'She – or one of her assistants – will come the moment we ask her to. And the first rule we need changing is this bun-fight to make it in time from clocking-in to getting to our stations. It doesn't give us time even to have a pee, and sometimes my stomach aches with wanting to relieve myself by the time it's dinner break.'

A cheer went up, which seemed indecent to Elsie when she thought of what had just happened, but she had to admit that if they were allowed to clock-in earlier, life would be easier. She herself knew the urgency of wanting a pee in the mornings, especially on these cold days.

As she thought of this, the bitter cold of January, which she hadn't felt so far, suddenly made itself known to her and she shivered. The same seemed to happen for all the women, as they now started to stamp their feet and wrap their arms around themselves. They'd had no time even to collect their cardigans from the hooks near the door of the yard that led to the lavatory block, let alone go to the cloakroom and get their coats.

The ringing of loud bells silenced everyone, as the ambulance, the fire brigade and the police swung their vehicles into the factory yard. Their appearance made the reality of what had happened come into focus again.

Elsie felt a tear drop onto her cheek, and yet she hadn't registered that she was crying. Now that the shock and bravado of protecting Peggy, and the call to arms, were over, it seemed to Elsie that everyone was thinking of the terrible tragedy of a young woman like Ruth falling into a boiling vat.

'Do you think she died instantly, Else?' Dot asked.

'I hope so, love. Surely no one could survive for even a second in the temperature of that water.'

The supervisor appeared at that moment and hushed all conversation. A burly man, whom everyone hated, Horace Chambers was a bully, and too free with his hands – something no one dared complain about, as they all knew he'd find a reason to sack you if you did. There was even talk of him forcing one girl to go the whole way with him in the lav. Elsie was afraid of him, as she felt his eyes on her all the time. Well, on her bust – not her.

'You've done it this time, you scum! Someone'll hang for this, I'm telling you. Mr Hawkesfield ain't taking no rap for this. I want to know who was responsible, or I'll sack the lot of you and have new staff in here by the time Mr Hawkesfield gets back from his Christmas break. Do you hear me?'

No one spoke for a moment, then Lucy piped up. 'You'll have to take on the Federation of Women Workers if you do, mate.'

'What, that fucking lot of troublemakers? You'll be the first out, Lucy Dalton. In fact, you can get your coat now.'

'I wouldn't advise that, Chambers. I'm a fully paid-up member of the Federation, and an active member at that. You don't want an all-out strike on your hands, and that's what will happen if you sack me.'

'I don't think so. None of this lot are members. They like their booze too much to spend a penny on airy-fairy stuff like women marching with banners. Get your coat. Now!'

Elsie felt afraid that he might turn on her next. If she lost this job, they'd be all right for a bit, but for how long? Mum's money might dry up, if her punter – and she wasn't sure if it was still Mr Hawkesfield or not – suddenly stopped wanting her to visit him. What would they all do then? Suddenly she didn't care. A young woman was dead, and all because of the rules of this awful place. Without thinking it through any further, she shouted, 'I'm joining the Federation. And if you make Lucy go, I'll go, too.'

'Ha! Hark at you! You won't be missed. You can get your coat as well. Have you looked at the gate, eh? Look: can you see how eager they all are? Seeing you standing here, they know there's a chance, and they're nearly killing each other to take the next place. Neither of you will be a loss.'

Without warning, another voice called out that she was joining the Federation, and if two went, she was going, too. This built gradually, until there was what Elsie would describe as a battle-cry of 'All out! All out!'

This stopped only when the doors of the factory opened. Then there was complete silence as the ambulance crew brought out a stretcher with Ruth, wrapped completely in a sheet, lying on top. All bowed their heads, including Chambers.

When the ambulance went past them and out of the gate, many of the women were crying. Ruth might have been a troublemaker, but she was a jam factory worker – one of their own, all the same.

There was still silence as one of the firemen went up to Chambers. After a few moments he turned to them. 'Right, I want everyone back in the factory. The vat is empty now, and I want that place scrubbed from top to toe. You, Makin, and you, Dalton, will clean out the vat. And we'll have no more talk of any federation. Am I being heard clearly?'

Elsie looked at Lucy. She could see that Lucy was having none of it. 'If you have any humanity, Chambers, you'd order that everyone has a mug of hot, sweet tea before they set back to work. Everyone has had a massive shock.'

To Elsie's surprise, Chambers agreed, and she began to realize that there was something in banding together and made her mind up to join the Federation.

After the tea, Elsie felt better, but dreaded the task ahead of her.

It was a couple of hours later, just before the dinner break, when Dot came over. Elsie hadn't found the cleaning of the vat – something usually done at night by the factory cleaners – too difficult. There had been several processes: scrubbing, then swilling it out several times, which entailed filling it with boiling water, then running it through and out of the tap at the bottom. This had been the hardest part, as each bucketful had to be lugged to the drain outside. Elsie was whacked.

'Mr Chambers wants to see us, Else.'

'Me and you? Why?'

'He's asking everyone a lot of questions. They say he's determined to pin the blame, so that Mr Hawkesfield doesn't get any backlash from the government or the police.'

‘I hope no one’s saying anything. Come on. Me and Lucy have finished here.’

‘What do you think of what Lucy proposed – are you really joining that Federation thing?’

‘I am. Lucy talks a lot of sense and will stand as our representative. She says that if enough of us join, we can change a lot of things. We’re daft not to. Look at what happened when we all stood firm. Chambers backed down.’

When they reached Chambers’s office – a sort of lean-to inside the factory, with only room for him to stand at a shelf-like desk, where he had a notebook out – they listened to him telling them that a grave occurrence had taken place, one that would have far-reaching consequences for all of them. ‘Now I have been told by all that I have spoken to so far that you two tykes were right behind Ruth. Is that right?’

They both nodded.

‘Well then, you should both know what happened, and you have to tell me. Remember, a young woman, only a few years older than yourselves, is dead. No one deserves to die that young, and in such a horrible manner. And if they do die, they deserve whoever caused it to be punished.’

‘The system caused it.’

‘What? That’s not what I wanted to hear, Makin. Now shut up with that talk, as you know where it will lead you. Tell me what happened, and what you saw.’

‘Everyone was rushing, and Ruth stopped to straighten her stockings. She was asked to move on, as we were all desperate not to be late at our stations. Ruth didn’t move and the next thing – well, the crush was too much and it happened.’

‘Just like that. No one pushed her? You two didn’t push her then?’

'No . . . No, we didn't! Honest, Mr Chambers, we were being pushed ourselves.'

'So you tell me, Grimes, but I'm not buying it. It's been said that you two had a few words with Ruth, while you were waiting to file in.'

'We didn't.'

'I heard that you did. And I heard that you, Grimes, poked Ruth and told her to get a move on.'

Elsie felt Dot shiver. She reached for Dot's hand in a way that Chambers didn't see and squeezed it.

'Everyone was telling her to get a move on. Ruth was trying to cause trouble.'

'Don't speak ill of the dead, Makin. How do you think her mum would feel, hearing that about her dead daughter, eh? Yes, she had a mum. Unable to walk, poor woman. Ruth was the only one bringing in any money, because her dad's dead. Who do you think will look after her mum now, eh?'

Elsie felt terrible for saying what she had. 'I'm sorry, but I was only telling you what happened. I shouldn't have said anything about Ruth. She was all right, most of the time. But why did she stop everyone, knowing they would lose their jobs if they were late at their stations? She could have straightened her stockings once she was off the bridge.'

'So you're saying she deserved what happened, are you?'

'No! You're twisting my words. She didn't deserve it, and no one made it happen. It was a crush, caused by a sudden hold-up, and for no reason – that's all I'm saying.'

'Well, I think you two are the culprits.' Chambers's face came near Elsie's, and his expression was menacing. 'In fact I think you will hang!'

Dot gasped, then fell to the floor, as if she'd suddenly turned into a rag doll.

'Dot? Dot! It's all right, Dot. We're not to blame, and everyone knows it.'

A heavy hand came onto her shoulder. 'Who is then, eh? Tell me that, or I'll see that you two take the rap for this.'

Elsie looked up into Chambers's dark, beady eyes and saw evil staring back at her. A terrible dread washed over her. *God help me!*

A scream that held agony pierced her eardrums. She looked from Horace Chambers back to Dot.

'Dot! No, don't, Dot.'

Someone came over, picked Dot up and slapped her face.

Elsie stared at Lucy. 'Wh – what did—'

The screaming stopped, and a sobbing Dot almost fell onto Elsie.

'She was hysterical. Someone had to help her, and the best thing is a short, sharp shock. Now what's all this about?'

Elsie told Lucy what Chambers had said.

'That's unjust, Chambers.' Lucy stepped backwards so that she was half in and half out of the office. Raising her voice, she shouted, 'Is there anyone here who will testify that Elsie and Dot are to blame for the accident?'

Not one person raised her hand. Elsie felt relief flood through her, but as she looked back into Chambers's eyes, her fear returned.

'Who's going to say that, where they stand a chance of being lynched, eh? No bugger. I have it written down what each person told me, and these two are mentioned time and again. I'm calling in the police on this.'

'You'd do anything to save your precious Mr Hawkesfield – even lick his arse. Well, this time, you can tell him, he'll have a hell of a fight on his hands. We have the might of an army of women workers on our side this time.'

'Ha! You think you do. You speak to each person in private and you'll know otherwise. In a crowd they're scared to be different from all the others, but when they're on their own . . .'

'When they're threatened, you mean.' With this, Lucy turned and strode away.

Elsie stood, trying to support Dot. 'Don't worry, Dot. He's just looking for someone to put the blame on. We didn't do anything. So he can't put it on us.' But inside, these brave words didn't help, as Elsie felt dread deep in the pit of her stomach.

Chapter Nine

Millie

Tired after the long car journey back to London, Millie stretched out in the tin bath Ruby had placed in front of her bedroom fire. This was something she still loved to do – laze in a steaming bath, with the blaze of the flames warming her. Much better than shivering in the bathroom that Papa had had installed a few doors down from her room.

'Eeh, there's a to-do downstairs, Miss Millie.'

Millie opened her eyes, not wanting to be disturbed, but knowing Ruby wouldn't do so unless it was serious.

'Your papa is storming about the place. He's called for his working suit to be made ready, and for a car to be at the front door. By, Larkson's going mad, saying the engine needs to cool before he can fuel up the car, but he's been given no time for that.'

'Have you heard any hint of what's wrong, Ruby? Has something happened at the factory?'

'Aye. Sommat bad an' all. The downstairs maid said she overheard your papa ranting about an accident, and a young lady being killed.'

Millie froze. 'Did she hear a name?'

'Naw. There were naw names, but when your mama tried to calm him, he did shout out that this could ruin him. Not just the scandal, but if the Board of Trade came down on him again for safety measures; and sommat about a Women's Federation interfering, getting the women to join it. He was raving.'

Millie put her hands on the side of the bath and stood up in one movement. 'Ruby, get my riding clothes for me while I dry myself.'

'Where are you going, Miss? Please don't go to the factory, or to that housing estate again. I really got it in the neck with a threat of being sacked, if it happened again. Me ma's frantic. She don't knaw how she can carry on, if I'm not here. She misses the North and all her friends, as it is.'

'If you swear that you'll never tell a soul, you can come with me.'

'Naw. Please listen to me, Miss Millie. If one of them's been killed, the mood amongst them could be very angry. Seeing you could trigger a violent outrage. I beg you.'

'Look, we'll drive the trap to St George's gardens, then you can take a note for me. I know where two of the factory girls live. All you have to do is go to the tenement blocks and ask anyone for Elsie, Dot or Elsie's brother, Cecil. When you find one of them, ask them to come to me in the park. If they won't, then ask if they are all safe and give my note to them. You can do that for me, can't you? I must find out if they are all right.'

'I don't knaw. Look, if you just want to find out who was killed, why not ask your mama? She probably knaws.'

'I'll try that first. But I do want to go out for some fresh air, so I'll dress in my riding clothes anyway.'

'I'm sorry, Miss. I – I knaw I should help you do whatever you want to, but in this . . .'

'Don't worry, Ruby. But you do need to toughen up. I may want to do any number of things I'm not allowed to. And I need a friend in this house – someone who can cover for me, and who I know is loyal to me.'

'Aw, Miss Millie, I'm all of those things. But you don't knaw your papa; not really knaw him.'

'Tell me, then. How can I know what you are afraid of, if you don't tell me? I know you are afraid of losing your job, but I wouldn't let that happen. But I also know there is something else you are afraid of.'

'It's not for young ears, Miss.'

'Poppycock! I am nineteen – twenty in May; you are only four years older than me. I am just getting my papa to stop treating me like a child. I don't wish to go through the same thing with you, Ruby.'

'But this is sommat as would shock and hurt you.'

'Does my papa try to molest you, Ruby?'

Ruby's mouth dropped open. Millie hoped against hope this meant that he didn't. But no matter the pain she would feel if it was true, because it would disgust her and break her heart, she had to know.

Ruby lowered her head. Her hands wrung in agitation, but she didn't deny or confirm anything – she didn't need to.

Wrapping the towel around herself, Millie went up to Ruby and put her arms around her. 'I'm sorry. Sorry that I have such a letch for a father; but mostly sorry for your hurt and humiliation, dear Ruby. Has anything happened yet or does he simply threaten you?' Swallowing hard, Millie tried not to cry, but when a tear plopped onto Ruby's cheek, her own floodgates opened. They sobbed in each other's arms.

Millie's grief was for her friend, as well as for her own hurt – she had learned so many bad things about her father in such a short time. *I have been blind to his faults and only saw Mama's, because Papa gave in to me at every turn and she seemed to be a sourpuss, who wanted to spoil everything I wished to do.*

But suddenly she saw everything differently. Mama wasn't spoiling everything; she wanted Millie to get away from all of this, never find out the truth and be shielded from falling from grace. And yes, Mama may even have feared that Papa's hold on the business was fragile because his ways might lead to disgrace, and she wanted her daughter safe and secure. Her means of trying to achieve this was misguided, but nevertheless Millie no longer saw her as the enemy, but rather as a victim.

As she cried out her pain, and tried to comfort Ruby's, Millie's mind questioned if her papa truly loved her, or if he saw her as a weapon to beat her mama with. *I have often cold-shouldered Mama, and counteracted her wishes by getting Papa to champion my cause against her.*

A great feeling of shame washed over Millie as these revelations hit her, and she made her mind up to put them right.

Patting Ruby on the back, she withdrew from her arms. 'Now that I know, Ruby, I will protect you. I may only be nineteen, but in these last weeks I have aged years in my knowledge of the world, and in my wisdom. I have had a peek into another world and have seen how the poor live; and a lot of what I have seen can be put down to my papa's actions. I have learned that I have taken after him, in his determination to have what he wants – only my needs are very different. I want justice. I feel compassion for those who are less fortunate. I would never step on them to better myself. You have a friend in me, Ruby. You need never be afraid of my papa again.'

'Eeh, Miss Millie, you mustn't do owt. Please . . .'

'Not doing anything isn't an option for me. I will do something, but you won't get into trouble. I will make sure of that. My father is a despicable man, but I must be careful, because it is vital that he carries on with his plan to take me into the business. Now, I will dress and go and see my dear mama, and let her know how much I love her and that I am on her side.'

Ruby dried her eyes. 'By, Miss Millie, you've turned from a girl into a woman – a strong woman – in five minutes! Eeh, I feel as though the whole world had better watch out, and not just your father.'

'And you're right, Ruby. I do want to put the world right. There is so much that is wrong, especially for women. Have you heard of the National Federation of Women Workers?'

'Naw. Was that what your father was on about?'

'Yes. Well, I have written to its leader, Mary Macarthur. I have read so much about her in my father's trade journals – not that he knows that I read them, I take them from the bin before the maids empty it. Anyway, I have explained who I am in my letter and how I need the help of the Federation to try to make things better for the women who work in my father's factory.'

'Eeh, Miss Millie, won't that lead to trouble for you?'

'Probably, but I am hoping not to be found out; you see, I have asked that any mail to me is sent in a plain envelope, which cannot be identified as coming from her or the Federation.'

'Eeh, that's grand, if risky to yourself, but I admire you

for it, Miss Millie. From what you tell me things do need to change for the poor women working in the jam factory . . . Ooh, wait till I tell my Tommy . . . I mean—'

'Your Tommy? Tommy Ryan, the stable hand?'

'Aw, Miss Millie, me tongue slipped. But aye, that Tommy: me and him are walking out.'

'Oh, Ruby, I'm so pleased for you, but why the secrecy?'

'Because we staff are not allowed to have relationships amongst us, and if we were found out we'd get the sack. And me ma would, an' all, as the housekeeper, because she'd be judged as allowing it. And that's your mama's rule, not your father's.'

'Oh, dear, another battle for me. I'm beginning to regret being me. Why can't I simply be a demure little lady who does as exactly as she is told?'

Ruby burst out laughing at this. 'You? Never, Millie, you've allus been a rebel!'

Millie laughed with her and her mood lifted, making her feel able to seek out her mama. She wasn't sure how she would approach her, and was afraid of rejection, but took a deep breath and marched determinedly down the stairs.

Mama was in her sitting room, seated staring out of the window. She looked startled when Millie walked in.

'Oh, Millicent, I wish you would tap on the door before you enter. You made me jump. And besides, this is my private sanctuary.'

This dampened Millie's enthusiasm for changing the world, but only for a moment. She took a deep breath. 'I don't wish to be impudent, Mama, but if I had done, you would have called out, "Not now." I didn't want to give you that opportunity. I want to talk to you.'

She looked taken aback, but she soon recovered. 'What about this time? Haven't you achieved all you wanted to?'

'No, all I wanted to achieve was having you love me.'

'Don't be ridiculous. Whatever brought this on? Of course I love you. Now, please, Millicent, I have a headache. I've had enough of being ranted at by your papa.'

'My father – I don't wish to call him my "papa" any longer.'

'Oh, and when did this change take place?'

Another deep breath. 'It took place the moment I learned who, and what, my father really is. And I don't like it. But, like you, there is little I can do about it.'

'Millicent! What on earth has happened to you? You seem like a different person. What in heaven's name do you mean?'

'I *am* a different person, Mama. I have grown up. I was a young girl up until the moment I ventured out of the protected world you wrapped me in. Then I saw and learned. And now I have to be an adult – about everything that is different in my world from the picture that I had of it.'

'I don't understand. Sit down, Millicent. What is all this nonsense you are talking? Are you feeling unwell?'

Millie smiled as she sat down. 'No, Mama, I am quite well. But I want you to know that I love you, and that now I feel I understand you, too – at least your motives in wanting a good marriage for me. I understand why you think that falling in love isn't a consideration, because it won't protect me from heartache. But if I married well, I would have some standing in society, and friends among those who have to put up with infidelity – as you have.'

Mama's face was a picture. She started to speak, but seemed unable to.

'I have learned that Father is not only unfaithful, but a

brute of a man, who uses others' fear to bend them to his will.'

'Millicent! I – I, well, I—'

'You cannot keep this from me by denying it all, or by forbidding me to say such things, Mama. I know them now. And I will do all I can to change things for those who are in fear of my father, and for those working as his slaves.'

A tear trickled slowly from Mama's eye. Followed by another. Millie watched them trace a path down her cheek.

'Mama. I love you. I don't want to hurt you. You know all that I have spoken of is true. Please may I hug you?'

'Just . . . just hold my hand. I am afraid I may break down if you do more than that.'

Millie jumped up and went to her mama's side and knelt down beside her. She took her tiny, cold, shaky hand in her own and held it gently, afraid that her mama might indeed break down. Her own tears spilled over when Mama stroked her hair.

'The day you were born, my beautiful daughter, was a happy day. Papa was so in love with me, and besotted with you. I trusted him with our lives, but he threw that back at me, and you and I have suffered. At least in how we were unable to relate to each other, because I made sure – well, I tried to make sure – that you didn't know anything about the other side of your papa. And then – misguidedly, it appears – I insisted on you having the very best chance of meeting someone who, as you say, would have meant that you were in the right circles to have confidantes. I haven't had that, and I have led a very lonely life.'

'I know what loneliness feels like, Mama. The upper classes can be very cruel to anyone trying to join their ranks by any means other than right of birth. And this is how my own loneliness was born.'

'I really didn't realize. I am sorry, my darling girl. But what will you do? Do you really wish to join your papa's business? From what I hear of his workplace, it's a very unpleasant environment.'

'I want to change that – and the way Papa's business is run – but I can only alter things from within. I need to learn the business and make changes gradually. Without being there, I cannot know what goes on, or how it might alter.'

'It will be a difficult world for you to adjust to, but I have already seen what a strong young woman you are. I will give you my blessing, but promise me you will tread very carefully?'

'I will.' Sitting up, Millie looked into her mama's eyes. 'Mama? Something has happened at the factory, hasn't it?'

'Yes, but . . . Oh, well, I suppose if you are going into jam-making, then you will witness these things. It's horrible. It has greatly upset me, and is why I was sitting here quietly. I was trying to come to terms with it. You see . . .'

Millie listened in horror to what Mama knew of the terrible details of the accident.

'Oh, Mama, that poor woman. Do you know her name?'

'No, dear. All I know, besides the accident itself, is that Chambers, the supervisor at Papa's factory, has caught the culprits – two girls. He says they deliberately shoved the young woman. Papa said he will personally see to it that they are hanged, drawn and quartered, as he put it.'

Millie felt extreme fear clench her stomach. 'I have to go out, Mama. Ruby is to accompany me. And, Mama, may I speak with you on one more matter?'

'What is it, dear, and where are you going?'

'It's about the rule you have that our staff must not get over-friendly with each other or they will be sacked. I am of a mind that we cannot help who we fall in love with. So if two of the staff do fall in love, they don't deserve to lose their jobs and have no chance of setting up home together, getting married and having children. It is so unfair on them.'

'Oh? Has it happened then?'

'It has, and the two concerned are terrified that you will find out. They may even end up leaving us and getting work elsewhere, whereas they could get a home near enough to travel to work and—'

'Oh? I . . . well, it is the usual rule of a household. I didn't think it through. I will tell the housekeeper that the rule no longer applies, but there is to be no courting while on duty.' Mother smiled then and lifted an eyebrow. 'Does that meet your approval, dear?'

'It does, Mama. Thank you.' Standing now, Millie impetuously planted a kiss on the top of her mother's head.

Mama gave what sounded like a happy giggle. 'Now, please leave this to the housekeeper to deal with. It is her place, and we mustn't interfere with the smooth running of her staff. But you haven't told me where you are going, Millicent?'

'Just out to get some air. It was stuffy in the car, and such a long journey. I feel like some fresh air.'

'If we'd had this conversation earlier, I might have come with you – especially with our new sense of companionship. I feel cooped up myself. But make sure you are back in time to dress for dinner. Papa will be in a foul mood, as it is – that's if he even bothers to show up for dinner.'

'I will, Mama.' The thought of taking her mama with her

made Millie smile, as she was sure her mother would have a blue fit at what she was intending to do. Although would she? Millie hugged herself. *Mama isn't the only one to find a new friend, in me. I think that I have found one in her, and it feels so wonderful.*

She would have skipped for joy, but for her worries.

She wasted no time getting ready and making sure Ruby understood that she must accompany her. Millie was soon heading out to the garden, with a note in her pocket for a very nervous Ruby to take to Elsie, Dot or Cecil.

Millie found it difficult not to blurt out her mama's new decision, regarding courting amongst the staff, when she saw Tommy jump back as Ruby tried to greet him with a kiss. Ruby giggled at him and told him, 'Millie knows all about us, and she won't tell on us, will you, Millie?'

She smiled. If only she didn't have to respect her mama's wishes and leave this matter to the housekeeper. She longed to put their minds at rest.

As they set off, Millie could hardly speak for the prayers she was sending up, begging God not to let anyone involved in the accident – or the accused – be Elsie or Dot. Her heart pounded with fear for them, for if it was one of them who'd lost her life, it would break her heart. If one or both of them was accused, then she would do everything she possibly could to help them. *I know neither of them could do such a thing – I just know it!*

Cecil did come to her, when Ruby found him, his face red, his eyes raw. What he told Millie filled her with anguish. Elsie and Dot had been arrested.

Chapter Ten

Kitty

Kitty had been on cloud nine. She'd been to see Gerry Flounder and found he still wanted to audition her. 'I'll tell you what, girl, so as I know you're not wasting my time, sing something now. I've no music set up, but I will give you an audition, as I need to know that you can sing to music, and keep time with it.'

Her nerves had heightened and her throat had dried, because so much was riding on this. With a job, she truly could change her life round. Taking a deep breath, she started to sing Elsie's favourite, 'I'm Shy, Mary Ellen'.

Gerry didn't interrupt her, and as she got into the flow, Kitty did the actions she'd seen onstage, changing her voice just as the actress had done for the part. When she came to the end, Gerry applauded.

'Bravo! Well, girl, you can sing, I'll say that for you – and act, too. You had me believing the words. Let's fix a date for you to come to my studio. I'll have a trio to play for you. Can you read music?'

'No, is – is it needed?'

'No, a lot can't, but you do need to have an ear for it.

The trio will play the song once, and you'll be expected to sing the words to the music the second time around. Producers and directors won't tolerate understudies who are slow to pick up a part.'

'What is an understudy?'

'My, you're green behind the ears, ain't yer? It's someone ready to take over if the lead singer is taken ill, or cannot do the show for whatever reason. You'll be at the theatre an hour before the show, and will stay there till the end. And you'll be word-perfect on every song and every line, and you'll know every stage direction and all the cues.'

This sounded so exciting that Kitty had immediately sent up a prayer that whoever she understudied would be taken ill. But then she felt bad, so she cancelled the prayer.

'And often the understudy gets a chance to star in a show of her own, once she's shown what she can do. All you need is that break.'

'So I won't audition for a starring role?'

'No. It doesn't work like that. You have to earn your stripes, so to speak. Now, about the pay. It ain't much, and I can't say that I'm taking you on yet. And you only get paid once the show starts its run, though you'll have to work hard, running up to that time with rehearsals.'

'Oh? I don't know then. I need to earn money. Maybe I'll just go to work in the pubs, like me mum did.'

'Don't be daft. You have to look on this as your apprenticeship. Find yourself something in the meantime. Maybe I can help with that, as they're always short of stagehands, and need women in the wardrobe department. If you make the grade, I'll ask around for you. Better that you work totally within the industry than have your loyalties divided.

Leave it with me. Now, let me see.' After consulting his diary, he made a date for the following Wednesday. Kitty couldn't wait.

When she arrived home, Kitty hadn't set her foot in the door before Cecil came running over to her. 'Mum, step outside – it's urgent.'

'What? What's going on, Son?'

'It's Elsie. Mum, she . . . she's been arrested.' With this, big as he was, Cecil burst into tears.

'Cecil – Cess, come on now, pull yourself together and tell me what's happened. I'm going mad with worry. What on earth could our Elsie do that would cause her to be arrested?'

When he calmed down, between sniffles and sobs he told her what had happened.

'What? God! Who told you, Cess? It can't be true. And Dot as well? Oh, Cess, no. Tell me, how did you find out?'

'I – I was working on the dock, when a bloke came to the stall and said that there'd been some trouble at Swift's. He said he'd passed by earlier in the morning and one of the women standing outside had said a girl got killed by falling into a vat of boiling water. I left me station and ran like the wind to the factory. There weren't no one about at first, but then the bloke that keeps the waste down, and that I speak to often, came into the yard. He said the police had just arrived back to do some more investigating and they'd spoken to the supervisor, then arrested Elsie and Dot! Oh, Mum, what are we going to do? He said he don't think they did it. That it's a cover-up.'

'I know what I'm going to do. Was the boss's car outside?'

'Yes, it was.'

'Right. You stay here with Jimmy and Bert. I'll be back soon.'

'Mum . . . Look, I have a secret. I'd never tell, as I was asked not to, but now I think you should know.'

Kitty sighed as Cecil told her about Richie's daughter, and how she had befriended Elsie and Dot. The implications were many. She should have guessed, that time at the funeral of poor Phyllis. But she didn't feel angry now, as she had then. The secrets were many, and she had a few herself.

'And you say that this Millie said she would help?'

'She did, Mum. And I think she will. She has to have some say with her dad, surely?'

'Don't you worry, me darlin'. I'm sure she does. Leave it with me.'

As she hurried towards the factory, Kitty didn't feel at all sure. Richie Hawkesfield was a hard man to fathom. If he didn't have a mind to, he wouldn't listen to anyone – not even his own daughter. *Yes, he'd see my Elsie, and Dot, hang to save his own skin.*

As she walked, she thought about the terrible accident. Elsie had told her many times that she felt afraid when they had to walk across the top of the vat. She dared not look down, as it made her feel giddy and she thought she might fall. Kitty had been shocked that it didn't have a cover on it, to stop an accident happening. But then – from all that she knew herself, and from what Elsie told her – corners were cut to make more profit. Richie needed a lot of money, not only for his fancy homes, which he'd told her about, but for his gambling; more than anything, for his gambling. She'd known a time when he'd cried on her shoulder because he'd lost a lot of money. He was in debt up to his eyes – or at least his factory was.

She doubted his fancy wife and daughter knew that! Well, it was one of the weapons she would use against him, to force him to have Elsie and Dot released. Never in a million years did she ever imagine she would think like this, but when it came to her daughter – and the man who had caused her pain for many, many years – there was no contest.

Reaching the factory, she saw one or two of the women coming out of the doors and making for the gate. She called out to them, 'Can you help me? I'm Elsie Makin's mum. Can you tell me what happened?'

One of the women came running over. 'I'm Lucy – Lucy Dalton. I tried to stop the arrest, but nearly got arrested myself. They didn't do it. You see . . .'

Kitty couldn't believe what Lucy told her. 'So, you're telling me this other woman ain't going to come forward and tell the truth?'

'No, and no one'll split on her. Not even me. I'm sorry. The only way is if she changes her mind and faces what she did. I mean, she didn't intend to kill Ruth, or harm her; she was just very angry at the delay. But all the girls and I will testify to Elsie and Dot not being responsible. We'll say there was fear of being late, and those at the back surged forward.'

'And you haven't said that already?'

'I did, but I was threatened with the sack. But by the time the trial comes, everything will have changed.'

Kitty couldn't take it all in, as she listened to how things were going to alter. 'So this Women's Federation will make changes, so you won't all be frightened of losing your jobs, and then you'll tell the truth? In the meantime, with none of you coming forward before then, me poor Elsie and Dot will have been convicted and will be in prison, terrified for their lives and going through God-knows-what!'

'I know, but no matter what you do, you won't change that. No one dare speak out until they're sure they won't lose their jobs. I'm sorry.'

'So your jobs are worth more to you than the lives of me daughter and her mate?'

Lucy hung her head.

'Look, I ain't blaming you. And I'm grateful to you for saying you'll stand up for them, when the time comes. But do your best to get this federation thing organized, Lucy. Please, do your best, and hurry.'

'I will. Ta, Kitty. See you around.'

Kitty turned and leaned against the gate. She had made her mind up that she would tackle Richie Hawkesfield, but not here. She needed to place herself where she could stop him as he went home, pretend that she wanted to be with him. Luckily she was dressed well, as she'd put on her Sunday best to go and see Gerry Flounder – the outfit she'd worn to the theatre.

Running as fast as she could, she made it to St George's garden and stood next to the road. Inside, she was dying from panic and pain at what had befallen her lovely Elsie, but on the outside she knew that if ever she acted any part in her life, she had to play this one to the full. She had to appear desperate to see Richie, and surely he would be feeling the same, because he'd been away for a couple of weeks and wouldn't have been getting what he most desired, unless one of his maids had looked after him.

She didn't have long to wait. She'd recognize his car anywhere – there were so few sleek cream-and-black cars around. Stepping out onto the edge of the pavement, Kitty waved him down and was pleased to see Richie swerve into the kerbside. His window was wound down and his head popped through.

'Well, hello. You're a welcome sight, and just what I need. Jump in.'

Kitty sank into the plush red-leather bench seat and slid across until she was near to him, her hand finding his crotch. 'Missed me?'

His 'Missed *it*!' would usually have hurt her badly, and she couldn't understand why it didn't. She laughed at his immediate reaction to her touch, which showed her that she might have some power over him, and she knew this was the way to wield it.

Richie grinned. 'Have you missed me? Or just *him* – and my money?'

She giggled. 'Both of the last two.'

'You're a naughty girl, you know that, don't you?' He slid down in the seat a little, so that she could reach him better.

As he moaned his pleasure, Kitty frantically searched her mind for how to turn this to her advantage. She knew that Richie was ruthless. Would he care if she threatened to expose their relationship?

Keeping up her caressing movements with her hand, and her own moans of pleasure, she tried to plan. 'Shall we go to our room, so I can do a proper job and have something in return?'

His reply was barely audible. 'Soon, but don't stop.'

This panicked her. If she satisfied him here and now, he might shove her out of the car with a couple of quid and leave her. She didn't want that. 'Only if you can be ready to give me some pleasure soon afterwards. Oh, Richie, I've missed you. I want to lay with you – I want more than this.'

'And you'll get it, I promise, but . . . don't . . . don't stop.' His long moan, and the feel of him pulsating, told her he'd climaxed.

Kitty couldn't enjoy the moment with him, nor had anything that she'd done aroused her; all she felt was worry that her chance was gone.

After a moment he calmed. 'Phew, that beats bashing it myself.' His laugh was a nice sound, and his look told her that he was pleased with her. 'Well, now we'll have to go to our room. I need to bath and change – better still, you need to bath me.' His eyes clouded over. 'You can be my slave. I like all my slaves to work in the nude and to object to my antics.'

'No, Mister, you can't use me like that. Me is a lady, you know.'

They laughed together as he set the car in motion. 'Oh, Kitty, I've missed you. Two weeks with only the maids to chase. But the only one I really want to have is still not playing ball. Even when I threatened her with the sack!'

This kind of conversation would normally have torn Kitty in two, but she felt nothing. 'She doesn't know what she's missing! But I'm glad she hasn't given in, or I would have missed out.'

'Never. You're in my blood, Kitty. My feelings for you run deeper than mere gratification, you know that. If circumstances were different and we had married, I would never have strayed. But you're not there all the time, and I have my needs and fancies. My darling daughter's maid, Ruby, is a conquest that I'm going to have, one way or another.'

Kitty wanted to scream at the way he spoke of his daughter's maid. She couldn't bear it. But she had to wait for the right moment. She *had* to.

He'd told her before, in this roundabout way, how much she meant to him, and hearing this had always made Kitty hope that Richie would never leave her again, and that eventually he would do what he had once promised and set her and her family up in a nice place, and they would want for nothing. But now she felt only contempt for him, although her snuggling into his body and laying her head on his shoulder belied this.

When they reached the house – once a private dwelling, but now two flats, the top one being owned by Richie – they ascended the stairs. She'd been surprised when Richie had first brought her here; surprised, and hopeful that his intention was for this flat to be hers. She'd planned each room out: the three bedrooms for the boys, one room for Elsie and one for herself; and hoped that she would still meet Richie at the hotel, but he'd never voiced this as his plan, and always brought her here now and not to the hotel.

'Brr, it's cold in here. Light the gas fire, slave.' Richie slapped her bottom.

Giggling, Kitty did as he bade, glad of the warmth immediately radiating into the room.

Richie sat down in the huge armchair next to the fire. He still wore his coat. 'Now you can get your clothes off, don a pinafore and make me a nice hot drink of tea; and put the water on for a bath, while I watch you. Then while it is coming to the boil, you can bring the tin bath out of the cupboard and place it in front of the fire. I don't feel like going into a cold bathroom. Oh, and I'm hungry. So before all that, pop down to the corner shop and get something for me – bread, butter and cheese will do.'

Kitty took a deep breath. 'No. Before I do any of that, I am going to tell you something.'

'What?' He looked at her, annoyance emanating from him. This would frighten her normally, but Kitty felt nothing but loathing for him. Richie's expression turned to one of anger. 'Can't whatever it is wait? I had all this planned in my mind, and now you are spoiling it.'

'I want my daughter out of custody.'

He sat up straight. 'What? What daughter? What are you talking about? God! Is . . . is one of those bloody murderers your *daughter*? Which one? How? I . . . mean, why didn't I know? For Christ's sake, what *is* this?' He stood up, his expression a mixture of anger and fear. 'Kitty?'

'One of the girls is my daughter, but they are *both* your daughters.'

His mouth dropped open.

'And either you free them, without charge, and take responsibility for the accident yourself, mate, or the whole bloody world will know how you haven't recognized them, and how they have been brought up in poverty – and that your ultimate revenge on them was to have them arrested for a murder they didn't commit.'

Richie sank back into the chair, his look one of defeat and yet utter incredulity. 'My daughters? But . . . how? Why didn't I know?'

Kitty felt relief and elation pulse through her – he was showing his shock, not ranting and denying it all. Not only that, but at this moment Richie had an air of defeat about him, giving her some hope that her plan was working.

'What would you have done, if you had known? Nothing. I thought you loved me – I was only sixteen! You told me you loved me, but before I realized why I felt unwell and was being sick in the mornings, which made me late for work, I was sacked and couldn't get anywhere near you to tell you.' Bitterness entered her then. 'Because you'd moved on – to my best friend – and I was barred from the factory. The gateman wouldn't let me in, and you ignored me when I stood and waited for you to go by, even when I waved you down. Then my mate fell pregnant with you, and I fell out with her, as I felt betrayed by her and . . .'

She hadn't wanted to cry. She'd told herself that she would do this in a cold, calculating way, but all the heartache and pain of yesteryear flooded through her and she sank down onto the sofa that faced the fire. 'I – I married, so as not to be shamed, but I deceived my boyfriend, I didn't tell him. When the baby was born, he knew it wasn't premature, and knew it wasn't his . . .' As she sat there, her mind replaying scenes of the brutality she had endured as a result, she could feel the sting of her husband's blows. The biting of his teeth, the burns of his cigarettes, and the pulling of her hair from its roots.

'But why have you never told me this before? I don't understand.'

'Because once it happened, neither of us could get near to you. You'd moved on to others; you were the big "I am" around here, and we were just two young girls from the slums. Even so, there was a moral code among our own, and to be pregnant and unwed was looked down on, as bringing shame to the neighbourhood. We had no choice but to inflict your kids on our innocent husbands. But by God, we paid.' She told him how it was for her, and how she suspected it still was for Beryl, and knew it was for his daughter, Dot.

'But if not then, why not later? We've been together on and off for years now.'

'Exactly! On and off, at your will! I didn't want that for

my daughter. I didn't want her to feel the pain of rejection. She deserves better – not that she got it. What I had to do to survive, after my husband killed himself, has meant more heartache than she, or any of my kids, should have to bear.'

'And what about your others – who fathered them? Not me. None of your sons are mine, are they?'

'No.' By now, Kitty felt only disgust at herself. 'Ha – they, poor sods, could be anybody's: from the milkman's, in exchange for a pint of milk, to the grocer's, for a box of food. But I had no choice . . . no choice.' Despite saying this, Kitty hung her head with the weight of her shame, but then the reason for it all came back to her and she raised her head and, with all the hate she held inside her for this man, spat out, 'You left me with no choice, you bleedin' bastard!'

Richie stood up, his anger visible in his stance, but she was angry, too.

Standing, Kitty told him in measured tones, 'And now I'm only giving you two options: you go to the police and get my daughter and her half-sister out of custody and cleared of charges, or I go to the local rag. They love a bit of scandal and will relish my story – they'll expose you for what you are. And, mark my words, it'll make such good reading that the national papers will pick up on it . . . I can see the headlines now: "Respected Businessman Causes His Own Illegitimate Daughters to Go to Prison and Face Being Hanged!"'

'Shut up!'

The stinging slap knocked Kitty off-balance. But she steadied herself on the arm of the sofa and managed to dodge his raised fist. Scooting around the back of the chair that he'd risen from, she screamed at him: '"And Then He

Beat Up One of the Mothers – a Woman Who Was Just a Girl When He Seduced Her!"'

Seeing him slump down onto the sofa, a picture of despair, she knew she'd won.

But as she basked in her victory, horror dawned when Richie suddenly jumped up and crossed the room. When he reached the door, he turned towards her. She recoiled from the look that she saw on his face, which spoke of his hate for her, and of the power he had over her. 'Don't think for one minute you've got the better of me. If this accident is found to be my fault, through safety measures not being in place, I could be the one in jail. And not only that, but I would lose everything.'

'Where are you going? What will you do?' Fear gripped Kitty.

In a voice that made her blood run cold he said, 'I wonder if the police will even bat an eyelid if they find another prostitute dead in the canal.'

Kitty ran to Richie, begging him, but in doing so she played into his hands, as he grabbed her, bent her double and rammed her head into the wall. Extreme pain overtook any ability to form thoughts about what would happen to her, as she sank into oblivion.

Chapter Eleven

Elsie

The cell was dark, but for a small light coming through the grid in the door. Elsie's body trembled, not just with the extreme cold that made her teeth chatter, but because her heart and soul were full of fear. She looked over to where Dot had been sitting on the bed opposite hers and bitterness crept into her. Dot had been taken out to spend five minutes with her mum.

Elsie wanted to be held, comforted and have someone standing in her corner, demanding justice for her, in the way that she'd heard Mrs Grimes screaming for. But nothing happened. Mum didn't come. And no matter how much she told herself that there must be a good reason, she felt abandoned. Left alone, to hang!

Oh God, help us. Help me and Dot. We didn't harm anyone.

Lucy came to her mind, and a small hope seeped into her as she remembered what Lucy had said about testifying for them. *Lucy's a strong and determined person. Surely any judge will listen to her?*

A sobbing Dot came back into the cell and sat down beside Elsie. Elsie took Dot into her arms and they rocked backwards and forwards, their despair weighing them down.

'What did your mum say, Dot?'

'Not a lot, though she ranted at the Old Bill, which didn't help. It's not their fault. But, Else, for her to come and show she cares like that, she must love me, and I've never thought she did. She told me she couldn't bear me to be in this situation, and that she believed in me and knows I didn't do it. She's never told me she loves me, but today she's shown that she does.'

'I'm glad, Dot. Maybe she's afraid to show her love for you, because of your dad.'

'Yes, she is afraid of him. He's been a brute to her. But I've felt nothing from me mum other than resentment. I've snapped at her at times, telling her that I didn't ask to be born.'

'At least she came as soon as she heard. I can't understand why my mum hasn't.'

'I'm sorry, Else. I know it's breaking your heart, but perhaps she don't know yet, mate?'

The key turning a few minutes after this raised Elsie's spirits, but when the door opened, it wasn't for the reason she was hoping for.

'Here you are, girls. I bet you're hungry, eh?' One of the policemen walked in, carrying two bowls of soup and two chunks of bread on a tray.

Elsie didn't feel a bit hungry, but didn't say so. She did tell him how cold they were, though.

'I'll see what I can do. We've some blankets for overnighters, which it looks like you might be. We're waiting for a bloke to come from another station to question you. He's a detective and he'll get to the bottom of this, don't you worry. Sounds like the usual sort of women's squabble to me, only it ended badly for you all. A tragedy.'

When he left, Dot had more hope in her voice. 'He don't seem a bad bloke, does he, Else? He don't seem to be saying it's our fault.'

'No, and that's good. I mean, if blokes like him don't really think so, then it gives us a chance. And I've been thinking: we've got Lucy on our side, too.'

They'd only just finished their soup – which Elsie had enjoyed more than she thought she would – when the key turned again. 'You've got another visitor, girls. And this one might help your cause, as it's only the daughter of the boss of your factory! You keep high company, don't you?'

'Millie? Millie's here!'

'She gave her name as Millicent Hawkesfield.'

Elsie felt a surge of fresh hope.

They were taken along the same narrow corridor they'd travelled along to get to the cell, and then through a door that led to a small room with a table and three chairs in it.

Millie looked pale and tearful as she greeted them with a hug. She told them how she'd heard of the accident and had feared it might be one of them who had died.

Elsie felt amazed that Millie thought enough of them to go to all this trouble. Someone of her standing would never usually even bother to look in the direction of folk so far beneath them as she and Dot were, let alone seek their friendship and want to help them. Millie was different from anyone she'd ever met, and Elsie found it all hard to understand. But Millie was lovely, and she felt an overwhelming feeling of love for her.

'Are you both all right? You're not hurt, are you? What happened? I only know there was an accident.'

As they came out of their hug, Elsie told the story, as agreed by everyone.

'Oh, Elsie, this is awful. That poor girl. How must her mother feel? I'm appalled at my father. To think that a simple change could have prevented her death. But why would someone say you two did it?'

'I don't know. I've thought and thought. We were directly behind Ruth, and all I can think is that someone told Chambers something, and he jumped on it and twisted it to make it look as though we were to blame and that none of it was the fault of his precious boss.'

'He licks your dad's arse, mate.'

'Dot!' Elsie felt mortified that Dot had voiced to Millie what all the workers said about Chambers. But Millie, after her initial look of shock, giggled.

'Oh, Dot, you don't say much, but when you do, it has real meaning. I've never heard that said before, but I can see how apt it is for someone like my father's supervisor, who takes the action he has. I've only met Chambers recently, so I don't know him, but he doesn't sound a very nice person. Anyway, back to your predicament. I'll try to help, I promise. I have some money of my own. I'll go to a solicitor and ask about engaging help for you. If you had a lawyer, he would soon get you out of here. But you mustn't say who is helping you.'

Millie put out her hands and took hold of Elsie's hands and Dot's. 'Don't be afraid. Even if I don't come to see you again, I will be doing all I can.'

'Ta, Millie. You're a real friend.' As Elsie said this, she felt a pang of guilt and wished with all her heart that she didn't know about Millie's father and her own mum. Shame washed over her – if Millie found out, would she break off their friendship?

'I'm so happy to hear you say that, Elsie. And I mean it

when I say I will try my best for you. But is there anything you need now? Anything I can try to get for you.'

Dot piped up, 'Me and Else are freezing in that cell, Millie. We weren't even allowed to get our coats when they arrested us. The policeman said he'd try to get us a blanket, but even that might not be enough.'

'One of you can have my cardigan. And Ruby, my maid, is in the foyer; she is wearing one too – I'll go and get hers.' As she said this, Millie was undoing her cloak. She wore a thick brown jacket underneath, which matched her long riding skirt, and then when she removed this, she had a lovely light-brown cardigan on. She took it off and handed it to Elsie, before saying that she would be back in a minute.

Elsie turned to Dot. 'I'll have this one, eh? You don't mind, do you, mate?'

'No, I don't care which one I have, as long as I have one.'

Although she felt she was being a bit selfish and would normally have offered first choice to Dot, Elsie had the feeling that by wearing Millie's cardigan, she'd feel that Millie was with her and she knew that would give her comfort.

Nothing Elsie had worn had ever felt as soft and luxurious as this cardigan did, when she slipped it on. The feeling it gave was like being hugged. It brought her mum to mind. Tears stung her eyes. Why wasn't Mum coming to her? She must know, because Millie had said that Cecil knew. Poor Cess. Millie had said he was distraught. *Oh, Mum. Mum, please come to me.*

'Are you all right, Else? You've gone very quiet, mate.'

Elsie nodded. She couldn't speak, as the lump in her throat threatened to choke her, but she swallowed hard. She didn't want to upset Dot any more than she was already.

When Millie returned with a grey cardigan for Dot, the

policeman's head appeared at the door. 'Just five minutes more, Miss.'

'Not if I chain myself to the door, as the suffragettes did outside Parliament.'

The policeman laughed and, despite all the anguish she felt, Elsie giggled, too. To her, Millie was a lot like Lucy. With this thought, she decided to tell Millie about Lucy and what she planned.

Millie's reaction surprised her. 'That's a coincidence, as that's exactly what I have been up to lately. I have written to Mary Macarthur myself, as I'm interested in hearing more about her movement. I think she, and women like her, will see to it that things change – you have to believe that. Now I have to go, not least because my poor mama will be out of her mind with worry. And if Father has returned home and finds that I have been gone for as long as I have, then I will be in a lot of trouble.' She took their hands again. 'I'm so sorry I have to leave you here. It is an awful place and you shouldn't be here, but try not to worry. I will be doing all I can to help you, I promise.'

Millie stood then and opened her arms. Both Dot and Elsie went to her and the three of them huddled together. When they parted, they all had tears running down their cheeks. A big void opened up inside Elsie as the door closed on Millie and she and Dot were escorted back to their cell.

It was the morning after their second night in the cell.

There had been hours and hours of anguish, tears and fear. And yet, somehow, Elsie had to be the strong one, as Dot had gone to pieces, despite the support of her mother coming each day, when Elsie hadn't heard a word from her own mum.

They'd both eaten the porridge that was brought to them, though the tears they shed had seemed to swell Elsie's throat, and the smell of the slop bucket turned her stomach. She made herself swallow every mouthful, to encourage Dot to eat. She knew they had to keep their strength up.

The policemen looking after them were kindly, letting them out of the cell to empty their bucket regularly and to have a wash. They'd brought blankets to them and always had a kindly word. But there was little they could do about their situation; just take care of them as best they could, until the detective they'd spoken of arrived. The policemen were able to tell the girls that he'd begun investigations at the factory and had spoken to Mr Hawkesfield.

Elsie knew things could be a lot worse for them and they were lucky to be treated so well, considering what they were accused of, but none of that mattered to her – she felt alone and abandoned.

When a policeman came and told Elsie she had to go with him, Dot jumped up. 'Don't leave me here, Elsie. Not on me own, please – I couldn't bear it.'

Elsie felt the last remnants of strength ebbing from her. She was exhausted, both physically and emotionally, and wished Dot could be a little braver. Despite this, she couldn't feel cross with Dot, and so she asked the policeman if Dot could come, too.

'All right.' He turned to Dot then, and what he said aroused fear in Elsie. 'But you're to be strong for your friend, as it isn't good news that we have for her.'

'Why, what's happened?' Although she asked, Elsie didn't really want to hear; she'd thought for hours and hours about why her mum wasn't coming to see her. Her mum, for all her faults, would move heaven and earth to get to her and do all she could – *if* she could.

'Your brothers are here. They say your mother hasn't been home since she left, the afternoon you were brought here. She told your eldest brother not to worry: she would get you out and home in no time, and that he was to stay with the younger ones. But she never returned.'

'No! Me mum? Where can she be? What's happened to her?'

'We don't know. With her only just being reported missing, we need to get the facts and start a search.'

When Elsie saw Cecil, Jimmy and Bert, it undid her. She ran to them and gathered them to her. Her sobs racked her throat, her tears wet their faces as she kissed them. She held them as if she would never let them go. Sitting down on one of the chairs, she took Bert on her knee. He hadn't spoken, but his little body trembled. She stroked his hair and spoke to Jimmy. 'Come here, mate, you look all in. Are you feeling unwell?'

He answered her with a fit of coughing. His visit to the doctor had resulted in him getting some oils to rub on his chest and some nasty-tasting medicine to take. Both had helped.

'Have you taken you medication?' He nodded his head. She'd never known her brothers so quiet. 'It'll work soon, love,' she told him. 'Take some deep breaths.' Looking up at Cecil, she saw that he was standing close to Dot. His arm was around her. Dot was weeping silently. 'What happened, Cess? Did Mum say where she was going?'

Cecil could only tell her what the policeman had already told her, then he added, 'She said she could sort it out. I had the feeling she meant that she could speak to someone and make everything right. I'm scared, Else.'

Knowing that she had to be strong for her lovely, lost-looking brothers, Elsie hid the dread inside her. 'Mum'll be all right, Cess. The Old Bill will find her. I've something I can tell them that might help them in their search.' As she said this, Elsie's dread deepened, because exposing her mum's association with Mr Hawkesfield meant that Millie would get to know about it. However, the implications of this paled beside her need to help find her beloved mother.

'Look after Bert and Jimmy, Cess, while I'm gone for a moment or two. Dot will help you. I'll be back soon.'

Looking up at the policeman who stood in the doorway, Elsie asked if she could speak to him in private. Outside the door, she told him in a hushed tone how she'd seen her mum meeting up with Mr Hawkesfield, then added, 'They seemed to know each other well, by the way they greeted each other. I reckon she might have thought she could talk to him and make things all right.'

'You're not suggesting Mr Hawkesfield has anything to do with your mum's absence, are you? Look, you know your mum as well as we do – we know her very well, in fact. I didn't say anything, but we think she probably couldn't take the anguish of it all and went and bought a bottle of gin and went to her mate's. The sergeant has sent one of my colleagues round there. I'm sure we'll find them both out of their minds on drink, and your mum oblivious to her responsibilities to them brothers of yours.'

'No, Mum wouldn't do that. You've got to believe me. She's changed her ways. But even if she slipped, she'd have come to see me first – I know she would. Even at her worst, she never left us alone overnight. She wouldn't. Please, please listen to me.'

'Let's wait till me colleague comes back, eh? If he has no

news, then I'll talk to me sergeant. I can't do any more than that. Now go and have five minutes with your brothers. But, Elsie, I have to warn you that if we don't find your mum, we can't let them go home on their own. They need an adult with them.'

'What? You mean . . . No, not the workhouse!'

'No, not the nippers, they're too young to go there without an adult. They'll be taken to an orphanage till all of this is sorted out.'

Elsie felt her despair deepen. How would the boys cope without each other?

'The older lad might have to go into the workhouse, unless he can prove that he has a job and can look after himself.'

'He can. And once Rene knows their predicament, she'll take care of them. You won't take them if Rene stays with them, will you?'

'We'll have to see. But don't get your hopes up. Rene hasn't got a good name with us. And though I know her to be the salt of the earth and she'll stick by them kids, me sergeant might not have any of it. But you needn't worry about the younger ones. The nuns will care for them, and they're kindly souls. I often have a cup of tea with them, and me and the lads raise money to help their cause. Now go back in, please, Elsie. I can't give you long. Detective Wilson is due here soon to question you.'

As she re-entered the room, Elsie asked Cecil, 'Have you seen anything of Rene, Cess?'

'No. I can't understand it. Mum said that Rene would be moving in with us, so I thought she might come and bring some of her bits and pieces, or be round like a shot if she heard about it all, so I don't think she can have heard yet. But I've not wanted to take Bert and Jimmy into that area to call on her. Anyway, I didn't want to leave the house, as I kept thinking Mum would come back any minute. But when she didn't come back last night, I made me mind up that I'd gotta come here this morning.'

'You did the right thing, Cess. Don't worry, mate. You kept the lads safe, and that's the main thing. You didn't know Mum wouldn't come back. Anyway, the Old Bill's sent someone round to Rene's now. They think Mum's gone round there, and she and Rene have drunk gin and forgotten about it all, but I know Mum wouldn't do that.'

'No, she wouldn't. She'd been to see that bloke about getting on the stage, and she was so sure she could make everything right.'

'And it will come right, mate. I know it will. But Cess, Jimmy: that might not be right away. You've got to be brave. You see – well, until they find Mum . . .'

Telling them what the copper had said about them all being split up almost broke Elsie, but she kept herself together. When she finished, Cecil had tears in his eyes.

'Be brave for the nippers, Cess. They've only got you to rely on. You'll be able to visit them, but it's important that you have someone at the docks who will stand up for you and say that you have work with them. Otherwise you may be forced to go into the workhouse.'

Wiping his eyes with his sleeve, Cecil told her that he knew one of the traders who would speak up for him.

'That's good. And there's some money in the pot. That'll pay the rent for a couple of weeks. And if you go and talk to Mr Wright, he'll see as you're fed – you'll be all right, Cess. Keep coming here to let us know what's happening to Jimmy and Bert. They'll be safe with the nuns. Then, before we know it, we'll be out of here, Mum'll be found and we'll all be together again.'

By the time she'd said this, Jimmy had sidled off his seat and was standing next to her, leaning his head on her shoulder. 'I don't wanna go with no nuns, Else.'

'Not even to look after Bert? Oh, Jimmy, I had you down as braver than that. Look, the nuns will look after you. You'll be warm and safe, and well fed. And me and Cess'll know that little Bert has you looking after him, till all this is over and Mum's back, and me and Dot are out of here. Can you do that, Jimmy?'

Jimmy nodded. He reached for Bert's hand. Bert smiled at him with the hero-worship smile he reserved specially for Jimmy, and Jimmy cheered up. 'I'll look after you, mate. Them nuns'll love us, won't they, Else?'

'They will, mate. Just like me and Cess and Mum do.'

'And me, Else. I love them, too, you know.'

'I know you do, Dot.' Elsie swallowed the lump in her throat as she saw Cecil tighten his grip on Dot, and Dot smile up at him. At that moment they looked like a courting couple, even though they were so young. And Elsie knew that, one day in the future, they would be together as that. And she knew she had to keep faith that this would all end and everything would be as it was. If she didn't, she would go mad.

Chapter Twelve

Kitty and Millie

Kitty fought through the fog that clogged her brain. The whir of a car engine drummed in her ears and, beneath her, she could hear the sound of wheels crunching on gravel.

Her thoughts gradually became clearer and slotted into some order. As they did so, her heart sank as the memories came to her. *Oh God, Elsie. My lovely Elsie. I was trying to help you!* Little by little, all that had happened pieced itself together.

When she opened her eyes, her fear deepened, as they couldn't penetrate the darkness. Nor could she scream, because something was wedged in her mouth. It soaked up her spittle, leaving her dry and retching against the intrusion. She tried to stretch her cramped limbs, but couldn't move. This showed her that she was tied up – not simply by her hands, but trussed, with her hands and feet secured together behind her back.

Panic gripped her, intensifying her fear. Writhing her body made her roll from side to side. *What kind of vehicle is this? I'm not on a seat, as there's nothing to stop me from rolling around. Am I in a van?*

Sheer terror made her heart bang against her chest. She couldn't breathe. Beads of sweat dampened her body. Pain burned every joint. How could Richie be so cruel? Although he was always calculating, and looked after his own interests, she never dreamed he could go as far as this. What were his intentions? *Is he driving the van?*

As she thought this, the vehicle gradually slowed and then stopped. Feeling frantic, Kitty couldn't allow herself to hope. Somehow she didn't think she was simply being kidnapped to keep her quiet until it was too late to stop the unjust action against Elsie and Dot.

The sound of a lock being undone and then a latch being lifted increased her fear, and only the beam of a torch relieved the darkness when the door opened – there was no moon. No houses with lights showing through the curtains. No sound except . . . water! The rhythmic ripple of fast-running water. She shook her head. A moan came from deep in her throat, but whatever was in her mouth prevented her from being able to form the words to beg.

Suddenly she was grabbed by a strong pair of arms and lifted as if she were a baby. The stale body odour that assaulted her nostrils told her this wasn't Richie.

The man's steps faltered under her weight, but his grip didn't loosen as she writhed in his arms. With every step the sound of the water grew louder. *No! Not . . . Please, God, help me!*

But no help came. Kitty felt the effort it took the man to lift her higher. Heard him grunting. Felt something hard beneath her – a wall?

When he tossed her, as if she was a bag of rubbish he was discarding, she felt herself falling a long way down and knew she'd been thrown from a bridge. She had but a moment to breathe in through her nose, before her body splashed onto the surface of the icy-cold water and swallowed her into its swirling depths.

Deeper and deeper she sank, her lungs bursting with the need to be released of the breath she held. She could deny them no longer and, although she fought against drawing in the water, she lost the battle.

With her mind screaming her love for her beloved children, Kitty knew a moment when her limbs were freed and she was sucked into a channel of beautiful light. Blinking against the brightness, she saw something come into focus – someone . . . 'Mum?'

'Yes, I've been waiting for you, mate.'

Her mum's arms were open. Her smile, so beautiful, encouraged Kitty to float towards her. When she did, Kitty felt a deep peace that held wonderment as she let go of her earthly being and embraced a greater love than she'd ever known before. All knowledge of anything she had been, or had known, drifted away from her, as her mum's arms enclosed her.

Millie pushed her breakfast plate away. She was too excited to eat.

Today she was going to see Elsie and Dot with some good news to give them. The last two days' visits had been full of Elsie's despair, as there had been no inkling of where her mother was, and her little brothers had been taken to the convent.

Cecil had a woman called Rene, whom Millie had heard spoken of, staying with him, and he was visiting Elsie and Dot and the boys every day. Millie, too, had been to see the little ones. She'd never met them before, but had found them adorable, and the nuns were caring for them with love.

Jimmy, whom Elsie had been particularly worried about, was well, and had been seen by a doctor and was being nursed by a lovely nun called Sister Margaret.

Both boys had sent letters to Elsie. Jimmy's was in lovely neat handwriting, which showed that – despite his illness and his missed days at school – he was an intelligent young man; Bert's was a scribble of what looked like an attempt to draw the tenement block they all lived in. Outside the building he'd drawn five figures, holding hands. This had wrenched at her heart, as Bert was obviously trying to connect all of his family together and put them back as they used to be.

Today Millie hoped to turn some of their despair into hope. She had managed at last to persuade her mama's solicitor to contact a lawyer, but he'd only done so when Mama had visited him and demanded it of him. Mama was proving to be a tower of strength. Millie suspected that a part of her was driven by her need to take revenge on Father. Nonetheless, once she heard the story, she'd been firmly in Millie's corner, and that helped.

Now a Mr Mortimer was going to visit Elsie and Dot tomorrow, and Millie couldn't wait to tell them.

A sudden crash forced these thoughts from her, as her father slammed his newspaper down on the table and sent his teacup flying, spilling the contents and smashing the cup to pieces as it landed on the floor. His face was deathly white, and sweat broke out on his forehead.

'Whatever is the matter, Richard?'

Father didn't answer Mama's question.

'Richard! Are you all right?'

His eyes closed, a noise like a deep groan came from him and his body collapsed forward.

'Father. Father!' The sound of her mama ringing the bell

that stood next to her on the table grated on Millie's fraught nerves as she ran to her father's side.

Mama didn't get up. Her expression held fear as she stared at his prostrate, unmoving upper body, slumped across the table.

Shaking her father's shoulder, Millie cried: 'Father. Father, wake up! What's wrong?'

In her anguish, the love for him that she had quashed came rushing to the fore, at the thought of losing him.

Behind her she could hear orders being shouted, as gently she was moved out of the way by Barridge, the butler, his voice commanding the housekeeper to send someone running for the doctor; and to tell Larkson, the driver, and Ryan, the stable lad, to come to the dining room as fast as they could.

With her mother tending to Father, who was now in his bed being examined by the doctor, Millie, trembling from head to toe, made her way back into the dining room. Ruby was close behind her. 'I'll get you some sweet tea, Millie. Eeh, what a to-do. I'm sure your father will be all right. Dr Stanley can work miracles.'

Millie sat down at the now-cleared dining table. Her thoughts were going over what had happened. 'Ruby, bring me my father's paper, please. I want to see what upset him, as it seems to me that he read something that gave him a deep and sudden shock.'

The paper was folded inside out. Millie instinctively knew that the page showing was the one her father had been reading. As she scanned it, the headline halfway down the page screamed at her: 'Second Prostitute Found Washed Up on the Banks of the River Thames'.

A body, thought to be that of missing prostitute Katherine Makin, known locally as Kitty, has been washed up on the banks of the River Thames.

Miss Makin has been missing since the day her daughter, Elsie Makin, and her friend, Dorothy Grimes, were arrested on suspicion of causing a death at Swift's Jam Factory.

Miss Kitty Makin was last seen when she left her home, stating that she would soon have her daughter and her friend freed. She was never seen again.

Oh, Elsie. Elsie, no. My heart bleeds for you. How are you going to stand hearing this news, my poor, dear friend?

The doorbell resounding in the silence cut into this agonizing thought. Millie's body froze. She couldn't have said why, but the sound, the newspaper article and her father collapsing all mingled in her mind and became one story.

Hearing Barridge say 'Please come inside, Officer' propelled Millie out of her statue-like state and got her running into the hall. She stared at the policeman who stood there. She heard him say, 'Sergeant. I am Sergeant Collins.' And then he asked to speak to her father. Barridge told him Mr Hawkesfield was with the doctor at the present moment but that, if the Sergeant would be kind enough to leave a note stating his business, he would see that Mr Hawkesfield got it. 'This is a private and urgent matter, sir, and I prefer to wait and speak to the doctor, to ask if I can have a word with Mr Hawkesfield.'

'Very well. Please come into the withdrawing room, and I will see what I can do.'

As soon as Barridge went up the stairs, Millie darted out, crossed the hall and then composed herself, before opening the drawing-room door. 'Good morning, Sergeant. I am Mr Hawkesfield's daughter, Millicent.'

The sergeant stood up, bowed his head and uttered, 'Miss Hawkesfield.'

Millie recognized him from the station. He coughed. 'Hmm, this is a mite awkward – you are friends with two of those we have in custody. I—'

'Yes, I am, but you won't mention that to my father, will you? Please, Sergeant Collins. He will stop me seeing them, and they need my help.'

'So I take it that you are working against your father in the matter of what they are accused of? You aren't there as a representative of Swift's Jam Factory, showing concern for two of its workers then, Miss Millicent?'

'No. And as I see it, there is no care for the welfare of the workers. I want to change that, but I can't if you expose me to my father.'

'I haven't any intention of doing so. And your business with those girls – which my constable assures me helps them a great deal – isn't connected in any way to my visit here, so please don't worry.'

'Thank you. Sergeant, may I ask: does Elsie Makin know about her mother's death yet?'

The sergeant looked taken aback. 'Yes, she does know and is distraught. She was told last night. She collapsed on hearing the news, and is now in the infirmary attached to the workhouse.' He coughed again and looked a little shame-faced. 'No other hospital will accept our prisoners when they need care, as we cannot afford to pay their rates.'

Millie couldn't swallow. *Oh, my poor dear Elsie. And Dot.* Knowing that Dot was nothing, without the support of Elsie, compelled her to ask, 'Is Dot all right?'

'We have allowed Miss Grimes's mother to visit her regularly throughout the day, as well as Miss Makin's brother, so she is bearing up and is more concerned for Miss Makin than for herself.'

'If only I had known about her mother's death, but I only found out this moment from my father's newspaper. I'll leave you now and get straight to the hospital.'

'I wouldn't advise that, Miss. Such places are not for the likes of you.'

'Well, they will be from now on, Sergeant. At least as long as Elsie is in there. By the way, I have engaged a lawyer who will take on Elsie and Dot's case. So I need to tell her that, too, as it might help her to cope . . . If anything ever can.'

'Quite. But – well, I shouldn't say this, but things are looking better for them both. There have been a number of enquiries made and people interviewed, as well as the girls each giving a statement. So they may not need the help of a lawyer. I hope not, because . . . off the record and in the strictest confidence, I believe they are innocent and that this charge has been trumped up by parties who need a scapegoat.'

'I'm glad to hear you say that, Sergeant. I'll leave you now. Thank you. It's good to know that if Elsie and Dot have to be anywhere, under this dreadful cloud of false accusation, they are in your care.'

The sergeant bowed his head slightly and smiled at her. 'You are very young, Miss, but you have a wise head on your shoulders. They are lucky to have your support.'

As she slipped out of the room, Millie wished she'd been brave enough to ask the sergeant's business with her father, but she knew he probably wouldn't discuss it; and somehow she didn't want to know, as she suspected he might confirm her fears. And yet how could her father possibly have anything to do with Elsie's mother's death? *It's inconceivable that Father knew Kitty Makin unless . . . No! Surely he wouldn't be one of her clients, would he?* This prospect shuddered through her, and the implications for her mother made her gasp. But then another thought came to her: *How would I ever face Elsie again?*

At the workhouse gate Millie was met by the gatekeeper, a sour-faced man whose face was pitted with scars, and with sores that had fresh, weeping crusts on them. He wore a collarless shirt that should have been white, but was thick with dirt, and the stale smell that came off him made her want to retch.

'Begging your pardon, Miss, but what's the likes of you want here then?'

'I am sorry to bother you, but can you please take me to the infirmary. I wish to visit a patient.'

'Visit? Visit? There ain't no visiting allowed, mate. This ain't somewhere you should be. You need to forget whoever it is. They rarely come out of the infirmary alive anyway.'

'What? Why?'

'Den of disease, it is. I couldn't let you into that – it would kill you. Just go away. Do yourself a favour, mate.'

'I can't. I have to see my friend.'

'Well, I ain't got no authority to let you in. If you can get that, things would be different, but I don't think you ought to. What's this friend's name? I'll take a message, if you want.'

'Really? Look, I'll give you the message, then if I find out you really have delivered it, I will return and give you tuppence.'

'I'll deliver it, and I trust that you'll keep your word.'

'It's for Elsie Makin – she came from the police cells. Tell her that Millie is thinking of her and doing all I can to get her out.'

'Right-o. Leave it with me. But mind you keep your promise.'

'I will.'

Millie almost ran for a few steps, just to get away from the horrid smell of the man, although her heart wasn't without compassion for him – or for anyone who had no alternative but to live in such a state.

At the police station she saw Constable Burns, who looked after Elsie and Dot.

'Morning, Miss, you're here early. Have you heard?'

'I have, and I tried to visit Elsie, but the gateman stopped me. How's Dot holding up?'

'Not very well. It's all a tragedy. They shouldn't be in this predicament, but they might not be for long. Detective Hadley has presented his case, and he's recommended that the charge is dropped. I'm waiting for my sergeant to come back. He, um . . . Well, he's out on police business.'

Millie didn't let on that she knew where he was. 'Has a lawyer been in touch? I have engaged one for them.'

'No. But that's good – he can speed things along. He can bear the brunt of the paperwork and then we only have to file it. In the meantime, do you want to see Miss Grimes?'

Dot looked awful. Her eyes were even more swollen and red raw, her hair was matted to her face, and a red and angry sore spread from her lip to her nose. As she held Dot in her arms, Millie could detect a similar smell on her to the gatekeeper's stench, though not quite so strong. She made up her mind to tackle Constable Burns about giving Dot a fresh prison gown.

'Sit down, Dot. I've heard the terrible news. What happened to Elsie? I only know that she collapsed.'

'She . . . she went into a deep faint when she was told about her mum. Oh, Millie, I can't believe it. Mrs Makin had given up being a prostitute, and Elsie was so proud of her. She was going to be a music-hall artist and—'

'It's all so sad. Do we know how this happened to Kitty?'

'I have thought and thought, and me and Cess talk of nothing else when he visits. All he knows is . . .'

Listening to what Elsie's mum had said, the last time her son saw her, sent a shiver through Millie. *Has my father anything to do with this? Please God, no.* But why would Mrs Makin think she could sort everything out, if she wasn't going to see someone who could do that for her?

Not knowing what to say, she hugged Dot again. 'You have to concentrate on getting well yourself, Dot. You can't let your spirits drop so low that you are ill, too. Elsie would want you to have courage.'

'I try, but I don't seem to be as strong as she is – or as you are, Millie. It must take a lot of courage for you to keep coming here, mate.'

'It does, yes. I would be in trouble with my father, if he knew, but my mother already does know. Strange how wrong you can be about someone. I always thought of my father as the one to lean on and go to in times of trouble, but he has proven to be a selfish man who hurts my mother a lot, whereas my mother is strong and supportive and very loving, in an honest way.'

'I know what you mean. My mum has come up trumps for me.'

Dot had only just said this when the door opened and the constable announced Mrs Grimes's arrival. When she saw Millie, she went sheet-white. 'Who . . . ? What? I – I . . . Dot?'

'This is Millie, Mum. I meant to tell you about her, but I didn't know how. She is—'

'I know who she is. What's she doing here?'

Mrs Grimes looked very afraid, and Millie felt uncomfortable in her presence, as the woman hadn't acknowledged her.

'She's a friend. Me and Elsie met her in the park one day, and we just got on so well, and she's been helping us. I – I wasn't sure if you'd be pleased or not, so I didn't tell you. I was going to, one of these days.'

'Didn't tell me? Well, I know now, and I'd thank you to leave, Miss. Me daughter's not a charity case. I can see to her needs. She doesn't need friends like you lot – you're the reason she's in here in the first place.'

'Mum!'

'Don't "Mum" me. Her father put you in here, and now she's salving her conscience by visiting you. Not on my nelly, she ain't. Kindly leave and don't come back, Miss!'

Dot began to cry. Millie was torn between her own humiliation and wanting to console Dot, but decided it was best to leave and return when the coast was clear.

As she went to do so, Dot cried, 'Mum, I won't let you do this. Millie has engaged a lawyer for us, and he's our best chance of getting out of here and to get off the charge.'

'A lawyer! I tell you, Dot, she's trying to make herself feel better about her rotten father. I don't want you associating with her – she can only bring us trouble.' When she turned to Millie, Millie was surprised by intensity of the fear in Mrs Grimes's face.

'Don't worry, Dot, I'll go. I'm sorry, Mrs Grimes. I don't wish to be rude. But nothing of what you have said is true, concerning my motives. It is as Dot has said: we did meet by chance and felt an affinity with each other – Dot, Elsie and me. We couldn't explain it, as I know this kind of friendship is rare; that is, if it has ever happened before. But it did happen, and that's that. We can't undo it, nor will we. No matter how much you or my father forbid it.'

'I think he would forbid it, Mr High-'n'-Mighty. Well, I'll live to see the day he tumbles off the high stance from which he looks down upon us all – and his antics are stopped. That will be the day I rejoice.'

Millie wanted to cry, but the tears running down Mrs Grimes's face cut into her. She'd never seen such anguish, or heard it manifest itself in such a vocal way.

Once she was outside and had begun to compose herself, Millie decided to visit the convent and check up on Elsie's little brothers. She hadn't far to go, as the convent stood behind St George's Church, almost opposite the workhouse.

Standing on the pavement, about to rattle the knocker on the big oak door, she was stopped in her tracks when someone called out her name. Turning, she saw Cecil. His face was as swollen as Dot's, and his eyes showed traces of the many tears she knew he must have shed.

'Oh, Cecil, I'm so sorry about everything. Especially your loss; it's all so painful and unbelievable.'

'Ta, Miss. I can't take it all in. I – I well, I feel all alone in the world.' His eyes showed his pain, and Millie wanted to take hold of him and hug him.

'It's not easy being the man of the house, I should think. Do Jimmy and Bert know what has happened yet?'

'Well, the police were going to tell the nuns, but I don't know if they have told me brovvers or not. I thought I'd come and check on them, and try to make them see that we will all be together soon.'

'Do you want me to come with you? I thought I would come along to check on them, too, but I can go away if you would rather be alone.'

'No, I'd like you to come with me, ta.'

When the door was opened by a small nun, Millie thought her smile was lovely, but how quickly it changed to a look of concern when she saw Cecil. 'Come on in, Cecil, I'll show you to Reverend Mother, she will need to have a word with you. Now what can I do for you, Miss?'

'I'm Millicent – Millicent Hawkesfield – and I am with Cecil. I'm giving him support as a friend. I've been here before, but I didn't meet you then.'

'Oh? Well, this is unusual, but I suppose you had better come in, too.'

Their walk to the Reverend Mother's office took them through many halls, all smelling strongly of polish. Their shoes squeaked as they walked, and in front of them the little nun's beads and keys jangled in time with her walking. Something didn't feel right to Millie, and she could feel the strength of Cecil's nerves.

On the little nun's knock, a sharp 'Come in' made Millie's trepidation deepen. It felt to her as if she was up in front of the headmistress for a misdemeanour, back in her school days.

When they entered, the voice belied the kindly face. There was nothing stern about the homely-looking woman who stood up from the chair behind her desk as soon as they walked through the door.

'Ah, you're Cecil. May I say that we are all very vexed to hear the news, and we have prayed daily for your mother, and for you all.'

Cecil nodded. Millie could see that he, too, was consumed by fear of what all this meant.

'Now, introduce me to your friend. I'm glad you have someone to support you.'

Millie didn't miss the slight look that showed the Reverend Mother was taken aback, on hearing who she was.

'I won't delve into how you young people became unlikely friends, as I have news for you, Cecil. I hope you will be able to see our actions as doing what we think best for Bert and Jimmy, in the circumstances that you all find yourselves in . . . We have found them a good place to become their permanent home. They left this morning.'

'No!'

'Now don't upset yourself. Think about it. They are so young and they need caring for. Even if your sister is found not guilty, how can you both properly look after your brothers? The family who have taken them will bring them up, and the boys will never again know what it is like to be without the basic things that every child deserves. They will be loved, educated, fed and clothed well, in an environment so far from here that they will soon forget their old life. Be happy for them, Cecil. And tell your sister to be happy, too.'

Cecil let out a racking sob, and tears ran unbidden and unchecked down Millie's face in turn. She felt at a loss as to what to do. The nuns were a law unto themselves, and it would be useless even trying to challenge their decision. Millie feared that Bert and Jimmy were lost to them forever.

Chapter Thirteen

Elsie

'You're free to go. And can I say that me and my men are very pleased this day has come. None of us thought you should have been here in the first place, and we have tried our best to ease the situation for you.'

'Ta, Sergeant.' Elsie couldn't say any more. She felt like an empty shell. Dot's hand came into hers. There was little comfort for her in the gesture. Not through any fault of Dot's, but because there was nothing that could touch this barren place, which had taken her soul and left her unable to feel anything.

In three days' time she was to bury her mum, and no one had yet been convicted of her murder. To Elsie, it was another day that she had to get through somehow. She didn't know how. No one had prepared her for all that she had to bear.

When she thought about her little Bert, and poor ailing Jimmy, it was as if her heart had been turned to stone. She was unable to let in the grief she felt at their loss. To do so would break her.

* * *

The moment was upon her. There was an eerie silence, broken only by the sound of the horse's hooves clip-clopping and the wheels of the dray grinding on the cobbles.

Elsie walked stiffly, holding herself together, unable to imagine her mum lying inside the plain wooden coffin, not moving, not feeling, not knowing that she and Cecil were there, walking behind her.

Cecil hadn't spoken for days, but then she hadn't wanted him to. His shoulder rubbed against hers as they walked. On her other side Millie strode silently, holding her hand. On Cecil's other side, Dot walked closely beside him, holding his hand.

Behind them walked Rene, who had been like a solid rock to lean on. Not counselling them to get on with life, or trying to make them see that what had happened was for the best – those words were what the neighbours had said as soon as Elsie arrived home. Rene loved them too much for that.

Walking next to Rene was Beryl Grimes – a surprising mourner, showing more grief than anyone. Elsie couldn't understand this, because although she and Mum had been good friends as girls, they hadn't spoken to each other for years.

Somehow, once the church service was over, they were back outside in the early spring sunshine, which was trying to warm them, but losing the battle. Elsie thought she would be cold forever.

The final walk across the churchyard, past many graves bearing the names of someone's dearly departed, gave Elsie time to steel herself for what was to come. She could see the looming hole next to the wall, in the shadow of a huge oak tree, flagged by a mound of earth – earth that would be shovelled on top of Mum. A shudder shook her body at this thought.

As the coffin was lowered, the pattern of the branches of the tree fell across it and the sun turned them into a blanket of what looked like lace draped over Mum. It disappeared, the deeper her coffin went.

Given a handful of earth, Elsie stepped forward. The sound of the dirt hitting the coffin reverberated through her. Still she couldn't feel anything. The knot in her chest tightened and reached her throat, making it difficult to breathe. *Maybe I could just stop breathing and be forever at peace, as Mum is. Be with her and Gran.*

Looking up, she saw a fresh grave close by. Ruth's face swam before her – and her fateful scream that awful day at the factory resounded in her head.

Stepping back from the graveside, Elsie didn't really register the small line of folk doing as she had, with handfuls of dirt – symbolizing that her mum's body was being given back to the earth, so that her soul could soar to heaven. Would she go to heaven? Did folk like Mum go to heaven? She thought of the stories of Jesus, and how he had befriended Mary Magdalene, a known prostitute, and this comforted her. Jesus knew Mum wasn't a bad person. The thought lifted Elsie and drew her to look towards the sky. A wispy cloud hovered above, and Elsie imagined her mum sitting on it, floating away. She imagined her smiling and waving. Unconsciously she lifted her hand.

'Elsie?'

She didn't want to respond to Millie. She wanted to stay inside this fantasy, because now she could see her mum. Her red hair was gleaming in the sunlight, her feet dangling off the side of the cloud in a playful way – a scene so beautiful it filled her with wonderment.

'Elsie, are you all right?'

Elsie looked away from her mum and back at Millie and nodded, wanting Millie to be reassured, but wishing to get back to watching her mum. But when she looked back, Mum had gone, and a fresh pain sliced through Elsie's heart. She gasped at the ferocity of it. The gasp released the tightness in her chest and opened her up to the enormity of what had happened over the last six weeks, since the accident that had changed her life.

She heard a sound like a moan. It got louder and hurt her throat, but still she wasn't aware that it was coming from herself; all she felt was the need to let go of the pain, scream it out of her body, but she couldn't register that this was happening until arms came round her and she was held closely in a circle of love.

'Elsie, I've got you. Oh, my dear, dear friend. I've got you.'

Another pair of arms came round her. 'Else, hold on. Be strong, mate. We'll help you. Me and Millie. You won't be alone, mate – not ever.'

But she was alone. She didn't have her mum, or Bert, or Jimmy; and Cecil wasn't Cecil any more. She would be alone for the rest of her life.

This thought died as Rene stepped forward. 'You've got me and all, Elsie.'

'And me,' Beryl Grimes said. 'I've not been the kind of friend I should have been, and I've a lot to make up for, and I'm going to start today. Your mum were me mate; we'd have defended each other, and cared for each other till the end, but for – well . . . secrets. But I think it's time I put all of that behind me now.'

Elsie could only extend her hand towards Dot's mum, who took it, then drew Elsie into her arms.

'I'm sorry, mate. Sorry for everything. For letting your mum down. For letting myself and my man down. I kept shtum to save something of my life, to try and salvage the love my Reggie had for me. But it didn't work, and I was the loser. I have something to tell you, and although it will be the end of my marriage and will cause God knows what kind of a rumpus, the time has come for you to know.'

Rene, who'd been standing like a statue, stepped forward. 'Not here, Beryl. And not anywhere. Some secrets are best left as that.'

'Rene, you've seen how things are with these three. They have a right to know.'

'Well, let's at least move away from here. We'll go home, to Elsie's.'

'All right.' Mrs Grimes turned away from Rene, 'Come on, Elsie – and you, Dot. And you too, Millie. Cos this involves you, as much as it does Elsie and Dot.'

This unfathomable turn of events had the effect of suspending Elsie's feelings. She looked at Dot and then at Millie. Both had a bewildered expression, but neither spoke.

It was the young woman accompanying Millie who broke the silence that had fallen.

'Eeh, Millie, lass, do you think as you should? By, your father would have sommat to say if he gets to knaw as you were here, let alone going to the housing estate.'

Her accent told Elsie that this was Ruby, as Millie had often spoken of her and had said that she came from the North of England.

Millie's cheeks flushed at Ruby's words, but she didn't admonish her. 'Don't worry, Ruby, we're going with friends.'

She turned then to face them all. 'Everyone, this is Ruby: she's my . . . my companion. She feels responsible for me.'

Elsie knew that poor Millie was in an awkward position, for she was trying not to humiliate Ruby, while at the same time making excuses for what she had said. But she had no need to. They all knew and accepted that anyone of Millie's class wouldn't be expected to mix with them; and that her maid – as they knew Ruby really was – would think it her duty to protect her mistress.

Elsie could do no more than nod her head, but Dot saved the day by carrying on as if nothing had happened. 'Mum, what is it? What have you got to tell us? How can you know anything that involves all three of us? And what about Dad? If he finds out you've been here, you'll be in trouble – let alone going back to Elsie's.'

'I don't care any more, Dot. I've paid for my mistake, over and over. I lost the friendship of someone I loved, and I lost the love that your dad gave me when we were courting. He stood by me, but that's all. I want to make amends now, and only the truth can do that.'

Rene had an urgency in her voice as she said, 'Think about this, Beryl. I know as the emotion of the moment has got to you, but Kitty wouldn't want this.'

'Rene, I'm only sorry that me and Kitty didn't get together and do this years ago. Everyone has a right to know these things about themselves. And at this moment these girls deserve to know the truth. They *need* to know.'

Elsie looked at Millie, and then at Dot. Her clouded mind wouldn't give her any clues, but by the way Rene was acting, she felt sure that what Mrs Grimes was going to say would have a deep and lasting effect on all three of them.

But nothing prepared her for what a sobbing Mrs Grimes

told them. 'Me and Kitty were mates, as you all know. Mates like you and Dot are, Elsie – and like you both are now with Millie. But I betrayed Kitty.' As the story unfolded, Elsie stared from Mrs Grimes to Dot, to Millie. Both girls had a look of astonishment on their faces, although Millie's was tinged with something else: fear? Horror? Repulsion? Elsie couldn't tell, and felt afraid of what Millie's emotions might be. Dot was transfixed, and it was she who voiced what they all knew to be the truth.

'You mean we're half-sisters? Me, Elsie and Millie?!'

'Yes, you are. Richie Hawkesfield fathered you all.'

There was a silence for a moment. Elsie looked over at Millie once more. Millie looked lost and, for the first time ever, as if she didn't know what to do. But Elsie understood, as she felt the same way too. But one thing was clear. *My mum loved Millie's dad! And was hurt by him going with Beryl. Which must have been while she was pregnant with me.*

'Look, girls, this needn't change anything. You're still who you are.' Rene was looking at Millie as she said this. 'This has been a shock for you, girl. It isn't every day that you hear what your dad's really like. I'm sorry for you, and I don't think Beryl should have told you. Can I help you in any way?'

'I – I don't know . . . I . . .' Millie looked from Dot to Elsie.

Elsie wanted to go to her, but couldn't move. *Oh God, Millie is my SISTER!*

As she thought this, the revelation sank in, and she and Millie moved towards each other as if propelled. Dot, seeing the movement, joined them. The three of them collided in a hug that wasn't joyous, but held comfort. It felt, to Elsie, as if she'd found the missing pieces in her life.

'Else . . . we're sisters! Oh, Else, I've loved you like one forever, and now you actually *are* one.' Dot kissed her cheek. 'And, Millie, I don't know what to say. You've had more of a shock than me and Else, but I'm glad you're my big sister.'

This seemed to break the ice, as Millie held them tighter. 'I am, too. So glad. This explains our bond, but I can't take in the enormity of what my father has done. He has caused so much hurt. And, well, I – I just don't know how to cope with it all.'

'None of us do. Me least of all. I ain't got me mum to talk it over with. Oh, Dot, Millie, I'm lost.'

As she said this, Elsie caught sight of Cecil. He stood looking as though he was in deep shock. And yes, almost as if he didn't belong. She had a sudden urge to mend the way the strain of their mum's death had distanced them from each other. 'I know something, though. I've got the best brovver in the world to share all this with, and to help me through it. Come here, Cess.'

She met Cecil halfway across the room and opened her arms to him. He didn't reject her, but didn't stay close for a long time. Elsie could feel how tense he was as he pulled away from her. 'Does this mean I'm related to Dot and Millie, Sis?'

'No. You have a different mum and dad, so you're only related to me.'

'What will happen now?'

'Nothing. Everything will be the same.'

'No, it won't, Elsie.' This, from Millie, surprised Elsie for a moment, but then she saw the smile on Millie's face. 'What I mean is that now I know you and Dot are my sisters, I will help you even more than I was always going to.'

Elsie didn't have time to answer Millie, as this hit a nerve with Beryl. 'My daughter don't need your help, or no one's. I'll thank you not to interfere with her or our business, Millie. I have enough trouble to face when I tell my Reggie. Being friends, well, that's all right. But I don't want my daughter having any more than that to do with you, or your rotten dad.'

'Mum, please. Millie doesn't deserve you to talk about her dad – our dad – like that. It takes two, as they say, and whatever he did, it took you to agree to it.'

This earned Dot a swipe across her head that sent her reeling. Shocked, after the benevolent side to Beryl that she'd seen all day, Elsie didn't know what came over her, but she couldn't remain silent. 'Don't! Don't use Dot like that. She's not your or your husband's punch-bag, and I'm sick of seeing her with black eyes and bruises all over her. She doesn't deserve to pay for what you did – you've no right to hit her like you do.'

Beryl slumped down onto a chair. 'I'm sorry, so sorry, Dot. I don't know why I do that. I'll change, I will, but I need time to adjust to everything. I've become bitter and twisted with it all, and yes, I have taken it out on you. And Elsie's right: you don't deserve it.'

Cecil dashed to Dot's side. He gently helped her up as he said, 'If anything good comes out of all this, it has to be that Dot's treated better. I've never seen anyone hit like that, and I'm with Else in what she says.'

Elsie was astonished. Cecil sounded and looked like a grown man: but then, with what they'd been through and all they had yet to face, they'd both grown up faster than most.

'I'll never hit you again, Dot. You're the best thing in my rotten life, and I love you.'

'Oh, Mum, it's all right – don't cry. You've never told me you loved me before. It was worth a clout to hear it. Will you stick up for me, when Dad beats me?'

'I will. I don't care a jot about him, not now. I don't care if he leaves, as long as I always have you, Dot. We'd be better off without him.'

Millie, who hadn't spoken, but stood as if in shock, stepped forward now. 'Despite what just happened, I want to tell you that it was a brave thing you did today, in telling us the truth of our relationship, Mrs Grimes. Thank you. I don't know how we will all go forward from here. I don't want my mama to know, and will try to keep this from her, but at the same time I do want to be with my half-sisters, and if they need anything, I want to help them. But I will respect your wishes. Remember: I'm here for you – for you all – if you need me.' Turning to Elsie, she said, 'I have to go soon, as I will be missed. But will you, Elsie, and you, Dot, walk with me and Ruby as far as the park? I can lead Fennie there.'

Ruby led the horse and trap on the road, and Elsie, Millie and Dot held hands as they walked. They didn't chatter much. Elsie told them she was in shock and couldn't take it in, and Dot said she felt the same. And Millie, poor Millie, just said, 'I can't get over what a ruthless and hateful man my father is.'

When they reached the privacy of the park, they hugged.

'Are you upset to find we're your half-sisters, Millie?'

'No! Oh, Elsie, I am over the moon. I have always wanted a sister, and now I have two. And I have felt very strong connections to you since the first day we met. It is all so incredible that I am having a problem coming to terms with it – but mostly from the point of view of what my father is capable of. How could he have done what he did in the first place – be unfaithful to my mother, but even worse than that, leave you both, his daughters, to live in poverty? And – and I cannot excuse him being party to you being falsely accused of murder! I am ashamed of him.'

'Millie, don't take all of his wrongdoings on your shoulders. I'm sorry that you've found your dad out. I cannot imagine what that's like for you, mate.'

'It's horrid, Dot. I did have an inkling of what he is like, of course, but to have to face the full truth of his ways has hurt.'

'Look, I know I've been bit quiet since we met, but I felt in awe of you. Anyway, I want you to know that I'm glad how everything has turned out, cos I think the world of you, and I know you are only doing your best. I'm sorry how me mum treated you. She's a Cockney girl through and through, and they have a lot of pride that stops them taking help unless it's from their own.'

'Oh, Dot, you have a lovely heart. Thank you. We'll find a way of sorting all this. I hate it that you have to return to poverty.'

'I'm not so bad. At least not while my dad . . . my step-dad's in work. But how you're going to manage, Else, I just don't know. I expect we'll both be sacked from Swift's.'

'I'll see that you're not. My father has to face up to his responsibilities to you. I will tell him that, if he doesn't, I will broadcast to everyone that he is your father.'

'But, Millie, if he recognizes us as his daughters, he wouldn't want us working as we do in his factory. It would humiliate him even further for folk to see him treat us as he does.'

'You're right, Elsie. Oh, dear, I don't know what to do for the best. I don't want you working in those conditions, either, but I can't change them on my own. I need you both there, as that will mean that when I am working with Mary Macarthur – who, by the way, I have now heard from – I can change things from within. You can help with that, by keeping the women informed for me, and by helping to get them on the side of the Federation of Women Workers. You can also be my link to Lucy.'

'I, for one, am willing to carry on at the factory, mate, if you can get us back in. It will be worth it to change things for everyone.'

'Me too, Millie. We're used to it. It's up to you to figure out how you can get us back in there.'

'I'll do that part. I've enough to get at my father about, without telling him about us. You see, thinking about it, it's better that he doesn't know you are his daughters. Do you think he will recognize you as the girls who were accused of killing that other poor girl?'

'I shouldn't think so. He wasn't there, and he never claps eyes on us – none of us. He goes up to his office by them side-steps and rarely comes round the factory. It's Chambers you need to see. It's up to him who gets work in the factory.'

'That will be easier. Father is still not well, but he's been making progress since . . . well, since he's been exonerated. You see, I haven't told you, but he was implicated in the death of your mother, Elsie . . . I – I'm sorry.'

'It ain't your doing, Millie.'

'Dot's right. None of it is your doing, Millie. What our parents did, we have to forget, and stay close together.'

'Thank you. I do love you both. We'll work this out, I promise. I will go into the factory as I normally do on a

Wednesday. I will speak to Chambers. Trust me, I will make sure he is left in no doubt that you have to be reinstated. In the meantime, Elsie, I have paid the undertaker, and you have the shopping that I bought for you. And there will be a delivery of coal for you, too. I will be thinking about you all the time, and will meet you both here in a couple of days: say, around two in the afternoon? I'll have been able to sort something by then. I want to improve things for you both – give you a better life.'

'I know you mean well, Millie, but I don't need you to change things for me, as me home's with me mum. And if she's on my side from now on, I'm going to be all right. You take care of Else. That's what's important to me, mate.'

'I will, Dot. Keep strong, my lovely sisters. I'll see you here in two days' time.'

Millie kissed them both and left. They stood a moment watching her go, then turned to each other and fell into each other's arms. Elsie felt her heart breaking. 'Oh, Dot. Dot.'

'Cry it out, me Else. You know, I still can't believe it, but it means the world to me that you're my sister.'

Elsie could only nod. She had a strange feeling in her. It seemed to her that she'd lost and gained. Gained a huge amount, but lost much, much more. How was she to carry on without her mum? When would she see little Bert and Jimmy again – if ever?

She felt as if she'd been sliced into little pieces, and although it was lovely to know that she had sisters, nothing could compensate for what had been taken from her.

Chapter Fourteen

Millie

Millie sat in the armchair next to the window of her bedroom, gazing out over the park. Her mind was in turmoil. She'd hardly been able to look Mama in the eye since returning.

She'd seen the hurt she'd caused when she'd rejected her mama, who had wanted to comfort her, but with the new-found knowledge she had, Millie didn't feel she could accept that comfort. She felt full of deceit and just wanted to be alone with the secrets she had to keep, but which burned inside her all the more because she hadn't wanted to keep anything from her mama ever again. But how could she tell her what she knew about Father?

She folded her arms across her chest, trying to ward off the pain of the crumbling remnants of the man she'd always adored, because now all his flaws lay bare, crowding in on her and breaking her heart. It was as if she'd gone out as one person – happy at last to be comfortable with her mama, and to have her love and support – and had returned as another.

The tear that seeped out of the corner of her eye, and which was quickly followed by more raining down her face, didn't give Millie any sense of release. Guilt assailed her. *I was so wrong.* Poor Mama must have felt very alone and isolated by her husband's behaviour at times. *And by mine. And now, with what I know making the bridge built between me and Mama so fragile, I feel lost.*

Was it really true? But then why would Dot's mother lie? And you only had to look at the three of them to see the truth of it all. They had the same eyes – Father's dark-brown eyes. And although Elsie had taken her red hair from her mother, Dot had the same-coloured hair as she and Father had; and the way Dot's hair curled was like his, and like her own did, if not brushed into the usual chignon style that she wore. Nor did the resemblance end there. Their features were very similar, too, and their height.

Oh, Father, how could you behave in such a way? How am I going to cope with knowing what I know? How am I going to be able to carry on? And yet I must, because not doing so would mean that I would jeopardize any chance I have of making life better for so many people.

Millie dried her tears and took a deep breath. She had to draw on any courage that she possessed, in order to carry out her plan to make her father's factory more like others, where the conditions were far superior.

She'd read about these other factories in the same trade journal that she'd found out about Mary Macarthur's existence, and her fight to better the lives of working women. In the article, Miss Macarthur had singled out Hartley's Jam Factory as being the model that all factories who employed women should follow. Well, if they could achieve that and still run a profitable concern, why couldn't Swift's?

A tap on the door interrupted her deliberations. 'Come in.'

'Eeh, Miss, what a morning! I'm still reeling. I've brought you a tray with some sandwiches, and a slice of Cook's nice sponge cake. You must be starving, and I knew you wouldn't want to join your mama for lunch.'

'Thank you, Ruby. No, I don't want to be with Mama just yet. Oh, Ruby, how am I to bear it all?'

'I'll help you, me little lass. You can talk to me whenever you want to. By, it's a real turn-up, this lot. I'm not surprised by your father, as you knaw; but to find out you have half-sisters, like you did this morning, well, I feel for you.'

'You know, I'm not sorry about that. I knew from the start they were special to me. I'm only sorry about the situation: the way they have had to live, and how my father treats them. God, he'd have seen them hang! Though, in his defence, I don't think he knows about them, by what Mrs Grimes said. But besides this, I'm worried about how my mama is going to be hurt, if ever she finds out.'

'If you ask me, she knows already. She's not daft, and many of us have heard her accuse your dad of having bastard children. I think she'll be relieved to hear that he hasn't got a son to usurp you – as us downstairs think that's her main worry.'

Even though Millie knew the servants gossiped, it felt strange to hear about it. As they went about their business she hardly noticed them, except to greet them first thing in the morning.

Changing the subject, she asked, 'How are you settling without your ma, Ruby? She was so pleased to get the post to look after Raven Hall, so that she could stay in Leeds.'

'Aw, I miss her, Millie. It's like me right arm's been cut off. And the new housekeeper's a tartar. But I'm that pleased for Ma; she was so happy when your mother appointed her to keep Raven Hall looking nice while it's unoccupied. She loves the little cottage that goes with it, and I reckon she loves the gardener-cum-caretaker an' all. Her letters are full of "He said that" and "He said this", and she loves how she can catch up with her sister most days, and with her old friends. She's so happy that I'm happy for her.'

'Oh, that's good. I did mention to Mama, before we went, how much you had said she misses Leeds, as I knew Mama was thinking about how to replace Mrs Davies, who wanted to retire. But I didn't know if she would take me up on it, so I'm so glad she did.' Brushing the crumbs from her skirt, Millie stood up. 'I feel so restless. I really don't know what to do with myself. I think I will go and sit with Mama, as she will have finished her lunch now. I don't want to eat, Ruby, I'm sorry.'

Downstairs, Millie was surprised to hear her father's voice coming from her mother's sitting room. What he was saying to her mama shocked her, as she'd had the impression that his involvement in everything had been denied beyond doubt.

'Damn and blast the whole lot of them! How dare they even think to question me about a prostitute's murder?'

'How can you think of even going with a prostitute? You're disgusting!'

'Here we go again. Well, you know the answer to that one.'

'No, I don't. A prostitute! That's scraping the barrel, isn't it? Lost your charms with the ladies and have to pay for it now, do you?'

'Shut up! You're obsessed. This is all your fault. If you could have forgiven me . . . But what's the use in going over that again? What I'm asking is that you make what the police are saying a lie. Play the loving wife, in public. Refute anything you hear. Say that I was here with you on the night of the murder.'

'And exactly where were you? Because you certainly weren't here, and I don't see why I should lie for you.'

'I told you. But I have no alibis. I simply drove and drove – I had to think. I did see the murdered woman, but only for a moment; she had some notion that she could persuade me to let her daughter out of jail. I told her to go away and then drove out of London. After a while I turned round and was shocked by how far I had driven. There were no garages open and I was short of petrol, so I pulled up and slept in my car. It was bloody cold and uncomfortable. But no one saw me, to verify where I was. You have to help me, Abigail. You *have* to. You're my wife, for God's sake! How will this look for you?'

'I actually see it as a way of getting rid of you.'

'What! You hate me that much?'

'Yes, I do.'

'What about Millie? Can you bear to hurt and humiliate her? Because if I am falsely accused and the charges stick, think about what this will do to her.'

'Yes, of course I am very concerned about Millicent. She and I have become very close, now that you are unable to influence her. She has found you out for what you are!'

Millie rushed to open the door. She didn't want her father upset with her, not now. She needed him on her side.

'Mama, Father, the whole household can hear you! Father, it isn't a good idea for them to hear you begging for a false alibi. Besides, they all know you weren't here, so even if Mama does testify, they can prove that's a lie. Just tell the truth, as you have told Mama, and get your solicitor to get a good lawyer for you.' Although she hated herself for saying it, Millie added, 'After all, there must be hundreds of men who have been with the poor unfortunate woman. Are they going to question them all?'

Her father looked aghast. 'Millie!'

'It's true, Father, and I do know your ways. None of it is my business, except when it affects me and . . . Well, I do need to talk something over with you, but not in front of Mama.'

Mama shocked Millie then. 'If it is about Ruby, darling, then I know and have discussed with your father his behaviour towards her.'

Father coloured up, then looked angry. 'How dare you talk like that in front of our daughter!'

'Father, I am a grown woman now. I have had to grow up a lot in the last few weeks. You can no longer keep things from me. But I do need to speak to you on another matter, too.'

'Your father has no secrets from me, my dear. If you take him to task on anything, he will already have goaded me with it, so please speak out, Millicent.'

Although Mama said this, and tried to sound as if she didn't care, Millie could see that she was shaking.

'Yes. Your mother is right. I am a pig of the first order, and whatever misdemeanour you meant to take me to task over, Daughter – who has suddenly turned into a woman – you can do so. But let me tell you, you can forget coming into the factory to learn the trade. You have obviously inherited the traits of your mama, which I would find unbearable. And just when I was looking forward to getting you ready to take over from me.'

'Don't be so silly, Richard! I would never let you do that. Business is no place for a girl. You know very well that you were simply humouring Millicent, and no doubt you have an heir among those children you have scattered everywhere.'

'Oh, you think you have the upper hand now, don't you? You think you have me downtrodden and you're going to stamp all over me. Well, that isn't going to happen, Abigail.'

Father turned to leave, and although Millie felt very afraid at this turn of events, and saddened too, she followed him, ignoring her mama calling to her to remain in the room.

Once outside in the hall, Millie spoke to her father in a tone that she hoped would make him heed her. 'Father, you will do well to listen to me. I know a lot more than you can ever dream I know. And I am on your side.' This wasn't wholly a lie, because although he had plummeted in her estimation, she still loved him and hoped to save him, as well as make everything right for Elsie, Dot and all the workers in his factory.

'Oh, for goodness' sake. If this is some kind of game, Millie. I know you're mad at me, but I do have to go and see a lawyer.'

'It isn't, Father. It is imperative that I speak with you.'

'Very well, come into my study.'

Once in the room that he called his study – much smaller than the one he occupied in Raven Hall – Father told Millie to sit down and tell him what she had on her mind. Now that the moment was upon her, her nerves jangled. *I have to pull this off, if I am to make any difference in the short term to Elsie's and Dot's life. I cannot support Elsie for long out of my allowance. And this way I can, in the long run, help her cope with her finances until we are all much older.*

'Before you begin, I have to say that I am shocked and

saddened that your mama has seen fit to use the new-found closeness you have to fill you with rubbish about me. Most of it is in her imagination.'

'Papa, Mama hasn't done that. I want you to allow me to go to the factory in your place and calm the workforce down. If we don't do something, we will have the whole factory going to ruin. I intend to instruct Chambers to reinstate the two girls who have been acquitted of the murder of that poor girl who died in the accident at the factory.'

'What! Good God, have you lost your mind?' He stood up from the large chair on the other side of the fireplace from her and stomped towards the door. 'I am not even going to discuss this matter with you. You shouldn't even know about it . . . How do you know?'

Swallowing hard to steady her voice, she told him the lie she'd rehearsed. 'I came to the factory the morning of the accident and saw a lot of workers outside. I didn't try to go in, because the mood of the women wasn't good. One of them told me what had happened. They said it was an accident, but that two girls had been accused of it. I acted without thinking and went along to the police station.'

'You did what? My dear girl, have you gone mad? I'm beginning to agree with your mother. You shall go to that finishing school, after all. You are a danger to yourself. You say you are grown-up, but you aren't. I am going to order that you are locked in your bedroom until a date can be arranged for you to be sent to Belgium.'

Millie stood. Making a snap decision, she told him more than she wanted to. 'Father, that isn't going to happen. Please listen to me. One of those girls knows that you were a regular customer of her mother – the dead prostitute.'

Her father stopped in his tracks on the way to the door

and reeled round. His face lost its colour. Millie feared for him, but was determined to carry on.

'I visited them in their cell for a few days, making sure they were looked after. I said I was concerned for their welfare, on behalf of my father's factory. One of the girls told me that she was sure her mother would approach you, and you would get her out. Now, if she has told the police this . . .'

Millie's fear deepened as she witnessed her father age before her eyes. He only just made it back to his chair before slumping down into it. She knew she'd taken a huge risk, but there was no other way, unless she told him the truth about Elsie and Dot being his daughters. That was far riskier.

But now, seeing how this news affected him so badly, the realization shuddered through Millie that her father really had murdered Elsie's mother. A deep sense of hurt gripped her then, and her whole world reeled, as it dawned on her that she had truly lost her father – at least the father she had loved so dearly.

Tears prickled her eyes. 'F – Father, I know it looks bad for you, but you can do things to make it all better. Show some compassion. Now that the girls have been found innocent and haven't been charged, reinstate them. And put some safety measures in place – a lid on the vat, for instance. And change some of the rules that are so difficult for the women to keep to – like the time they have from clocking-in to getting to their stations.'

'Oh, Millie, Millie. Everything is so simple to you. Black and white. Well, the big world isn't like that. If you give those scum a little slack, they'll take up the whole rope and run rings around you. Besides, all of what you say will implicate me, and it will look as though I am trying to cover up my guilt. And . . . well, there are other factors. Things you know nothing of. No. We must never let those two girls into the factory again.'

'And how will that look? Just as bad. They didn't do what they were accused of. They were dragged to a cell, and one of them has since lost her mother. And as a consequence, her little brothers, too. And on top of that, they have now lost their jobs, even though they have done nothing to deserve to.'

'How do you know all this? What have you been up to, Millie? You are frightening me. You're putting your life in danger by mixing with them. And after I forbade you. I really will have to think seriously about sending you away, for your own safety.'

'I just told you: I visited them. All of this happened while they were in that cell. I saw the devastation it cost them – in particular the daughter of the murdered woman. I am trying to help you, Father. You have always said that knowledge is power; well, now that you know the facts, you can act in the best way possible to put right the false accusation against them.'

'I don't think it was false. Someone pushed that girl. It wasn't an accident.'

Feeling despair, Millie bowed her head. She was losing the battle and had alienated her father in the process. Now he would no longer trust her.

'Millie, I know you think you are doing the right thing, but you really don't know what you're messing with.' He was quiet for a long time then, with his hands in a praying pose, his chin resting on his forefingers. When he spoke after a long moment, what he said surprised her. 'Look, you may have something. I will get my foreman to set them back on.

I haven't a clue which two girls they are, and wouldn't stand a chance of finding them.'

'Thank you, Father. I know I am inexperienced, but sometimes a woman's intuition is right.'

'I have never thought of you as a woman, Millie – not really. But now I can see that you have grown up very quickly.' Again he went quiet, and again he surprised and pleased her when he spoke. 'Millie, I have to say that I have been very impressed with how you have taken to learning the everyday running of the factory, and how much you have picked up in such a short space of time. Your negotiation of the supply of bush fruits from the small market gardeners looks as though it will bring us a much bigger profit than dealing with the large farms in Kent. How did you do that?'

'I went to the library and researched the workings of the market gardeners who are based in Kent. They mostly do just that – supply weekly markets. But I wrote to a few of them, and they were very positive in their reaction to my enquiry. One gardener on his own cannot supply enough to us, but they tend to be situated very close to each other, so if we bought from, say, a dozen of them, they could club together to pay for transporting the fruit to us.'

Warming to her theme and the obvious interest that her father was showing, Millie told more of what she had learned. 'They are family-run businesses and so their overheads are small, making their prices very competitive. They are also dedicated and specialize in a certain product, which they are very proud of. This means they are less likely to include fruit in our orders that would rot quickly – a blight that we suffer with our present suppliers, and which is a source of loss to us. Besides, not only would that be alien to the way they work, but it would jeopardize them keeping our custom, which those I have heard back from say they would value.'

'That was very good work. And you did it all on your own initiative! I think we will need to take a trip to have a look at these places, and we shall see whether they make the grade or not. Look, despite being a woman, you obviously have a good business head, which pleases me greatly. I need an heir, and you are the heir I have. I know other women who are very successful in business. There's one in the North who runs a huge coal-mining company. She was the only child, and her father had faith in her. I am willing to have faith in you, Millie, but you must show me that you are ruthless enough to deal with the rabble we choose our workforce from – and with a strong hand.'

Millie nodded, not wanting to confirm that she would work in that way, but not wanting to jeopardize the new-found confidence her father was showing in her.

But then suddenly it occurred to her that, with what she intended to do on Elsie and Dot's behalf, she had the perfect way of making her father believe that she could be the person he wanted her to be. 'I can do that, Father. I will prove it to you by going into the office tomorrow and dealing with Chambers. He needs to know that I have your authority, so I will be grateful if you could write a note to that effect. And I want you to leave things to me for a few days. Let me find out for myself what the problems are, and how to handle things. I can't make too much of a mess in a few days, can I? You rest a while longer. See your lawyer and get everything settled. And then, when you return, you will be fully recovered. You have to remember what the doctor said about your heart.'

'Yes, I agree. I'm sorry I got so very cross with you, my

dear. I was shocked and am very upset at how everything looks as though it is stacked against me. You do believe me when I say that I was only driving around that night, don't you?'

'Father, of course I do, but I wish I hadn't heard so much about you lately. And it wasn't from Mama. I overheard you both arguing that night when I first rebelled against going to finishing school. A lot was said between you then.'

'I can't excuse myself to you, Millie, and neither am I going to try. A man is very different from a woman, so you wouldn't understand. There are things I would like to school you in, so that you go on to have a happy marriage – not the misery your mother and I have endured. But I cannot. It isn't fitting for me to do so.'

Millie felt herself blush. She probably knew far more than he realized, because in an all-girls' school everything was discussed. But she knew that, in this, she was on her mama's side, and would be just the same as Mama if her husband was unfaithful to her.

'Talking of marriage, it won't be long before your mama will try and get you suited, though she has been thwarted in her original plan. But, well, there are a lot of eligible and rich bachelors who are not aristocrats. This is a new age, and new money is very much richer than old. So when the subject comes up again, I might suggest that we entertain more, especially in Raven Hall. I have a lot of business associates in the North who have sons of marriageable age, and there is a shortage of daughters of the same standing for them to marry. You will have the pick of the bunch.'

Despite the pain she was in, for all her father had done and what she imagined he had done, Millie couldn't help giggling at this. 'Father, stop it, you are worse than Mama!

I don't want to marry for a long time. I want to put right a lot of what is wrong and unfair in the country first.'

Her father groaned. 'You're not thinking that you're another Pankhurst, are you?'

'No, I want to help everyone – not just women, although I am interested in making things better for women.'

'I can't believe we are even talking like this, when you are going to take a much bigger role in running the factory, as you will see a lot of what looks like ill-treatment and slavery. I know it is there and I am a party to it, but it is the only way to make more money. And working in any other way simply makes the workers soft. So you will have to get used to it.'

'I don't agree. A happy, well-cared-for workforce is surely more productive, because they wouldn't want to lose such jobs and would want to please a good boss.'

Father put his head back and laughed out loud. 'Ha, you've a lot to learn, my girl. An awful lot. Now, I have a headache. I need some fresh air. I will go to see my solicitor and chat with him about having a lawyer ready.'

When he left the study, Millie sat back in the chair. Had she done the right thing? Should she have thought up another story to convince her father to let Elsie and Dot back to work in the factory? Should she even be thinking that such a course of action was the right one for Elsie and Dot, or was it just to further her own cause?

She sat bolt upright as this came into her head. *I'm using them! Just because I want to change things in the factory, I'm using them*. Why had she even thought Elsie and Dot should return to the factory? Wouldn't it be better to try and help them in some other way?

A tear seeped out of her eye. But then Millie told herself that she had to be strong; and once she was part of the Federation of Women Workers, she would be, because she would have their support. But did she really want to fight her own father? Fight him in an underhand way, by working to further the Federation's cause against him, and other bosses like him?

She knew that she did. But at all costs? This she didn't know. However, she did realize that the cost to all of them could be very high. And yes, she was up to the challenge herself, but had she given Elsie and Dot any choice?

Making up her mind that she would keep a close eye on things and ensure both girls were all right, Millie felt reassured. Getting up, she went in search of her mama, who would be wondering what on earth was going on.

Millie found her mama sitting back in her chair with her eyes closed, but not looking relaxed. Not wanting to disturb her, she went to withdraw, but Mama called out, 'Come in, Millie. I have been waiting for you.'

Millie walked over to her and laid a hand on her shoulder. 'I'm sorry that you go through so much with Father, Mama.'

'Oh, I'm used to it, dear. Come around here and sit at my knee. I love it when you do, and I can play with your hair.' Once Millie had squatted down, her mama asked, 'So what was all that about?'

'Oh, I was just trying to persuade Father to do the decent thing and undo some of the harm he's caused.'

'I doubt he will take your advice, darling. Tell me: how did everything go this morning?'

'Sad, very sad.'

'I'm sorry. But I do wish you hadn't gone. I have had a terrible morning worrying about you. And now that you have done this, what's next?'

'I want you to give your blessing to me working with Father. I have to do this; those workers need my help. And, Mama, thank you for the part you played in getting a lawyer to represent Elsie and Dot. He wasn't needed in the end, but it meant a lot to me that you believed me and helped me.'

'It was the least I could do, and I will try to get used to the idea of you going in a completely different direction from the one I had planned. But please, never let your father know about the lawyer. I have enough trouble with him as it is.'

'I won't. But, Mama, you do seem to be able to stand up to him. Whenever you have words, he is the one who ends up storming out of the room.'

'I know, but then he forgets, while I suffer more and more.'

Millie put her head on her mother's lap. 'I wish I could make things better for you, Mama.'

'You have enough on your plate, dear. You have a world to put to rights. Besides, you *have* made things better. A whole lot better. You have become like a friend to me, as well as a loving daughter, and that has made up for it all.'

'We should go on an outing together, Mama. Maybe a shopping trip to the West End? And go to the theatre and have dinner. I would love that.'

'Oh, that sounds wonderful. You know, Millicent, I really think you can put the world to rights, as you have already started on my world.'

This warmed Millie's heart. *I wish I could make things better for everyone, especially Elsie and Dot – my two lovely sisters.*

Chapter Fifteen

Elsie

Elsie stirred. Always awake these days before the knocker-up arrived, she turned over for the umpteenth time, still unable to get used to the emptiness of her bed, even though four and a half months had passed.

Cecil now slept in the fold-down bed in the living room, which Mum had originally bought for Rene. Rene slept in Mum's old bed, and often snored gently – a soothing sound that made Elsie feel less alone.

Stretching her legs out, Elsie felt her heart aching, because although she knew she wouldn't, she still hoped to feel the familiar little feet at the bottom of the bed and hear the giggle as she tickled Bert with her toes. The usual dread of another day without her mum and little brothers assailed her, bringing with it a feeling of despair.

They say that time heals. How much time will it take? Her grief hadn't lessened one bit.

She talked often with her mum and felt that she was happy, which helped, but it didn't take away the longing to hear her voice, or to feel her arms hugging her. Every day Elsie promised her mum that one day she would find Bert and Jimmy, and that all four of them would be together again. But that seemed hopeless, for appeals to the nuns fell on deaf – if kindly – ears. Each time she visited the convent, the nuns told her they were praying for her and Cecil on a daily basis, and they were pleased to inform her that her brothers were well, cared for and, above all, loved. They never said they were happy, and this worried Elsie.

Turning over again and dragging the heavy coat that covered her from where it had nearly fallen off the bed, Elsie wrapped it around her, but didn't get any comfort from it. Sighing, she wished she could get up, but that would disturb Rene and Cecil and wasn't fair on them.

So instead she lay thinking about all that was happening.

Things were moving along towards a strike taking place at the factory. And this gave Elsie a feeling of hope, and yet she worried about the stories that circulated. One in particular, of how sixty women went on strike a few years back and were immediately locked out and their jobs taken by others, filled everyone with trepidation. Despite Elsie knowing how difficult this would be to carry out, if everyone walked out, she still worried that maybe they wouldn't, and that she would be one of a few who did and were sacked.

But what could she do? Millie was convinced that the strike was the right way to go. She spent a lot of time trying to help Elsie and Dot see that.

The three of them met as often as they could in St George's churchyard gardens. It was a time when they could be the sisters they were meant to be, and they hugged each other and helped each other – mostly Dot and Millie helping Elsie, both in an emotional sense and, as far as Millie was concerned, in a practical sense too, as she brought Elsie clothing, money and food, whenever she could. Dot was fine and was a lot happier now, so Millie didn't worry so much about her.

'Are you awake, mate?'

Rene's voice coming suddenly out of the silence made Elsie jump. 'Yes, I just can't go back to sleep.'

'I know. I'm the same. I could murder a Rosy Lee.'

Rene was one for rhyming slang now and again, and it always made Elsie smile. 'As soon as Mr Munster's been, I'll get up and make one.'

'You're a good girl, Else. He shouldn't be long; I heard the dawn chorus a while ago, so it must be getting towards the time he comes.'

'I was awake for that – noisy things, birds.'

'Lovely, though. Makes you feel hopeful of something good happening. Not that it ever does.'

The sound of a match striking resounded in the room. Smoke wafted over. Elsie had always hated the smell of cigarettes, but had never been subjected to it this early in the morning. Getting out of bed, she opened a window.

'Are you hot? I were feeling chilled meself.'

'A bit.' Elsie drew in a breath of air; she couldn't call it fresh, as smog hung just above, making the gas lights hazy, and the smells from the docks and the all-night factories tainted the air. The cry of 'Wakey, wakey!' in the distance told her that the knocker-up was on his way. She waited, watching his progress and seeing lights come on in every house he visited.

'Good morning to you. You're up bright and early, Elsie, girl.'

'Morning, Mr Munster.'

'Were the bedbugs biting?'

'No, but I don't sleep well these days.'

'Well, you've plenty to keep you awake. But another day has dawned, and maybe this one will bring something better for you. I hope so, girl.' With this, Mr Munster moved on and raised his pole higher, to knock on the railings above. 'Me old legs don't get me up and down the apple and pears, to knock the upstairs flats up, so I rely on this method. Seems to do the trick.'

'Yes, I can hear movement above. Well, better get the kettle on. See you about, Mr Munster.'

Closing the window, Elsie turned and lit the candle.

'He's a lively old soul, considering the hour. Ha, me and your mum often met him when we were on our way home after a night's work. He always had a cheerful word for us. "Busy night, ladies," he'd say. Every time, without fail, those were his words. Anyway, you take your time.' Rene threw the covers off. 'I'll go through and see that Cess is awake, and get the fire going and the kettle on.'

'Ta, Rene. I'll be through in a mo. I had that nice bath last night, so I only need enough water to swill me face.'

'Consider it done, love.'

Though she had some habits, like smoking in the bedroom, that Elsie found hard to get used to, Rene was a godsend to her and Cecil. They didn't know how they would have carried on without her. She hadn't been out at night since she'd moved in, but had talked more and more lately about those times, and Elsie wondered if she was thinking of going on the game again. She hoped not. Rene was a strong woman and could easily work, but from what Elsie knew, she had never known anything other than working the streets. And she knew Rene found it hard to ask for money for her fags.

As Elsie began to dress, the sun rose, lighting the bedroom

with its warming rays. She loved the summer months when it was light early.

As she brushed her long tresses, she remembered how her mum's hair used to tickle her when she leaned forward to hug her. Wiping away the tears that filled her eyes, Elsie made a determined effort to shake off the sadness. Cecil suffered enough of his own heartache, but it was worse for him to see her cry and looking sad. She didn't want that. Coiling her hair, she clipped it on top of her head, then fastened her mob cap in place, before donning her undergarments. These were her mum's, and not only did she love wearing them as it meant she held her mum close, but having her large breasts supported made Elsie feel much more comfortable. Once she'd slipped on the long grey cotton frock that she always wore to work, she went through to the living room.

'Morning, Sis.'

This was all she got from Cecil these days – no morning hug. 'Are you all right, Cess?'

'Yeah.'

'He's hunky-dory, aren't you, young man? Now there's tea in the pot, and hot water in the bowl, and I've cut some doorsteps off that loaf you brought home from Millie. I'm going back to bed with me Rosy Lee and me old hag.'

Cecil looked at Elsie. His grin warmed her heart. 'She means her fag.'

'I know, Cess. Ha, she's a one. I'm sure that ain't the right slang. She makes it up when she don't know it.'

'Last night she said, "Your custard pies look like an unmade bed." I haven't a clue what she meant.' Cecil giggled when Elsie told him. 'Custard pies? Eyes?'

'Unmade bed? . . . Nope. Can't get that one.'

Cecil was laughing out loud now.

Elsie, too, found that her giggles were turning to a belly-laugh. She couldn't have said why, as it wasn't that funny, but she couldn't stop. Nor did she want to, because the laughter felt good. And hearing Cecil laughing lifted her heart.

Impulsively she opened her arms to her brother. He came to her, if sheepishly, but she didn't mind that. The fact that they were reaching out to one another was enough. They hadn't done that since the day of the funeral. Having Cecil hold her to him, as he was taller than her now, gave Elsie more comfort than anything had done since everything in her life went wrong.

'We'll be all right, Else.'

'We will, Cess. We need to stick together and help each other through this.'

Cess let her go, but took hold of her hand. 'And we'll find Bert and Jimmy one day, won't we?'

'Yes. Nothing will stop us. Though I don't know how. Maybe they will find us when they are old enough, as we'll still be in the same place.'

'I might be, but I'm not so sure about you, Else. I think you'll be leaving next, now you've found a fancy sister.'

'I'll never leave you, Cess. I promise. Not until you're settled, and that won't be long now. Look at you – a handsome young man; you and Dot will soon be walking out as a proper couple.'

'I hope so. But then Dot's me girl, no matter how much her fear of her dad keeps us apart.'

'I know. So how can we ever part? Our strong bond will never lessen, Cess. I know we won't always live together, and will make our own lives, but we'll visit, like other families do. Our kids'll be cousins. And you'll make a smashing uncle, and I'll try to be the best aunty ever.'

'I know you will. Well, I think we should go. I've a chance of being set on to a full-time job today. Old man Palmer wants to retire and leave his stall to his son, Phil. Phil said he was seriously thinking of taking me on to replace his dad, so I can't be late.'

'I'll keep me fingers crossed for you, Cess, though I'm sure the job is yours. Be good if you could bring in a regular wage.'

Out in the street, they were soon joined by Dot. Elsie couldn't believe the state of Dot's face. 'Not again, Dot. Your mum promised.'

'It wasn't her; it was me dad, but he's gone, Else. He's gone at last.' Dot looked afraid and was shaking all over. 'He's got another woman. After all Mum has put up with from him, he's been seeing some floozy – a widow with a nice little house in Streatham. Mum told him to go and take his dirty underpants with him. He went to clout her, but she was too quick for him, so he turned on me and . . . he . . . he knocked me for six. Mum couldn't stop him. I mean, she did pick up the poker.' Something didn't ring true about this, and Elsie wondered if once again Dot's mum hadn't helped her.

'Oh, Dot, luv. Are you sure you're all right?'

'I'm . . . Yes, I'll be all right. He's gone, and good riddance. Mum cried, though.'

'She cried over your dad!'

'Well, it wasn't exactly like that, Cess. It was more because I was . . . Because I was hurt, and she didn't know how we'd manage. I told her we'd find a way. Anyway, I'd rather starve than live with him any longer.'

As she said this, Dot fell in step with Cecil and took his hand. 'We can show how we feel for one another now, Cess, as I ain't scared any more. Can you meet me tonight? I thought we'd go for a walk.'

Cess coloured and looked back sheepishly at Elsie.

'Don't be daft, Cess. I know how you both feel. I told you this morning how it would be. I couldn't be happier for you. Ha, imagine: if you marry Dot, you'll be me brovver and me brovver-in-law!'

All three giggled at this, and Elsie felt the atmosphere lift and something of her old self coming back to her. She'd never be the same again, but as her gran always said: 'No matter what is happening in your life, you've no need to go around with a miserable mug on you.'

'My, isn't that a sound to please the gods?'

Curly was out sweeping the pavement, as usual, when they came up to his shop. But Elsie didn't feel as friendly towards him now – not after what he'd said to her mum that time.

'Man, you not happy with Old Curly then, Elsie? That look you gave me could have struck me down.'

It was Cess who answered. 'We don't forget how you disrespected our mum.'

Curly had the good grace to lower his head and touch his forelock. The three of them walked on.

'Hey! I'm sorry, man – but what's a man to do when faced with such a beauty as your mum was? Call in tonight and I'll make it up to you. Pie, mash and liquor all round, on the house.'

'Ta, Curly, but you'll have to include Rene and Dot and her mum.'

'Done! I've done a bad thing. Old Curly don't mean no

harm, and I feel me heart breaking now that your mum's gone.'

They didn't answer this, but smiled and waved and went on their way, glad to have a free supper to look forward to.

'Mum'd be proud of you for standing up to him, Cess.'

'I know, and she'd be pleased with the result, too, knowing we're going to have our bellies full tonight.'

They giggled, and to Elsie it felt good, as it made her feel as if Mum was still part of them, because at last they had talked about her in a light-hearted way.

Lucy joined Elsie and Dot at dinner break. 'I've news for you. The dock-workers are coming out on strike today. The Federation has contacted me and told me everything is ready, so this is a good time to get the women out, as it could mean the men will back us. So will you let the boss's daughter know?'

Lucy had never questioned why they had access to such an important person. She simply accepted that they had met and had become secret friends, maybe because it helped her cause to have Millie on her side.

'Oh, Lucy, I'm scared. Me mum's on her own from today, as me dad's left, and we'll both be relying on me wage until she can get a job for herself. I can't go on strike now.'

'I'm sorry to hear that, Dot.'

'Don't be – we're not.'

'Well, striking is our only way, Dot. And it has to be all of us or it won't work. Besides, the Federation isn't just telling us to do it, but will back us, by helping to provide food and even money if anyone is in dire need. You have to join us. I need to go to the others saying that you two are with us. That will encourage them, as you're held in high esteem since you were both willing to take the rap rather than shop Peggy.'

'Oh, Lucy, you know what happened last time. Hawkesfield replaced those who walked out, and they got nowhere, merely finding themselves out of work.'

'This is different, Elsie. This is big. Them at Pink's Jam Factory will lead the way. It will look as though it isn't organized and is a spontaneous downing of tools, but the word is going around, and the Federation hopes that once the women see Pink's lot, it will spark a mass walk-out of women workers.'

'Do we know when?'

'In one week's time – the tenth of August.'

Suddenly all trepidation and doubts left Elsie. 'I'm in. And I'll spread the word.'

'Else!'

'You heard, Dot. No one will suffer – there will be help for us from the Federation. And if everyone walks out, then how will they replace us all? Some of the women have skills that need to be passed on before anyone can take their place.'

'You're right, Elsie. Come on, Dot. I promise you, everything will be all right.'

'I suppose.'

'Good. I'm going to spread the word now. Some'll be afraid, but when they see that what Lucy predicts will happen does take place on the day, then they'll follow us, you'll see.'

Elsie didn't feel as confident as she sounded, and still she had this niggling worry that something else had happened to Dot. But she had no time to consider this thought, as Lucy was in full flow now.

'I don't know about you, but I'm going to make a day

of it, girls. I'm wearing me Sunday best under me overall and, as we walk out, I'm going to throw me pinny off. It'll be like a carnival, I tell you.'

Lucy left then, and Dot looked worriedly at Elsie.

'Come on, Dot, smile. Let's both wear our Sunday best, eh?'

'Ha! You mean the only other frock I've got to me name, don't you?'

There it was again, a different Dot. Elsie chose to ignore it. 'Well, I could bring one of the two that Millie has given me – your mum needn't know. But maybe now she's on her own she won't be as touchy about Millie giving us help. They're lovely, Dot. There's a blue one that's the colour of cornflowers and has little yellow daisies on it. It falls straight to just below the waist and then there's box pleats to the ankles; it wouldn't half suit you. The other's a plain green. It looks like a two-piece, as it has a mock-jacket top. I love it. Neither feel as though they have been worn. What do you think?'

'I'd love that. Ta, Elsie.'

'And if anyone asks how we afforded them, let's say they turned up at the church jumble sale and we got them for a penny.'

When they left the factory that night, Cess was waiting for them.

'I got it, Else. I start tomorrow. I'll be working six days a week, from six till six, so I'll be leaving for work before you both, but I'll meet you as you come out at night.'

'That's good news, Cess. And what about the wage?'

'Five bob a week to start, but the best bit is that Phil's going to teach me to drive his van and then I can take deliveries out for him, as he has a round once a week and he wants me to fetch new stock for him as well. I'm that excited. He says he'll give me a rise to seven shillings then, but if I sell well to the householders, I'll be in for a bonus.'

'Oh, Cess, that's wonderful. We're easily going to manage all right now.'

'Not only manage, but have a few treats. Me first treat is going to be for Dot.'

'Oh? And what you thinking of, Cess?' Dot coloured as she said this, but her smile shone from her as she looked up at Cecil.

'Well, we'll go for that walk we talked about, after we've had our pie and mash, but soon I'm going to take you to the seaside, Dot.'

'The seaside! Oh, Cess, that'd be wonderful. But we can't go without Else.'

'No, don't worry about me – I'll be all right. You two go and have a lovely time.'

'Dot's right, Else. I weren't thinking, but now she's said it, I wouldn't enjoy myself if we left you at home. I should have thought.'

'We can wear them frocks again, Else. Oh, it'll be lovely.'

'I'd love it, ta, Cess. But ain't the seaside a long way away?'

'I've heard a lot say that you can get a train and be in Brighton in two hours. I'd have to save a bit first.'

'We can all save towards it. We'll find out how much, and then we'll put some in a pot each week.'

'No, Dot, I want this to be my treat. I'll work it all out. We'll go when I have enough.'

Elsie had never seen Cecil be so forceful, but then, with a full-time job, he probably felt more of a man than he had been believing himself to be for the past couple of years.

When Dot took hold of his hand and grinned up at him, Elsie felt a little wistful. She'd never had a boyfriend and wondered what it felt like. She'd had a few who showed her that they fancied her, but she'd never been interested. Life had always been about looking after her brothers and trying to keep going. Maybe one day she'd meet someone.

She fell into step behind Cecil and Dot until they reached Curly's. Just as he said he would, he had their supper all ready.

Dot surprised them all by going into his shop to wait for the food to be packed up. Curly didn't remark on this, but Dot did. 'I've always wanted to be friendly with you, Curly, but my dad would have scalped me if he caught me talking to you.'

'I know, Missy. Old Curly knows how the land lies around here – don't worry about it. You enjoy your supper, and spread the word how good me food is and I'll be a happy man.'

Outside, Elsie linked arms with Dot, as Cecil insisted on carrying the two bags full of hot food.

'That was good of you, Dot. I'm still a bit mad at Curly for the way he treated my mum, but then Mum were known for the trade, so we can't altogether blame him.'

Dot didn't say anything, but then it was a funny subject to talk about.

'Anyway, after supper I'm going to the park, as you'll be otherwise engaged.'

Dot surprised her by being cross at this. 'Why should you say that? I'm only going for a walk!'

Taken aback by the tone of Dot's voice and how cross she sounded, Elsie thought it better not to say anything to this, and was glad to hear a softening in Dot's tone as she said, 'Anyway, I won't be out long. But I can't come and see Millie. I don't want to leave my mum too long. I've been thinking about how she was when my dad left, and I don't think she was really glad. I think she was hurt and, to start with, she'll need me to be with her whenever I can.'

Elsie couldn't understand this and thought Mrs Grimes should be pleased to get rid of her husband. But there was no accounting for feelings of love, and maybe Mrs Grimes did love her husband. When she fell in love herself, she hoped it was to someone really nice and good – not like Mrs Grimes's husband, and definitely not like the man who had fathered her and Dot.

Chapter Sixteen

Elsie

'Oh, Millie, I'm so glad to find you here, luv. It's getting so late – gone seven!'

'I know, I've been waiting for almost an hour and was just about to give up, as I'm already late getting home. Only dinner will be delayed tonight, as Father had an engagement after work. I only have a few moments, though.'

They hugged one another and Elsie could feel the tension in Millie. 'I would have come sooner, Millie, love, but I had a hot supper to eat and I was starving. I'd had nothing since breakfast, and that was only the bread you brought for me. But I've got some news that will cheer you.'

'About the strike?'

'Yes, and about Cess.'

When she'd told her all her news, Millie gave her a lovely smile. 'Oh, that's wonderful. But I feel sad for Dot, even though it's for the best. She's looked on that man as her dad, and I know how it feels to lose your respect for a father figure. So be gentle and understanding of her, Elsie.'

Elsie knew she should be, but since what had happened to her mum, she found that other people's troubles – even those of her half-sisters – didn't touch her like they would have done previously.

'Anyway, your other news is music to my ears. Tell Cecil that I'm so pleased for him. You know, after Cecil helped me that day when my horse threw me, I asked my father to set him on at our house, gardening and helping out wherever he was needed, but he didn't do anything about it.' Millie sighed. 'Anyway, he's settled now and I'm sure it will work out for him.'

'Oh, it will, and he has some big ideas now that he's going to be a man of means.' They giggled together over Cecil's plans to go to Brighton.

'You are lucky. I would love to go to the seaside. I have been, of course, but only when I was little.'

'Why don't you come? It'd be lovely. You'll save me playing gooseberry to Dot and Cecil.'

Again they laughed together.

'I might just do that. I've been invited to visit my friend Bunty, so I could use that as an excuse to cover my absence – she's a friend I made at school and am still in contact with.'

They chatted on excitedly about the prospect of a day out together for a few moments, and Elsie thought it would make her day really special to have Millie along. She hoped, with all her heart, that Cecil would agree.

It was Millie who changed the subject. 'Now, the strike. I do know a bit about it, as I am in regular contact with Mary Macarthur. She's such a wonderful woman. I want to be like her one day.'

'I think you already are. It's only your loyalty to your mum that stops you being more active.'

'It is. I can't bear to cause her hurt. Anyway, what's the mood in the factory like? Do you think they will all join in?'

'I think so. Your dad's going to get the shock of his life.'

'I know. I do worry about that. I know he is a bad man and deserves his comeuppance, but I feel terrible that I'm part of what could be his downfall. Still, I can't help myself. I have to be on the side of justice, and I have tried to talk to him about the conditions that you all work under. He simply won't listen. I can't believe the terrible accidents that occur, and yet some of them could be avoided.'

'Do you think we'll win? I mean, not just more money, but safety measures, like your father buying a better-quality jam jar that isn't so likely to explode? It's that happening that causes a lot of the injuries. One poor girl was blinded.'

'Oh no! I feel so guilty about things like that. I think my father will have to agree. He cannot afford not to. The factory must stay in production. Even a day lost will be a disaster to him. If he falls behind with his orders, there are plenty of others ready to take our customers from us.'

'Oh, Millie, if the factory went—'

'Don't worry. From what I have heard, there is a possibility that every factory is coming out, so all of them will be behind with their orders. The customers won't get their jams and pickles any sooner by switching, in this instance. No, it will all work out, you'll see. Now I have some cake for you, although it sounds as if you've been well fed tonight.'

'Ta, Millie. It'll keep. I still have that tin you gave me that first time. I'll keep the cake in that, and me and Cecil can take it to work with us.'

'Well, I have to go. I won't see you till after the strike. Good luck.' As Millie opened her arms and Elsie went into them, Millie whispered, 'I do love you, Elsie. I'm still reeling from learning you are my sister, but I'm so happy about it.'

'Me, too. And I know Dot is. I promise I'll be more understanding of her. After all, what's a big sister for?'

As they came out of the hug and Millie mounted her horse, Elsie felt bereft at the thought of them parting. She didn't think it would happen, but she wished with all her heart that one day they could always be together, like proper sisters.

On the morning of the tenth of August there was excitement in the air as everyone trampled to work. The calling out to one another held a kind of joy, and the air seemed to zing with anticipation. Most of the women looked more as if they were going to church than to face the daily grind. And yet the word 'strike' wasn't mentioned by anybody.

As they neared the factories, the mood changed to one of nervousness, and as Elsie looked round, she was filled with doubt as to whether the women would go through with the plan. But she needn't have worried.

With the windows of the factory open, to combat the intense heat, there was suddenly a different sound coming from outside than the usual toing and froing of horses and cars and the mingled factory sounds. For a moment it took them all by surprise, and Elsie heard a few ask, 'What is it?'

'It's what we've been waiting for, girls. Look! Thousands of them. Women against the hardship we're put through.' Lucy sounded jubilant. 'And just look at those banners the women from Pink's are carrying. "We're not white slaves, we're Pink!" Ha! Come on all, down tools!'

'Oh no, you don't.' Chambers's voice boomed across the factory floor. 'Anyone who downs tools and joins that lot can forget about coming into this factory ever again. I'm warning you.'

At this, Elsie felt indecisive for a moment.

'Don't listen, girls. Come on – hurry up. Off with your overalls. Let's see your Sunday best, and your best foot forward.'

'You're done for this time, Lucy Dalton. You can get your overall off and collect your cards – you're sacked!'

'You can't sack me. I'm on strike. Follow me, girls.'

Lucy threw off her overall and let it drop on the floor. Underneath she wore a bright-red blouse with a bow at the neck. It looked lovely with her ankle-length light-grey skirt. Seeing her courage gave Elsie the determination to follow. She too threw off her smock.

'Oh, Elsie, your frock! It looks wonderful.'

'Ta, Lucy. Are you ready, Dot?'

Dot didn't look very brave as she took her apron off, but when she stood there in the stunning frock, she seemed to grow in confidence. 'I'm ready, Else. Lead the way, Lucy.'

As they walked towards the door, with Chambers shouting after them, they became aware that others were gradually following suit. Chambers was almost hysterical, which caused a few to resume work.

Once they reached the door, though, there was a crowd of women behind them. Lucy gave a huge cheer as they passed the bottom of the stairs that led to the office. Elsie looked up and saw the door open and an astonished Mr Hawkesfield come out onto the landing. Behind him came Millie. She smiled down at them, but jumped as her father yelled, 'What the . . . Get back to your stations this minute. Anyone who leaves will lose their job. There's a crowd at the gate waiting to come in. Chambers, lock the door!'

Elsie looked back to see Chambers trying to make his way there, but he didn't stand a chance. The swell of women had grown and now formed a sea of bright colours, as all showed off their best dresses.

Lucy dashed forward and opened the door. It was a relief to get through it, though the heat outside was almost as intense as that inside the factory. Elsie broke out in a sweat that wasn't altogether caused by the heat, but generated by excitement and fear. There was no turning back now.

A massive cheer went up as they appeared at the gate and the women from Pink's encouraged them on.

Once out of the gate, they pushed themselves into the massive surge of bodies. Although she felt exhilarated, Elsie's fear was still with her, but now it was for the safety of everyone, although all kept on their feet. The atmosphere was as if the circus had come to town. The streets were lined with cheering men, who shouted words of pride. Some were saying, 'There's my Mabel', or Peggy or Ada; and then a voice came to her that she knew, and Elsie saw Rene waving to her. 'Well done, Else, girl.'

She felt a bubble of joy fill her. It was as if she was being freed from captivity, and it was akin to how she felt when she was little and was let out into the street to play, because Mum hadn't come home drunk and could watch over Cecil.

Clinging onto Dot's hand so that they didn't get separated, Elsie laughed with her, as they once did as children. 'We're on strike, girl!'

'We are, Else, we are. And it feels good. Look, there's me mum. MUM! Over here!'

Beryl Grimes caught Dot's eye and waved. She had a mug in her hand, and it was then that Elsie noticed the carts with several well-dressed women dispensing drinks and sandwiches. One had a trumpet hailer: 'Ladies, want for nothing. We are here to support you. Keep going, that's right.'

As they came up to the Peek Freans Biscuit Factory, another loud cheer went up. Elsie and Dot joined in, as the gates of the factory opened and the women who worked there came out in their droves. To Elsie, it felt as if everyone was on holiday. The blistering heat didn't dampen anyone's spirits, although a few around her fainted and were looked after by the striking dockers and transport workers, who carried them away from the crowd to the Federation women.

'That's Mary Macarthur. Look. Over there, Elsie.'

Elsie looked over in the direction that Lucy pointed, to see the lady with the loudhailer. She was a tall young woman with short, thick, wiry fair hair that stuck out at the sides and a very pretty face. At that moment Mary Macarthur looked over at them, caught sight of Lucy and beckoned her over.

Lucy grabbed Elsie's hand and took her with her. Elsie kept hold of Dot.

'Mrs Macarthur, isn't it wonderful!'

'It is, Lucy, if a little frightening.'

'These are the girls I told you about. Elsie and Dot.'

'Hello, I am so pleased to meet you. I wanted to say that, through Lucy, I followed your case, and never have I known anyone show so much courage in the defence of a working colleague. Though of course we were so saddened to hear of one of the workers meeting her demise in such a terrible way. Practices – bad practices – were changed as a result of this terrible accident, but that isn't how it should be. They should be changed before such things happen. However, I applaud you both for your bravery, and want to say how sorry I am to hear of your tragic loss.'

'Ta, Mrs Macarthur' was all Elsie could manage, as it seemed to her that she was in the presence of a great lady, and that overwhelmed her. Dot was, as usual, struck dumb.

'Now, girls, this is just the beginning. I want you all to stay strong. The dockers' leader, Ben Tillett, is going to help us become more organized. So we want you all to remain on strike until our demands can be met. We want a higher wage for you all; longer break times; and safety measures to be implemented. We will support you along the way. There is nothing that we cannot provide. So please pass the word along that no one should break the strike, and all who seek our help will get it.'

It was seven days later that everything the striking women asked for was granted by the employers. During that time Elsie enjoyed the comradeship she found, working alongside the Federation workers. They visited some poor homes, which made hers seem as if she and her family were rich. Ada's was one of them. Five children – and Ada and her man – lived in a cottage with one room downstairs and one up. Elsie had known poverty, but what Ada endured she hadn't known the likes of. Damp blotched the walls. No rugs covered the stone floor, and there weren't enough chairs for all the children to sit on.

When Elsie went back to Ada's with a food parcel from the Federation, Ada was in tears.

'I can't go on much longer, Elsie, girl. Me man ain't in work and, without my wage, I can't pay the rent. It ain't just food we need, luv.'

'I'll see what I can do, Ada. I'll talk to Mary Macarthur about your case.'

The Federation responded by paying two weeks' rent and providing more food for Ada and her family. Elsie's heart sang, and yet she felt the sadness of Ada's lovely man, as he couldn't be the breadwinner for his family.

On the seventh day they received news that Elsie couldn't believe. From now on, she was to receive nine shillings a week, with overtime that would be paid as a percentage of her wage. Ada, who had recently become a jam-maker, would receive eleven shillings. Her larder was full now, and some furniture and rugs had been delivered, as well as sacks of coal for when winter arrived. To Elsie, this was a lesson in how the masses could fight back and make a difference, and she thought that never again would she fear doing so.

Lucy didn't come back to work when the strike ended. The Federation offered her a full-time job. Elsie was pleased for her, as she had a calling for the work. She was to be the factory contact, if everything slipped back again and they needed the help of what was now their own union, with all of the women workers of Swift's paying their dues to the Federation.

With her extra earnings, Elsie was able to let Cecil keep a shilling of his wages for his own use. His pride at having money in his pocket warmed her heart.

The idea of the seaside trip was gaining momentum, and Cecil was happy that Millie was coming too. Elsie thought secretly he was glad, as he'd become a little nervous about being looked upon as the one to take care of them all, when he'd never stepped outside their own area before. Millie was much more worldly-wise.

Three weeks later, they were all sitting on a bench in the park, a place that felt like home to Elsie – the home where she could be with Millie.

'So, Millie, we want to go to Brighton on Saturday, the ninth of September. Is that possible for you, luv?'

'It is, Elsie. It'll be so lovely to escape this heat and feel some sea breeze. My mama is travelling to our home in Leeds the day after tomorrow, and Father is joining her at the end of the week. I'm going on my visit to my friend Bunty for a few days – you remember, I told you about her invite? Well, she surprised me by telling me that her mother is really keen to have me visit. It seems the worm can change. But I will be with you on Saturday. And, best of all, as my parents think I will be away and will be looked after by Bunty's maid, they are taking Ruby with them. I'm so pleased for her. She so wants to see her mother.'

'Oh, will you manage on you own?'

'I will, Dot. Bunty is sending a car for me, and Ruby has already done my packing. But I will have to meet you all in Brighton. I can travel from Bunty's. I will tell her that I am going to visit an old aunt, and ask if she will arrange to take me and my luggage to the station to catch the train.'

'But what will you do with your luggage? You can't drag it around Brighton.'

'Oh, that's no problem. I will put it into Left Luggage until we return that evening. One of our family cars will pick me up, once we get back to London, as I have told them that Bunty can only put me on the train, as her family's drivers are needed. Anyway, I'll aim to be in Brighton by eleven-ish. What time will you be there?'

They all looked at Cecil. Cecil coloured, started to speak, but before he could do so, Millie said, 'You can catch a train from London Bridge to Brighton and, if you go there beforehand, Cecil, they will tell you the times and you can buy the tickets, in readiness. Try to take a train that will get you there at roughly the same time as me. Then I will wait on the station in Brighton for you. Or, if I'm not there, you can wait for me. How does that sound?'

Cecil looked relieved. 'Simple, mate, although whether it will be, I don't know.'

'It will be, Cecil. I promise you.'

'I'll come with you, Cess. I'd like that.'

Cecil looked gratefully at Dot.

'Why don't we go tomorrow evening, eh? We can walk to the station.'

'All right. I'll wait for you when you come out of the factory.'

With this settled, Dot said she had to be home in the next fifteen minutes or so and went to leave. Faithful Cecil rose to go with her. Millie hugged Dot. 'I can't wait to spend a day with you all, Dot. It's going to be amazing.'

When Dot hugged Millie back, Elsie felt, for the first time, that Dot was really letting Millie get close to her. She wouldn't say the relationship between them was strained in any way, but that Dot held back a little of herself, where Millie was concerned. Now that seemed to have evaporated, as Dot spoke to Millie.

'I can't wait, either. I'm going to love being with you, where we don't have to be secretive and nobody knows us. We've had a few looks, when we're here. Though not many of our neighbours come this way, or would know who you are, if they did, so it hasn't caused any problems. Well, I'll be off. See you in the morning, Else.' A quick hug and she was gone.

'I cannot stay too much longer, Elsie, but Saturday is something I'll look forward to so much.'

Just as Millie said this, her horse reared and strained against the post that Millie had tied her to. Millie ran to Fennie to calm her. 'What happened? What spooked you, lovely lady?'

A stone whizzed past Elsie's head. She ducked, but it caught the horse and sent her kicking her legs up in the air. Her nostrils flared; her neigh was a painful sound. Millie clung onto her rein, but was losing the battle.

Elsie could see that the culprits were a small gang of boys who stood at the entrance of the park. One of them shouted, 'What's that posh bit doing around here? Come to look at how the poor live, eh? Get back to your own end.'

Another stone flashed by. This one missed its target, but Fennie was spooked and reared once more. Elsie ran to Millie's side and grabbed hold of the rein. Never before had she felt a force like the one that tugged against her and Millie.

'What's going on? Let me help. You boys, stop that, now!'

The voice sounded different from any local, and yet it wasn't as posh as Millie's. Elsie looked at the young man it belonged to and implored him, 'Help us. Please, we can't hold her.'

The man grabbed the rein. 'Steady, girl. Steady.' His hand stroked Fennie's nose. 'There now. All's well. Calm yourself.'

Elsie couldn't take her eyes off him. His skin was dark and his deep-black eyes scanned her, as if he was sizing her up, then looked at Millie in much the same way. 'You can both let go now. But be careful. I can see that a couple of the boys have hung back. They are show-offs who might want to be seen to win the battle.'

Elsie didn't answer him, but grabbed hold of an exhausted-looking Millie. 'You're all right, Millie, love. Hang on to me. I'll get you to the bench.' Once there, she shouted at the boys, 'I know who you are – you're from the top flats. You'll be in trouble for this.'

At this, the boys scarpered.

'Oh, Millie, you're shaking, luv.'

'I'll be all right. I just need to get my breath back. As long as you and Fennie aren't hurt, that's the main thing.' Millie looked over to where the young man had now soothed Fennie and was stroking her mane. 'Thank you kindly, sir. I don't know what would have happened if you hadn't have stopped to help us.'

'My pleasure. I'm Leonardo Lefton – known as Len. I work in my father's bank down the road and I often walk this way, but you are always too busy talking to your friends to notice me.'

Millie blushed. For the first time ever, Elsie saw a vulnerability in her when dealing with a stranger. 'Oh, I thought . . . I – I, well, I thought maybe you were a visitor to London.'

'Ha! Most people think that. I have taken my looks from my Italian mother and her many brothers. My name comes from my maternal grandfather, and though I have lived in London all of my life, I always look as if I have come from sunnier climes. And you are?'

'Millicent Hawkesfield, and this—'

'The Swift's Jam Factory Hawkesfields?'

'Yes. This is my si . . . friend, Elsie.'

Len turned towards Elsie and smiled. Elsie thought him beautiful. As she looked into his eyes, a feeling overcame her that made her heart race. Her breath caught in her throat, but before she could speak, Len had turned away from her and was showing his concern for Millie. 'Do you live far from here? May I accompany you to your home? I can drive the horse.'

Millie, still flustered, nodded and allowed Len to take her hand and guide her to the trap attached to Fennie. Elsie felt as though she was being shut out of their world for a moment, but Millie turned back to her before she stepped up into the trap and put out her arms. Elsie went into them.

'Are you sure you'll be all right, Millie, love?'

'I'll take care of her. You have no need to worry. I know her father well. Do you have far to go, Elsie?'

Just hearing her name on his lips made Elsie quiver. 'No, I live over on the estate.'

Len showed no repulsion, but simply smiled and asked if she would be all right.

'Yes, ta. I know them lads – they won't harm me. Their mums would scalp them if they did. It would be Millie who was their target. They resent anyone who has more than they do.'

'Yes, you can't blame them. But they do need to be taught that this kind of attack, especially on a woman, is wrong. But then I expect all the unrest is fuelling their desire to fight back, and it is understandable.'

'I'll make sure they're punished. Their dads'll be very angry about what they did.'

'Good. Well, goodbye, Elsie, and I hope I see you again.'

As Len said this, he climbed into the trap where Millie was sitting and took the reins of the horse. The smile that he gave Elsie sent her reeling. She hardly noticed Millie waving to her as they drove off.

Turning towards home, Elsie wanted to hug those boys, not have them punished, because they had brought Len to her, and she knew her life would never be the same again.

Chapter Seventeen

Millie

Millie had never felt so shy in all her life as she did sitting so closely to Len. She couldn't understand what was happening to her, or the effect Len was having on her.

He was adept at handling a horse and trap, having told her that he had horses of his own on his father's country estate in Kent and missed them during the week, when the family lived in their apartment in Knightsbridge. 'My father is a partner in a large bank in Knightsbridge – Harlington & Lefton's. He works there, and I run the smaller, family-owned Lefton's Bank on Dover Street. I walk through St George's gardens to get to Borough Underground and, as I said, have often noticed you there.'

'Oh? I'm sorry, but I have never seen you before.'

'No, you were always deep in conversation, hugging or giggling with Elsie and, often, one other girl. Forgive me for saying so, but you seem an unlikely group of friends – I mean, well, so obviously from different backgrounds, and from classes that don't usually mix.'

'I – I . . . We met by chance and just got on so well. They are both lovely girls.'

'Elsie is certainly down-to-earth and doesn't seem to have any resentment in her, which you can come across in those who are poorer than us. Mind you, they don't realize the problems we have with those who are more fortunate than us. They think we are the elite and are accepted everywhere, but we are the middle-rich, so to speak.'

'Yes, I know what you mean. I have experienced being looked down on, and this gives me a natural empathy for Elsie and her class. If only all of this class-divide didn't exist, what a happier world it would be.'

'Maybe, but that will never happen. Tell me, what do you do with yourself all day, other than seek out the less fortunate to befriend?'

Len was really surprised to hear of Millie's role in her father's jam factory, but then it was rare for a girl to take up such a position.

'Father doesn't have a son, or any male relatives. Mama has a cousin who has a son, but Father doesn't get on too well with Mama's side of the family. When my grandmother was alive and visited often, they always clashed. Grandmother won, though. I often think that I take after her, because I, too, can be very determined to get my own way. And if I can't, I get it secretly.'

'Like your friendships? I can't imagine them being condoned.'

'What the cat doesn't know about, the mouse can enjoy.'

'Ha, I don't see you as a mouse, and I doubt your parents do, either. They probably despair of you.'

They both laughed at this, and Millie began to relax. 'They certainly will, seeing me brought home by a stranger! I shall be in for a dressing-down from Mama, for not having my maid to chaperone me.'

'And I agree with her. You could have got into a lot of trouble tonight, if I hadn't happened along. Though Elsie did seem to be able to handle those boys. You should be more careful, Millicent.'

'Millie. And please don't lecture me. You don't know what it is like to be a woman restricted in your movements, and told what you can and can't do!'

'Oops – sorry. Hit a raw nerve, have I? Are you one of those who fight for the rights of women? Will you be campaigning with the likes of Mrs Pankhurst? Smashing windows, et cetera?'

'Maybe. Yes, I think I will, in time. I do feel passionately about how we are perceived. I am far removed from the embroidery-wielding, obedient woman who puts up with everything her husband does. I believe that women have a lot to offer. I believe there should be equality in the way all classes of women are treated. Working-class women should have good conditions to work in, and be paid well for what they do. But, above all, they and all women should be respected and listened to.'

'Bravo! My sentiments exactly. When I take a wife, she will be loved, respected and will be my partner in all decisions.' He'd slowed the horse as he said this and looked into Millie's eyes. 'Would I be the kind of man who would suit you, Millie?'

Millie felt her colour rise and her cheeks burn, but she held his gaze.

Len smiled then. 'Sorry. That was a bit forward of me, but I . . . well, I would very much like to be your friend and to see you again. May I?'

'Yes, I would like that.' She wanted to shout for joy and say that she wanted him to be more than her friend – her lover even! But this thought made her blush more deeply, and confusion seized her. 'I – I . . . Oh, look, we are here. I cross the park to get to the stables, so if you turn into the gate ahead.'

Without speaking, Len steered the horse deftly through the gates.

'Will you come in to meet my mama and take refreshment? Then I will instruct our groom to take you to the station.'

'Thank you. I would like that.'

Len, too, seemed to have a shyness about him now. Millie wondered if he was sorry for what he'd said – not the forwardness of it, but in a regretful way.

Mama was shocked at first that Millie should come home with a strange gentleman, and that she hadn't been chaperoned by Ruby. But Millie could see that she immediately fell for Len's charm.

Over a cup of tea she told him, 'I have met your father. I was sorry to hear that your mother died. I met her once. She was a beautiful woman. You certainly have her features. Thank you so much for taking care of Millicent. I despair of her and her antics at times.'

This embarrassed Millie, but also shocked her, as she hadn't thought to ask Len about his family.

Len didn't refer to 'her antics', as Mama had put it. 'Thank you. Yes, we miss her greatly; it was a short illness that took her from us very quickly. And yes, I have heard my father speak of you. He met you at a dinner given by his bank, I believe.'

Millie sat listening to them chatting. She hadn't seen her mama this animated in a long time. She looked beautiful in her grey silk blouse and long, slender grey skirt. So elegant and graceful.

Occasionally she would glance in Millie's direction with a look that told her she was very pleased at this turn of events. Millie knew that Mama had her paired with Len in her mind, and was probably already imagining the wedding. But somehow Millie didn't mind. All she minded was that Mama was hogging Len's time.

When he put his cup down and announced that he must leave, Millie stood up. 'I'll call for the horse and trap to be brought round to the front for you.'

'Thank you.' After saying goodbye to her mama, he stood in the hall with her. 'You cannot wait to get rid of me, I see.'

'Not at all. I'm so grateful to you.'

'Does that extend to seeing me again? You did say you would – has that changed? I would love to take you to dinner one evening. Tomorrow, for instance.'

'I – I don't know. You will have to ask my father. There, you see. You are able to make all your own arrangements, but I . . . I need permission. Besides, I am going away tomorrow and won't be back until Saturday evening. My parents will be away until next week.'

'That's not a no, then.'

Before she could answer this, Barridge opened the front door and they both saw her father's car coming up the drive.

'Well, there's no time like the present to get permission.'

'I must warn you that Father isn't in the best of moods. He is seething about the concessions that the strikers won.'

'Hmm, I heard about that. Well, then, maybe not the best time. May I call to see you on the Sunday after you return? Please say yes.'

Nothing was going to make her say otherwise. 'I would like that. Come in the afternoon and, if it is still nice, I will have tea served in the garden. If not, we do have a lovely summerhouse at the bottom of the garden – we can take tea in there.'

'Wonderful. I will see you at three on Sunday. Now I will just greet your father, and I see that the horse and trap are ready for me, so I will leave you now. Goodbye, Millie. I'll be thinking about you every minute till Sunday.'

Although she blushed again, Millie felt a surge of joyful heat warm her body. After watching him greet her father, she turned and went back to sit with her mama, thinking how wonderful it was that a day could make such a difference in your life.

Bunty showed her pleasure at seeing Millie again by running to her as she stepped out of the car. 'Oh, Millie. Millie, I'm so pleased you are here at last. I missed you so this term. It was frightful, and I am dreading going back.'

Millie laughed as she was caught up in Bunty's hug. Then, as she stood back and they held each other at arm's length, she could see that in the months since they had last seen each other, Bunty hadn't changed one bit. She still wore her fair hair pulled back in a ponytail, with tiny ringlets escaping and bordering her pretty face and lovely blue eyes. The same height as Millie, Bunty was inclined to carry a tiny bit of weight, which gave her a rounded, little-girl look. Unlike herself. Millie now felt years older than her friend.

Bunty expressed this, without actually saying it. 'What has happened to you? There is something different about you.'

'Quite a lot. You can't begin to imagine. Not that I can tell you everything, but yes, I have changed. I've grown up. I've had to.'

'Well, I suppose I will have to soon. I am being prepared

for the marriage market. I will make someone a wonderful wife, don't you know?'

'Ha, Bunty, you're a one. You haven't lost your sense of humour. I, too, am still considered to be marriage material. I'm just waiting for some poor man with a title who cannot keep his pile without my riches, and I'll be snapped up. But, oh, I don't want to be.'

'Well, you might be sooner than you think. And it would be so wonderful. Jeromy! Yes, my brother – the younger of my two brothers – is looking for someone to marry. Father has told him that the whole of our fortune is going to Adrian, the eldest. Either Jeromy finds a rich wife or he must become a vicar. He is appalled. But then he remembered meeting you, and *voilà*!'

'You mean, you only invited me so that Jeromy could try and woo me?' This realization hurt Millie badly.

'Well, not altogether. I wanted to see you too, and, well, it all just happened to fit in with Mother's plans for Jeromy. I thought you would be pleased. After all, it is what you came to the same school as us for, isn't it?'

At one time Millie would have laughed at this, but now her new, changed self felt humiliated. Without thinking, she blurted out, 'No, it isn't why I came to your school, but it is why my parents sent me. You know how unhappy I was about it all. Besides, I am engaged to be married, so you're too late. And I would like to go back home right now!'

'Millie! No, Millie. Please. I'm sorry. I thought you would be so pleased at the prospect of getting what you have sought – and of being related to me. I don't understand. And you say you are engaged! You should have told me. I feel a fool now.'

They were still standing on the gravel driveway of Bunty's

family retreat, Audley's Wood in the county of Hampshire. The beautiful mansion, not overly large, had enchanted Millie at first glance, as she had been driven up its very long drive. She knew it wasn't a quarter of the size of their mansion in Surrey, and wondered at the son of such wealth having to beg for a rich wife.

'*You* feel a fool? Bunty, you have humiliated me. Please ask your driver to put my luggage back in the car and take me home. I cannot possibly stay, and I never want to see you again. I thought you were my friend, asking me to visit because you wanted to be with me, but you're just like all the other girls I schooled with.'

Tears were streaming, unbidden, down Millie's face. She felt completely stripped of all dignity.

'Oh, Millie, I can't believe how this is turning out. As soon as my father told Jeromy, I thought of you, and he was so pleased, as he remembers meeting you once and found you so pretty. He's really excited to meet you again and get to know you. Are you really engaged? I haven't seen an announcement. Can you not give Jeromy a chance?'

'No! I want to go home.'

'Ah, Barbara, there you are. Why must you keep our guest standing on the driveway? It was most unladylike of you to rush out and greet her like that. So you are Millicent? I am very pleased to meet you.' Turning to look at Bunty, the lady who had joined them, and whom Millie knew to be Bunty's mother, said, 'Well done. Yes, she will do nicely.'

Bunty tried to cover this up by saying, 'Millie, this is my mother, Lady Standing.'

Millie pulled herself up to her full height. 'I will *not* do nicely, as you put it, Lady Standing. And I would ask you to kindly request your driver to take me home at once.'

'What? What on earth is this? Bunty? And why is Millicent crying?'

'I think, Mama, she had some idea that she was just coming to stay with me as a friend. I cannot understand it myself. I would never invite the likes of her to our home, if you hadn't agreed that I should because of Jeromy's fancy to look her over as a possible wife. The others at school would ridicule me for doing so. Anyway, Millie does not see a good thing when it is offered to her, so as far as I am concerned, she can return home when she wants to. Goodbye, Millie.' With this, Bunty turned and walked towards the house.

Lady Standing wrung her hands together. 'Oh dear. I do apologize. It seems that you feel insulted by us. Very well. Gables, please take Miss Hawkesfield back to wherever you picked her up from. Goodbye, Miss Hawkesfield, and please forget this encounter. I doubt it will be repeated by any family of worth, and I believe that will greatly disappoint your mother.'

'It won't, actually. She is like me – heartsick of her daughter being treated in this manner. Goodbye.'

With this, Millie hurriedly got inside the car.

On the way home, her humiliation and tears turned to giggles as she suddenly realized that she'd won another battle for women like herself – lost between the classes. Besides, she could contact Len and have him visit sooner.

'Glad to see you looking happier, Miss, if you'll beg my pardon in saying so. But you were very brave back there, and it was good to see. You haven't missed much. Mr Jeromy is a womanizer.'

Millie didn't know what came over her, but she laughed out loud at this. 'You don't have to beg my pardon to speak to me, Gables. My father may be a rich man, but I am not anyone special and have never considered myself to be. I'm sorry that you have another long journey ahead of you.'

'It's not a problem. I would drive you anywhere, Miss. Would you like me to stop somewhere so that you can get a pot of tea? They didn't even offer you any refreshments, or let you . . . well, I mean, like the ladies say, powder your nose.'

Millie burst out laughing this time. She liked Gables. 'Yes, please. Can you make it an inn? Thank you. And I will buy you a cup of tea, too – you must need it.'

By the time Gables dropped her back at home, Millie had begun to worry about her plans for Saturday. How would she pull off going out and getting a train to Brighton? Not that she couldn't do it, but the staff – or at least the new housekeeper – would be up in arms about it, and would be sure to tell her mama and her father that she left for a whole day without a chaperone. They would be surprised, as it was, that she was back so soon, and the gossip amongst them would be rife.

Unable to come up with a solution, and not wanting to forfeit her trip with her lovely sisters, Millie decided that she only had one aide to call on. Writing a note, she asked Barridge to see that it was delivered to Len's bank.

Len called round to the house the very next day. He was upset when he heard how Millie had been treated, but not surprised. But he was astounded by her story, because Millie had decided to tell him the truth about herself, as she felt anything else would be deceitful. Besides, how could she ask him to help her if he didn't know her real motives – to be with her sisters?

'I know it is scandalous, but my father isn't what he seems. He . . . well, he hurts people and . . .'

'I'm not exactly shocked by your revelations about your father, Millie. I have heard my father speak ill of him many a time. It seems that he even made a play for my mother once and had to be told, though it was awkward for my father, because your father is a valued customer of his – or was.'

'Was?'

'No. No, I meant . . . I – I mean, of course he is, but after that incident when he upset my mother, Father isn't best pleased with him.'

'I'm sorry, I really am. I'm ashamed of him.'

'It isn't your fault. But I'm taken aback about how you have found all this out, about Elsie and the other girl you speak of; and yet you have befriended them and help them, and are desperate to be with them. I must say that I admire you, and it confirms to me what a very nice person you are, Millie.'

'Thank you, but surely you would do the same?'

'No, I don't think I would. I think I would run a mile from half-brothers who were the illegitimate sons of my father. And I'm sure everyone but you would do so, especially when they are . . . well, you know.'

'No, I don't. When they are what?'

'Oh, Millie. I'm sorry, I didn't mean . . . Well, I did, but it was very ignorant of me. It's difficult. But luckily your sisters – or at least the one I have met – are different from others who have been brought up like them . . . Oh, dear, you're going to hate me now. I can only say, in my defence, that it is the way I have been schooled. But I can change. With your help, I too can see the world as a place where all should be treated equally. Can you forgive me?'

They were sitting in Millie's back garden. The sun was still beaming down, even though it was six in the evening. Millie swatted a fly that was buzzing around her. 'Of course. I understand, but only because you can see the error of your ways – unlike Bunty and her family, who think it is a God-given right for them to behave that way and would never change.'

Wondering at herself for speaking so openly to someone she barely knew – although she felt as if she'd known him all her life – Millie tried to explain further. 'Maybe it is because of people like Bunty and her family – and the way I have been treated by their like, since my parents first put me in their world – that has made me how I am. When you've experienced the treatment that I did yesterday, and for years, then you want to protect others, not inflict the same treatment on them. I was very lonely when I came across Elsie and Dot. I never dreamed that befriending them would turn out how it has, and yet I was strangely drawn to them. As they were to me.'

'Yes, I can see that. I have never experienced anyone snubbing me, but then I have only dealt with the aristocrats of this world on a business level. And believe me, I have seen their arrogance. They are a breed of their own. A lot of them are living from hand to mouth, and yet most could turn their fortunes round if they were willing to do even half a day's work each day, but basically they are extremely lazy. They have servants to do everything for them.'

'Yes, you're right. It is arrogance that they have, and a side to them that makes them uncaring of anyone's feelings. Anyway, I need to ask you a favour. It is a huge one, considering that you hardly know me, but . . .'

Len was shocked once more as she told him about her

trip to Brighton and how it was now difficult for her. 'Millie, are you sure about this? You really feel safe going to the seaside on your own?'

'I won't be on my own, once I get there.'

Len was silent for a moment. Millie waited, taking in his handsome face as she watched him struggle about what to do. She hoped against hope that he would help her.

'I won't give you the cover you ask for, Millie. I would worry myself all day as to what was happening to you. I know it seems simple to you, for me to have an invitation sent over to you to spend the day at my home, but it isn't. However, I will accompany you, if you can accept that and don't think it will be looked upon as improper?'

'Yes. Yes, I will. Thank you. I really cannot see anything improper about it. I have been badly treated and had to return home. And you, who have met my mother and been approved by her, have offered to take me out for the day. Oh, Len, thank you. But you will be all right with everyone, won't you?'

'Of course I will. Despite what I've said, I would never be anything other than polite and friendly to anyone. It's just that I wouldn't actively have sought their friendship, as you have.'

Millie understood this. She knew that what she'd done, by instigating a friendship with Elsie and Dot, was unusual and not the 'done' thing. After all, didn't she keep it from her mama for a long time, and still did from her father? The only reason being that she knew it wasn't expected behaviour and would upset them.

When Saturday dawned, Millie was overtaken by nerves. What would Dot and Cecil think of this new turn of events?

She knew Elsie would be fine. She'd met Len and, for the short time they'd been together, she seemed to like him. And how would it seem if it ever got found out by her mama – gallivanting off with a man she'd only just met, and alone! But all this left her once Len arrived to pick her up. He looked different in his casual clothes: a cream-coloured linen jacket, brown slacks and a straw boater. She might even say rakishly handsome.

When Barridge had finished fussing over her and settling her into the front seat of Len's car and closed the door, Len gave her a look that sent shivers down her spine and made her blush with pleasure.

'You look beautiful, Millie.'

She smiled her thanks. If only he knew how many outfits she'd put on and taken off again, before settling on this frock, which she hadn't worn before. It was the latest fashion – navy-and-white vertical stripes, with the bodice cut into the waist, adorned by a huge white collar with points that extended to her waistline. The skirt was tulip-shaped and fell to her ankles. She'd teamed this with a straw hat in white, with a navy ribbon around its brim and hanging down the back. Her hair was tied loosely into the nape of her neck. She'd liked the effect, and could see that Len did, too.

Glowing with happiness at the prospect of the day out, and of being with Len, Millie couldn't wait to reach Brighton. The train journey seemed interminable, but pleasurable at the same time, as she and Len talked and talked.

'So, tell me about yourself, Millie – and I want to know everything, from when you were born.'

Millie laughed. 'How long is the journey? My life story could bore you for most of it, as I was a lonely child as a young girl and into my womanhood, and spent most of that time like a square peg in a round hole.' She gave him a brief outline of how her life had been. 'It is only recently that I have a sad – and, some would say, interesting and at times uplifting – tale to tell, but you know most of that. What about you? Your turn to tell me all.'

'Well, in the loneliness stakes, I wasn't quite as badly off as you. But being an only child, I did experience some of what you spoke of: lonely feelings, that is. But only at home. I went to a day-school and was very happy and popular there. I found learning came very easily to me and I ended up in Oxford – there's many a tale to be told about those days, but I think I will introduce you to the boisterous, sport-loving Boat Race cox that I was in those days in small doses, because even relating it is too much for me in one long narrative. Anyway I am twenty-five now and a settled, sensible gentleman banker, with no ambitions other than to marry the woman I fall in love with and have ten children.'

'Ten! Good gracious, why as many as that?'

'Well, I want my children to have a very different childhood from the one I had – not that mine wasn't happy, but I'm sure, as an only child, you understand. Apart from the loneliness we have spoken of, all expectations are upon you to achieve, to be the best at everything. And, as you know, it is not always nice being solitary, with all the focus on you.'

Millie hadn't thought of this; not that she had ever got as far as thinking of having any children. But now that the idea was planted, she found herself agreeing.

'I like that. I too will add having a large family to my wishes for my future. But ten? I might draw a line at four maybe.'

Len gave her a lovely smile. 'Nearly halfway to my total. Well, I suppose the actual number is up for discussion, but I would never agree to have only one!'

Millie blushed. Len had said this as if the matter rested between them to decide. Something in her hoped it would turn out like that.

One thing she did know – she was now converted to wanting a large family herself. And she wanted to giggle at the prospect, as she imagined them and all the fun they would all have.

When at last they arrived and got off the train, Elsie, Dot and Cecil were already there. The girls looked lovely in the frocks she'd given them – especially Elsie. She looked stunningly beautiful in the lovely straight-cut green frock with its mock-jacket top, which flared out at the hipline and had a lace inset over her bosom, which allowed a very feminine and pretty cleavage to show.

Dot looked pretty too, in the blue frock with little yellow daisies on it, which flared out from her tiny waist. Neither girl wore a hat, and Elsie's red hair looked glorious, tied loosely into her neck and left to flow down her back. Cecil looked very smart in his knee-length sandy-coloured breeches and brown jacket. He wore a cravat that wasn't quite tied correctly, but it made Millie beam with pride at the effort he'd made. And for the first time she saw him as a young man – a very handsome and muscular young man.

Elsie greeted Len with a dazzling smile and, for a brief moment, Millie felt a pang of jealousy as Len held Elsie's gaze. Something quivered through her – a small fear. But she soon dispelled it and forgot it, as she was caught up in loving hugs and excited chatter, and then in explaining to them why Len was here.

'Well, he's very welcome, ain't he?'

Dot and Cecil both agreed, and Cecil again made Millie happy when he offered his hand to Len. 'Nice to meet you, guv.'

Millie saw Len suppress a giggle. She had to herself, because she hadn't ever thought of Len as 'guv'. It seemed more a term for a boss than a friend. But then Dot topped it.

'It is, and it's lovely to have you with us, mate.'

Letting his laugh go, Len told them, 'And it's a pleasure to be with you, too, mate and guv.'

They all laughed at this, and Millie felt the ice was broken and they were in for a lovely day. If only she could dispel the strange feeling she had about Elsie. It was as if she feared her as a rival, when Elsie could never be that. She was just her lovely sister, wasn't she?

Chapter Eighteen

Elsie

As they walked off the platform, Millie chatted on, explaining in greater detail how it all came about that she'd brought Len with her. Elsie was appalled on hearing of Millie's humiliation by her so-called friend, and didn't think she would ever get used to Millie being treated in such a way, or having folk who looked down on her as a lesser person than themselves. But although she made the right sympathetic noises, she wasn't happy with the way Millie spoke about Len. It was as if he was her boyfriend, and gave Elsie a jabbing pain in her heart.

Elsie didn't like having a fifth person along. Dot and Cecil would be taken up with each other, and she had wanted to have Millie to herself for the day. *Maybe it's the loss of that which is making me feel as I do?* But she knew it wasn't; it was this feeling that she had for Len, and seeing that Millie had it, too. But worse than that, it was seeing Len return Millie's feelings. This was a bitter pill to swallow. Loving Millie as she did, Elsie didn't want to be a rival to her.

As they were caught up in the hustle and bustle of the

Brighton crowds, the atmosphere of happiness and a good-time-had-by-all feeling, Elsie let these emotions drift from her and threw herself into having a good time.

Around them was a hub of noise and activity, to the background sound of a street organ playing and colourful market stalls, which lined the streets, their owners calling out their wares. 'Fresh fish brought in this morning from Newhaven: you don't get no fresher than that, lady!' And 'Spanish oranges, fresh from the boats, too. Come and try – sweet as sugar, they are!'

This gave Elsie a vision of sorting the rotten things, and she could almost feel the sting from the juice getting into her torn hands. Her mind reeled back to where she didn't want to be: the jam factory.

Millie's cry of 'Let's go to the Royal Pavilion – I've always wanted to visit it' cast any thought of the factory from Elsie's mind, as she answered, 'The Royal Pavilion? That sounds posh.'

'And expensive,' Len cautioned. 'It will cost sixpence each to get in. I saw an advert for it on the train.'

'What is it? Some sort of palace?'

'It is, Dot. It was built by King George IV, Queen Victoria's uncle.'

Len took up the tale from Millie. 'Yes, and Queen Victoria almost demolished it – at least the interior. She found it too small for all her children to be housed in, so she took everything out of it and distributed them around her other homes – paintings, carpets, furniture, all gone. But she did return quite a lot of them, so it will be lovely to see them.'

'Is it still a royal palace then? Will they let us in?'

'Yes, of course. But no, it's not a palace any longer, Cecil. Queen Victoria sold it to Brighton. Now it's a place to hold events in – art exhibitions, bazaars and music concerts, that sort of thing. And there are some lovely gardens. I think it will be fun to visit, but costly,' Len told him.

Elsie thought sixpence an enormous sum, especially when you realized there were five of them. That would mean the total cost would be half a crown! She could feed herself, Cecil and Rene for three days on that. She was about to say so when Millie jumped in and said that she would pay. 'I would love to treat you to a visit. Please let me.'

'I'll go halves, Millie. One shilling and threepence each – how about that?'

Cecil dug his wallet out of his trousers. 'No, Len, we can't have you treating us like that; you've only just met us. We'll split it three ways: tenpence each. Here you go.'

'Fair enough. Come on then. We'll have to walk along the promenade, but you'll soon spot it – it's magnificent, according to the pictures I've seen of it.' Len took hold of Millie's hand as he said this, giving Elsie's heart a jolt, until he turned to look at her. 'Come on, Elsie. You hold my hand, too.'

When her hand touched his, it was as if something pulsed through her body. And yet Elsie knew without a doubt that she'd lost any chance of being his girl, because his grip was no different from the way Cecil would hold her hand; whereas with Millie, Len tucked her hand through his arm. How could this happen? How could she fall for the same man as Millie – a man Millie was far more suited to? But then she'd heard that you can't choose who you fall in love with.

The Pavilion was truly magnificent, although Elsie felt she wouldn't have appreciated the grandeur of it, but for Len and Millie. But she was excited to see there was a bazaar going on, with such wonders for sale as lavender bags, beautiful embroidery, all manner of cloths and clothes, too, beside curiosities that intrigued her.

But her attention was taken up by the chandeliers and paintings, which she knew the great Queen Victoria had also looked upon, and by the vibrant colour of the wall-papers. The grand staircase, whose spindles and banisters looked like bamboo, but which Len said were fake, was so beautiful. It was difficult to believe what Millie was saying: that Queen Victoria hadn't liked it very much. Elsie was glad, though, that the Queen had returned some objects to the Pavilion, because now everyone who visited could gaze on their beauty.

'What is there not to like, Elsie? How could Queen Victoria have called it a strange, odd, Chinese-looking thing, both inside and out, and have thought that most rooms are too low. Not only that, but she also complained that she couldn't see the sea.'

'She must have been used to something much grander perhaps? I don't see how you could call these ceilings low. I haven't got a feather duster long enough to reach the cobwebs, I know that much.'

Millie laughed at this and put her arm through Elsie's. 'Oh, I do love you, Elsie, you're so funny.'

'And I love you too, Millie. Ta for coming today. I never thought I'd go on a trip like this.'

'You've Cecil to thank for that. Talking of which, he and Dot seem to be getting closer and closer. It's lovely to see, as they look so happy in each other's company.'

Elsie noticed that Len was engrossed in a painting a few steps ahead of them, so she thought to broach the subject on her mind. 'They're not the only ones. You and Len seem to be getting on really well, Millie.'

'You noticed! Well, yes, I do like him. What do you think of him, Elsie?'

What did she think of him? She couldn't stop thinking about him, and hadn't since the first time they'd met. But should she tell Millie this? Should she tell her how Len made her tingle all over, and how she longed to be held by him? And how, when he glanced at her, her legs turned to jelly?

'Elsie?'

'Oh, I think he's a smasher and just right for you. He'd make a lovely brovver-in-law.'

'Really? You wouldn't mind? I – I mean . . . Oh, I haven't even thought of him as a . . .'

Elsie felt sorry to hear the usually confident Millie sounding so unsure. She knew Millie had guessed how she felt, and was feeling bad about it. She decided to treat it all lightly. To this end, she giggled – something she felt least like doing – then leaned in to whisper to Millie, 'He's not my Rosy Lee. I mean, I like him, very much, but not as a boyfriend! He'd leave me standing, with him being all educated, and I'd feel forever out of my depth. But for you, he's perfect, Millie.'

'I have no idea what a Rosy Lee is, but I'm so happy to hear you say that, Elsie. I thought, well . . . I thought you had fallen for him.'

'Me? No. He's handsome, and any girl would swoon over him, but I like a more ordinary lad. And a Rosy Lee is a cup of tea – and I'm dying for one, right now!'

'Oh, I wanted to look at the stalls. But we can do that after.'

By the time they came out of the pavilion, Elsie felt a lot better about the situation between herself and Millie. She knew what she'd done was the only way. She loved Millie too much to hurt her by going into rivalry with her over a man – even an adorable, wonderful man like Len. So to lighten things even more she suggested, 'Let's go and have a paddle, eh? I'd love to cool my feet in the water. I've never stepped into sea water in my life.'

They crossed the road and were on the promenade. The sea looked like a beautiful lake, but the pebbles to get to it didn't look too inviting.

'Come on. You're not going to chicken out are you, Elsie, mate?'

'You go first, Dot. I'll follow.'

She watched as Cecil took Dot's hand and began to run towards the sea. Dot's screams were a joyful sound that spurred Elsie on. Stepping onto the beach, she too ran towards the water, stopping just before she reached it to take off her shoes, then crying out with the pain the pebbles caused her until she reached the water's edge. Looking towards the horizon, Elsie gasped. How could there be so much water leading to nothing?

'Bet I put my feet in before you do, Elsie.'

Elsie picked up her skirt and ran in, laughing at Cecil, with his trouser legs rolled up, as she did so, then catching her breath at the coldness of the water.

'You, young man!' The irate voice directed at Cecil came from a woman with a rolled-up sunshade, which she was waving in the air. 'Leave the beach at once! This is a ladies-only hour! Go on, be off with you.'

Cecil's face was bright red as he looked round and then up towards Len, who stood on the promenade, his hands raised in a shrug, his face grimacing, as if to say that he hadn't known.

'You'd better go, Cess. Don't worry about it, we weren't

to know. Len stayed up there as he didn't fancy taking his shoes and socks off.'

'Well, if Cecil has to go, I'm going!'

'Me too, Dot. Wait up. I'm coming with you.'

As Elsie reached her shoes, Millie caught up with her. 'Are you sure you're all right, Elsie? I'd hate to hurt you, only I thought—'

'Of course I am, you daftie. Let me get me shoes on, then I'll give you a hug.' Getting her boots on was not an easy job with wet-stockinged feet, and Elsie envied Millie slipping her feet into those comfy-looking pumps.

But she was amused at Millie saying, 'We should have taken our stockings off – we're going to get blisters now.'

'What? And show all we've got to everyone? That'd be a peepshow and a half.'

'I suppose that's why it's ladies only at certain times, to allow for privacy.'

'Oh, I don't know. Look around you, Millie. If you looked like most of these women, would you want to lift your skirts to have a dip, if there was a man within two hundred yards? They've made the rule to hide their own embarrassment.'

'You could be right. Oh dear, I know it's naughty to mock, but look at those two. If they even sat down to take their stockings off, they'd never get up again.'

'Millie!' With this pretend indignation, Elsie burst out laughing. 'Come on, I'll race you back, seeing as though I've already lost the race that Dot challenged me to.'

By the time they reached the promenade they were both giggling like schoolgirls. Elsie's hair had come loose and hung around her face. As she gathered the ribbon and flicked her hair back to catch it in a ponytail, her eyes caught Len's. His look was one of shock. He stared at her, and Elsie knew that her resolve to forget her feelings for him was never going to be successful. But she had no choice other than to learn to live with them, for as he looked away and into Millie's eyes, she saw something between Len and Millie that was different from the way he looked at her. To Millie, he gave a look of love.

For Elsie, at that moment, the day was spoilt and she wished Len hadn't come with them – or come into their lives at all.

Somehow she endured the rest of the day and the journey home and, exhausted, managed to sleep well.

The next day when she rose, Elsie felt unsettled and sad, so she took herself along to the churchyard. She sat next to the grave leaning against the wall, talking her problems over with her mum. This helped her, and strengthened her resolve to try and forget Len – at least in the way she had been thinking about him. And she steeled herself to be in his company without longing to be in his arms.

I can do this, Mum. I can. You did. You had to carry on without the man you loved . . . I hope it wasn't Millie's dad, but I think it was, from what you said about loving the man who'd fathered me. But oh, Mum, I wish I could shake this feeling that he had something to do with your death. It's eating away at me.

When she arrived home, she found that both Cecil and Rene had gone out. The walls of the flat seemed to close in on her, and her sadness at the loss of her mum, which always came out in private moments, overwhelmed her. She cried her eyes out, lying on her bed, knowing that some of her tears were for a love she would never realize.

* * *

When Monday dawned, Elsie felt less like going to work than she'd ever done, but somehow she dragged herself there. She stuffed every strand of hair into her mob cap, annoyed at it for betraying her.

Dot's incessant chatter as they walked to work – going on and on about the wonderful weekend and all they'd done – nearly drove her mad. So much so that she changed her mind and couldn't wait to reach the factory. She was surprised, when they did, to see the boss's car outside. Millie had said that her father would be away all next week.

Set to washing jam jars again, Elsie threw herself into the work and lost herself in the rhythm of the new system Lucy had implemented before she left. Suddenly, her name was called. Turning, she saw Chambers gesturing to her to go to him. *What now? I just want to be left alone.*

'Get yourself into the stores and fetch some more jam jars. Leave these two to carry on. With this new method, you're getting through them, and I don't want you running out. We've a rush job on, and need to keep a steady supply to the fillers.'

This was a job Elsie loathed. She wasn't strong enough for it, but dared not say so, because one of the criteria for working in the factory was that you were strong enough to haul heavy loads.

'Go on. Grab that trolley and get a few boxes of jars. And do it now!'

Elsie jumped. Her nerves were on edge, and had been since her mum's murder. It was as if Chambers knew this, because he seemed to pick on her every moment that he could. Sighing, she grabbed the trolley and went towards the stores. Her objection wasn't solely because of the heavy work, but because the storeroom was a big, lonely place.

She liked to be where there were people and noise and she could keep herself busy, to give less time for dwelling on all that was in her mind.

Making her way backwards into the stores, Elsie let go of the door to manoeuvre the whole of the trolley through it, before going back to the light switch, hoping to get there before the door swung closed and she was left in darkness.

But the door banged shut. Standing still, she listened. Her fear was making it difficult to move. There wasn't a sound, other than the muffled activities of the factory floor. Telling herself not to be silly, she moved slowly in the direction of the light switch, holding out her hand to feel for any obstructions.

When she reached the wall, she ran her hands over its rough surface, trying to locate the switch. A warm, clammy hand covered hers.

Elsie's heart banged against her chest. Sweat broke out over her body. She couldn't speak or cry out, as fear held her like a statue.

The hand came round her and covered her mouth. A great strength lifted her, as if she was a doll. Struggling for all she was worth made no difference. Whoever had hold of her was oblivious to her kicking, even though she landed a few heavy blows to his shins. Suddenly she felt herself toppling forward and landing heavily on what she knew were the sacks of packing material used to steady the jars in the crates.

A noise made her think someone had come into the stores, and she hoped with all her heart that they had, and that this would deter her attacker. But nothing happened; no one came to help her or to frighten this beast off her.

The weight of the man took the breath from her. Before

she could recover, his hands lifted her skirt. Her mind screamed what he intended to do. With an extreme effort, propelled by sheer terror, she bent her back. The movement dislodged him. Scrambling to her feet, Elsie stumbled in the direction of the door and groped once again for the light switch.

The store flooded with light. Grabbing the door handle, she turned it frantically. Locked! Frenziedly she shook it with all her might, but it didn't budge.

'You won't get out, so why not come back here and do as I ask. I'll pay you well.'

Elsie swung round, then gasped as she looked into the face of her boss . . . her own father! 'No, I don't want to. I've never . . . Please, just let me go.'

'Oh no. I've been watching you. You have something about you that gets to me. Now, why not be a good girl and let me have my way, eh? I always get it in the end.'

'No. No, I don't want to.'

'I'll pay you well. How does three pounds sound? You lot will do anything for a bit of money.'

'No. Please let me go. I won't say anything. I won't tell on you.'

'You won't get the chance, as you'll be sacked. Now what's it to be? Play ball and line your pockets, or have no job?'

Elsie watched him come closer to her, and her throat constricted. When she could feel his breath on her face, she shrank back.

'I'm warning you. I will force you, and then you'll get the sack. But I mean to have you.'

'You – you're my father!'

For one split second there was a look of horror on his

face. Then one of disbelief, as he shook his head from side to side. She heard him utter, 'My God!' as he backed away from her.

'I don't want anything from you. I just want my job, and to be left alone. I'll never say anything about this. Please, Mr Hawkesfield. My mum, she was murdered; and my little brovvers . . . were taken off me. I need my job, for me and my other brovver.' The tears rolled down Elsie's face, and yet she wasn't conscious of crying, only of feeling a deep desperation.

'You're Kitty's daughter! But I thought . . . I mean, when did you return to work?'

'A bit ago, sir.'

'Look, I'm sorry. I didn't realize. But it makes no odds to your standing. I'm not recognizing you as mine. Nor do I want anything to do with you.' He stood tall, his expression evil. 'And if anything about this gets out, you'll be sorry. You may even end up like . . . Anyway, I can promise you, you won't want to live.'

Elsie wondered what he had been going to say; it was as if he was threatening to torture her or even kill her. And what did he mean by 'end up like?' Like what? Her mum! Yes, she was sure he was going to say that she would end up like her mum.

His tone was lower – more menacing – when he spoke again. 'So you are the one who told the police that I had a relationship with your mother, aren't you? You put them on to hounding me, didn't you? Well, I'm glad she's dead; she was a filthy prostitute who'd go with anyone.'

'Don't talk about my mum like that!' Strength came into Elsie that she didn't know she possessed. She looked into the eyes of her father and lifted her head in defiance. 'I've changed my mind, and I'll tell everyone what you just tried to do to me. And I don't care what happens to me. It was you who set my mum on the path she took. You didn't stand by her, when she found herself pregnant. Folk like you should be stopped, with all your money and your power. You're rotten, and I'm ashamed to know that you're my father!'

With this, a change came over him. His face went blank. His mouth dropped open.

Elsie stood, transfixed, as he slumped to the ground. Cowering against the door, unsure what to do, she willed him to get up. But he lay very still and she knew instinctively that he was dead. *Oh God, help me. Help me.* Turning, she banged on the door.

'Get away from that door. There's no helping him now, but you can help me.'

Chambers appeared from behind the shelves. Elsie stared at him. His flies were unbuttoned, showing all he had. She couldn't sort this out in her mind for a moment. Then it dawned on her. *Oh God, it was him that I heard. Mr Hawkesfield wouldn't have taken any notice because he thought Chambers was just locking the door.*

It was all too clear what Chambers had started to do to himself. Elsie felt sick.

'No. Please don't . . . No – o – o!'

Chambers had hold of her wrist and was pulling her away from the door. When he reached the sacks Hawkesfield had taken her to, he growled, 'I heard everything, and can make things very nasty for you. I'll make it look as though you killed him – your second murder, as I still believe you had something to do with Ruth's death. I'll say that I witnessed it this time – that is, unless you play ball. Now lie down and get your knickers off.'

Elsie couldn't speak. Her mind filled with the terror of the prison cell, and showed her once again the possibility of being hanged. Tears leaked from her eyes and mingled with her snot as she lifted her frock, pulled down her knickers and stepped out of them.

Chambers's voice was low and gruff as he bade her lie down.

The sacks took her weight. Elsie closed her eyes and thought of her mum – floating on the cloud, saying she would look after her. Then a pain seared through her groin and she took in a deep breath that held a groan.

'I knew you'd like it. Good girl.'

This brought Elsie fully conscious to what was happening: the feel of Chambers inside her, the stink of his breath, his sweat droplets wetting her face and his guttural moans.

'No-o-o!' In one movement she arched her back and rolled over, dislodging him. She sat up.

Chambers's face contorted and a filthy, deep moan came from him, then he slumped down onto the sacks.

Elsie scrambled up and put her knickers back on. 'You're disgusting. A disgusting pig!' Her body slumped and she leaned against the shelves.

'Shut up! Shurrup, I tell you!' Chambers got a handkerchief out of his pocket and wiped himself, and then the mess he'd made on the sacks, before buttoning up his flies. 'Don't even think of saying anything. You're a bitch – a tease. This is your own fault. You've driven me mad for weeks, flaunting yourself as you go about your job. Your overall's been undone and you're only half-clothed underneath.'

'I haven't! Not in that way. It was hot – boiling, unbearably hot. We all loosened our clothing.'

'But not everyone looked like you – and you knew it.

Then you went out on strike and helped that Lucy. I told Mr Hawkesfield to sack you, but he had other things on his mind. He'd have paid you well. You'd have wanted for nuffink. Nuffink! And all that about him being your father – you tried that on, didn't you? Now this is what's going to happen.' He'd done the last button up and came towards her. Elsie turned and went to run, but he grabbed her. His face came close to her, his tone menacing, and he told her, 'Like I said, I ain't convinced that you had nuffink to do with that Ruth's death. And now this. Well, I ain't leaving it there. I don't trust you not to say anything about what I just did. So I'm going to make it look as though you killed Hawkesfield.'

'No! I let you do that thing to me, didn't I? You promised! And I won't say a word – I can tell you that for nothing. I wouldn't want a soul to know what you did. I'd rather die first.'

Chambers looked into her eyes for a long moment before he said, 'Help me to move him. We'll put him behind the shelves. Look, this is the story then. Mr Hawkesfield told me he was coming in here to do a stock-check. Then I sent you in to get some jars – we'll put some boxes on the trolley, so that it looks like you started to do that. Then you went round the back of the shelves to get the bigger jars, and you saw him on the floor and, in your panic, you banged on the door and called me in. Right?'

Elsie nodded.

'Get his other arm then, and pull for all you're worth.'

Desperate for this to work, Elsie put all her strength into pulling the body.

Panting for breath, Chambers told her, 'Now I'll put some crates onto your trolley. You get that broom and sweep where we've dragged him. And be quick about it. I'm saving your skin here. That bloody cleaner's never swept this floor in a month of Sundays – you can see a trail in the dust.'

Elsie felt she was going to retch. She swallowed hard as she put her back into the sweeping.

With this done, Chambers said, 'Now, you run out and make a fuss. Tell someone to go for the doctor. Say that you've found Mr Hawkesfield collapsed, and that I'm with him.'

Elsie had no problem obeying this order. She ran out of the storeroom, making a sound between a yell and a moan, which told of how she felt her world crashing down around her once more.

Chapter Nineteen

Elsie

'What is it? Elsie, love. Oh dear, come on, mate, you're bound to have these moments. Get yourself together or they'll be sending you home. And you know what that means – someone'll soon take your place.'

Elsie slumped into Peggy's arms. 'No, no, it's . . . it's Mr Hawkesfield – he needs a doctor! Quick, Peggy, he's . . . he's dying!'

'What? Good God! I saw him go into the storeroom earlier. How long have you been in there?'

'I don't know. Chambers sent me . . . He's in there with him. I – I didn't see him – the body . . . I mean, Mr Hawkesfield. I found him just now and banged on the door, and Chambers came in. Help him, Peggy. Send someone for the doctor!'

Peggy looked at her for a moment. Her look held disbelief, but she shouted orders, then held on to Elsie and guided her to the canteen.

'Sit down. I'll go and see what's what. And I'll get someone to send Dot in to sit with you. It'll be all right. You've had a shock, but you'll be all right. I promise.'

* * *

'Elsie? Elsie, mate, what's up? You've been gone ages. There's a right commotion on the main shop floor.'

'I was stacking the trolley, Then . . . then . . . It's Mr Hawkesfield. Oh, Dot, he's dead!'

Dot looked as though someone had taken all the stuffing from her. Her face went white, her hand reached for a chair and she sank down onto it, her bottom making a thud as it hit the wooden seat. 'Dead? How?'

'I don't know. I – I'd put a few cases onto me trolley. I went round the back of the shelves to look for some bigger jars, and there he was!'

'Oh, Elsie. What's going to happen now? They won't think you were responsible, will they?'

'Oh God, Dot – no. They can't do that. He – he must have collapsed.'

Dot was quiet. She looked awful. Elsie couldn't comfort her, because to do so would open her own floodgates, and she didn't want that. When Dot's hand found hers, she held it, trying to convey strength, and yet using it as an anchor for herself.

The door opened and Peggy came in. 'Well, the doctor's on his way, but I'm afraid Hawkesfield's a goner. Good riddance, I say.'

Neither Dot nor Elsie spoke. Elsie couldn't. Despite what had happened – what Mr Hawkesfield, her own father, was going to do to her, and the unhappiness he'd caused her mum – he was Millie's father, and Millie loved him. And although she hadn't got used to the idea, he was her father and Dot's, too.

For all that, he had been a vile man, and Elsie felt repulsion shudder through her as she thought of how he'd also been a greedy, thoughtless man, who, for as long as she'd known him, had taken, not given. How her mum could have loved him was beyond Elsie. And how she could have fallen out with her best mate over him, and not have the support of that friendship, was hard to understand. Elsie knew she would have stood by Dot, but she mustn't judge her mum. They say that love is a powerful thing that can change a person – and her mum's love for that pig of a man had certainly changed her. *Will my love for Len change me?*

'Here you are, I've made you a cuppa. You both look in a daze. I know it's been a shock, but you'll soon forget it.'

'What do you think killed him, Peggy? Does a man just die like that? I mean, fall over dead?'

'He's the first I've ever known, Dot. But he collapsed a couple of weeks back, didn't he? Or so I heard. Maybe he had a weak heart of something. Who knows? Anyway, God knows what will happen to this place. He's only got that daughter of his, as far as I know, and I can't see a girl taking over, though she seems to like being here. It'll most likely be sold, but where does that leave us in the meantime?'

Elsie didn't have an answer to this. Millie was very much on her mind, and she wished she could go to her – be the one to tell her he didn't suffer. But then could she do that, with the lie she would have to tell about having found him, and with all that she'd suffered at the hands of Chambers, still trapped in an ugly ball inside her? Would talking to Millie make it all come out?

Elsie felt Dot fidget beside her. She looked up and saw a tear running down her cheek. 'Dot? Dot, it's all right. We'll be all right.'

'Oh, I'm sorry, Dot, mate.' With this, Peggy moved to stand next to her and put her arm around Dot. 'I didn't mean to upset you. Sup your tea, mate. It'll calm you. It's all a bit of a shock for everyone. Even Chambers isn't shouting the odds and making us all work through this one.'

As if saying his name conjured him up, Chambers walked through the door. He didn't have his usual composure, but gave Elsie a warning look that sent a fear through her so deep that she found it hard to breathe. Then he turned from her and asked, as if nothing was wrong, 'Is there any of that tea left in the pot, Peggy?'

'Yes. Help yerself.'

'Don't get cocky, mate. This don't mean that you can slack. Get me a mug of tea poured, then back to your work. And you, Grimes. But not you, Makin. The police want a word – they're with the body now.'

Seeing that Dot was reluctant to leave, Peggy linked arms with her and took her away. Chambers didn't waste a moment before setting on Elsie. 'Now, you remember what I told you, or you'll be in big trouble.'

Elsie's hate for him intensified. 'I don't see what more you can do to me that's worse than you have done already.'

'Don't be bloody insolent to me, you slut born of a slut!'

Elsie didn't know what happened to her, but something inside snapped and she flew at Chambers. He stumbled backwards and landed on a chair. All reason left Elsie, as she flailed at him with her fists, screaming at him, 'You vile, hateful creature! You'd sell your soul to the devil for a penny, and you'd lick his arse for a favour! Everyone knows how you were in Mr Hawkesfield's pocket. You arranged everything this morning, and then you did that thing to me. You—'

'What the blazes? Elsie!'

Elsie stopped her onslaught and stood and stared at Sergeant Collins as if he was a ghost.

Chambers was the one to speak, and what he said – and the condescending way he said it – betrayed his scheming, sneaky ways more than anything else could have done. 'It's all right, Sergeant. She's had one shock on top of another, and sees me as the instigator of it all. I can understand it. It's not every day, is it, that you are accused by one of your workmates of murder, then your mum's murdered and then you find your boss dead?'

'Quite.'

'She has some twisted notion that, because the evidence I gathered about the accident here led to her arrest, I am responsible for her mum being in a position of trying to get help for Elsie, which led to her mum being done in.'

'Is that what she was doing? We didn't know that. Who did she turn to?'

Elsie was surprised at this, because she was sure she'd told the sergeant that her mum had gone to someone to get help – and who that someone was. But she'd never told Chambers or anyone who would tell him, so how did he know that, and what made him say it now?

Chambers stuttered his reply. 'I – I don't bloody know, do I? She . . . well, that's what folk are saying she did.'

'Who? What folk? I would like to speak to them. I'd like to know what they know. Names, please, Mr Chambers.'

Chambers's face drained of colour. His lips quivered and droplets of sweat ran down his face.

'I'm waiting.'

'I – I don't know who. It's just gossip. Look, I went with a prossie and she told me. All right?'

'What prossie, and when? All of them are well known to us. Could you pick her out, if I lined them up?'

Chambers shook his head.

'Oh? Why not? You looked at her, didn't you?'

Chambers didn't speak.

Elsie stood, transfixed. She understood now that the sergeant was trying to trap Chambers. She looked from the sergeant to Chambers as the realization hit her: *He believes Chambers knows what happened to my mum.* She wanted to scream at him, to tell him that it was Mr Hawkesfield her mum had gone to see, but she caught the sergeant's eye and he warned her, with a look and a slight shake of his head, not to speak. Then he turned his attention back to Chambers.

'Do you own a van, Mr Chambers?'

Chambers stood. His sudden movement sent his chair crashing to the ground. Elsie hardly had time to register what was happening, before Chambers ran for the door. But the sergeant caught up with him and wrestled him to the ground.

'I take it you do own a van. A bit affluent for a jam factory supervisor, aren't you? Are you paid extra for doing dirty jobs then? Is that why you can afford what no one else of your standing can, eh?'

'Let go of me. None of it's true. I didn't do anything. She's the one – I caught her with Hawkesfield just now. At it, they were. The shock of seeing me killed him. She's as bad as her mother, nothing but a prossie. She killed Hawkesfield!'

The sergeant looked over his shoulder at Elsie. His expression asked a question of her, but she could only stare back at him. She heard the click of the handcuffs, watched the sergeant go to the door and heard him call, 'Constable? Ah, there you are. Get this heap of scum into the carriage. By my thinking, he's going to be a guest of ours for quite some time.'

'Yes, guv.'

Then the sound of the door closing, and Elsie knew the questions would come. Could she answer them – should she? What of Millie?

'Elsie, am I right in thinking that something happened today? I mean something more than you finding Mr Hawkesfield dead?'

Elsie could only nod as embarrassment crept over her. The sergeant was a man – how could she tell him what had happened? Besides, telling him would open up a can of worms.

'Look, I know how it is, and I can guess what Mr Hawkesfield's game was. We know his ways. However, there is nothing we can do to him now. But am I guessing right that Chambers had something to do with what happened?'

Elsie nodded.

'You need to tell me, Elsie. You need to make a statement. I'm thinking that Chambers did Mr Hawkesfield's bidding, no matter what he was asked. Now we know that Mr Hawkesfield was one of your mum's customers . . .'

Elsie flinched.

'I'm sorry. This is going to be very painful for you, but in the end you will have achieved justice for your mother. Don't you think that will be worth it?'

'B – but others will be hurt . . . and I—'

'Hawkesfield's family? You're very friendly with his daughter, aren't you? How did that come about? Oh, I know she said she was looking after your welfare because you worked at the family's factory, but that never rang true with us. What's the connection, Elsie? Why are you so concerned about protecting Miss Hawkesfield, even going so far as not wanting to catch your mum's killer?'

Elsie felt trapped. There was nothing she wanted more than to have her mum's killer hanged, but so much else would crumble.

'Elsie, please. We will help you all we can. Look, think of it this way. If Chambers goes free, the chances are that he will kill again – you won't be safe. He has lost his source of power, because that's what Mr Hawkesfield gave him in exchange for favours: power, and more money than he could possibly earn as a supervisor. He'll come to see you as a threat, as you know too much. Men like Chambers have no scruples; they are cunning, they wheel and deal to get what they want, and they don't care what they do to get it. There is no choice, Elsie. You have to tell me everything.'

A sob escaped her. 'I – I have to see Millie.'

'Miss Hawkesfield? I don't think . . . Look, as you are a witness, I can make you tell me. I don't want to do that, Elsie.'

'If I tell you, then please, please, Sergeant, let me speak to Millie. Let me go with you to tell her about her dad.'

'All right. What about Dot? Because I have a feeling she is involved. I even have an idea what this is all about. My constable grew up around here, and he has a theory about you and Dot and Hawkesfield. Do you know what I'm getting at?'

Elsie lowered her head. Her tears dripped onto her pinny as she nodded.

The sergeant released an audible sigh. 'There's a lot to go through, Elsie, but you can do it – for your mum and your brother. Cecil deserves to know that your mum's killer has been brought to justice.'

'Yes, but at what cost?' she almost whispered, even though she wanted to scream it out.

'There is always a cost. And often it is the wrong ones who have to pay. There will be a lot of scandal, Elsie – we can't avoid that – but none of what comes out will be your fault. You are the victim. We will protect you.'

'I – I just feel so alone.'

The sergeant coughed. Then he blew his nose loudly. 'Tell me everything, then I'll get Dot for you, and we will all three go and inform Hawkesfield's family. You can both come with me.'

'Can I tell Millie? Please, Sergeant, please let me.'

'We'll go together. I have to formally give the news to the next of kin, but I can allow you to have a moment with Miss Hawkesfield, while bearing in mind that she may want to be with her mother and not listen to what you have to say.'

At the end of her telling, Elsie waited.

The sergeant had his head bent, and had pinched his lips between his forefinger and thumb. When he looked up, he said, 'Elsie, I'm so sorry, but I can't leave you with Miss Hawkesfield after what you have told me has happened to you. You need to be examined by a doctor. Look, I will take you with me, and Dot. But you will have to leave with me, as I will need a doctor's evidence.'

In the sergeant's car Elsie and Dot held hands. 'What's this all about, Else? Have you told the sergeant about us?'

'I had to. You see . . .' Telling Dot the truth about what had happened to their father, and what Chambers did, cost Elsie dearly. Dot put her arm round her, and Elsie leaned her head on Dot's shoulder. 'It's all got to come out, Dot. Everything.'

Dot was silent for a moment. When she spoke she sounded

fearful. 'You mean, about me mum going with Mr Hawkesfield and . . . Oh, Elsie. I can't bear it. What about Millie? Neither she, nor me mum, deserves this.'

'None of us do, Dot.'

'No, I didn't mean . . . Oh, Else. You're least deserving of it all. And for that thing to be done to you.' They both cried and held onto each other in a tight hug.

'Listen to me, both of you.' The sergeant turned in his seat, next to the driver. 'If things go the way I think they will, you won't have any say in what comes out. I'm sorry. Really sorry for you both. You didn't ask for any of this. But there is very little I can do. You will have to be brave and very strong.'

'Will you drop me at home, Sergeant? I need to tell me mum,' Dot said.

'Yes, but we can't come in with you. It is vital that we get to Mrs Hawkesfield as soon as we can.'

'Dot?'

'I have to do this, Else. Me mum must know. I – I need to be with her. Tell Millie that I'm sorry – really sorry – and will always be there for her. But me mum comes first.'

Elsie felt the last shards of her world splinter as Dot got out of the car and didn't say goodbye or turn to wave to her.

Leaning back, she closed her eyes. *It's all over – everything. I've lost all I had.*

When they pulled up outside the house, Elsie was surprised to see that it wasn't a huge, imposing building with a long drive, as she had imagined, but then maybe Millie's Leeds home was like that. This one was large and double-fronted, with six windows on the front and a huge oak door.

The outside was deceptive, because when the door was opened by the butler and they were shown in, they entered a huge hall with a staircase spiralling up from it and many doors leading off it. They were shown into the room on the left, a lovely room in soft greys and deep reds. 'Mrs Hawkesfield is not at home, sir. She is away for another week. Miss Hawkesfield is here.'

'May we speak with her, please?'

When the butler left the room, Elsie implored the sergeant again to let her see Millie alone to explain.

'I cannot do that, Elsie. I have already explained that I have a duty to inform her formally. And then, if she wants to, she can have some private time with you.'

The door opened and Millie walked in. She looked at Elsie and then at the sergeant. 'Elsie? Are you all right? What has happened?' Her voice shook, her face drained of colour and she again looked from one to the other.

'Please sit down, Miss Hawkesfield.'

'Is it bad news? I mean, what . . . ?'

Elsie, who'd not spoken, left the sergeant's side and hurried to her half-sister. 'Oh, Millie. Millie.'

Millie held herself stiffly and stared into Elsie's eyes. 'Father . . . Is my father hurt?'

Seeing Millie looking so lost, so afraid, gave Elsie the strength she needed to cope. But, more than that, to help Millie to do so. 'Sit with me on the sofa, Millie.'

She allowed herself to be guided to the sofa.

'Millie, there's bad news. I'm so sorry, but I'm here for you. I'll help you.'

Elsie held onto Millie's hand as the sergeant told her, 'Miss Hawkesfield, I'm very sorry, but there is no easy way of telling you that your father passed away about two hours ago.'

'What? No! How? . . . Elsie?'

Elsie put her arm round Millie. 'We think it was his heart. He . . . he didn't suffer, he just folded and . . . died. Oh, Millie. Millie, I know your pain.'

'Miss Hawkesfield, we need to inform your mother. How is it best to do that?'

Millie looked up, her face ashen, her expression unreadable. 'Where is my father?'

'They took his body to the hospital. If we can contact your mother, then we can follow whatever instructions she has for us.'

'They have recently had a telephone installed in our home in Leeds. Father went to oversee it – he was to stay, but he came home . . . He never said he was ill. He was agitated, but he didn't look ill.'

'My dear, when he collapsed last time, and I wanted to talk to him, your doctor told me that your father had a weak heart. He intimated that he was in danger of going out like a light. Did your father not tell you this?'

'No.' Millie shook her head.

'Can we get you anything, Miss. A cup of tea – or water?'

'No. I'll be all right. Thank you for bringing Elsie with you.' As she said this, Millie held Elsie's hand tighter, and Elsie could feel her trembling.

'Look, I think it best that you give me the address where your mother is, and I telephone the local police to go and see her. They will help her all they can. Has she the means of transport to get home? If not, I can arrange that for her, too.'

'Yes, we have a car and driver in residence at our Leeds home. He will bring her. Or she may want me to go up to her.' All of this was said in a shocked whisper.

The sergeant looked at Elsie. Then he took a deep breath. 'There is more to the story, Miss Hawkesfield. We have a man in custody. Things . . . well, there are some unsavoury facts to come out, about your father and what he was possibly involved in. I think you may need to ask your solicitor to engage a lawyer. As for the details, Elsie wants to tell you those herself. It is unavoidable that you know them, I'm afraid. Now, is there anything I can do for you? Can I contact anyone to look after the factory, or to close it for a while?'

Millie looked even more dazed than before. 'Chambers – he . . . he'll look after things.'

'He cannot do that.'

Millie's head swivelled round to stare at Elsie, as the sergeant told her that Chambers was the man in custody.

'Elsie, what's happened? Please tell me. I can't take all of this in.'

The sergeant was quiet as Elsie told all that had happened. Millie simply stared into Elsie's eyes.

'My God, Elsie! Oh, my poor darling. And my father is to blame. What we thought happened actually did – your mum did go to my father . . . And Chambers! Oh, Elsie.'

They collapsed into each other's arms.

'Girls, I can only say how very sorry I am.'

Millie composed herself a little and nodded at the sergeant, before turning back to Elsie. 'Oh, Elsie, what are we going to do?'

'I don't know. I thought you'd not want to know me, Millie. I've brought nothing but pain to you. But I didn't mean to. I didn't. And Dot . . . Oh, Millie, Dot wouldn't speak to me. She . . . she's afraid that her mum won't be able to stand all the scandal. Because everything will come out: how your dad is ours, and how he might have had a hand in murdering my mum.'

'Me not want to know you! Oh, my dear Elsie, how can you forgive what my father has done to you?'

They clung together once more, each feeling the other's pain; both lost, not knowing what would happen next or how they would cope with it.

Chapter Twenty

Millie

Millie sat with her mother in her sitting room. The sergeant had just left, after delivering the news that Chambers had been charged with the murder of Katherine Makin, Elsie's mum, and saying that Father had paid him to carry out the killing.

Mama had been quiet for a long time. When she spoke, her voice was steady. 'I knew he was wicked, but this! I wish . . . No, I don't wish that, otherwise I wouldn't have you, my darling.'

Millie had sat down on the rug at her mama's knee. She didn't know what to say or do. When Mama next spoke, what she said didn't seem to accord with the news they'd heard.

'We will have his body taken back to Leeds and arrange for his funeral to take place there.'

'Yes, Mama.'

'Our solicitor in Leeds holds your father's Will, but I happen to know that he has left everything here in London to you, and the house in Leeds to me, along with a sum of money for us both. I want you to think about what you are going to do, dear. I advise that you sell everything and let us go home together. I don't want either of us to be in London when the horrid trial takes place.'

The moment had come. Millie couldn't put off telling her mama the full truth any longer. 'Mama, there are more shocking things about Father that I haven't told you yet. Oh, Mama, I'm so sorry, but I'm going to have to hurt you even more than you are already hurt. But I want you to hear this from me, not read about it in the papers.'

'Don't cry, darling. Whatever it is, after this, nothing about your father will shock me. I feel so much for you in all of this, as I have known about your father's weaknesses for a long time.'

'I know you suspected this, Mama, but . . . well, Father has another two daughters besides me.'

'Oh God! And you knew this?'

'Yes, Mama, and . . . and I know them, too.'

'What? You mean those girls you've been helping? The funeral you went to – it's them? They are your half-sisters!'

'I found out at the funeral. I didn't want to hurt you. I thought I never need tell you. But . . . but it will all come out. You see, there was more to Father's death . . .'

By the time Millie had finished telling the whole sordid tale, both she and her mama were sobbing in each other's arms.

'That poor girl. How is she? Was she hurt?'

A small sob of relief came from Millie. Mama wasn't condemning or blaming Elsie. 'I think she must have been, but with the shock I had over Father's death, I didn't pay the terrible thing that happened to her much attention. I need to go to her, Mama. I haven't seen her since she came here with the sergeant to tell me. He – he took her to a doctor, straight from here. That was two days ago.'

'Yes. You must go to her. She has been through a terrible ordeal. If she wants to come here, bring her back with you and we will care for her. Bring them both.'

This both shocked and pleased Millie. 'I will ask them, Mama, but Elsie has a brother and a . . . well, sort of aunt, and Dot lives with her mum. I cannot see either of them wanting to leave them and come here. But I will see that they have all they need and . . . Mama, I need to get the factory open again. We—'

'No, Millie – you can't, darling. How can you?'

'There's the workers to think of – they must all be frantic with worry over their jobs – and there are orders to fulfil. Some of which I was involved in securing. I have to do something. I've spoken to Len. He said he will help me. He can get a caretaker manager in, someone who knows the business well. I will go tomorrow morning and meet this manager and make a statement to the workers. Len has the payroll and he is contacting all the workers today.'

'Millie, no. You can't do that! I accept that you have to get the factory open, but please leave it to Len and this manager to deal with. The workers might turn on you. You could be in danger.'

'I won't be. They need to hear the truth from me, and my plans. I think they will respect me for that. The women who work in the factory are Cockneys and I have found that they are a different breed, Mama. They are strong, they stick by their own and they pull together. Father has left a terrible legacy, but I want all of these women – my workforce – to know that neither you nor I are responsible. I think I should tell them about Dot and Elsie, too, and give them better positions – shares in the business even. But all of that will come in the future, and Len will advise me along the way.

He was shocked, but very understanding. As soon as the Will is read, he wants me to have a meeting with his father. In the meantime, he is dealing with my requests through our solicitor.'

'Oh, Millie, I don't know where we got you from. You are good and kind, clever and very courageous. I'm really proud of you.'

'I got those traits from you, Mama. You have shown them all, especially courage. All these years you have kept your dignity and thought of nothing but protecting me – not that you went the right way about it, but I forgive you for that.'

They smiled at one another, and Millie rose. Kissing the top of her mama's head, she told her that she would instruct Ruby to call the car for her, as she didn't feel like riding her horse to Elsie's.

When she arrived at Elsie's, Millie was greeted by both Elsie and Dot. She'd been worrying about Dot and the way she'd reacted to poor Elsie's plight.

The three of them went into a hug. None of them had a dry eye when they came out of it.

'How are you both? I'm sorry I couldn't come sooner. I've been with my mama. She needed me, but she is feeling stronger today.' She didn't really have to ask Elsie, for her gaunt look and sore red eyes told her what an awful two days she must have had.

'Come in, Millie, and you, Ruby – that's if Millie thinks . . .'

'Yes, Ruby knows everything. But I'll leave my driver sitting outside.'

'Eeh, lass, I'm right sorry for you all,' Ruby said. 'I've

never known owt like what's happened, especially to you, Elsie.'

'Ta, Ruby. Sit down, both of you. Would you like a mug of tea? I've just made a pot.'

When they were all sipping their tea, Millie asked after Cecil.

'He's still at work – he's getting on really well and works long hours. Speaking of which, I heard that we're expected back tomorrow. A messenger came.'

'I am opening the factory again tomorrow, but you two don't need to be there. You see, I feel I must make an announcement to the workers, and I want to ask your permission to tell them the whole story – everything. They need to know that you are my sisters.'

Dot's gasp was audible.

'Dot, you have to realize they will find everything out when the trial begins. Then they will feel as though we have been deceitful. I think it much better that they are told from me – it will nip any gossip in the bud.'

'But me mum . . . She's broken-hearted. She can't bear it all.'

'Dot.' Elsie spoke in a gentle voice. 'You know, luv, there's been tittle-tattle about you not being your dad's for years. You know how it was – how your dad told everyone that your mum wasn't having his kid, before they married. Then, with your mum not having any more babies, how the story has kept going. I think Millie is right. If everything is told to our workmates, then they can't speculate, or get a shock when the trial comes. And your mum has accepted that everyone will have to know then.'

'She has, but she ain't happy. And how will it all look, when we go back to work? They're all going to think we get favours, because of who we are.'

'Dot, I understand your concerns. It is going to be awful for me to stand up and admit to everyone what my father was really like, but I am hoping that, in being honest with everyone, they will be understanding of me and how I feel, and of both of you.'

'But they won't accept us the same way.'

'Yes, things will change – they are bound to. I am not at liberty to say how everything will work out, as my father's Will hasn't been read, but I will look after you both. You're my sisters. I couldn't do much up until now, but now that my mama knows, I can. I want you both to come and live with me.'

Millie saw Ruby swivel her head and knew this had shocked her. Dot and Elsie looked astounded.

'I can't. I can't leave me mum, Millie.'

'I know, Dot, but I wanted to ask you, and it is a genuine request. I want you both near me, and to know that you're all right.'

'And I can't leave Cecil, Millie. Or Rene, although she has gone back to her old ways. I think a lot of her, and this is her home.'

'I don't think you should worry about Rene, Elsie. I don't know why you don't kick her out. She's thrown your kindness back in your face and is causing you problems now.'

Elsie didn't answer this from Dot.

'I understand, and I knew those would be your answers. But I won't leave you living here. I will sort something out. Mama is going to live in Leeds – she has friends up there, and a cousin of her own age – so I will have the house to myself. Maybe, if Cecil agreed, it would be easier for you to live with me, Elsie? I would love him to come, too. But we can talk about everything, once the funeral is over. In the meantime I'm going to give you both enough money to cover your wages and more, as I don't want you working on the factory floor any longer.'

They both thanked her, and Millie could see the relief on their faces. Then Elsie surprised and pleased her by saying, 'I want to come in with you tomorrow, Millie. I want to face all my mates and keep my head held high. I haven't done anything to be ashamed of. And I think they'll appreciate you, and us, being honest with them.'

'Thank you, Elsie. I think it will be better if you do come with me. But after I have said my piece I won't stay at the factory, and you can leave with me if you want to.'

Elsie nodded. 'I'll make me mind up as it happens.'

'Yes, that's a good idea, and, Elsie, we won't say anything about what Chambers did to you. Have you heard from the sergeant? Has he prosecuted Chambers for that crime, too?'

'Yes, he called round. He said the doctor confirmed there was evidence that I'd been – well . . . there was bruising and . . . blood, which showed I had been—'

Millie put out her hand to Elsie. 'I'm so sorry. I hate what happened to you, my dear Elsie.'

There was a silence, which Dot broke. 'I'm coming in tomorrow, too. I've decided. I can't leave you both to face it. Mum will have to understand. Like you say, everyone is going to know soon anyway.'

'Oh, Dot, are you sure? I think seeing us all together will make a great deal of difference.'

'I'm not sure of that, Millie – you don't know these women – but I feel bad about how I treated Elsie. You know that, don't you, Else? I need to start making that up to you now. I'll be by your side, mate, no matter what you have to go through.'

Millie watched her sisters hug. It tore her heart to see how frail Elsie was. Reaching for her bag, she took out an envelope each. 'There. Now while I am in Leeds, if you need anything, you can call on Len. He is helping me with everything, and will help you with anything you need him to. I have written on the envelopes how you can contact him. You see, the funeral is to be held in Leeds.'

'Oh, Millie, if it had been here, we would have come – wouldn't we, Dot?'

Dot didn't answer. Millie understood. This was all so much more difficult for Dot, who saw everything in terms of how it would affect her mother. Millie wondered if Mrs Grimes had changed, in the way she said she would at Elsie's mum's funeral; or if she was still controlling Dot, using different tactics than beating her.

Millie's nerves jangled the next morning. For all her bravado the day before, now that she had to carry out her plan to speak to all the workers, she wondered if she was up to it. A message had gone out to the factory workers that she would address them, before any vats or any machinery were switched on. Now, as she stood on the bottom step of the stairs that led to the office and looked round at a sea of faces, she wished she was anywhere but here. Swallowing hard, she began.

'Good morning, everyone. Most of you know who I am, but for those who don't, I am Miss Hawkesfield. I'm addressing you today to try and allay your fears, and to put you in the picture about things that you will find out, once the trial of Mr Chambers begins. I thought it only fair that you, as my loyal workforce, should know a few things about the factory's future and, therefore, about your own.

'This here is Mr Ellington. He is very experienced in our trade, and is going to manage the factory for the time being. I know you have a lot of grievances and that your working conditions are not what they should be. I mean to change that.'

A few mumblings arose at this.

'But I cannot do that overnight. Mr Ellington will work closely with you over the next few weeks, and he will see where there are faults and will put right what he can – reporting to me if there are any major problems that haven't an easy way of fixing them. But you will appreciate that I have my father's funeral to attend, and I need to be with my family.'

Again a few mutterings – one comment reached Millie's ears and pain shot through her on hearing 'Good riddance'. She'd coped well, but today she was feeling the loss of her father more than she had done in the last few days. Happy memories had visited her during the night and had got her weeping for what might have been.

'You will all be paid for a full week this week, as it wasn't your fault you couldn't work. But may I ask you to pull out all the stops to try and fulfil the orders that we have? If anyone can work overtime, please put your name forward to Mr Ellington and he will sort out the hours for you all. Any extra hours done will be paid at a time and a half.'

The mutterings this time were favourable, but Millie wondered how that would change, now that the moment was upon her.

'I – I want to give you some information, which some of you who have worked here for many years may already have surmised. It is painful to me, in that I have to stand here and admit what I have found out about my father.'

There was a hush. All eyes were on her.

'I am telling you this because the nature of the trial will involve my late father, and because I want, above all, to recognize my sisters . . .'

Heads turned. The women had shocked expressions.

'Elsie and Dot, well, they . . . they are my half-sisters.'

More than a mumble burst out then. Mr Ellington stepped in. 'Please, everyone. Please give Miss Hawkesfield a chance. This is very difficult for her. She has no obligation to be this honest with you all, but she respects you all. Please quieten down and respect her.'

This did the trick. Millie doubted that any of them had thought she was doing this out of respect for them.

'I understand what a shock this is to you. But you need to know, because in due course both Dot and Elsie will leave the shop floor and work alongside me, as we – with the help and advice of others – take over the running of this factory. Now I know we are only young, and that is why I have said it will all be done with the help of others. You, too, will have a part to play. Elsie and Dot know what needs changing, and will work closely with me to make those changes, but both – like me – have been through a great deal and need a break from work for the time being. Their absence will give you all time to adapt to their new status in the business, and in life. They, like me, didn't ask for any of this to happen to us. And we need your understanding and cooperation to help us adjust, and to make Swift's Jam Factory the very best place for its workers, and the very best producer of jam.'

There was a complete silence for a moment. Then a woman who stood at the front said, 'I'm Peggy Farrow. I've worked here for more years than I care to number. I think what you've done today, Miss, was a very brave thing, if you pardon me saying so. And I, for one, am with you. With all three of you. It's no surprise to me, what you've told us. Just a confirmation of what I thought was the truth. I didn't like your old man; he was rotten through and through. But I like you, and I'm willing to work for you.' She looked around her. 'It sounds to me like we've landed on our feet at last, girls, and we can help make this a success. What d'you all think, eh?'

A cheer went up and shouts of 'You're right, Peggy' and 'I'll give it a go'. Another woman spoke, once all this quietened down. 'I want to say that although what Peggy said about your old man is the truth, I, for one, am sorry for you. He was your father, and no doubt you had a different view of him than we did. It sounds to me as though you've had a lot to take on board these last few days. And, like Peggy, I think you are a brave young woman. And if anyone can keep this factory going, you can.'

After the cheer died down, Millie swallowed the lump in her throat and reached for Elsie's and Dot's hands. 'Thank you, everyone. I am very grateful to you all. We all are.'

'Right, come on, ladies. Let's have you all back to your stations, please.'

'Oo-er, we ain't been called "ladies" before, Peggy.'

'No, we ain't, but if we behave right, that's what we should be called, Edna. So let's do as Mr Ellington says and get to work. We've orders to fulfil.'

As the women filed to their stations, Millie turned to go up the stairs. 'Will you come up with us, Elsie and Dot?'

When they reached the office, Millie could see that it was all a bit overwhelming for her half-sisters.

'If you want to go home, it's all right to do so. But if

you can wait a while, I thought we'd go to the tea shop together and have a cup of tea, as I won't be able to see you both for a while.'

'We'll wait. It just feels strange, don't it, Dot?'

'It does. Like we don't belong anywhere now. Not on the factory floor, nor up here.'

'That will pass. Don't worry about it. I promise I'll be with you every step of the way until you grow in confidence.'

Both girls nodded, but didn't look convinced. Millie felt sorry for them, because Dot was right: it did seem as if they belonged nowhere at the moment, but she would change that. However, she couldn't do anything until she knew the exact terms of the Will, and had her meeting with Len and his father, to hear how the finances of the business looked.

'I only have a few questions, Miss Hawkesfield,' Mr Ellington said, 'and then I am sure I will cope until you are back next week. Firstly, I understand that if any bills come in, I am to refer them to Mr Lefton?'

'Yes. He has said he will come in each day to make sure you have everything you need, on the financial side of the business.'

'Good. Well, I am a little concerned that I cannot be on the factory floor all the time. I rather liked the attitude of the woman called Peggy. What do you think of her?'

'Yes, she seemed to be able to rally everyone, and everyone listened to her. What are you thinking?'

'I wondered what Miss Grimes and Miss Makin think of her being made up to supervisor? I need someone to keep everything flowing downstairs.'

It was Elsie who spoke up first. 'Peggy's a good woman and a good worker. She has a temper, but that keeps the rest doing as she bids; and while they all love and admire her, they are wary of her, too. You'd do right to make her supervisor, Millie – don't you think so, Dot?'

Dot, as usual, was struck dumb, but did nod her head.

'Well, that's settled then.'

'I'll put her on a trial period.'

'Thank you, Mr Ellington. And thank you for stepping in like this. You come highly recommended.'

Millie thought she couldn't thank Len enough for bringing Mr Ellington to her, or for all he'd done since her father had died – yes, besides being her friend, Len was their bank manager and adviser, but he really had gone the extra mile for her.

'If there's nothing else, I think we would like to go now, Mr Ellington.'

'Of course. No, everything is fine. I have toured the factory a number of times while it has been closed and know all about the workings of it. I'll make sure the orders are sent out on time, even if I have to join the workforce and be hands-on! My first job will be to get Peggy to choose a few workers from the gate. I've a mind that she knows most of them and will know if they are good and reliable. Then I'll work out a shift pattern with the workers and try to keep production going for at least fifteen hours each day.'

'That is all very reassuring to me. Thank you. Goodbye, Mr Ellington.'

'Well, what did you think?'

They sat in the almost-empty tearoom on the corner of Staple Street, sipping hot tea. Millie had ordered a plate of biscuits, but none of them had touched them.

'I think you did well, Millie. Really well, and the women took it all in a much better way than I thought they would.

It felt very strange to be – well . . . known for who I really am. It's as if, like Dot said, we don't belong in any world now. Not our own, and not yours.'

'That will change, I promise you. And mostly it will be down to how you handle it with those you live and work with. When they see that you haven't changed, they'll soon be as comfortable as ever around you. But, you know, you aren't on your own with these thoughts, as I feel out of my depth, too. I never dreamed that at such a young age I would have so much responsibility. I only know that I'm going to do my best. And with your help – both of you – I might stand a bit of a chance.'

'I'll be all the help I can to you, Millie. But I need time. I can't just change my life. And there is so much to face in the near future, with the trial and everything. And much more to come out, which the women I've known all my life will learn of.'

'I know, Elsie. All we can do is support each other. We can get through this if we stick together. We can.'

Elsie looked down at her hands.

'Millie's right, Else. We're all in the same boat. And what one has to face, we'll face together.'

Elsie smiled at Dot. And then she turned to Millie and smiled at her. 'We will, won't we, Millie?'

'Yes – everything. As three young women, we're nothing on our own, but together we're a force to be reckoned with.' She held out her hands to them, and each took hold of one.

They didn't speak again, but sat there with their own thoughts, and Millie sent up a prayer that she could be strong enough for these lovely sisters of hers, and make their world a better place. And she wished to make them feel safe and comfortable, and not lost in the new world they were entering. Her second prayer was for help in the task she had ahead of her: to make the factory a success and a good place, where the workers were happy and their safety was paramount.

Chapter Twenty-One

Elsie

Elsie stared out at the rain. The long, hot summer that had extended into the early part of October had finally given way to what autumn should be like. But she didn't care. Her mind wasn't in a place to care much about anything, other than how her life was and how it could be. Getting up from the sofa, she crossed to the fire and gave it a poke. She'd been listening to Dot moaning on about how things were, and felt like screaming at her.

'Look, Dot, luv, things have changed for us, whether we like it or not.'

'I know, mate. All I'm saying is that I'm not sure I want them to. Oh, I know we haven't had the best of lives, but it was the life we knew – what we were born to – and I don't know if I can adjust or not.'

Elsie understood. She'd gone over it herself many times, turning her mind in somersaults – one minute feeling excited, the next afraid, and the next that she wasn't ready for change. But into all this came the nightmares, the feeling of being alone with the horror of what had happened to her, which no one spoke about. No one asked her how she was feeling. If they had, she could tell them that she was going mad.

'How much do you think things will change then, Else?'

Elsie lifted the kettle and went towards the scullery. 'Only as much as we want them to. We can carry on being us, living where we are, or we can take what Millie is offering.'

'My mum don't like charity.'

Elsie escaped through the door and ran the tap, letting the noise of filling the tin kettle carry her thoughts away. But however much she tried not to let them, her feelings crowded in on her. She rubbed her stomach. She knew she was ratty with Dot because of having her monthly, more than because of Dot going on. Her head ached and she just wanted some peace. No, she wanted to turn the clock back. Drawing in her breath, she went back through to the living room.

'Dot, it ain't charity. Hawkesfield was our dad! He paid nothing towards our upkeep, nor cared a jot about us all our lives. We're entitled to something now.'

'So what're you going to do?'

Elsie thought for a moment, going through the motions of putting three scoops of tea leaves into the pot – three, huh! She'd seen the time when she'd used yesterday's dried-up dregs.

'I think we should have somewhere decent to live. For me, I'd move in with Millie tomorrow, if Cess would come, and I've talked to Rene as well. She ain't happy doing what she's doing, but she didn't see another way, and she didn't like living off me and Cess. I've some suggestions to discuss with Millie about Rene. I think she could be very useful to Millie, with her dressmaking skills. And I think she could set herself up as a dressmaker. I'm going to ask Millie to fund her.'

'That'd be good for Rene, but where would she live?'

'She said she'd be happy here, if I kept the tenancy going, till she got on her feet. But if I decide not to live with Millie and to find a better place than this, she'll come and live with me.'

'That sounds good, but I can't believe you'd be happy living in a big house like Millie's, mate. Ha, you, Elsie Makin, with a maid!'

Elsie couldn't help laughing with Dot. 'Here, drink your tea, and stop making fun of me. Anyway, that's what I'm saying now, but with the quandary I'm in, I'll probably change my mind later.'

'Look, luv, now you've put it that way – you know, Hawkesfield owing us – then I think Mum might accept a decent place to live and me having a better job, so that I can keep us.'

'There you go then. Oh, Dot. I just want to escape from here for a while before the trial begins. I can't take much more. My heart bleeds for Jimmy and Bert, and my mum. And on top of that . . . Anyway, Millie's would be ideal for me.'

'I know. What you've been through, no one should go through in a lifetime.'

They sat silently for a moment. The rain beating on the window made Elsie feel even more depressed. 'I'm all right, most days. But I wish Millie would come home soon, so we can talk and make our minds up.'

'We need that. Especially as the factory will be closing soon till the oranges come in after Christmas. That could be a funny time for us, with all the women out of work and us looking like we're in clover.'

Again they fell silent. The squeak of the letterbox and the

sound of a letter plopping onto the floor startled them both. It was a sound they rarely heard. Elsie immediately thought of Millie and jumped up. 'It's a letter!'

'I thought that much, when the box squealed. You need some oil on that, Else. It's like ours; it only gets used every quarter when the bills come in.'

'Ha, I know. But this is a real letter! And it has a Leeds postmark.'

'Millie! Ooh, open it Else.'

'Fetch me a knife from the drawer, will you? I ain't ripping open the only letter I've ever had in my life, mate.'

After carefully opening the envelope, Elsie read the letter out. She was a better reader than Dot, who'd never done very well at school. Spreading out the lovely pale-blue paper on the table, she sat on one of the hard wooden chairs:

'Dear Elsie and Dot, my lovely sisters,

I hope you are both all right – especially you, Elsie. You have been so much in my thoughts. I stood behind my father's coffin and I wanted to go and kick it, to avenge what he did to you and your mother. But I couldn't. You see, he was such a different person towards me – a loving father who indulged my every whim. I am grieving, and yet torn by feelings of disgust and hate, knowing the person he often was. Can you understand that?'

Elsie looked up at Dot, who stood looking over her shoulder. 'I can. I had something of those feelings over my mum. Not that she was anything like Hawkesfield, but I do wish I could forget some memories.'

Dot's face had paled, but then, Elsie thought, she had

her own memories to deal with. The only saving grace for Dot was that she had been able to see things change. With her so-called dad gone, her mum had been different towards her and her home life was a lot better now.

After giving the hand that Dot had pressed onto her shoulder a little tap. Elsie read on:

'The Will has been read, and it is as my mama told me. I now own the factory and the house in London, and Mama the house in Leeds. We are both to receive a large sum of money from Father's private investments and, as I say, you two, my dear sisters, will share in the fortune that has come to me.

As for the factory, the meeting with Len and his father is fixed for the day after tomorrow – Thursday morning. I have no idea what the state of the business finances are, but I have been thinking that if they are as they should be, then I am not going to close the factory altogether at the end of October, but put the women on part-time. I want us to make pickles as well as jam. Father talked about doing so, and set me to find a good supplier of dried shallots. I haven't been idle over these last two weeks since the funeral, but have contacted the farm I found and placed an order. It isn't a large order, as it was too-short notice, but it will be a trial run, and I have searched the library for a good pickled-onion recipe. All we need now is to find an outlet for the stock, but that can come later. Besides this work, which won't keep the workforce busy for long, I intend for the women to give the factory a good clean – all the machinery and paintwork and floors. I know some of this is done every evening, but I want a good deep-down clean. I hope you like this idea.'

'Oh dear, it all sounds good, but do you think she is running before she can walk, Else?'

'I do a bit, although if Mr Hawkesfield was already thinking of going into producing pickles, there may be some plans in place. After all, he set her to find out about shallots, didn't he?'

'Yes. What else does she say?'

'None of this will involve you both, or indeed me. I am going to keep my manager on for six months while I sort everything out. I have telephoned him to ask him to start to put all my ideas into action.

I didn't tell you about him, did I? His father owned a jam factory in Liverpool, but although Mr Ellington ran all the practical side of the business, as he is doing now for me, he was never allowed to take part in the business decisions. Then suddenly his father sold out. Not long afterwards Ellington senior died, and it was found that he had run the business into the ground, leaving more debts than assets, so there was nothing for Mr Ellington to inherit.

He and Len went to the same school and they'd always stayed in touch, so when I was left without Father to run the business, Len thought of Ellington. So, you see, the man needs a job, and at the moment I need him. Also, he was always telling his father to go into pickling so as to make the business all-year-round, and he has researched this line. He is very keen to help me get that side of the business up and running.'

'Well, she seems to have a diamond geezer in Ellington. I can't see her needing us in the office, can you?'

'I don't know, Dot. We'll have to see.'

'I'm not much for it, Else. I can't work out figures and things, nor write letters. And as for speaking on a phone, I'd rather run a mile!'

Elsie laughed at this. Dot didn't take umbrage, but laughed with her. 'Well, we'll soon know our fate, as it sounds as though Millie will be home tomorrow – or at least travelling home. Anyway, there's more:

'Well, both, I think that is all, except to tell you a little about my second home – Leeds. The house is very grand – large and imposing, standing in its own grounds in Ravensprings Park . . .'

The description of the park spoke of it being very beautiful – a haven. But it was hearing about Leeds that most fascinated Elsie.

'Though Leeds is an industrial and coal-mining town, it is full of wealthy folk who own these concerns and yet, in contrast, many poor, underpaid workers.'

Elsie wondered about the workers and how their day-to-day lives were lived. Her impression of the North was that it was a drab, cold place, with all the men wearing cloth caps and the women downtrodden and beaten. But then wasn't that the same the world over? Look at Dot. She'd had her fair share of beatings.

At this thought, Elsie suddenly realized that Dot, although free of her dad, and with her mum changed, still seemed sad. Looking up at her, Elsie was shocked at how drawn Dot's face was, and how her eyes were sunken in their sockets. She hadn't been the same for a while now. Not so caring; tired-looking and sad . . .

'Dot?'

She lifted her hand off Elsie's shoulder. Her eyes had no life in them as she looked enquiringly at Elsie.

'Dot, are you all right, mate?'

'Yes . . . Why?'

'You don't look well. Is your mum really treating you right? She's not still bullying you, is she?'

'No . . . No! Why should you say that? Mum's different now. She needs me. Sometimes that's hard for me, as . . . well, I have to make different decisions from what I want to.'

'Like leaving me when I needed you.'

A tear plopped onto Dot's cheek. 'I – I needed you, too.'

This shocked Elsie. How could Dot have needed her, or anything from her, at such a moment? When her life had been torn into shreds and she'd been dragged from grief, to be violated in such a way?

Dot suddenly crumbled and fell to her knees. Her hands were clinging onto Elsie's skirt.

'Dot! Dot, what's wrong, mate? Tell me. Dot?'

An agonizing sob ripped from Dot as if it had been wrenched from her. Fear gripped Elsie – the fear of knowing she was going to hear something dreadful; something she wouldn't know how to deal with. Bending over Dot, she tried to scoop her into her arms.

Dot rested her head on Elsie's knee. 'Help me, Else. Help me.'

'I will, Dot. Whatever it is, I'll do all I can for you, luv.'

'Me . . . me dad, he – he did that thing . . . He made me mum watch. He . . . raped me . . .'

Dot's sobs rasped from her, choking her. Snot ran from her nose. Her body slumped further, dragging Elsie off the chair till she was kneeling beside a prostrate Dot.

Torn in a desperate agony of hurt, for Dot and for herself, Elsie gathered Dot close to her. Together they rocked in a rhythmic motion as they sobbed out their pain.

Elsie calmed first. 'Come on, luv. Let's get off the floor. I won't let go of you, I promise.'

They rose while still holding hands. Elsie had a feeling of being emptied out – drained of all that had hurt her; and then a sensation of being consumed by her need to help and protect her beloved sister.

'I'll help you, Dot. We'll get through this, mate – we will.'

'How? How, Else? I'm having a baby!'

Elsie stood stock-still. Slowly, she willed herself to move. She guided Dot gently towards the sofa, sat her down and brushed her hair back from her face, holding the damp curls away from sticking to her cheeks. 'I'll get you a towel, Dot. Hold on.'

This seemed a stupid, futile thing to say, but Elsie felt she needed to do something practical. Hurrying across to the cupboard next to the fire, she pulled out a towel from the pile on the shelf and took it to Dot. 'Wipe your face, luv, and let's talk, eh?'

When Dot managed to calm a little, they sat holding hands. 'He was hitting me mum, and . . . and I tried to stop him. Then he turned on me. He went to hit me, but his face changed. His eyes seemed to glaze over . . .'

Elsie shuddered. Memories of her own attack reverberated through her.

'He turned from me and went to the door to lock it. Me and mum looked at each other. We didn't know what he had in mind. He came back into the room. Grabbed Mum. Shoved her onto one of the wooden chairs at the table . . . Pulled her cardi off and used it to tie her to the chair. Mum must have realized what he was about to do, and she went to stand, but he punched her and she lost her balance and fell to the floor, still tied to the chair. I froze as his voice growled out, "Now, you're going to watch me give your bastard daughter what you won't let me have." I – I didn't know what he meant . . . He . . . Oh, Else, it hurt. I – I felt repulsed. I couldn't stop him. He was like an animal. A powerful animal!'

'I know. Oh, Dot.'

Chambers's sweaty face came back to Elsie. She smelt his stinking breath, cringed against the feel of him, as she clung to Dot.

'And, Else, I haven't seen my monthly since.'

Elsie swallowed down her own fears and heartache, but then remembered that she had had her monthly, and even had it now; and she recalled how she hadn't let Chambers finish his business inside her. Relief mingled with her love and heartbreak for Dot. 'Don't worry, Dot. Does your mum know the plight you're in?'

'Yes. She's talking of sending me away. She says it's the only way. That we're to tell everyone I'm ill and need to spend time in the country. She's going to invent an aunt in the Midlands. But really she's contacting one of them places. I don't want to go, Else. I don't want a baby, but I don't want to go away to one of them homes for unmarried women. You know what they're like – they're cruel places.'

'That's not going to happen, Dot.' Elsie couldn't think

of a solution, but neither could she believe that Mrs Grimes could do such a thing to her daughter.

'We'll think of something. We'll get Millie to help us. I know she will.'

'How? What can she do? There's only one thing I want to do, and that's visit Ma Sawyers.'

'No. Remember Emma Townsend? And Viv Rowling? Both dead – and why? Because they went to Ma Sawyers. Don't do that, Dot. Please. We'll find a way.'

The door opened and Cecil walked in. He dropped his bag and ran over to Dot. 'What's wrong? What's happened?'

Dot didn't greet him, but simply hung her head. Elsie felt at a loss. In her confusion as to whether to tell Cecil or not, she blurted out, 'What are you doing home at this time? You haven't lost your job, have you, Cess?'

'No. Trade's slow with this weather, so I was signed off. But more to the point, why are you crying? What's wrong with Dot?' Saying this, he went down on his haunches in front of her and took Dot's writhing hands in his. 'You can tell me, Dot. There's been something wrong for a while now, ain't there?'

She nodded. Elsie wasn't sure whether to leave them alone or stay. But Dot made her mind up for her, as she took one of her hands from Cecil and reached for Elsie's as she said, 'Something bad happened, Cess.'

Cess didn't speak, but stared at her, his expression changing from concern to anger, to concern again, as Dot broke down at the end of her telling. Then the strangled word 'Bastard!' came from him, and a tear ran down his cheek. 'Was it before . . . ?'

Dot nodded. What Cecil meant, Elsie had no idea, but what he said now made her feel proud of him.

'We'll get married, Dot. I'll take care of you, I promise.'

Dot stopped sobbing and looked up, her look one of beautiful love.

As they held each other and the shock of this statement wore off, Elsie began to think about this turn of events. Was it possible for Cecil to marry Dot? They were old enough – Cecil was now eighteen and Dot nineteen.

Within seconds of this seeming to be a solution, and one that Elsie thought her brother was a hero for making, Dot's demeanour changed again. Once more she hung her head. 'Mum would never allow it. I know she wouldn't and, without her consent, I can't marry.'

'We'll run away then. I don't want anything bad to happen to you or the baby, Dot. I love you, and I will take care of you both.'

Elsie thought Cecil had always shown a maturity far beyond his years, but at this moment she saw him as a man. A good, kind man. She could think of no better solution for Dot than to marry the man who loved her, and whom she loved. And she would support them with all her heart.

'Well, there's only one way to find out what your mum thinks, Dot. You and Cess go and talk to her. Go on. You might be surprised.' Something else occurred to Elsie then. 'And tell her that you can move from this area – all of you can. Millie will see to that for you. So there won't be any gossip, as no one will know, will they?'

'Except all the workers in the factory.'

'No, they won't, Dot. As my wife, you won't work in that factory. I'll take care of you.'

'And you'll have what Millie has promised to share with us, too, so that will set you up.'

Cess looked quizzically at Elsie as she said this. Elsie

explained what Millie had said about her inheritance. 'I mean she'd didn't say share it – not as in each of us having a third – but that she will make sure we are taken care of. She . . . well, she wants me – all of us – to move into her house with her, but Dot said her mum wouldn't let her do that. Anyway, Millie said if that wasn't suitable for us, then she would insist on housing us in a decent home. If you two marry and don't want to live with Millie, then I will.'

'Blimey, mate, that'd be going up in the world.'

'I know. And I don't know yet if I can get used to it or not, but I love Millie and know I could live with her.'

'Well, it ain't for me, but we could take the offer of a better home, Cess, couldn't we?'

Cess looked confused for a moment. Elsie guessed he was thinking of how he would wish to support his own wife, but Dot didn't give him time to protest.

'Of course we can. What's stopping you? Mr Hawkesfield was our dad, and we are entitled to live better than we do. We're owed it, Cess.'

'But what about your mum, Dot? You know how she is with me. Leaves me standing on the doorstep if I call. Doesn't speak to me; well, only grudgingly. And although some of that's improved, I'm not sure I can live with her. I thought you'd move in here with us.'

'Think about it, Cess. How can you and Dot move in, with Rene being here? There's only one bedroom. If you won't accept a better place from Millie, then you're stuck, because the same situation applies to Dot's mum's flat as well. Where would you all sleep? Anyway, all this discussion when we should be celebrating. You just asked Dot to marry you, and she said yes! I reckon that calls for happiness, not worry.'

Cess smiled. It was as if he realized for the first time what had happened. He gently pulled Dot to her feet and held her close to him. 'I love you, Dot, and I don't care that we're only young. I know I want to spend the rest of my life with you.'

Dot giggled, but then pulled back from Cecil. 'Cess, you are sure about the baby, aren't you? I mean, look how my dad was with me.'

'I am sure, Dot. I will take care of the baby as if it was mine. It . . . *will* be mine. Anyway it will be born when you're married to me, so no one will know any different.'

Elsie's heart swelled with admiration for this brother of hers, but her mind caused her some doubts. The presence of a child in a home who wasn't fathered by the husband could be a source of resentment that could fester over the years. And what about Mrs Grimes? Dot's mum had changed lately, but Elsie knew she hadn't really changed. She'd somehow got a hold over Dot, so that Dot didn't do anything without putting her mother first. How would that affect Dot and Cecil's marriage? A shudder went through Elsie, and suddenly what had seemed like a dream solution contained worry for Dot and Cecil's future.

Chapter Twenty-Two

Elsie

Two days later Dot and Cecil still hadn't found the right moment to speak to Dot's mum, and Elsie had offered to do it for them.

As she finished washing the breakfast pots, she wasn't surprised when the door opened, letting in the sound of Big Ben striking nine chimes, and Dot popped her head round it.

'You're early today, Dot. Are you all right?'

'Yes, ta. I haven't even felt sick this morning. I woke up starving. Mum had only got a loaf in. She won't let me spend any of the money Millie gave me on food for us.'

'She's not still playing the I-don't-take-charity card, is she?' Rene asked, her fag drooping from her blood-red lips.

'You know what she's like, Rene.'

They all did, and it worried Elsie, because Mrs Grimes's attitude didn't bode well with regard to accepting living in a better place provided by Millie.

'She won't budge on the stance she's taken, and she is still waiting on a letter from a convent in the Midlands.'

Elsie didn't know what to say.

'She thinks it might come today and told me not to be long round here, as I've to pack.'

'Bloody hell – she's a one, is your mum. Always has been, and they say a leopard can't change its spots. Well, she don't seem able to.' Rene puffed out a cloud of smoke as she said this, then looked as though she'd seen the light, as she turned her head to one side to avoid the cloud and her expression animated her face. 'Just a mo, though. Look, mate, this could work in your favour. Go along with her and then, when you've to travel, insist that Cecil takes you, and not her. But don't go to the convent-thingy; instead, you and Cecil find a home together up there. That Millie would give you enough for that, surely? And by the time your mum finds out, you'll be married and there's nothing she can do about it.'

They were all quiet for a moment. Elsie couldn't sort in her mind all the pros and cons of this suggestion, although many of them came to her. The first con was the nuns reporting Dot not turning up. But when she voiced this, Rene had an answer.

'Can you write like your mum, Dot?'

'Yes, I've had to do it many times, when me and Else wanted to skip school. Why?'

'You write to that convent, girl. You tell them that you – you being your mum, in this instance – thank them very much, but you've made an alternative arrangement.'

Elsie began to see that this could work, but her heart was heavy at the thought of not having Dot and Cecil near her. 'Can't you and Cecil just speak to your mum, Dot? She might surprise you, and think you getting married and moving somewhere different in London is a good solution.'

'She won't, Else. I know my mum. And for her to send me away shows how strongly she feels about me getting rid of this baby.'

'Don't forget what she herself went through, Dot. She may be sacrificing her own happiness at having you close to make sure you don't go through the same thing she did.'

'I know, Rene, and I do think that's motivating her. And that's what makes me think she'll never accept me marrying Cess. She believed she'd be all right, married to the man she loved, but she wasn't . . . Perhaps I – I should do it her way, and me and Cess get married later.'

'Dot, do you reckon as it'll be any different then? Men don't forget. If Cecil was that way inclined – and I know he ain't – he'd be bitter anyway. Your dad would have been. But Cecil ain't like that, so why put yourself through having to give your baby away? It's the most painful thing in the world, you know.'

A silence fell over the room.

'I – I mean, not that it happened to me, but it happened to a mate of mine. Drove her mad, it did. Ended up topping herself, poor sod.'

'Yeah, but did she have to face the father being the man she'd thought of as her own dad all her life? That's what's getting to me. I don't want any reminder of him – or of what he did to me.'

'Look, Dot, I'm going to speak straight to you now. Have you and Cecil ever lain together – you know . . . Have you two ever done it? I mean, in all these years, that bastard never knocked a tin lid out of your mum, did he? How come he's done it to you, when he only had you the once, eh?'

Dot coloured. She looked from Rene to Elsie, her lip

quivered and then an expression of enlightenment suddenly lit up her face. 'You mean it could be Cess's baby?'

'If you've let him touch you, it could.'

'I – I did. After, I mean. Well, I wanted Cess to be the first. We'd been near to it a couple of times, and then after my dad . . . well, I wanted to blot it out. Only it didn't, it only felt dirty and I cried. And Cess cried. I made him feel shame, and I didn't mean to. We ain't been the same since. He ain't even tried to . . . I – I know he's offered to marry me, and that made us both happy, but, well, we weren't happy – not deep down. Oh, Rene. Do you reckon my baby could be his?'

'Yes, I do. And you can stop all this nonsense about making each other unhappy and blaming other things for it. Be honest with each other. I've never seen a love like you two have, mate. I'd give my eye-teeth for it. Don't spoil it by dwelling on another man having stolen a bit of you. You didn't give consent – you were forced. Forget it. If you don't, Cecil won't, and it'll eat away at you both. I've told this to you, haven't I, Else? And you seem to be coping better.'

Elsie didn't feel that she was, but she nodded. It was easier to put on a brave face now, but inside – that's where the hurt and repulsion were.

'Anyway, girls, I'll always be a listening ear and a support to you. I do know what you're going through. But I have to get going now.'

'You're a busy bee, Rene. Where to this time?'

'I'm going to see Gerry Flounders again. You have to keep on top of these fellas . . . Ha! I didn't mean that. But he said he might have work for me, and out of sight is out of mind. And I really fancy theatre work.'

A knock at the door got them all standing still for a moment.

'I'll go. I don't know – every time someone knocks on the door, I have this fear that I'm back in my cottage and can't pay the tallyman. I always want to run and get under the table.'

Elsie and Dot could relate to this and they both giggled.

Rene came back into the room. 'It's that young maid of Millie's. Come on in, Ruby, luv.'

'Hello . . . Eeh, I've not interrupted sommat, have I?'

'No, come on in, Ruby. Has Millie sent you, luv?'

'She has. Here you are: it's an invitation for you both to join Millie at her home for tea today.'

Elsie read the note:

'Dear Elsie and Dot,

I cannot wait to see you and would very much like you to join me this afternoon. I take tea at around 4 p.m., so, I thought that would be a good time for you to come. Please bring Cecil with you, if he is home in time. Ruby will come back with my driver to fetch you, so you have plenty of time to get ready.'

'What does she mean, get ready? Will I have to dress up?'

'Naw, Elsie, you look fine. She'd mean sort out what you were doing, and you might want to brush your hair – that sort of thing.'

'Ta, Ruby. Well, I, for one, am going and it won't take me long to get ready.'

'Eeh, I'm glad. You'll cheer her up. Millie's been a bit down since she came home yesterday. Though she was excited to be going to a meeting this morning.'

Elsie wondered if she could cheer anyone up, as she was hoping to be cheered up herself. 'What about you, Dot?'

'It'll be too posh, Else. I won't know how to act.'

'You don't have to act; just be how you always are with Millie. She needs us, Dot, I can tell.'

'You go. Me and Cess had talked about having tea together one evening. We can go to the pie shop. I need to talk to him, after what Rene's said.'

Elsie nodded. She was still reeling from the revelation that Dot and Cecil had done that thing, but part of her was glad Dot was going to meet Cecil, because Dot was right: they did need to talk.

'It's just me then, Ruby. Would you like a cup of tea before you go? You can tell us how your wedding plans are coming along.' Over the last few weeks Elsie felt as though she had got to know Ruby really well, and found her to be a lovely young woman. She'd talked about her plans to wed the stable lad.

'Married, eh? Have you a wedding gown yet, Ruby?'

'Naw. There's been no time, Rene, but I must sort sommat out soon.'

'I could make you one, if you like.'

'By, that'd be grand.' Ruby clapped her hands and did a little jig. They all laughed out loud at her antics.

'So when you've finished dancing, when is the wedding?'

'It'll all happen in the spring, Rene, so we've plenty of time.'

'Good. But hang on a mo. I'll get some of my drawings. I want to sort through them, so that I have some to take with me. I'm going to see someone about some work in a bit.'

Rene hadn't been out much since she'd latched onto the idea Elsie had given her about starting her own business.

She'd often sat for hours drawing clothing designs and seemed a lot happier.

'Eeh, Rene – they're grand. By, Elsie, just look at them. I'd love this one, and the price is sommat as I can afford an' all.'

'Well, it's a bit of an estimate, but if that price suits you, then that's what I'll charge you. Anyway, you can pay me in stages. I'll find out how much the material will be, so if you can make your first payment enough to cover that, then give me a bit more when we have the first fitting and the balance when the frock's ready, that would suit me. Now will you be having bridesmaids?'

'Aye, I will. Miss Millie for one.'

Elsie had noticed that, when speaking to anyone other than her and Dot about Millie, Ruby always referred to her as 'Miss Millie'.

'And I am really friendly with the downstairs maid in the family's home in Leeds, but it would be difficult for you to make her frock, as she couldn't come down here. Me wedding'll be up in Leeds, you see.'

'If you can get her measurements, I can make the frock and guarantee it will fit her.'

'Ta, Rene. Let me have a price, and I'll see if she can afford it. I think she will, as she's very thrifty, but I know she's sweet on one of the farm lads on the estate and if she's thinking of marrying him, she might not be able to be me bridesmaid, as she won't afford the dress.'

'Well, you find out. And I'll let you know what first payment I'll need for your frock when you return later today. That's if I can leave now, as it'll take me half an hour to reach Petticoat Lane Market. There's a stall there that sells some wonderful fabrics.'

'Right-o. I'll bring some money back with me when I come to pick up Elsie. I have to be off now, but I'll be back just after three, Elsie. By, I'm that excited.'

Millie was at the door when they arrived later that day. The butler was right behind her. Elsie had to smile, as it seemed a race between Millie and him as to who was going to open the car door. Millie won, and her butler looked most annoyed, turning on his heel and going back inside.

Elsie could hardly get out of the car before Millie had her in a hug. 'Oh, Elsie. I'm so happy to see you.'

As they went inside and the butler took her coat, Elsie was glad that he didn't show any disdain at her old green coat. It had been her mum's and had seen better days.

'Come in here, Elsie. Barridge, would you see that tea is served to us?'

They went into a different room from the one Elsie had been in before, but just as beautiful, in soft greens and deep reds. 'This is – was – Mama's sitting room. I will use it as mine now, although it will be Mama's whenever she visits . . . Oh, Elsie, I'm missing her already. I feel as though I'm rattling around in this big house by myself. It's as if my whole life has been turned upside down— Oh, I'm sorry, Elsie, I – I . . .'

'No, don't worry. I know exactly how you feel, and that means that we are more understanding of each other.'

When Elsie sat down, her body sank into the soft cushions of the sofa – it felt as if she was being hugged. Millie sat next to her and was quiet for a moment. The way she was wringing her hands told Elsie something was bothering her.

'Is there anything I can help you with, luv?'

'I don't know if anyone can, Elsie . . . Well, I'd better

say it: you see, things aren't as I was always led to believe. My father had even more bad traits than we knew. He was a gambler. He – he appears to have embezzled money from the business to feed his habit, and to have lost heavily.'

'Oh no, Millie! What does this mean for you? Will you be all right?'

'Yes, on a personal level, because Father invested his savings well, and also had a property portfolio that neither Mama nor I knew anything about. And that is worth a great deal and has been left to me. But on the business front, Swift's Jam Factory is in danger of failing badly.'

Elsie didn't know what to reply to this. She had no knowledge of business and property portfolios, or even what that meant, and felt completely out of her depth.

'But you're not to worry, Elsie. I know all this is difficult for you to grasp. It is for me, too, and I do have some knowledge of it. But I want you to be involved and to have the full picture. And you don't know how much it means to me to have you to share my worries with.'

Barridge brought the tea in then and they fell silent while he fussed over them. Once he'd left, Elsie asked what Millie intended to do. 'Did Len have any answers for you?' Just mentioning his name made Elsie's heart flutter.

'He did. He suggested that I put Swift's up for sale, but that's not an option for me. I feel passionately that I need to honour my promises to the workers, and somehow – oh, I don't know – pay them back in some way for the wrong my father did them, and you and Dot and your mums. Especially your mum, Elsie, and you. I'm ashamed of Father, and want to put right the bad things he did.'

'You can't do that, Millie, and you shouldn't feel you have to, luv. Why not take Len's advice?'

'No, Elsie. I need to do this, and I need you with me, backing me all the way. And Dot, too.'

At the mention of Dot, Elsie involuntarily took in a sharp breath. Millie picked up on her anguish.

'Is Dot all right? You didn't say why she didn't come. I've been concerned for her. I . . . well, I know she is ruled by her mother, but there seems to be something else. The way she reacted to your plight – I don't know, maybe I'm just being too sensitive at the moment.'

'No, you're not. There is something wrong. Well, not wrong . . . Dot's having a baby.'

'What? Cecil and Dot?'

'Yes. It might be Cecil's. We're all hoping so. Oh, Millie, I came with such a lot to tell you, and to ask you, and now I find that you have extra worries of your own, and I don't want to burden you further.' Elsie's cup rattled in its saucer as she leaned forward to put it down. The sound was different from any she'd heard before, as it was beautiful china that her tea had been served in, and not a thick pottery mug.

Millie reached for her hand. 'Remember what we once said: whatever we have to face, Elsie, we will do so together. Tell me all about it.'

In her anguish over all that she'd heard today, Elsie shed a tear as she told Millie what had been troubling Dot.

'Poor Dot. I can see now why you say that you hope the baby is Cecil's. And so do I. But, as you say, they cannot get married without Dot's mum's consent. And I can't see her giving that, either. This going away, as Rene suggested, sounds the best solution – at least until Dot's mum can be told and accepts the situation. But it might be worth Dot trying her mum's tactics. I think her mum is still controlling her, by using emotional blackmail. I hate that, but Dot could use it by telling her mum that either she accepts the situation and allows her and Cecil to marry, or they will run away together and she will never see Dot again.'

Elsie thought about this for a moment. And yes, she could see it working. She smiled at Millie. 'You know, Millie, you have a way of solving problems. I think you can make a success of Swift's. And I will help, though I don't know what I can do. What is your plan?'

'The only one I have is to put my property portfolio up as collateral at the bank and take out a huge loan to prop up Swift's with. I firmly believe that, with the modernization I have in mind and diversifying into other lines, such as pickles and bottled fruit, the factory can be saved.'

'And does Len agree?'

'In part, yes. The business part of him does, but the part of him that has fallen in love with me doesn't. He wants me to be as all men wish their wives to be—'

'Wife!' Pain prompted this outburst from Elsie. *Oh God, how am I to bear it? I love Len . . .*

'Ha! I know, it shocked me, too. But in a nice way. But yes, it's true. Len and I are in love!'

'Oh, I . . . it's so sudden. Oh, Millie, I don't know what to say.'

'I'm just as astonished. I always dreamed of falling in love and marrying and having children – all of that – but now that the falling-in-love bit has happened, and like a bolt out of the blue, I'm not sure.'

'You're not sure that you love Len?'

'Oh yes, I'm sure of that. But marriage? I have so much to do and, with Len's negative attitude towards me doing it, I'm not sure I want to take the step towards marriage for a long time.'

Elsie smiled – a smile that cost her so much. If she had the chance to marry Len, she would, right here and now. The thought of her never having that chance made her feel a sense of hurt and extreme disappointment.

'Anyway there's plenty of time for marriage. I don't think Len fully knows who I am yet. I'm nothing like he imagines. I have fights to fight, and battles to win, and I can't do that within the restrictions of marriage.'

What about loving to do, and your man to fight for? Elsie didn't voice this, but she knew these things were what she would concentrate on, if only she had the chance. *Oh, Len. Len.*

Millie gently shook Elsie's hand. 'Elsie, are you all right? You said you had a lot to tell me, and I brushed over Dot's problem, but I will help, I promise. All that Dot and Cecil need, I will give them, and I will support them and the child. I'm sorry. I have so much on my plate at the moment that I only seem able to give my mind to that.'

'No, it's all right. I did come armed with problems, but you have enough of your own . . .'

'No. Tell me about them.'

'It's difficult, because it seems like I'm coming cap in hand – as if you are expected to fork out your money to solve my worries, and you ain't. I don't want you to think that.'

'Your money, too. Look, I haven't had time to sort anything out, but I do have intentions. I now know the extent of my fortune, and the lack of fortune concerning the jam factory, and I need to balance that out. You and Dot are Father's daughters, too. You have as much right as I do to everything. And I am going to see that you get your fair share. I don't want you to have to come begging to me.

I want you to be able to use your own money to look after yourselves.'

'Oh, Millie, you don't have to.'

'I do. Oh yes, I do, Elsie. I need to. And Mama agrees. Len, too. And to that end, he wants to see you both, to help you to open a bank account and to advise you on the way.'

Could she bear that? Elsie looked out of the window: the rain still on pounded the glass – the world still turned. Nothing had stopped because her heart was in turmoil.

'Elsie, I'm sorry. Am I going too fast for you? Does it seem as though I am taking over your life?'

Elsie shook her head. 'No. It seems as though you are going to make a big chunk of it better, but I have . . . I have so many holes in my life that you can't fill.'

'Oh, Elsie. I want to. I want to help you all I can. I love you, Elsie. I love you as if we have known we were sisters all along. I feel a special bond with you.'

'And I with you.'

They hugged. As they came out of the hug, Millie said, 'Come here to live, Elsie, please. I need you. Really need you to be by my side. Dot is going to be all right now. Oh, I know she has a few hurdles to get over, but she and Cecil are in love. That's plain for all to see, and they must make their life together. My settlement – or, rather, our father's settlement for his daughter's future – will help Dot and Cecil with that. And you say that Rene has gone back to her old ways; well, we—'

'She hasn't. She changed again. She only did that because she couldn't stand being beholden to me and thought herself a drain on what little me and Cecil had. But she does have plans, and that's another thing I was going to tell you about, Millie.'

Millie listened, then clapped her hands in joy. 'That's wonderful. Of course I – we'll help her, but where will she live? There is room here, but I don't think Rene would feel comfortable with that, do you?'

'No. And it will take me time to adjust to doing so.'

'You're going to come and live with me? Oh, Elsie!' With this, Millie jumped up and did a twirl. 'I'm so happy. You don't know what this means to me.'

Millie's joy seeped into Elsie and she felt her spirits lift. Millie bent and took her hands and lifted her up. Together they swung round, their laughter echoing around the house. 'Oh, Elsie. Elsie, I have longed for you to say yes.'

They stopped twirling and fell into each other's arms. 'It won't be for a while, Millie. There's a lot to sort out. Dot and Cecil need to be settled, and Rene. But then I will, and in the meantime, if you'll have me, I will come and stay a few nights at a time.'

'Have you! I feel like kidnapping you right now.'

They laughed again and Elsie felt she could do this for Millie, despite having to watch Millie and Len's love blossom. Millie, for all her bravado and her need to set the world to rights, was very lonely, deep down. Besides which, she was the sister Elsie had always longed for and, when she was with her, she always had the feeling she could cope with anything.

'Elsie, I want us all to go away for a holiday. We need that.'

'Millie, Millie, how can we? You have so much to do, and I have a lot to sort out.'

'Everything will take time, and Ellington is doing a wonderful job as foreman. I just need to get away. Breathe in some sea air.'

'But it's cold and wet. Ha, you're mad!'

'I know. Please, Elsie: me, you, Dot and Cecil.'

'I'll see. Where would we go?'

'Barmouth. It's in Wales. I own a cottage there. I didn't know I did, or why my father bought it, but it sounds wonderful and has been used as a holiday home for a long time. It's managed by a local agent and brings in quite a tidy income each year. Going to the seaside has become very popular.'

Excitement zinged through Elsie. She didn't care that she'd never heard of Barmouth and that Wales seemed a million miles away, or that the weather was likely to be horrid. Suddenly she wanted, with all her heart, to go to Barmouth with Millie. 'Yes. All right. Let's do it. Oh, I'm all giddy with it now.'

'Ha. Me, too. Very giddy.'

Millie's antics had them both bending over with laughter and Elsie felt some normality enter her, and she hadn't felt normal since her mum had died. It felt good as she allowed the hope and happiness that Millie had given her to seep into her.

Chapter Twenty-Three

Elsie and Millie

Barmouth was beautiful. The cottage was nestled into a rock face and looked out towards a wonderful view over the bay, where fishing boats were moored beside a huge wreck of a boat resting out its last days on the sand. To get to the cottage they'd had to walk down some slate steps, which took them past the rooftops of other cottages that were built on a lower level of the hillside.

'Eeh, we could sit on them roofs, Millie.'

'You can, Ruby. I'd be too scared. Just take care. I don't want any of us slipping.'

'By, you're getting fussy in your old age. I've seen the time you'd have skipped down these.'

Elsie didn't join in this banter, though it made her smile. She was too taken up with the views and the vastness of the ink-blue sea, which seemed to glitter in the rays of the low November sun. And although tired, because the train journey had seemed to go on forever, she felt lifted by the brushing of the salty breeze on her face.

She'd been so looking forward to this week with Millie and Ruby, though she felt sad that Dot and Cecil couldn't make it and worried about them, as well as missing them so much and feeling even more alone than she had before they left. Dot's mum, true to everyone's expectations, wouldn't give her permission for Dot to marry Cecil, and so they had taken the path Rene had suggested.

They had written, and were staying in a hotel in Leicester for the time being. Dot was missing her mum and was eager for news of her, but said they were both so happy and were convinced now that the baby belonged to Cecil. They found Leicester a lovely city, and were glad to say that Cecil had managed to get set on, working for a market trader, although the settlement Millie had made on both Elsie and Dot was more than enough to keep them for years, besides the weekly allowance, which Millie had insisted on giving to both Dot and Elsie, being enough on its own to keep them easily in rent and food.

Dot hadn't said anything about marrying, but Elsie couldn't think of the alternative and just hoped they didn't get into trouble. As it was, no one knew them there, so Dot said that she wore a wedding ring and no one had questioned them. Her other big news was that she had bought Cecil a car. Imagining this was too much for Elsie – her younger brother driving a car! She never thought the day would come.

It felt strange, exciting and frightening, all at the same time, to have a bank account, but wonderful to have been able to set Rene up. She'd started by making Elsie a couple of outfits for this trip, and had some work from the theatre and a commission to make some winter clothes for Millie; and, of course, Ruby's wedding gown. And she would soon be looking for a little shop of her own, so she was going to start making outfits to display in her window to show off her talent.

They had reached the door of the cottage and stood for a moment while the man Millie had hired to drive them around, through the agent who looked after the cottage, unlocked the door and moved two of their three trunks inside. He looked hot and sweaty, even though there was a chill in the air.

'I'll get your last trunk, ma'am.'

Stepping inside took them to a world none of them had ever known.

'It's like a doll's house!'

'Aye, it is, Millie. By, we've some small cottages in Leeds, but nowt like this.'

Elsie didn't pass any comment, but she was enthralled. A fire roared in the grate that seemed to take up most of one wall, with just enough room each side for a dresser, both of which were laden with pretty china. There was a table at the back of the room covered with a lace cloth, with a bowl of apples in its centre; and a small two-seater settee with wooden arms, covered in a flowered material in a pretty blue, faced the fire. Each side of this were two matching chairs. The floor was a shiny-grey slate, with a knitted rug covering its centre. The walls had been distempered in a very light lemon colour. The curtains at the tiny window matched the settee and chairs.

'I love it! Come on, let's see where the doors lead to.'

Millie and Ruby followed Elsie as she went towards one of the three doors that led off the cosy living room. One was a bedroom with two beds in it. The walls were the same lemon colour, and the beds were covered with a crocheted pink throwover and looked lovely. A chair, low and on rockers, stood under the window, with a dressing table and wardrobe taking up the opposite wall.

'You and I in here, Elsie. We'll get the driver to drag our trunks in for us.'

'Pity it's not a three-bed room or we could all stay together.'

Millie looked surprised at this. Elsie didn't say any more, but thought the incident, though small, marked the glaring difference between herself and Millie – one that she could surmount, but a difference all the same.

The next room was a much smaller bedroom, and this one, done out in a similar way to the bigger one, was claimed by Ruby, who seemed happy with her lot. Finally there was a kitchen through the last door. Although Millie had said, 'Ah, the kitchen', to Elsie it was more of a scullery, holding only a large pot-sink, a stove and a line of cupboards. A door that led off from this went into a walk-in pantry, and this was full. A ham hung from the ceiling, and cheeses and butter sat on the shelves. A loaf stood next to this, wrapped in a lily-white muslin cloth and still giving off the aroma of having been freshly baked.

'I'm starving. Is anyone else?'

'I could eat a horse, as my mum used to say.' Elsie was shocked at how easily this reference to her mum slipped off her tongue.

'Eeh, you lasses. Well, shift yourselves and see to the driver, who's just come back in, and I'll make us all a sandwich.'

As they sat in front of the fire, eating doorstep-sandwiches filled with ham – something Elsie had never imagined Millie eating – Elsie reflected on how easily she'd fallen into this friendship with Millie and Ruby. And how it seemed no time at all since it was only her and Dot, with all the troubles they had at home. For her part, she'd go back to them in a shot, with her mum alive and the boys around her; but she wouldn't put Dot back there, and nor would she not have Millie in her life.

In the quietness caused by the three of them feeling exhausted and munching away, Elsie allowed herself to think about Bert and Jimmy. She wondered what they were doing now, and if they'd changed at all in the last few months. She could almost feel little Bert's arms round her and hear Jimmy's hacking cough. Was Jimmy better now? Were they together? Did they go to loving homes? She wondered if she would ever know.

Wiping away the tear that tried to escape from her eye, Elsie looked over at Millie and saw that she'd closed her eyes. Poor Millie had been through the mangle and had been wrung out twice, and she'd handled it all with such dignity and courage. *I wish I had that courage. I wish I didn't keep crying about everything – my heart bleeds tears constantly. How did it happen that I am so alone?* For that's how it felt, as if everyone she knew and loved had been taken from her. Oh, she'd made new friends and found a sister – well, two, but then Dot had always been a sister to her.

Even in love, she hadn't been lucky.

A hand came into hers and she looked into Ruby's eyes. She hadn't noticed Ruby moving to sit beside her on the settee. In a whisper she said, 'It's always when it's quiet that I visit the bad things in my life. Like missing me ma. Eeh, I'd give owt to be up in Leeds with her now.'

'I know, luv. Maybe one day you will be. But don't forget: your groom lives down here in London. You wouldn't want to be away from him, would you, mate?'

'Naw. But he's from the North and would go back there, an' all. But it is how it is, and dwelling on it don't help none. I'd never leave Millie. Especially not now. Most of her staff are new, because a lot went up north with Mrs Hawkesfield.'

'You're lucky, having a young man to love and who loves you. Millie has that, and Dot, but mine hasn't come along yet.' Len flashed into Elsie's mind, but she brushed the thought away.

'It'll happen and, when it does, you won't knaw what's hit you.'

Elsie smiled. She wanted to say that it had – and no, she hadn't known what had hit her – but she couldn't.

The breeze whipped around them as they walked along the promenade the next day. Elsie held onto her bonnet, and noticed that Millie was doing the same. She looked at Ruby, then had to call out as Ruby's smaller bonnet was whipped off her head.

Laughing, they all ran after it, but a child let go of his friend's hand and ran from the other boys and the nun he was with and stopped its progress with his foot. He turned and grinned. Then his face changed and he screamed, 'Elsie!'

Elsie stood for a moment, staring, not believing what she was seeing. 'Bert! Bert, oh, Bert!' Her legs seemed to gain wings as she ran towards him and gathered him up. 'My little Bert.' Tears ran down her face as she clung to him.

'Where have you been, Elsie?'

He didn't sound like Bert. 'I've been waiting for you, Bert. Where's Jimmy?'

Bert's face dropped. 'Jimmy went to heaven. I don't see him any more.'

Elsie almost lost her grip on Bert. It seemed to her that her inner self had drained, leaving her trembling on weak legs. A part of her wanted to scream out the acute pain that had sliced through her heart, but she gasped in air and held Bert even tighter.

'You won't leave me again, will you, Elsie? You'll take me back to Mum and let me live at home, won't you? I cry every night.'

'Put that child down at once! Bert, how dare you disobey my orders and run away from the group? You are the most disruptive child I have ever known.'

Elsie turned to see a nun hurrying towards them – her face pinched into mouse-like features by her veil.

'He's my brother. I'm entitled to hold him, and I'm not letting him go. He's coming with me.'

'What? No, you don't! I don't care who you are: you cannot come here and abduct one of the children in my care. Hand him back at once or I will have the law on you.'

Millie stepped forward. 'There is no need for that. My solicitor will make my sister a legal guardian of the boy, then we will collect him. Sister, may I introduce us? I am Millicent Hawkesfield, and this is my half-sister, Elsie Makin. She is the sister of this child, Bert Makin. He was taken away without her consent, when adversity hit the family.'

'And you didn't think to help her then?'

'I did help, but the circumstances in which the child was taken were beyond my control. We had no way of knowing where he was, but I can assure you there is now a loving, comfortable and wealthy home awaiting him with us, because a lot has happened since he was taken. We are now able to give him the very best of everything that he will need in life.'

'Well, I have no idea what you are talking about, although you do seem to be a level-headed young woman. But I have to warn you that children in care are only released to a family. Not to single young women. And, with this child, even a family couldn't cope with him, and he landed back with our order.'

'We are family. Bert's my brother. I cared for him all his life. I wasn't able to for a very short time and he was taken away.'

'I understand that you are a criminal, young lady. There will be no chance of you taking the child.'

'She is not! Elsie was falsely accused. She does not have a criminal record.'

'I don't want to go with Sister, Elsie, don't make me. Please don't make me.'

Elsie could only hold Bert; she had no words – no promises she could make.

'Bert, you remember me, don't you?' Millie asked. Bert nodded at her. 'Well, dear, Elsie and I can't stop you going back with Sister today, but we promise you that we will be working to get you home with us. Won't we, Elsie?'

'Yes, Bert, we will. We'll get you home, mate, I promise. Try to be a good boy until then.'

'Will Mum come with you to fetch me, Else?'

Elsie was at a loss. How could she tell him their mother was dead? Once again Millie saved the day. 'We'll see, Bert. But we don't want to leave here to fetch anyone and then have to come back. We want to leave here with you.'

'All right. But you will come back?'

Elsie snuggled her head into Bert's neck. Despite her pain, she found enough courage to blow onto his soft flesh, making a sound like a balloon losing its air. Bert giggled. 'Course we will. And we'll come to see you every day, if the Sister will allow?'

'Well . . . I . . . It's not my decision, but I can see the boy loves you and that you love him, so I will put in a good word for you with the Reverend Mother.'

'Thank you so much, Sister. May God bless you for your kindness to these lost children.' At these words from Millie, Elsie looked round at a sea of faces looking on in astonishment. She watched as Millie ruffled the hair of one little girl. 'I am sure it must cost the convent a lot of money to care for them so well. They all look lovely and are a credit to you. I will speak to your Reverend Mother on my first visit, if she will be kind enough to give me an audience, as I would like to become a benefactor to your wonderful cause and contribute funds on a regular basis. I own a cottage nearby and intend coming here to Barmouth frequently. I would love to visit the children and get to know them each time I come.'

'Oh, well . . . I'm sure the Reverend Mother will be very welcoming to you. You have to understand, though, that we do a very difficult job, and not all children are happy in our care. Some never settle and will tell all sorts of lies about us.'

'I do understand – don't worry. I'm sure it isn't easy for you, or for them.'

The Sister coughed. 'Well, I have to go. Come along, Bert. Say goodbye to your sister.'

'No, Elsie. Don't make me. Please don't make me.'

'Bert, I promise you I have no choice – or they will put me in prison. Do as the Sister says. And be good. I will come tomorrow, I promise.'

'We'll see. You can come, but it is up to the Reverend Mother as to whether you will be allowed in. Our convent is the St Augustine Convent. You will find it on the Aberystwyth road, just outside Barmouth – you can't miss it.'

'Thank you. Please allow Elsie a moment to calm Bert and get him to go with you.'

The Sister huffed, but didn't object.

'Bert, please, mate. I will come tomorrow, and I'll sit outside until they open the gate, if the Reverend Mother doesn't let us in. Go now. And keep thinking about coming home.'

'All right, Else. I'll think about sitting on Mum's knee, and you tickling me, and Cess playing football in the street with me.'

Elsie swallowed hard and put a smile on her face. 'Good lad. See you tomorrow then?'

With this, she set him down, and Bert lined up with all the other children to be marched away. His eyes never left hers, his head swivelling this way and that to keep her in his sights, until they all went round a bend and disappeared from view.

Elsie slumped against the sea wall and plonked herself down on it. A wail came from her that joined the calls of the seagulls, sending those that had settled around them soaring into the sky, amidst a scurrying of flapping wings and squawks of protest.

'Elsie. Elsie, oh, my poor Elsie.'

'Eeh, lass, you're sent more than most to bear. I'm so sorry. By, me heart's breaking for you.'

'Jimmy . . . Jimmy, why? Why?'

'There is no reason for these happenings, Elsie. I – I don't know what to say to comfort you. Maybe he was very sick. Jimmy was never well, was he? Maybe he grew too weak to stay here, so he went to his rest.'

Nothing that Millie or Ruby could say would soothe Elsie. Living without her brothers had been a terrible ordeal, not knowing where they were or if they were all right, but she had thought them safe, and that they would meet again one day. Now . . . 'I'll never see him again, Millie.' A pitiful moan came from her. 'Never! And little Bert doesn't know about Mum. How am I to tell him? How?'

'Don't. Not until we get him safely home, then we can protect and help him – and try to shield him from some of the pain this will give him.'

'Home?'

'My . . . our home, Elsie. Please, please move in soon, so I can take care of you.'

'Aye, and me. I'll devote meself to you both.'

'Oh, Ruby.' Millie spoke gently to Ruby. 'We know you would like to do that, but don't forget you're getting married and will have all sorts of responsibilities, and even, well, maybe . . .'

'A babby, you mean, Millie? Aye, I will as quick as I can, an' all. Just think, Elsie, if I have a lad, then Bert can play with him and teach him to play football.'

Elsie calmed a little. 'Yes, he'd like that. Bert's a caring little soul. All right, Millie, I will move in. Rene's settled now and wants to take the flat over, though if she finds a shop with a flat above it, she'll want to move into it.'

'That's such good news. We'll sort everything out, I promise. I'll get you back to the cottage to rest, then I'll go out to the post office and phone my solicitor. Hopefully he'll be able to recommend someone local who can help us to get custody of Bert.'

Elsie felt as if her legs had turned to lead when she tried to stand, but she managed it. A few folk around them were staring at her, but she put her head down and walked past them.

* * *

Back in the cottage, Elsie ran to her room and flung herself onto the bed. There she wept her heart out. *Jimmy, my lovely Jimmy. Why? Why?*

When a calmness settled over her, Elsie had a picture of her mum cuddling Jimmy. Mum was smiling and Jimmy was giggling. The peace this brought to her enabled her to ease her anguish and fall into a deep sleep.

Millie left her to sleep, but didn't rest herself, for she was on a mission to get everything to turn out right – well, as far as she could. The phone line to her solicitor wasn't good, so she went along to see the agent who looked after her cottage.

'Pleased to meet you, Miss Hawkesfield. I trust everything at the cottage is to your liking?'

'Yes, it's lovely. But I need your help, and it is urgent.'

After listening to her, Mr Schale stood for a moment, one hand on his hip, the other drawing his forefinger and thumb along his beard in a stroking movement. A man of her father's age – mid to late forties – he was short and inclined to carry more weight than he should, but he had a pleasant face and an easy manner.

'Well, now, I think your best bet is Rod Mahoney. He's a fiery solicitor with a reputation of getting what he wants done. And, as it happens, he has an office above mine. It's a dusty old place with nowhere for visitors to sit, and Rod has no manners, so he will keep you standing, but if you can take his ignorance, you won't go far wrong with him championing your cause. I'll nip up and see if he'll see you now.'

Rod Mahoney was all that Mr Schale had said he was, and more. His bushy, unkempt red hair met his equally bushy beard and framed his grumpy-looking face. A tall, portly man, he had the look of someone who wouldn't tolerate fools lightly. Millie felt a little intimidated by him.

'So, you're trying to get one of those scallywags out from the grasp of the Sisters, eh? Well, I wish you luck. You'd better have good grounds for doing so. Don't come to me with no hairy-fairy tale of falling for some little bugger's big blue eyes and thinking you can be the mother to him that he's never had. Most of them would make mincemeat of you, young lady.'

'No, it is nothing like that. I will tell you from the beginning – that is, from when the child was taken from his sister. It's not an easy story for me to tell, as it involves my father and a posthumous allegation that he murdered the child's mother.'

Mahoney looked astonished. 'Good grief!'

'Ahem, I think Miss Hawkesfield will need to sit down to tell such a story. Please feel free to interview her in my back office. I can have my secretary make you both tea.'

'That's very kind of you, Mr Schale. Yes, I would like to sit down. There is a lot to tell, but you should know it all, Mr Mahoney, if you are going to take the case.' Millie not only needed to sit down, but to escape the stuffiness of the small, cluttered office and the cigar smoke that choked the air.

Once she'd told her tale, Mahoney sat for a moment, his hands held as if in prayer and his chin resting on his fingers. He pursed his lips a number of times before he said, 'I'll want to know how this young woman – your half-sister – lives now, as that will come up, if this has to go to court.'

'I don't wish it to go to court. I thought you would know if we can legally take the child home. And my sister will be living with me. I – well, we both, only it is in my name – own a jam-making factory. I also own a large house in London, with a full complement of staff to take care of us. The child will be loved, cared for and have all his needs met. I will pledge to see that he gets a good education and will set him on the path to achieving a sound career.'

'The little bugger will fall right on his feet, by the sound of it. Well, I don't see a problem. As the child is related to Miss Makin and she now has a stable home to offer him, this should be easy. You carry on buttering up the Sisters, make your first donation and become a patron of the convent. My job will be much easier then, as they are unlikely to raise any objections to the child going with you. In the meantime I'll go and have a word with the local judge, submit the paperwork applying for guardianship of the ragamuffin, and I think you'll be collecting him in a matter of days. Or my name isn't Mahoney!'

Feeling like skipping with joy when she left the office, Millie – happy with the outcome – had a sudden urge to go to the shops to see if there was a child's outfitter, so that she could buy some outfits for Bert. And a toy shop to get him something to play with. But she decided against this, thinking those lovely things to welcome Bert should be Elsie's prerogative; she herself was simply to provide the support that Elsie would need, in order to be able to think of these things and carry them out, which wouldn't be easy for her.

Her mind turned to Jimmy, and she wondered how he had died and where he was buried. Feeling restless about everything, she promptly turned into King Edward Street as a sign proclaimed 'St Tudwal's Catholic Church'.

The building looked newly built of grey bricks, with one small, square clock tower. Next to the church was a house, which she assumed belonged to the priest. The door was answered by a ruddy-faced housekeeper, who looked more like a farmer's wife. She had her arms folded and glared at Millie. But after hearing her business, she softened. 'I'll fetch Father Bryn to you.'

The priest greeted her in a friendly manner and was able to answer her questions. 'Wait here while I get my coat. I'll show you where the child is buried.'

As they walked towards the church the priest said, 'Sad it was – very sad. No one likes to bury a child. But I attended this one in his final hours, and he was better being taken to his rest. I gave him the Last Rites, as the nuns had put him through his first Holy Communion, and he died so peacefully, almost with a little smile on his face.'

'What was wrong with him? I know he had a bad chest, but . . .'

'Pneumonia, the doctor said; measles and pneumonia. He was very ill.'

When they reached the plot of almost freshly dug soil, Millie felt a wave of sadness come over her. 'Thank you, Father. God rest his soul. I'll come back tomorrow with his sister. But can you tell me who I should see about having a stone erected for Jimmy?'

'You can't do that for a year. You have to let the ground settle. But if you come back to the house with me, I'll write the funeral director's name down and where he has his place, and you can talk to him about it.'

When Millie arrived back at the cottage, she felt exhausted. But she mustered the strength to go in to see Elsie. Telling her the good news first got Elsie sitting up and smiling.

'That's wonderful. Wonderful. Oh, ta, Millie. You're a real pal.'

As Millie hugged Elsie to her, she thought that's what she had to be, besides being a sister: a real pal to Elsie, because she was certainly in need of one, especially now that Dot had left.

Chapter Twenty-Four

Elsie and Millie

Elsie and Millie stood in the hallway of the convent. The high ceiling and hollow bareness of the place made Elsie's nerves jangle. The Sister who'd greeted them had told them to wait while she told the Reverend Mother they were here. They'd watched her glide away, her shoes squeaking on the polished floor.

'It doesn't seem like a loving place for children,' Elsie whispered to Millie.

Millie seemed struck dumb, which was making Elsie feel even more afraid, as nothing usually daunted Millie.

Although Elsie listened hard, she couldn't hear a trace of a child in the building. Worry joined her nerves and churned her stomach. What if the children were treated cruelly? There were always stories about places such as this, and the strictness of the nuns. To Elsie, it seemed wrong that these women, who'd chosen not to marry or have children, should be in charge of other people's children. She knew they were meant to be holy and do God's work, but rumour had it that they did so grudgingly and that made them resentful, which they often took out on the children, or on the unmarried mothers they were supposed to be kind to.

A door opened and the nun returned. 'Reverend Mother will see you now. Come this way.'

'If she smiled, her lips would crack and bleed, I reckon.'

'Shush, Elsie. She might hear you!' Millie stifled a giggle behind her hand. 'This has got to go well, for us to stand a chance.'

'Please speak as little as possible while in the public areas of the convent. This is the silent hour – a most inconvenient time for you to call. And, I might warn you, your voice carries in this hall.' This was said in hushed tones, which didn't sound angry, just matter-of-fact.

Elsie felt her cheeks burn and she had a job to control the silly giggle prompted by her nerves. But she swallowed hard and had herself under control by the time they had walked along a narrow, winding corridor and stopped outside a huge oak door with a central doorknob.

The Sister knocked on it and then whispered, 'It isn't easy to smile here. You have to be happy to smile. I know what you are here for, and I hope you succeed. Little Bert's a lovely boy, and this isn't the place for such a sensitive soul.'

Elsie's fear of the place deepened. She looked into the nun's coal-black eyes and saw deep sadness there. She wanted to take her in her arms and comfort her, but the nun held herself stiffly, as if warding off any such reaction.

'Enter!' The word was snapped out as if the woman uttering it was in a vile temper.

Once inside the room, they stood in front of the Reverend Mother's desk, waiting for her to speak again. A thin woman, with thin features – a long nose, pinched-in cheeks and a jutting chin – she looked them both up and down.

'You're very young. What do you know about bringing up a child?'

'I've done it all my life, Reverend Mother. My mum . . . she wasn't always around, and I took care of Bert and . . . and Jimmy.' Saying her lovely brother's name stung Elsie's heart.

'Yes, I have read the notes on the poor child – his mother a drunk and a prostitute. His sister accused of murder. I take it that is you? Not a very good recommendation, is it?'

'I didn't do it. I was falsely accused of causing a fatal accident in the jam factory.'

'The factory that you told Father Bryn you owned?'

'That was me, Reverend Mother. I have recently lost my father, and the factory has been left to me. However, I have also recently found out that Elsie is my half-sister, and so she is now part-owner of the factory.'

'I see.' The Reverend Mother turned her attention to Millie. 'I understand that you wish to be a patron of this convent?'

'Yes, I do. I recognize the wonderful work you do here and thought the upkeep of the convent must be a heavy burden to you. I wish to make a donation, and then contribute a regular amount each quarter. I also want both Elsie and I to be allowed to visit the children when we are staying in our cottage, which will be twice a year.'

'Why would you want to visit the children?'

'I just love children and, if I am to be their benefactor, then it is a natural thing for me to do.'

'Check up on them, you mean. Oh, I know what the general perception is about convent orphanages, but we do not mistreat our children. We bring them up to have good values, and we provide everything for them. If we chastise them, it is because they need it, and not to feed any perversion that lay-people seem to think women who choose to live our way of life have.'

Elsie felt ashamed, and she could feel Millie's discomfort. But Millie saved the moment, as only she could. 'All of that shone through to us when we met the children yesterday. And that is why I was moved to wish to do something in appreciation of your work and, hopefully, to make it a little easier for you.'

The Reverend Mother didn't reply to this. She stared at Millie, and then at Elsie. Elsie felt a bead of sweat trickle down her back. It was as if this woman could see into your soul. And it didn't seem that she liked what she saw. But then suddenly she smiled. 'I like you. I like you both. You show guts. Not many women do, and they generally perpetuate the myth that we are incapable of anything other than being the little woman at home. Well, some of us are different. And I think you two are.' She rose. 'We need women like you to make a difference. To change things.'

'We are trying to. We were both involved in the strike in the summertime this year. Me behind the scenes, as it was very difficult for me – my father was still alive and running the jam factory. But Elsie was in the thick of it, banner-waving and standing firm.'

'Good. That was a start. But there is much to do to raise the profile of women. You two should be looking to do that. And yes, we would be very grateful to have you as a patron of the convent.'

She put her hand out, and Millie shook it. 'Thank you, Reverend Mother.'

'But don't think that, in being so, you will have the automatic right to take one of our children from us.'

Elsie couldn't believe this. Fear gripped her. 'We don't want to take a child from you. We just want my brovver home!' Her voice shook with emotion, but when Millie took over the plea, she sounded calm and in charge of the situation.

'We're grateful to you, and to the nuns of the convent in Bermondsey, for all you have done for Bert, and all you did for Jimmy. They were lost to Miss Makin through no fault of her own. And we know that you have cared for them. But we have found Bert now, and are capable of giving him a loving home. That is all we are asking.'

At the mention of Jimmy's name once more, the realization came to Elsie that she couldn't take him home. She wasn't able to stop herself, and her body crumpled. Tears wet her face. Millie's arm came round her to support her. The Reverend Mother skirted her desk and pulled up two chairs that had been standing by the wall.

'Sit down. I'm sorry, I should have asked you to do so before. Can I get you a drink of water?'

Elsie shook her head. The kindly tone the Reverend Mother was now using was the last straw for her. She put her head in her hands and sobbed.

'Elsie. Oh, Elsie, I shouldn't have mentioned Jimmy. I'm sorry.'

Elsie shook her head. 'No, I want to. I want to know what happened.' She looked up. 'Did . . . did he suffer?'

The Reverend Mother was back round her own side of the desk. She sat down slowly. 'Jimmy was very poorly. I and my nuns took turns nursing him – we never left his side. We kept him as comfortable and restful as we could. He . . . he received the Last Rites and smiled when Father Bryn completed the Sacrament. Then he whispered, "Tell

Elsie . . ." And then he died. The smile didn't leave him. I'm sorry, so very sorry. We tried to save him, we did everything we could, but in the end he was a child of God. And I am sure He has work for Jimmy to do that he can only do from his heavenly seat. Maybe that is why you are here now. I mean, what are the odds that you came for a holiday to Barmouth and found your brother? I think Jimmy's first task was to reunite you.'

Through her tears and anguish, this lifted Elsie. The Reverend Mother was implying that she was to be reunited with Bert. She looked up into a changed face – one that held compassion and kindness.

'Yes, Elsie, we won't be objecting to any application put forward for you to become the legal guardian of Bert.'

'Thank you, thank you . . . Ta, Reverend Mother. When?'

'I don't see any reason for a delay. We can have Bert ready to go very soon.'

Elsie felt some of her pain lift. Millie turned to her, her eyes full of tears, her smile wide. 'Oh, Elsie, I'm so pleased . . . Reverend Mother, I have begun the process of Bert's legal guardianship and that may take a few weeks.'

'No matter. We don't need to have it in place. We choose a family for our children, and that is that. But for your own purposes, yes, carry on.'

'Were Bert and Jimmy put with a family? Because that is what we were told.'

'Well, it's history now, but initially, yes. But they didn't settle. Little Bert was very disruptive, and poor Jimmy was constantly poorly. Anyway, the family lives in this area, and so it was all arranged between me and the convent in London. And so, rather than take them back there, they came into our care. Sometimes, with older children, we have to try several placements, although that is always far more difficult with more than one family member, as we like to keep them together.'

'Thank you. I would have hated them to be separated.' Elsie found she couldn't say any more than this. Her throat had tightened. *But they are: my lovely brothers are separated now. Oh God!*

Millie's hand came into hers. Elsie squeezed it, trying to gain courage from it. If she broke now, the Reverend Mother might refuse to let her take Bert.

'Well now, I am going to get Sister Rose to take you both into the nuns' sitting room to have a cup of tea, while I sort out for Bert to be made ready.'

Millie gave Elsie's hand a little shake. Elsie turned. 'At last, Elsie! I can't believe it. This is wonderful, and far more than we expected.'

'Oh, Millie, my heart is torn.'

'I know. I wish I could heal the hurt for you, too. Look, as soon as you are ready, we'll visit Jimmy. And we'll go to the undertaker's and order him a headstone. He's resting in a lovely place under a tree. We'll take some flowers, too.'

'Yes, all right.'

Although she said this, Elsie didn't feel like doing it. She didn't want to visit Jimmy in a churchyard. She didn't want her last goodbye to him – when she couldn't even remember what she had said – to have been before she went to work that day. She wanted everyone to be home with her, how they used to be.

In that moment she even felt resentful of Dot, for taking Cecil. Thinking of Cecil, she still had the task of writing to him with the news of Jimmy's passing. She knew that, as for her, the news of Bert coming home would be overshadowed by that of Jimmy's death.

But these thoughts were taken from her as Bert came bounding into the sitting room, his arms outstretched, his face beaming. 'I knew you'd come for me, Else.'

Elsie accepted him jumping at her, and hugged him to her. 'Bert. Oh, Bert.'

'Don't cry, Else, or you'll make me unhappy. I've been happy since I saw you.'

'I know, darlin'. I shouldn't cry, but some of them are happy tears.'

'Oh? How do you cry happy tears?'

'Ha, you'll learn. Come on, let's get you back to Millie's cottage.'

'I want to go home to Long Lane. I want to see Mum and Cecil.'

Sister Rose interrupted then, and Elsie was so glad that she did. 'Pick that small bag up, Bert. You can carry that. This way, everyone. Reverend Mother needs you to sign some papers and then you can go. Have you got transport?'

Millie answered. 'Yes, we have a cab waiting outside for us, thank you.'

'That'll cost you. You must have been here an hour.'

Neither of the girls answered this.

Back in the Reverend Mother's office, the nun came straight to the point. 'Well, I have two documents prepared. One is our release of the child into your custody, and the other is for your pledge, Miss Hawkesfield. Will you pay the first amount in cash?'

'No. I will write you a cheque, and then I will post a cheque to you every quarter.'

Reverend Mother watched closely as Millie wrote out the cheque.

'Fifty pounds! That's very generous of you – thank you very much.'

'I want some of it to go to whatever the children need, and for it to be dedicated to Jimmy's memory, please. But after this, whether you spend it on the children or on something to make the Sisters' work lighter, I don't mind. I will leave it up to you.'

'Of course. We desperately need two new prams, so that we can take the babies for a walk, and some toys for the older children. And new beds for the boys' dormitory . . . Oh, umpteen things.'

'That all sounds exactly what I intended to help you with.'

'Good. I will keep you informed. I have your address on the release papers for Bert. Now I will have to say goodbye.'

Taking Elsie's hand, she said, 'God bless and help you, Miss Makin. I will pray every day for you. And for you Bert. I want you to visit one day – a fine young man. And of course we pray for Jimmy, too; or, rather, I pray to Him to help me with this and that, as I know Jimmy is in heaven.'

The moment was upon her. They were back at the cottage. Bert had explored, behaving like a caged animal who'd been let free, screaming with delight at everything. Now he was sitting quietly, enjoying a glass of lemonade and looking very thoughtful.

'Why didn't Mum come on holiday with you, Else? She'd like this place.'

Else felt Millie's and Ruby's eyes on her. 'She would . . . But, Bert, you know how you have me to look after you?'

Bert looked intently at her and nodded.

'Well, Mum's gone to look after Jimmy. Otherwise he wouldn't have anyone, would he?'

A frown creased Bert's brow. 'I don't want her to. No! Mum will stay with me, Else.'

'She couldn't, Bert. She . . . she's happy in heaven. I'll look after you, darlin'.'

'No! I want Mum. Else . . . make Mum come back. Please.'

Elsie gathered him into her arms. For a moment Bert resisted, his voice cross. 'No, Else. No!'

'Oh, Bert, my darling. If I could make Mum and Jimmy alive again, I would. But I can't. I'm sorry, me little darlin'.'

They cried together, rocking backwards and forwards. Bert's sobs were pitiful. Elsie's hurt her throat and rasped her chest. Millie and Ruby cried, too, dabbing their eyes and looking lost.

After a moment Elsie gently put Bert down and stood up. 'Let's go for a walk, eh? You and me, Bert. Let's go along the promenade, shall we? We can take some bread to feed the seagulls. You'd like that, wouldn't you?'

With the resilience that only young children have, Bert rubbed his fists in his eyes. 'I'll have to put my coat on. The wind whips you sometimes.'

'Yes, I'll put mine on as well, as it is cold. But we can keep warm. We'll walk fast and then we'll play "Catch" on the beach.'

'I'm on first. You have to catch me, Else.'

'Easy, mate, I'll give you a few seconds' start and I'll still catch you.'

'No you won't, our Else! I can run fast now. Sister Rose said I have the wind.'

Despite herself, Elsie laughed at this. Bert smiled, not understanding the joke, but happy to see Elsie smile. And she realized in that moment that, yes, their lives were sad, but they had each other; and Cecil and Dot, Millie, Rene and Ruby. And, together, they had to go forward and live a happy life. Mum and Jimmy would want that for them. She would move in with Millie and, with her allowance, she would do all the things Millie had suggested – and see that Bert had the very best chance in life that he could have.

She'd make it her mission to get Dot and Cecil home. She'd make Mrs Grimes see how she could gain a whole family by allowing them to marry, and how she could have Dot close to her then; and not only Dot, but her grandchild, too. Yes, she would achieve this, even if she had to wear Mrs Grimes down.

And she would see that Jimmy had a lovely headstone – an angel praying, because, in his short life, Jimmy had been an angel. And she would come to Barmouth often with Bert to visit Jimmy, and to keep ties with the convent, as she'd liked the Reverend Mother and Sister Rose.

As for Swift's Jam Factory, she wouldn't care if she never saw it again for the rest of her life, but it was Millie's passion. Lovely Millie – the saviour of her. Well, Millie deserved something back from her, so she would devote herself to learning everything there was to learn about the factory, and would help Millie all she could to make it the success it could be.

But first there was the trial. She had to be strong for that, because so much would come out about her mum and about . . . Chambers's rape of her. And the whole horror of the man who had fathered her – the man her mum had loved since she was a girl. How could love be so blind?

And then there was Len. She tried hard not to let herself think about Len. He belonged to Millie. But that wouldn't stop Elsie loving him for the rest of her life. She would have to find a way to live with that – maybe even in the same house! No, she couldn't do that. She would make a home for herself and Bert, when Millie married Len.

Oh, Len, how will I be able to bear seeing you married to Millie?

Somehow, she knew, she would have to find a way. She took hold of Bert's little hand and looked down into his eager, tear-stained face and knew she could do anything, as long as she had him to care for. For in Bert's look was all the love and trust in her that she could not deny him.

'Come on, buggerlugs – it's me and you against the world, so everyone had better watch out. What do you think, eh?'

'I think I am buggerlugs, and me and you will sort them all out, Else.'

'Ha, you've got an old head on your shoulders, my lovely Bert. And you don't know it yet, but no matter what happens, you're my saviour.'

Chapter Twenty-Five

Elsie

Life had settled down into a pattern, although often Elsie didn't feel part of it all. She functioned and did whatever was asked of her, and enjoyed it most of the time.

She and Millie had gradually eased themselves back into things, spending a day, then two days and now up to three days a week working at the jam factory. Elsie's role wasn't specific; she was mostly a support and an assistant to Millie, but they had many a giggle together, and the last couple of months had passed without her really noticing them doing so.

Millie was in the throes of setting up the pickled-onion production. The women had taken to it well and seemed to enjoy the different skills they were learning. Many of the warehouses that stocked their jam had given them orders and, although not large in quantity, it was a start, and had kept most of the workforce busy during what would normally be the closed season.

Those not involved on the production line had been retained after the big cleaning operation, on a three-day week basis. These were the new intake that Jim, as they now called Mr Ellington, had taken on. They were painting and reorganizing the storeroom – a room that Elsie still hadn't visited since that awful day. Millie's idea was to make it a totally different place, so that it didn't relate to the horror that had happened there. This was for herself, too, because although she hadn't seen their father's body in that room, she was acutely aware of it being where he had died. Elsie didn't know if the changes would make a difference to her, but at the moment she couldn't bear to enter the room.

As the pickled onions weren't in such mass production as the jams and marmalades, they didn't need a large area to store them, so shelving had been erected along the wall between the factory and the canteen.

Elsie stood looking down through the office window. She'd never seen the factory floor looking as it did now, and was only just getting used to the different smell of it: the sweet aroma of fruit and sugar boiling was now replaced by that of onions and vinegar – one of the things she didn't like about the new set-up; the other was the streaming eyes of the women involved in peeling the shallots, but that had improved since she'd suggested that masks should be worn.

The welfare of the women was something Elsie took to heart, and it was slowly becoming her remit. She'd even toyed with the idea of becoming a welfare officer – a position that Millie had found out Hartley's had in place and, as Elsie understood it, someone who was completely dedicated to the well-being of the workers. Elsie really liked the idea, and she and Millie had spoken about it a lot lately.

But for now her attention was drawn to how lovely the factory floor looked, as it had been prepared for something that had never happened before: a Christmas party. This was the last day before they closed the factory for a week for the festive season – Christmas Day was only four days away.

Brightly-coloured paper chains were draped around benches, and one of the tables, normally used to fill the jam jars, had been cleared, covered in a white cloth and was now laden with food and bottles of sherry, which she could see Jim was busy opening and filling small tulip-shaped glasses with.

There was an excited buzz about the factory floor. The women could be heard as they called out to one another. Some of their comments made Elsie giggle, but also feel glad that Millie hadn't arrived yet, as the banter was perhaps a little lewd for her ears.

''Ere, Peggy, girl, you going to make up with your Arthur for Christmas and let him have his oats then? He's been complaining, down The Elephant, that you've turned your back to the wall.'

'I might do, Ada. But he's to spend less time in The Elephant and Castle and more at home, first.'

'Bet you miss it, don't yer?'

'A bit, but I ain't like you, girl. And mind you're careful over Christmas, or you'll have another bun in the oven and that'll set yer right back. You're only just getting on your feet after the strike.'

'Ha, don't you worry. I've perfected a family-planning method. Once I'm satisfied, he has to make do with an 'and-job.'

The laughter at this set the place alight and put a light-heartedness in Elsie that she didn't think she could feel. There was nothing like the banter of the women to cheer you up. Her giggle turned into a belly laugh as she saw Jim scurrying towards the office steps, his face bright red.

'The natives are at it again! We've made them too happy – we should cut their wages.' Jim was laughing as he said this. 'I've never known the like. I thought Liverpool women could be brassy, but these Cockneys take the biscuit.'

'It's all music to my ears, Jim. This place has changed beyond recognition, and for the better. It was mostly quiet, except for the production noise and the odd bit of chatter – a place of misery.'

'Elsie, you have seen so much, and been to hell and back in your life. I've never said anything, but I do feel sorry for you. And if there's ever anything I can do for you, I would be glad to.'

This was a new Jim. Mostly he was pleasant but very businesslike, with his main focus being the running of the factory floor. 'Thanks, Jim, but I'm all right. My life's nothing like it was a year ago, but I'm coping. It's as I have said many a time: Bert is my saviour. Full of life, to the point of being very naughty at times, but always loving and cheerful. He keeps me sane.'

'His naughtiness is his way of coping. He's kicking against the raw deal he's been dealt. Don't be too hard on him.'

'You sound as though you have experienced some of what he's been through, Jim.' Elsie couldn't believe she was having this conversation. It was one she had never thought to have with Jim; she had hardly viewed him as a person, simply an efficient and much-needed addition to this new life that she and Millie were leading. But now she was seeing a kind and thoughtful man.

'I have. I had a twin brother.'

Elsie saw his pronounced Adam's apple move as he swallowed hard. 'Had?'

'Yes, he – he was killed. My father crashed his car, and

we were both in it. Father was angry with us, as usual, and was shouting at us to shut up. We were giggling, John and I. John had picked up a worm that had been lying on the wet pavement; it had probably come out of the grass verge. It was wriggling over John's hand . . . Anyway, Father turned to look at what we were giggling at and veered off the road, then tried to compensate by braking hard. John . . . John was thrown through the windscreen; we were due to celebrate our tenth birthday the next day. My father – always a grumpy man – became worse after that.'

'Oh, Jim, I'm sorry, mate. I know how you feel. And Christmas brings it all back to you.'

'It does. And, well, I – I'm conscious of this being your first Christmas without your mum and your little brother, Jimmy. I'm glad you're going to see your other brother, though. It will be good for Bert, too.'

All of this shocked Elsie. It was as if she was in the room with someone she'd known forever, instead of with Jim Ellington the foreman.

'Thanks, it is hard. Last Christmas was so good, but I never dreamed how different this one would be.'

'I'm glad it was – you will have those memories to help you. I was lost without John, and still am. I've spent the last few years trying to cope with my father's increasingly bad moods and irrational behaviour, and now he has gone, too.'

Elsie wanted to go to him and enclose him in her arms. 'What are you going to do this Christmas, Jim? Are you going to visit family in Liverpool?'

'I have none. My mother died soon after John. A broken heart, they said, but I have since found out it was cancer. I've no aunts and uncles or cousins. I do have some friends in Liverpool, but they are all married, or thinking of becoming so, and are very tied up in their own lives.'

'Why don't you come to us? I know Millie would be very happy for you to. She, like me, had no idea you were going to be on your own.'

Elsie still couldn't believe she was having this conversation with the man she'd only ever talked to about work-related things. Now she was trying to imagine what life had been like for Jim during his time in London. She knew he lived in a flat near Tower Bridge, but that was all. She hadn't thought about the person behind the quiet, efficient front he presented.

She liked this new Jim. She hadn't disliked him before, but now she found that she was really at ease with him and knew he was someone she could make a good friend of.

'I'd like that, thank you, Elsie. I – I wonder, would you do me the honour of coming to dinner with me one evening? I would like to talk some more to you, and be a listening ear for you.'

Even more taken aback, Elsie heard herself say she would like that. But would she? Was Jim getting ideas about her? She didn't want that. Her heart had already been taken, and she didn't want to raise Jim's hopes.

'I can see the prospect worries you, Elsie, but it needn't. You have no need to be afraid. I – I am only trying to be a friend.'

A voice cut into the awkward moment. ''Ere, Josie, what's your Ron like then? You never talk about him. He seems a quiet chap.'

Then Josie's distinctive loud voice, not knowing how it carried up to the office. 'The quiet ones are the worst. I bet that Mr Ellington's a right hot piece. Especially if he's anything like my Ron.'

Elsie coloured, but didn't have time to react before another voice drifted up amidst the cackling laughter. 'And nice with it. I wouldn't mind getting him into me bed.'

'Not if I get to him first, yer won't.'

Elsie was mortified. Peggy was old enough to be Jim's mother.

'I'd smother him with love, like a son. And I wouldn't let any of you randy lot get anywhere near him. So get on with your work and let's get this batch done. We've a party to enjoy before we go home.'

Elsie saw Jim's face light up with a smile that turned to a giggle. 'And I'd love Peggy as a mum. Phew! I thought she had other plans for me for a moment.' At this, he burst out laughing, and Elsie couldn't help but join in. Yes, she really liked Jim and was warming to him more and more by the minute.

'At least you know the women like you. That's something not given lightly, Jim. They weigh people up and see if they're worthy first. You've passed muster.'

Jim still had the smile on his face that Peggy had prompted. It changed his otherwise pleasant, but non-expressive face into a handsome one, and Elsie thought what nice eyes he had, now that they had life in them and twinkled with amusement. Dark brown like her own, they were always serious-looking, with the brow that framed them often puckered into a frown. She took the whole of him in for the first time. A tall, slender man, he wore his moustache – which was sandy-coloured, matching the colour of his unruly hair – in a neat pencil line. His chin was square and his cheeks clear-cut.

'Do I pass muster with you, Elsie?'

Her cheeks burned once more as she realized she'd been

staring, so she covered her embarrassment by giggling. 'You'll do.' But then his face changed and she saw that, despite him saying he only wanted to be her friend, he was actually thinking of far more than that. 'Jim, I – I do only want us to be mates.'

His face clouded. He looked down, but then almost as if his expression hadn't given away his disappointment, he laughed. 'Mates it is. Ha, I've never had a mate before. But I'll think of myself as a Cockney lad if I have one.'

The moment lightened and Elsie relaxed. She laughed with him. 'You've a lot more hurdles than that to jump before you're one of us. For a start, you'd ask me to a pie-and-mash supper and a pint at the pub, and not to dinner.'

His laugh became a belly laugh, which Elsie had never thought to see Jim give way to. 'Pie and mash and a pint it is then, me ol' darlin'. Or shall we wash it down with a cup of Rosy Lee?'

Their laughter joined, and Elsie could feel that a bond was forming between them. And she knew that she welcomed it. Yes, she liked Jim: she liked him very much.

The huge doors that slid on screeching wheels opened, drawing their attention to the window to look downstairs. All of the women had stopped working and were looking towards the gaping hole.

'What's going on? We're not expecting a delivery, are we?'

Jim looked concerned. 'Not that I know of. Oh, it's Millie. What is she waving through?'

They didn't have to wait long, because a truck chugged through the door. Elsie gasped when she saw what was sitting on the back of it. 'Me gran's piano! Millie's brought me gran's piano from me old flat! I can't believe it.'

'You can play?'

'Yes, me gran was a pianist in the music halls, and she taught me. Well, Jim, it looks like Millie's plan is to introduce you to another Cockney tradition – the good old singalong.'

'Sounds good to me. I'll go downstairs and make sure that the work is all complete. I can see the women scrubbing down, though I'm sure I can leave it to my new mum to take care of it.' Jim winked at her.

Elsie followed him downstairs and watched the transformation from ordinary Jim to Jim the manager, dealing with everyone in a polite, respectful way and getting a good response from the women, as they did as he asked.

Elsie greeted Millie. 'Millie, you never said! How wonderful! Mate, you've topped any Christmas these women have ever had. A party and a sing-song in the jam factory. Never been known, or thought it would ever happen.'

Millie hugged her. 'And I've two men in my car waiting to join in. Oh, here they come.' Her face lit up as Len came through the door, holding Bert's hand.

Elsie's heart jolted painfully. The picture of the two people she loved most in the world, lit by the winter sun, caught her breath. Bathed in the light, Len looked beautiful to her. She wanted to run to him. To hold him and feel his lips on hers. Instead she acted in the way she had schooled herself to, over the last few months, and greeted him in a friendly way. Then, to further cover her feelings, she put out her arms to Bert. He ran into them. Lifting him, Elsie swung him round. 'Hello, buggerlugs.'

Bert giggled. 'I've come to the party, Else.'

'I can see that. And I'm so happy.'

'I'll be happy when we get to see Cess. Are we really going to see him tomorrow, Else?'

'Yes, really, really.'

'Will he remember me?'

'Who could forget you, eh? Yes, he and Dot will remember you. Cess used to cry every night because he missed you.'

'I cried at night, Else. Not in the day or I'd get a pasting, but at night I wet me pillow, and . . . well, I wet me bed sometimes, and got a leathering for that.'

Elsie drew in her breath. Bert had said a few things that worried her about his time with the nuns. 'Who punished you, mate? Was it all of the Sisters?'

'No, just Sister Bernard. I was frightened of her. She shouted a lot and clouted your ear if you did wrong.'

Elsie made up her mind to talk to Millie about this. But for now she wanted to be happy – needed to be. 'But most of the nuns were kind, weren't they?'

'Yes. Sister Rose was the best. She used to tell Sister Bernard off. They used to have a right barney, I tell yer.'

Elsie laughed and felt the happiness seeping back into her. Her conversation with Jim, and listening to the women, had put it there, but it had been threatened by the sight of Len and her worry over how awful Sister Bernard was. But she would cope with both – Len she would put back into the corner of her heart that was solely for him; and she would deal with the question of Sister Bernard in the new year. She felt safe in the knowledge that the cruel woman was contained for now by the lovely Sister Rose.

Around her the atmosphere was getting very lively and it seemed as if the laughter would lift the roof, as the women downed their first sherry and tucked into the sandwiches and cold pies laid out for them.

Jim came over to her. 'So, this is Bert? Hello, young man.'

'Hello, but I'm a boy, not a young man yet. What's your name?'

Jim's face lit up once more and his laugh rang out.

Elsie caught Millie's look of surprise and went over to her. 'Who'd have thought – our dour Jim, eh?'

'What's lit him up like that . . . Elsie! You're blushing. What's been going on?'

Elsie laughed. 'Nothing, except that what you are looking at is a very lonely man with sadness in his heart, who has found a friend – me.' She told Millie what had gone on before she arrived.

'Oh, Elsie, I had no idea. I'll invite him for Christmas, right now. Elsie, I'm so happy for you.'

'No, Millie. Don't be getting the wrong idea. I only want to be friends with Jim. Well, I want us all to be friends.'

They looked over to where Jim was talking to Len. Both men were smiling. 'Oh, but wouldn't it be lovely if it became more than that? Look, those two are old friends; it would be great if their wives were sisters.'

'Millie, don't turn into your mother!'

They laughed. 'Sorry, Sis. I promise I won't, but still . . .'

Elsie gave her a mock-clout. 'Stop it!'

When they had composed themselves Millie said, 'Well, are you pleased to see your piano?'

'Oh, I am. What a lovely idea, Millie. Thank you. I will play it, once you've done your bit.'

'Yes, I'd better get on with our surprise for the workforce. Len finally approved, when he saw the number of orders that we have for the pickles, and future orders for our jam. Come on.'

With this, Millie went into the middle of the room and

Elsie followed her. Once there, Millie put down the bag she was carrying and clapped her hands. The women fell silent and turned towards them.

'First of all, thank you from me, Elsie and Dot – who sends her love from Leicestershire, where, as you all know, she is staying with her sick aunt and taking care of her—'

A voice interrupted, 'Ooh-ahh, and where's Cess then?'

This earned the speaker a slap on her wrist from Peggy. 'Shut yer mouth for once, Jean, and give your arse a chance. It talks more sense than you do.'

The other women laughed, but Elsie felt mortified as she caught sight of Len's shocked face. She felt that she would go down in his estimation, as these were her people. This thought made her realize that she had to speak up – yes, they were her people and they deserved her explaining things to them, even if what she said was only a half-truth.

'Cess is also staying in Leicester. You all know, as it is no secret, how much he thinks of Dot – and she of him – so much so that he couldn't live without her. He followed her up there and has found himself a job. A good job, and he is supporting Dot in looking after her aunt.'

'Good for him, but I bet you miss him, Elsie, luv.'

'I do, Ada. Me and Bert are going there tomorrow to see them.'

'Well, you give them both our love, Elsie. We all miss Dot.'

'Thanks, Peggy. Now, can you all please let Miss Hawkesfield say her piece. You lot don't change – you love a bit of gossip!'

Laughter went up at this and the tense moment passed.

'Well, as I was saying, thank you. Now before one of you pipes up that you can't spend thanks . . .' Millie smiled her lovely smile, and once more the women laughed out loud.

'You'll be one of us yet, Miss.'

Elsie could see that this, from Ada, pleased Millie, who came back with 'I try, but you are a unique bunch, and I'm glad to be thought apprenticed to become one of you.'

A spontaneous burst of applause brought a tear to Elsie's eye, and she could see that Millie was touched, too.

When it died down, Millie went on, 'Well, ladies, this wasn't meant to be a long speech. Just a thank you, and to wish you a happy Christmas; and may we all have a happier 1912 and a very prosperous one.'

Another cheer went up.

'Finally, there is an envelope in this bag for each of you. Elsie and Mr Ellington will distribute them. They are a thank-you that you can spend, and are the first bonus of what will be a yearly payment – the amount to be determined by the year's profits. So continue to work hard, and know that everything you do is appreciated by us.'

A stunned silence followed. Elsie understood. Never before had the women's work been appreciated, let alone rewarded.

'Oh, and one more thing. You all saw the piano arrive. Well, once the giving-out of the bonuses is complete, Elsie is going to play for you, and I hope you will all sing along.'

This time the cheer almost raised the roof. Peggy shouted, 'Three cheers for Miss Hawkesfield, Elsie, Dot and Mr Ellington. Hip-hip!'

Mr Ellington shook hands with every one of the women and added his personal thanks to them, as they went around handing out the packets. Each contained a shining new crown – or five bob, as the women muttered in astonished tones when they ripped open their envelopes.

The atmosphere tingled with joy and happiness. But then it became more like The Elephant and Castle pub where, Elsie suspected, most of the five bobs would be spent, when she took her seat at the piano and began to play 'Alexander's Ragtime Band'.

Some of the women began to dance – well, jig would really describe their swinging each other round – and laughter filled the air. Elsie thought she'd never seen Swift's Jam Factory like that, and never thought to see the day she would. She'd heard that good could come of evil, and right now she knew for sure that it could.

She wouldn't let herself dwell on the evil, even though she would have to face it in the new year – Chambers's trial was set for April. But somehow she didn't have the same dread of it that she used to have, for now, as she looked around, she knew she would have plenty of support; and, yes, love, to sustain her through it. After all, she was a Cockney girl, and they looked after their own – they would do that for her.

A tug came on her sleeve and Elsie looked down at Bert. She had a job to hear him over the rendition of 'Let Me Call You Sweetheart', which the women were belting out.

'Else, can I sing a song? I know a Christmas one.'

'Yes, darlin'. The very next one. Is it "Away in a Manger" that Mum used to sing to us?'

'Yes, I want to sing it for her and for Jimmy.'

As the song she was playing came to an end, she lifted Bert onto her knee. 'Listen, everyone, as the party is coming to an end . . .' A collective 'Ahh' went around the room. Elsie smiled at them. 'I just want to say that I have a special treat to finish with. Bert is going to sing for us.'

The women all applauded. Bert blushed, but beamed at the same time.

When Elsie played the first few bars, Bert's beautiful, sweet voice rang out. 'Away in a manger, no crib for a bed . . .'

Silence fell, and Elsie saw the women begin to sway in time to the tune. Some of their faces smiled benevolently, while others had tears running down them. These matched her own, as she heard her mum's beautiful voice joining Bert's.

At that moment the winter sun shone a beam of light through the windows, and Elsie felt some warmth trickle into her and begin to melt the icicle of pain that had stabbed her. Bert sang on. Jimmy was now standing beside him. And Elsie was taken back to the time when she and Bert had met him from school one night, and Jimmy had been feeling well and was full of fun. He'd held Bert's hand as they had crossed the churchyard gardens and tugged at her hand. 'Come on, Else, you said we'd run.' She had laughed down at him and hurried her steps, but that hadn't been good enough, as Jimmy had pulled harder and begun to run. She could see him in her mind's eye. But then he'd stopped and given in to a fit of coughing.

Jimmy wasn't coughing now, but was laughing, and a great peace descended on her. Jimmy winked and then disappeared.

'Be near me, Lord Jesus; I ask you to stay
Close by me forever, and love me, I pray.
Bless all the dear children in your tender care,
And fit us for heaven, to live with you there.'

As the song came to an end, Elsie knew that Jimmy was fit for his place in heaven and was happy, as was Mum, despite everything. And they weren't crying; they were laughing with Gran. And yes, they were with her and Bert, and they'd never go away and leave them.

As the cheers went up, Elsie hugged Bert to her, and he looked up into her face. His smile filled her with joy. And she decided to take that joy and go forward, nurturing it, for she knew she would be all right now. And she would make sure that Bert was, too.

Letter to Readers

Dear Readers,

Thank you for choosing my book. I hope you enjoyed getting to know Elsie, Dot and Millie in the first of the Jam Factory trilogy.

Book two – May 2021: *Secrets of the Jam Factory Girls* – continues their journey to a time when secrets have to be kept. Secrets that, when revealed, cause heartache, tragedy and division.

Book Three, in Winter 2021, will see their courage and anguish as husbands and brothers go to war, and the help they give to those in need, especially objectors.

Writing a book is like taking steps through the unknown for me, as my characters come to life, taking me on a voyage of discovery – an exciting, but sometimes tense, experience through many emotions. This is what I want for my readers too.

I love the research process, and have often combined my love of travel with visiting the area I am writing about. However, the circumstances that prevailed when creating this trilogy meant having to rely on the internet. I became engrossed in learning about the lives of the girls who worked in our factories in the late nineteenth and early twentieth centuries – their fight for better conditions and their down-trodden lives, which the Cockney girls tackled with the true grit and humour they are known for. If you would like to know more, I have listed the resources overleaf.

If this book is your first introduction to my work and you

would like to read more, you can find a list of my back titles in the front of this book and stocked in WHSmith, Waterstones, online or to order from all good bookshops as well as when browsing in your local library.

To find out more about me, my work, my talks and my book-signing events – or to book one of these with me – I can be found here:

Website: **www.authormarywood.com**

Email: **marywood@authormarywood.com**

Twitter: **@Authormary**

Facebook: **facebook.com/MaryWoodAuthor**

I look forward to hearing from you.

Much love to all,

Mary x

Research

My thanks to the following sources:

www.exploringsouthwark.co.uk – a wonderful source of information on Hartley's and Pink's jam factories and the practices of the time – Hartley's came out with flying colours, not so Pink's on whom I based my Swift's Jam Factory.

Amanda Wilkinson's 'J is for Jam Maker' – www.victorian occupations.co.uk

The strong and caring Mary Macarthur and the National Federation of Women Workers – spartacus-educational.com/TUmacarthur.htm

Ada Salter, a woman of strength, courage and conviction. Millie is set to be in the same mould as this remarkable woman – menwhosaidno.org/context/women/salter_ada.html

Acknowledgements

Many people have a hand in bringing a book to publication and I want to express my heartfelt thanks to them all. My agent, Judith Murdoch, who stands firmly in my corner, whilst propping me up when I need it and encouraging me forward. My editor, Wayne Brookes, who is always there for me, whose care means the world and who makes me laugh. I love him to bits. Victoria Hughes-Williams, who does a wonderful, sensitive structural edit of my books, keeping my voice and tightening my work. Editor Alex Saunders and his team, Samantha Fletcher and Mandy Greenfield, who all do an amazing job of editing and checking my research, till my words sing off the page – I always say, an author is nothing without her editors and I am so lucky in mine. Thank you.

Thanks, too, to Ellis Keene, my publicist, who works towards getting exposure for my books and me, and meticulously organizes events to ensure I am taken care of on my travels. The sales team, for their efforts to get my books onto the shelves. The cover designer for my beautiful covers. And last but by no means least, a special thanks to my son, James Wood, who reads so many versions of each book, advising me on what is working and what isn't as I write my draft manuscript, and then helps with the read-through of the final proofs when last-minute mistakes need to be spotted. All of you are much appreciated, and do an amazing job for me.

My thanks, too, to my special family – my husband, Roy, who looks after me so well as I lose myself in writing my books, and is the love of my life. By my side for almost sixty years, I couldn't do what I do without him or the love and generous support that he gives me. My children, Christine, Julie, Rachel and James, for your love, encouragement and just for having pride in me. My grandchildren and great-grandchildren, too numerous to name, but all loved so very dearly and who are all in my corner cheering me on. My Olley and Wood families, for all the love and encouragement. You all help me to climb my mountain.

And I want to thank my readers, especially those on my Facebook page – 'Mary Wood Author'. The love and encouragement you give me, the laughs we have and all the support you show makes my day. You are second to none. Love you all, thank you.

If you enjoyed

The Jam Factory Girls

then you'll love

The Forgotten Daughter

by Mary Wood

Book one in
The Girls Who Went to War series

From a tender age, Flora felt unloved and unwanted by her parents, but she finds safety in the arms of caring Nanny Pru. But when Pru is cast out of the family home, under a shadow of secrets and with a baby boy of her own on the way, it shatters little Flora.

Over the years, however, Flora and Pru meet in secret – unbeknown to Flora's parents. Pru becomes the mother she never had, and Flora grows into a fine young woman. When she signs up as a volunteer with St John Ambulance, she begins to shape her life. But the drum of war beats loudly and her world is turned upside down when she receives a letter asking her to join the Red Cross in Belgium.

With the fate of the country in the balance, it is a time for bravery. Flora's determined to be the strong woman she was destined to be. But with horror, loss and heartache on her horizon, there's a lot for young Flora to learn . . .

Available now

The Abandoned Daughter

by Mary Wood

Book two in
The Girls Who Went to War series

Voluntary nurse Ella is haunted by the soldiers' cries she hears on the battlefields of Dieppe. But that's not the only thing that haunts her. When her dear friend Jim breaks her trust, Ella is left bruised and heartbroken. Over the years, her friendships have been pulled apart at the seams by the effects of war. Now, more than ever, she feels so alone.

At a military hospital in Belgium, Ella befriends Connie and Paddy. Slowly she begins to heal, and finds comfort in the arms of a French officer called Paulo – could he be her salvation?

With the end of the war on the horizon, surely things have to get better? Ella grew up not knowing her real family but a clue leads her in their direction. What did happen to Ella's parents, and why is she so desperate to find out?

Available now

The Wronged Daughter

by Mary Wood

Book three in
The Girls Who Went to War series

Can she heal the wounds of her past?

Mags has never forgotten the friendship she forged with Flora and Ella, two fellow nurses she served with at the beginning of World War One. Haunted by what she experienced during that time, she fears a reunion with her friends would bring back the horror she's tried so desperately to suppress.

Now, with her wedding on the horizon, this should be a joyful time for Mags. But the sudden loss of her mother and the constant doubt she harbours surrounding her fiancé, Harold, are marring her happiness.

Mags throws herself into running the family mill, but she's dealt another aching blow by a betrayal that leaves her reeling. Finding the strength the war had taken from her, she fights back, not realizing the consequences and devastating outcome awaiting her.

Can she pick up the pieces of her life and begin anew?

Available now

The Brave Daughters

by Mary Wood

Book four in
The Girls Who Went to War series

When Sibbie and Marjie arrive at RAF Digby, they are about to take on roles of national importance. It's a cause of great excitement for everyone around them. Perhaps they will become code-breakers, spies even? Soon the pair embark on a rigorous training regime, but nothing can prepare them for what they're about to face . . .

Amid the vineyards of rural France, Flors and Ella can't bear the thought of another war. But as the thunderclouds hanging over Europe grow darker, a sense of deep foreboding sets in, not just for their safety but for the fate of their families . . . With danger looming, as the threat of war becomes real, Flors and Ella are forced to leave their idyllic home and flee. Can they make it to safety, or will the war have further horrors in store for them?

'Wood is a born storyteller'
Lancashire Evening Post

Available now